Border Crossings:
A Catherine James Thriller

By Michael Weems
Copyright Michael Weems 2010-2012

Thank you to Heather Wren for helping edit.

"The accomplice to the crime of corruption is frequently our own indifference." - Bess Myerson

W9-AVB-365

PROLOGUE

The afternoon lay quiet except for the crunch of dirt beneath tires on an old worn out trail. A white and green Ford Explorer bounced along the dirt road, kicking up the desert floor and scattering it to the wind. In the passenger seat a young man's hazel eyes peered out from under the shadow of his green ball cap towards the searing sun. "It's awful hot," he said. It was more a premonition than a comment on the weather.

In the driver seat sat a squat man, brown-skinned with a wispy mustache that flickered with the air blowing in through the vents. He raced along the road with eerie calm for someone so consistently close to a cataclysmic crash at any second, skipping and sliding the SUV around each bend like a seasoned drift racer. He glanced down at the temperature gauge on the dashboard which read 94 degrees. It could be well over 150 degrees in a confined metal space, an oversized oven. "Yeah," he agreed, "they might already be dead." He reached in his shirt pocket and pulled out a well-worn toothpick and placed it between his teeth as he continued slipping along. The other said nothing, only watched the desert pass them by.

In front of them, Guadalupe Peak, the highest point in Texas at an elevation of 8,749 ft, rose up in the Guadalupe Mountains National Park. Before them lay the dirt road designated for 4x4 vehicles only, and somewhere out in the canyon region sat an abandoned metal trailer which had six young women locked inside and left for dead.

As they passed a campground sign the ranger in the passenger seat pulled the crudely drawn map from his shirt pocket, a fax they'd received not 10 minutes ago. He matched up the line drawn on the map with a trail he saw ahead. "There," he pointed, "that's it." The SUV made a sharp turn that sent him sloshing against the door while the driver barely shifted his weight. They turned on an offshoot where a sign that read "No Vehicles Beyond This Point" sat crooked on an old post. Nearby, a Gila monster sat flicking its tongue on a rock, curiously watching the great green and white beast roar past him.

They followed a trail along McKittrick Canyon just south of the New Mexico border. There lay the only natural source of water in the park in the form of a small creek on the Eastern side of the massif.

After about a mile and a half they came to a ridge they followed until it ducked down into another miniature canyon. There, they saw the small pull-behind trailer, old and discolored, not much bigger than the discount economy size available at any local moving truck rental facility. The sun was glinting off the less worn parts of its metallic exterior and rust was eating at its joints. The SUV rolled to a halt, its catalytic converter crackling as though desperate for breath after the race it'd just run. The two rangers exited quickly, yet apprehensively. They'd found a dead hiker several months back and both had learned it took some roots under your feet when greeting death out in the desert. The combination of sight and smell the heat could render human remains in just a short time could easily bowl over the unprepared.

And death's handiwork there was. Before they even approached the trailer they saw their first victim. A man's body lay stretched out on the ground, blood soaking his chest and iridescent green-bellied flies buzzing the newly dead flesh. The passenger approached but didn't have to go far. "Oh, yeah, this one's gone," he announced, seeing the man's open eyes staring unnaturally at the blazing sun, a few flies licking the wetness of his pupils.

The driver took his toothpick out of his mouth and tucked it away. "Damn," he muttered to himself. It wasn't a good sign for the rest of them.

He headed to the back of the trailer, but there was a massive padlock securing the door. "Hey!" he called in Spanish, "anyone in there?" He rapped on the side of the trailer but heard nothing. Then he put his hand on the trailer door and was nearly burned by the heat. *Chinga madre!* he cursed. "It's too late," he told the other, "it's like a hot grill."

His thoughts went to dark places, imagining bodies inside the trailer littering the floor like remnants of the holocaust ovens, charred grotesquely like a cannibal's Memorial Day weekend barbecue celebration. He turned and headed back to the SUV to call it in. As he did the other ranger strolled to the trailer and palmed the padlock, feeling its weight and heat.

"God, can you imagine?" he asked. "What a horrible way to go." As he spoke he thought he heard a faint clunk from within the trailer. Then, from a small hole in the rust near the bottom, a finger poked out. It was painted in crimson from its tip down to where it disappeared within the crevice, and as it poked out the rusty edges of metal cut against it like tiny teeth. The ranger noticed that some of what he thought had been rust around the hole was instead dried blood, someone's efforts to expand the tiny little opening with their fingers. Then a voice, if it could be called such, called out weakly.

"Hey!" he yelled excitedly, "hey, they're still alive! I've got a finger over here." He called to the people inside, "Hold on, we're going to get you out!" He bent down quickly and touched the finger. It immediately curved and tried to grip him and he heard the faint sounds of someone trying to talk, though he could not make out the words. The voice was a whisper, raspy and desperate. "I think maybe there's some bolt cutters in the truck," he told his partner.

"No, bolt cutters won't work. Lock's too thick." The driver was now doing his best to run to the truck in an odd sort of gait from a hip that'd been a bit off most all his life, although he'd never bothered to get a medical opinion on the matter.

The other stayed holding to the finger and tried his best to say something helpful, "We're going to get you out, just hold on."

The driver returned from the Explorer with a shotgun. Besides buckshot, they had a box of deer slugs in the glove box, which he loaded. He walked back towards the lock with a determined grimace, pushing the shuttle of the gun to place with its distinctive clicking.

"You think that's a good idea?" asked the other.

He shrugged. "Better move out of the way." In a loud voice he called out to those inside the trailer in Spanish, "Get back away from the door! I'm going to shoot the lock." There was no response, but the finger retreated and he heard the faint sound of movement. He angled his shotgun down in such a way that it would only catch the lock and the very right edge of the door. Then he pulled the trigger and the shotgun let off a blast, which resounded off the rocks around them. In the distance the Gila monster retreated to a shadowy crevice. The lock thudded in its place but the ring of the loop unclasped, freeing the latch. He put down the shotgun and grabbed the handle of the doors, which was also burning hot, and swung them open.

A wave of heat poured out as though cracking open a broiler, followed by the sickening stench of urine, vomit, and skin that had begun to burn slowly against the metal. The ranger with the shotgun held his arm up to his nose in an effort to block the odor. His younger peer came around his side and his heart froze with what he saw. "Christ."

Inside the trailer were six young women, all lying next to each other. Their clothes had been stripped off in an apparent effort to cool themselves and spread out on the floor of the trailer in an attempt to provide some protection from the surface heat. The rangers could see some of them not only had heat blisters on their arms and faces, but burn marks on their arms from prolonged exposure to the metal. The walls of the trailer were covered in dings and dents and along the bottom edges were tiny pinpricks of light where rust had eaten through the metal leaving small holes, many of which were now spotted with bits of blood. They had struggled against their prison before succumbing to the heat. The inside of the trailer looked like a trap in which the prey had flung itself against the walls over and over, beating itself with every effort of escape.

Two were undoubtedly dead, their faces sunken in and eyes staring forward in similar fashion as the corpse on the ground outside . . . the death stare looking beyond the mortal world. Three others lay completely motionless and the rangers didn't know if they were alive or dead. The sixth and final, the only one conscious, peered at the rangers, her nude body withered and tinted with a greenish discoloration, drained of an unnatural amount of fluid.

Her skin had the appearance of an old woman, her body the gaunt and lethargic bend of a withered, dry reed before it breaks. Her arms were wrapped around one of the other girls. Her tortured hands, swollen and splayed awkwardly revealing dozens of cuts, rested on the other's motionless chest. Her cracked and bleeding lips quivered as she tried to say something.

"Water," she pleaded in her native tongue. The cooler outside air brushed against her face and she held her head up to its breeze as her eyes rolled back and she lost consciousness.

Chapter 1

He sat in the parked car staring at the photograph in his hand, his right thumb circling the face. He'd been this way for several minutes now. Finally, he tucked it inside his shirt pocket and picked the gun up off the passenger seat. He opened the door and began walking down the darkened street, the gun held in his hand, tucked away in his sport coat pocket. He turned the corner and proceeded a few more blocks toward the neon sign. There in front of its red glow he waited in shadow.

The young men inside ordered another round, a pile of shot glasses already stacked in a small pyramid on the bar. A couple in the corner watched them apprehensively until one of the men noticed them looking on, "You got a problem, *puta*?" he asked the man. The onlooker quickly looked away. "That's what I thought." He smiled at the girl, "Hey, *chica*? Why don't you drop that pussy and come hang out with some real men?"

The couple quickly got up and left, leaving money on the table for their drinks with plenty of change to spare. The other men laughed at them.

"Later, *puta*," one called after them.

"I'll see you around, *chica*," said the first man to the departing woman. The man outside watched the couple leave from his shadowy alcove. "Let's get out of this shithole," said the first man to the rest. "We can go to Maricel's place and have her call up some friends."

Another finished the last shot on the table, licking the salted rim and tossing back the tequila. "Let's do it," he said, adding the glass to the top of the pyramid. They all shuffled out without paying. The bartender knew better than to offer them a bill. They came in once or twice a week drinking his establishment dry and there wasn't a thing he could do about it. It was simply another cost of doing business in the shadier parts of Chetumal, Mexico.

They swaggered out into the night with hearty laughs, getting into a metallic gray Chrysler 300, which stuck out like a sore thumb on the impoverished street. Its over-sized chrome wheels reflected the dilapidated storefronts condescendingly.

As the driver put the key in the ignition, one of the others pointed out a man walking towards the car on the sidewalk. He stood some feet away but under the open sky's light they could see something was distinctly off about the man. He was staring at the trio with a look of profound hatred. He wasn't a man of intimidating size or build, but his gaze was so cold it was enough to falter the three men's bravado. As he came along the car, he stopped walking, turned towards them slightly, and proceeded to simply stand and stare at them.

"Who the fuck is this guy?" one of them asked. The vehicle started, but still they remained, staring back at the man as he stared at them. They had been momentarily quieted by his unnerving demeanor but the moment passed quickly. They were not the type to be easily intimidated, particularly when there were three of them and one of anyone else. The driver hit the power window, ready to ask the brazen man if he had a death wish looking to be granted, but what happened next happened quickly and the driver had just enough time to realize his initial fear had been the best idea his rarely conversed with common sense had offered up in a long while. He wasn't afforded much time to regret not heeding it.

The man's hand appeared from the sport coat, a gun in tow with his index finger already in place on the trigger for introductions. The driver opened his mouth to yell *Oh, shit,* but the quicker bullet rendered him constipated as the word *shit* never made it out.

The man on the sidewalk calmly began firing. First was the driver, whose head was halfway out of the window and whose lips were just in the *O* shape preparing for his last exclamation, when *POP!* His forehead caved in like Gallagher was in town, and the bullet made a messy exit to the back seat where it found the rear passenger's third rib. Before the other two had time to flee or reach for guns of their own they had stashed in interesting places, the man was already firing at them, his finger pulling the trigger, releasing, and pulling again in a steady rhythm. He fired ten rounds, seven of which hit their mark of flesh, and those that were astray were not much so and would have found their mark but for the flailing inside the Chrysler.

Seven seconds later the men lay motionless, the car's interior redecorated in blood-splattered windows in a piece Pollack aficionados would have admired. The man stood staring in disgust with the gun still raised, his hand shaking, but only slightly. He looked around to see who else was on the street and may have seen the massacre, but there was no one. The few people in the bar had heard the shots, but didn't dare come out to see what had happened. The bartender was inside, crouched down behind his counter, quickly dialing for the police with a 20-year old shotgun on his lap. A man in a nearby apartment had heard the shots and ran to close his window blinds, not even peeking to see who was outside.

The man on the sidewalk lowered his weapon and looked down at the gun in his hand, pondering its meaning in this world. He'd been worried about how he'd feel afterward . . . about whether or not he could live with himself; becoming something so similar to that which he claimed foe. Much to his relief, he was feeling fine with it for the moment. There was no remorse. Perhaps that'd come tomorrow, perhaps not. But as he stood there looking upon the death he'd brought to them, he just felt right. Hell, who was he kidding? As he turned around and disappeared back into the shadows he had to admit killing them had felt pretty damn good.

Chapter 2

Taylor slumped into the couch with her backpack and exhaled deeply. Kendra heard her from the kitchen and poked her head out. Just as she figured, Taylor looked whipped.

"Test not go so well?"

She blew her platinum blond bangs out of her emerald-esque eyes. "He asked about shit we never talked about in class. I have my notebook right here," she explained, as she unzipped her backpack and pulled out a large yellow binder, waving it as though it were the final rule of law on the matter. "Half the stuff he was asking about was stuff he specifically skipped. That's just such crap."

"Are you going to say anything?" Kendra knew Taylor was the type to say something.

"Oh, I asked him after the test."

"What'd he say?"

"He said it was all out of the outline and just because he hadn't talked about it in class didn't mean it wouldn't be on the test."

Kendra went back into the kitchen and unscrewed the zinfandel. They'd given up buying the stuff with a cork in it. By this point in their lives of financially distressed educational co-habitation, they didn't give a damn whether the wine was corked, screwed, or came out of a plastic baggy in a cardboard box for that matter. She brought Taylor a tall glass and said with as much empathy as she could muster, "Yeah, they're dicks like that sometimes."

Taylor took the wine and leaned back in defeat, "I bombed it."

"Oh, you always think you bombed it and you always end up with an A or B, so stop stressing."

"No, I really think I bombed it. I literally don't remember seeing half that stuff. I mean, I read it . . . some of it, at least . . . but Jesus! Who remembers the vague stuff from some obscure chapter that he never even mentioned in class. I went looking for one question afterward and it came from a footnote . . . a freaking footnote . . . on some chapter from like the third week. Who's going to remember that?"

"Nobody," said Kendra. "That's the point. They always try to throw that stuff in there that nobody ever saw so it's not too easy. They can't have everyone acing their tests or they'll get canned for being soft. So don't worry about it. I guarantee you most of the class definitely didn't read the assignments and if he didn't talk about it they probably never saw it, unlike you who at least maybe saw it before, but don't remember it all now." She lifted her own glass. "Here. Here's to your last midterm and the start of our kick ass spring break. No more worrying about tests, no more cramming until two in the morning, and no more stressing about stuff that's already behind us. It's time to kick back, relax, and enjoy!"

She wasn't feeling quite so Zen, but Taylor toasted nonetheless.

An hour and two glasses of wine later brought a knock on the door, much to Kendra's relief as she was failing miserably at getting Taylor to stop worrying about midterms and start worrying about having fun.

Jamie burst into their apartment like a shining beacon of college debauchery. She had sandy-blond hair, double D's she regularly referred to as "her girls", and wore a pair of mini shorts which barely made it over an ample, yet shapely, rear end. "Spring break, bitches! Who's ready for Mexico!?" She swept through their apartment like a whirlwind, quickly finding the *vino* and pouring herself a tall glass in which she tossed a few ice cubes and a spritz of soda from a two liter in the fridge. Then she gracefully slid between Taylor and Kendra on the couch, shifting her rear side to side to make room between them. "Cancuuuun," she said slowly, "Doesn't it just sound sexy? But that's tomorrow, ladies. So the real question tonight is . . . who's up for Sixth Street!? I'm ready to get shit-faced."

Her enthusiasm was infectious, her smile a challenge to all in its presence to dare mope while in the light of its glory. Taylor forgot about her test and smiled. Spring break officially had begun.

Chapter 3

With one foot in front of the other she sped her way to an hour of freedom. The beat of *Motorcycle's* "As the Rush Comes" carried her like a drug, bass thumping in her eardrums like the rhythm man's drum on ships of old.

It filled her, moved her, letting her push always for more. The heat and her exhaustion were saying stop and rest, but the music said go, go, go! And, the music almost always won. It was eighty-five and climbing and she had a good sweat going, just like she liked it. She put her thumb down and tracked the mp3 player to another motivator, Armin Van Buuren. She passed him on the left, a middle-aged man of average fitness, thoroughly sweat-drenched in the humidity. He was momentarily distracted from his jog by the black haired woman's figure as she passed. She had a distracting type of figure. Shapely legs, not overly long, but well proportioned and toned with thick thighs like the seasoned runner she was, stemming from a thin waist and a rear end that could make any pair of jeans look good. Like any courageous, red-blooded, recently divorced and trying to get in shape for the ladies kind of man, he pepped up his step.

His mark was lost in the sounds of the music and the feel of the trail beneath her running shoes and did not notice him until he was almost even with her. She glanced over to see him running powerfully next to her, his chest high, an attempt at a half-smile through his deep breaths when he saw her blue eyes glimpse at him by her side. They continued on another quarter mile or so before she realized he was making a supreme effort to keep pace with her. She glanced one more time just long enough to catch a fading tan line on his ring finger. *Ahhh,* she thought, *I got ya, tiger.*

There was only a month left before the Dallas Big D marathon and if there was one thing she wasn't going to have, it was a pickup artist distracting her from her training. It was hard enough to get time in during lunch for a run these days. She flicked the mp3 to a secret weapon of hers reserved usually for end kicks, and cranked it.

The small smile crept in first, accompanied by adrenaline and power as though she were in tune with the player. Her body responded with the volume, jetting her off to a stunned and somewhat dismayed would be suitor who realized quickly he was out of his league in more ways than one. Seeing now the show would be for naught, he slowed to a crawl and dropped his hands upon his knees, the sweat pouring from him as he inhaled deeply. He couldn't help but wonder what song the mystery woman just selected. But alas, he'd never know. Catherine James was gone, baby, gone, nodding her head to the music as the beat played on.

Chapter 4

Yesenia sat on a bus with no air conditioning and filled to capacity. The heat pressed in around her, but she didn't mind. There was a pleasant smell of food, *churros* and *tamales* others had brought for the trip. Ortiz had arranged the trip for her, for a price, of course, and like everyone else on the bus she was headed north. The windows were down and Yesenia watched the Mexican desert pass her by, wondering what new adventures she'd have. It would be tough, she knew, but the optimistic spirit of her fellow passengers energized her and filled her with confidence.

"Do you know Fernando Ortiz?" She asked an older woman next to her in an attempt to strike up a conversation.

"Who? Fernando Ortiz? No, *hija*, I don't think so."

"Oh, okay. I didn't think you would. He's back in Mexico City. He's the man who planned my trip for me and found me a job over the border."

"Oh," said the woman, "How nice. My son lives in Texas. I finally got my papers to go and visit him and his family. They just had a baby."

"Oh," said Yesenia. "That sounds nice, too."

"Did you say Fernando Ortiz?" asked a voice behind her. Yesenia turned in her seat to face a girl about her age, maybe a little younger, with coffee colored eyes and a happy, rounded face.

"Yes. Are you going to work for his friend, too?" Yesenia asked.

"Yup," said the girl. "I'm Silvia," she told her, "Silvia Arce."

"Yesenia Flores," she responded, and they both touched hands.

"It's good you two girls already have jobs lined up," said the woman next to Yesenia. "They're so hard to come by. Where are you going to be working?"

"I don't know yet. It's just temporary work at first," said Yesenia.

"Just enough to get by until we find other jobs," agreed Silvia.

"Well, be careful," said the woman. "Pretty girls like you should watch out for each other if you're going to be working together. You're awfully young to be on your own."

"Tell that to my stepfather," said Silvia. "To hear him tell it, I'm an old woman who should have been gone ages ago."

"She's right, though," said Yesenia. "We should talk and get to know each other a little. It'd be nice to already know someone before we get there."

Both agreed. Yesenia and Silvia talked so much on the rest of the way that eventually the woman sitting next to her got slightly annoyed and asked Silvia if she'd like to switch seats. So the girls sat by each other and shared their stories all the way to the border. Silvia had just turned 18 and had left home because her mother had remarried to a man who didn't want Silvia around. She had lost contact with her real father years ago. Her mother had told her she was an adult now and needed to find her own way in life, maybe go north. She had tried telling Silvia it had nothing to do with her new husband, but Silvia knew better. So, heeding her mother's last bit of advice on what direction she should take, she found herself here.

Yesenia's story was similar. Her father had been a brick maker in a small village called Santa Rosanna where she'd grown up as a child, but he had died the year before from a heat stroke. Her mother had passed two years before that from breast cancer. She'd been living with her sister's family in Mexico City for the last year, but it was two married couples, three children, and Yesenia all sharing a three-bedroom apartment. Now 19, Yesenia had decided it was time to leave the city. She wanted more out of life. She'd found a flier that advertised work up north and made a call. The man didn't have anything for her, but he knew someone who might, who turned out to be *señor* Ortiz, a well-dressed, grandfatherly type of gentleman she met shortly thereafter. Against her sister's concerns and warnings, Yesenia had agreed to pay him two thousand dollars out of the wages she'd earn once across the border and now the adventure had begun.

The girls talked for hours and eventually Yesenia found herself nodding off. Sometime later the older woman who was now behind them was tapping her on the shoulder. "We're nearly there," she whispered, "if you want to get your things ready."

They reached Reynosa just after 10:00 P.M. There, Yesenia and Silvia were both met by a woman who said she worked for Ortiz, and that they should come with her. They said their goodbyes to the woman on the bus and went with the new one. She drove them to a house in a beat up truck and told them not to get too comfortable, because they could leave at any moment. She had a cell phone with her and told them they were waiting for a phone call. As soon as she got it, they were going to leave. "I hope you slept on the bus," she told them, "because you're going to have to walk for a little while, then cross the river."

The two girls had barely sat down when the woman's phone rang. The person on the other end did most of the talking. All the woman said was, "*Si, si, entiendo, bueno,*" and then hung up. "Let's go," she said.

They got back in the truck and drove for about 10 minutes before stopping on the side of the road. There, others were also apparently preparing to take the walk to the river. "You'll go with them," said the woman in a whisper to the girls. "There's a truck on the other side and you two get on with everyone else. Ortiz has already arranged this, but don't talk about where you're going to anyone and don't mention his name. You don't want any trouble if someone else gets caught and starts dropping names." Yesenia and Silvia recognized a few people from the bus they had arrived on, but there were many other new faces. All told, there were between sixty and seventy people, Yesenia guessed. Finally, a man told them all to follow him, and they started walking.

They reached the Rio Bravo River, or Rio Grande as it was called on the U.S. side, in the middle of the night. It was a desolate area with no buildings, nothing but the dirt, brush, and the river, with the exception of a tiny red dot that periodically appeared before them in the distance. There by the river was an old Toyota T100 pickup, a 4x4 with its bed piled high with cargo under a tarp. As the crowd of people approached they were met by two men who wore jeans and boots. One had a cowboy hat and held a rifle; the other had a large knife attached to his belt. He also had a small laser pointer, which he put in his pocket.

"Line up here," said the one with the knife on his belt. All complied. The man with the rifle said nothing, but he glared at the lot. "Across this river is the States," said the man with the knife again. "There is a truck waiting in McAllen that will transport you north to Houston." He walked to the back of the pickup truck, which had a large cargo covered in black tarp. "There are some very important things to remember. No talking. No unnecessary noise of any kind. No smoking. The border patrol can see a cigarette from miles away. And once you cross the river, if you see headlights or people with flashlights start coming towards you, you run! If you get caught, you don't say a damn word about the rest of us. You keep your mouth shut or there'll be trouble waiting for you when they send you back." He pulled the tarp back and revealed some rubber inner tubes and a load of bundles, all wrapped tightly in black plastic like square blocks, each about the size of a suitcase. "Those of you who can't swim will use the inner tubes." He pulled one of the big square bundles from the back of the truck and said, "The rest of you will cross the river with one of these," said the man.

One of the women protested, "But what of our things? We can't leave our own things behind, but we can't carry our things and those as well."

"These float," said the man. "You can put your stuff on top of them. If there aren't enough inner tubes, those who can't swim or aren't very good can ride on these but don't break the wrapping and don't lose it. If you're handed one then this is your ticket on the truck. No bundle, no ticket. Do you all understand?"

Everyone nodded and the man began handing them out. There were sixty-eight people and only fifty bundles, so not everyone had to take one with them. There were only five inner tubes, though, and over a dozen people said they either couldn't swim or weren't very good, so they were given bundles to float on first. It was decided that the children would use four of the inner tubes, two children to each one, followed by an old woman who was given the fifth. After that, the others who couldn't swim well were given a bundle, followed by the older people, the women, and what was left of the men.

"What's in these?" Yesenia asked Silvia.

"Shhh," said one of the men who had taken the bus with them. "Don't ask. Just don't talk about it until you're on the other side."

Those with bags of extra clothes bundled them up and held tightly to them as everyone waded into the water. It was very cold, but didn't seem to be moving too fast, nor was it very deep. "This isn't so bad," said Yesenia.

"Careful," said the same man. "It drops in a moment and there are hidden currents. It's dangerous to cross here, but there's less border patrol."

No sooner had he spoke than the water rose from Yesenia's waist to her shoulders as the bottom began to drop away. She and Silvia both had bundles, and she was thankful to see it did in fact float as she'd been told. A few more steps later the bottom was gone and she was having to dog paddle to stay afloat. She'd tied her bag of clothes and meager possessions around her back and as the water soaked them they became surprisingly heavy. As a child she had learned to swim in the Nigales River, though, and so she was still able to move forward without much concern.

Other people in the group were not having it so easy. One woman, with two small children with her, was struggling to keep their possessions from being caught up in the current, which Yesenia now discovered was in fact present beneath the seemingly calm surface. The mother had a bundle she was using for assistance as her two children clutched an inner tube which a friendly man had offered to pull for her.

As Yesenia and Silvia moved forward, little circles whipped around them and she occasionally felt a sudden, jerking sensation when she was caught up in one. Silvia was struggling next to her and Yesenia had to reach out on one occasion to keep her from being pulled suddenly downstream.

Finally, they reached the other side. A few others had made it before them and all were met by the scariest looking man Yesenia had ever seen. An unlit cigar hung from his mouth, which he chewed on, and he had both a knife on his belt identical to the other man's and a pistol sticking out of the front of his pants. As she got closer she saw that the man's eyes weren't quite right. One eye looked straight, but the other wandered off to the side in an abnormal manner. Next to him stood two more men, one with a shotgun and the other seemingly unarmed but twirling a black tube in one hand. She didn't know it, but it was a night vision scope the second man held.

All of a sudden a blood-curdling scream broke the silence over the gurgling river. "Help! Help!"

The cockeyed man told the other with the shotgun, "Go see what that's about and shut 'em up."

He ran down towards the river and shouted back, "A kid's caught in the current." One of the woman's two children sharing an inner tube had fallen off when a swirl whipped the inner tube around. The man who had offered to help her had just managed to grab the tube again, but the little boy wasn't able to hold on and was now moving quickly down the river. His mother pushed off her bundle and tried to swim after him, but she wasn't a strong swimmer. "He's going downstream!" yelled the smuggler with the shotgun.

"Well, get after him," shouted the other.

Yesenia heard the pounding of boots as the other man ran down the riverbank. The woman was still screaming and the man pulled his pistol and started towards the river, "She's going to bring the patrol down on us, stupid woman." Yesenia was terrified the man was going to shoot her, but instead he walked down to the edge of the bank and yelled at her, "Hey! Shut up! Are you trying to get us caught?"

"My son!" she yelled to him in tears. "He can't swim!"

That's when the man noticed the woman had let go of her bundle and it, too, was now being pulled in the current. "Shit!" he yelled. "Look!" He shouted to the man that had already taken off downstream. "Get the bale!"

"What about the kid?"

"Fuck him, get the bale!" yelled the one with the wandering eye. He glared at the boy's mother.

Seeing that the smugglers were no longer trying to save the little boy, one of the other immigrants who had already crossed quickly took off his shirt, dropped his belongings, and took off down the bank. "Stop!" yelled the man with the cigar, but it was too late. The young man was gone in a flash.

Out in the river others were coming to the woman's aid. When they finally got her and her other child ashore, she started running down the bank. "No!" yelled the man with the cigar, but the woman ran anyway, a moaning wail trailing behind her as she sobbed, "Save him! Save him! He'll drown!"

"Shit!" cursed the man with the cigar again. He returned to the rest of the immigrants, telling them to put the bundles in front of them and stay where they were. "If anyone else runs off, I'm leaving all of you here," he warned. Everyone stood still as statues, quietly dripping and huddled together as they waited for the others to return, everyone wondering what would happen next.

The minutes that dragged by were filled with fear and apprehension. Nobody knew if the little boy was dead or alive. The man with the strange eyes and cigar began to grow impatient and angrier as the minutes stacked one atop another. "What the hell is taking so long?" he cursed.

Suddenly, someone appeared from the darkness. It was the young man who had taken off after the boy. Directly behind him came the little boy, wrapped in his mother's arms. He was crying and she was hushing him gently. He'd been saved. Yesenia said a little prayer to herself, thanking God.

A few minutes later the other smuggler returned, but this time things were not so well. He did not have the missing package with him.

"Well?" said the one with the cigar and straying eyeball.

The man shook his head. "It's gone."

"What do you mean 'it's gone'?"

The fear on the other man's face was evident. He held his hands up, "I don't know what happened to it. I was running after it, but it was out in the middle of the river. I was going in after it, but then it was gone. It's dark and they're black, I lost sight of it. I don't know if the plastic got ripped and it sank or what, but I saw it one minute and then it was gone the next."

"Damn it!" cursed the one with the cigar.

"Also, I'm pretty sure I saw some headlights in the distance. I think we'd better go, boss. We're sure to have set off a sensor or something with all that noise and movement."

The man chewed on his cigar and eyed the woman and her little boy like a lion sizing up wounded prey. His right hand fell to the grip of his pistol and his fingers played upon the handle. "That bale was worth more than you can make in year," he told her.

The woman looked horrified. She held her child close and eyed the smuggler's gun. Everyone held their breath. "I'm sorry," she said. "My son can't swim."

He stared at her with fire and death in his eyes, as though he'd love nothing more than to kill her where she stood. "Stupid woman," he spat, his body easing and his hand moving away from the gun. The woman let out a slight sigh of relief. Then, to the other two smugglers, he said, "Let's go."

One of them started pointing to people and told them to pick up a bale, continuing to use them as muscle to move the smugglers' packages. "No talking," he said as they began to walk.

The young man who had saved the boy picked up his belongings and placed them on top of a bale he'd been told to carry. The woman with the little boy, having lost her bundle, walked up to help someone else with their belongings, but the fierce one with the cigar saw her and held up his hand. "Not you."

"What?" she asked.

He walked up to her with a venomous stare and said icily, "I said not you. No bale, no ride."

"But . . ." said the woman, looking at everyone else as though hoping they'd say something on her behalf, but no one did. Nobody could afford to lose his or her passage. The woman's eyes filled with tears, "But, I've already paid half," she told him. "My husband is waiting for me. We've saved for two years."

"No." He moved his hand back towards his gun for emphasis.

Some people in the group looked upon with woman with pity, while others, like Yesenia, felt too ashamed to look at her. They wanted to help her, to demand that the smugglers take her and her children with them, but they were all too frightened. With no help, the woman would have to return to Mexico, forfeiting the money she'd already paid. Her husband would be smiling and joyously waiting for his family that was not coming.

The group began to follow the smugglers into the darkness. The woman stood crying, her two children by her side, but the man wasn't moved. She watched everyone walking away and looked out into the darkness that was the United States, apparently contemplating her options.

The other smuggler who had given chase down the river had lingered and as he walked by guessed her thoughts. "You won't make it," he said flatly. "It'd be stupid to even try. He won't let you on the truck and without a vehicle out here . . ." he looked at her children, then back at her, "just go back."

Having no choice, she picked up two of the inner tubes that were left by the bank and told her children they had to cross again. The one who'd almost drowned looked terrified and refused, but she told him they didn't have a choice. He began to sob fiercely. The last thing Yesenia saw of them was the woman crouched down trying to comfort her child to prepare him to swim back across the Rio Grande.

After an hour and a half of navigating the darkness, the group hit upon a worn path where a truck was waiting. It looked like a small moving truck, one used for transporting fruit or furniture. The smugglers directed the people inside the trailer. "No noise," said one as the group had begun whispering among themselves, thankful the walk was over. He told them to stack the bundles in the back and then when everyone was inside he closed the trailer door. A thud and click could be heard as the door was secured. Then they were all left in darkness.

When the engine groaned to life and lurched forward, Yesenia leaned over in pain, clutching her arms. They burned and ached from carrying her load.

"Who are they?" asked Silvia, who was also rubbing the muscles of her arms trying to chase the burning sensation away.

"*Palleros*," said the man who had talked to them by the river. "Coyote smugglers. They get paid to sneak people across like this. These are moving drugs, too. They're dangerous people," the voice said. "I wouldn't have agreed to this if I knew they were moving drugs, too."

"Is that what these are?" asked Yesenia. The bales were now stacked at the back of the trailer and she could smell a deep, leafy smell coming from them.

"Marijuana," spoke the voice, "worth a fortune north. That woman is lucky they didn't shoot her for losing one. If they weren't so worried about the border patrol, they probably would have. If we get caught with these, we'll all be in big trouble."

"Shhh," came one voice.

"Stop talking about it," said another.

As the truck bounced along, someone else whispered, "I hope they make it back across okay."

Yesenia did, too, and made a little prayer for the woman and her two children. Then she sat huddled with Silvia against the wall. They looked at each other, both thinking the same thing, but saying nothing. Their new life in America had not began well.

Chapter 5

Jamie swung her bag on the bed and fell in behind it. "Spring break in Cancun," she said. "How awesome is this going to be?" They had been planning it for weeks.

Kendra put her own bag on the other bed in the room, followed by Taylor, who looked at the two beds already claimed and asked, "Okay, so who am I sleeping with?"

Jamie rolled her eyes with a playful smile, "I'm sure the guys back in the elevator would love to hear you ask that."

"Funny," Taylor responded. Three guys in the elevator, all complete with a beer in one hand and a set of Cheshire grins, had eyed the girls like hyenas licking their chops over a dismembered wildebeest.

"They were such pervs," Kendra added.

Taylor stretched her arms out and walked onto the balcony. They were on the 12th floor of the Hutton Cancun hotel, right off the beach with a view like a postcard. "Wow," she told her friends. "You've got to come check out this view. I mean, just wow, look at this place."

Jamie and Kendra stepped out to the balcony to a pristine blue ocean brushing against white sand with a blue sky void of so much of a wisp of a cloud. It was utterly perfect.

Someone whistled and Kendra looked up and to the right to see two guys standing on another balcony. "Hey!"

"Oh, great," said Kendra. "There's more of 'em."

"We got a case of ice cold beer up here if you girls want to come up!" said a friendly voice.

"Maybe later," said Jamie dismissively. "Oh, they're just boys," she told Kendra. "Besides, it is spring break. Boys are kind of the point, right?"

As they looked around they saw plenty more partygoers at their best; either standing on their balconies, down at the pool, or spilling out to that beach Taylor just couldn't believe was actually right there in front of them.

"This is gorgeous," she said.

"I told you!" said Jamie. "And you didn't want to come. I bet you've changed your mind now, huh?"

As much as she hated to admit it, Jamie was right. Taylor had been planning on going home for spring break and the idea of being crowded into a hotel with every drunken college kid who'd seen one too many MTV Spring Break specials hadn't exactly struck her as the best of times at first. But she'd been persuaded and looking at the view from her balcony now, she was glad. "It's pretty damn cool," she admitted.

"Oh, Taylor, did it hurt?" Jamie asked sympathetically.

"Did what hurt?"

"When they finally removed that stick you've had up your ass for the last two weeks," she said with that same contagious smile.

"Ha, ha, very funny."

Jamie, ever the outgoing one, threw her hands over her head and let out a loud "Whoo!" She was echoed by no less than four guys.

"Oh, my God!" said Kendra. "Check them out!" The hotel rose like a pyramid with sides jutting out adjacent to one another around the pool below, and somewhere around the sixth floor were two girls who had ventured out unto their balcony completely topless.

One of the guys above who had invited them up for a beer yelled out to the topless duo, "Oh, baby, I love you!" The girls waved and blew him a kiss.

"What a couple of hookers," said Kendra. "Hey, look at him," she said, pointing at one pale fellow down at the pool, "He looks like someone stuffed the Pillsbury dough boy in a pair of surfer shorts." The young man, who obviously traveled from somewhere way up north with very little sun, stalked the pool down below with his buddies, his bulbous belly quivering as he went.

"Check out that one over there," said Kendra, pointing to another young man. "Is he wearing a T-shirt or is that his tan lines?" Closer inspection revealed it to be a farmer's tan.

"Yikes."

"That looks painful," Taylor noted. "Sun screen. Get some, dude."

"Look at the hoochie in the ass-floss," said Kendra, pointing to a girl who was parading around the pool in her thong.

"Hey, I brought a thong," said Jamie.

"Oh, Lord."

After they put their things away in the room, Jamie asked, "So what do we do first?"

"I think we should go check out the beach," said Kendra.

"I'm all for that," agreed Taylor. "That water looks unbelievable."

An hour later the girls were spread out on beach loungers and drinking large frozen margaritas. Jamie, absent a thong but wearing instead a flowered two-piece with sufficient coverage for her curvy frame, turned onto her stomach and unsnapped her top to tan without lines. "This is the life," she said.

Taylor was staring out at the water, her green eyes dazzled by the blue of everything she saw, and took a long sip, "Mmmhmm. Are we going swimming later?"

Kendra raised her sunglasses and looked out to the water. "I don't know. I don't want to get saltwater in my hair before we go out."

Taylor licked a bit of salt from the rim of glass as she took another sip. "Speaking of which, what are we going to do tonight?"

"I say we grab a couple of cute and semi-sober guys and hit a club," offered Jamie.

"Sounds fun," said Kendra.

"Bah!" answered Taylor. "Do we have to? Let's just go ourselves and have some fun, a girls' night out."

"Okay," said Jamie, "but boys will be part of the equation this week, just so you know. You can't avoid them forever and I'm not picketing just because you're on boycott."

"I know, I know." It wasn't exactly a boycott. Taylor had had a long-term relationship that recently went down in a spectacular ball of fire and wasn't particularly fond of the male gender at the moment. Her boyfriend decided they were getting too serious and broke up with her right before midterms. *Asshole,* she thought to herself. It wasn't that she was so much in love with the guy, but just that he dropped the bomb right before midterms, like she didn't have enough to worry about.

"You should have a fling," Jamie announced.

"What?"

"Yeah, it would make you feel better. Just find some cute guy, let him flatter and gush about how awesome you are . . . and you are awesome, by the way . . . and you'll feel way better."

"Thanks, but I'm not really feeling the fling thing," said Taylor, "particularly not in Cancun on spring break. Sounds like a pop queen gone actress bad movie. 'She was the girl who had it all until her heart was broken,'" Taylor recited in her best movie announcer voice, "'until a chance encounter on spring break showed her how to love again.'"

"Oh, God, that is bad," laughed Kendra

"Oh, you know what I mean," said Jamie.

"Ooh, there's a leading man for you now," said Kendra, as a fat guy walked by with two arrows drawn on his large belly, one pointing up towards his face, the other down to his crotch. Next to the arrows he'd written, "Free rides for hot chicks."

Jamie looked over and started cracking up. "Wow."

"Gross," said Taylor. "That is absolutely disgusting, and JAMIE! . . ." she raised her finger and pointed it towards her friend, "If you whistle at that guy to come over here I swear to God all your clothes are going in the pool."

Jamie cackled. Her friend knew her too well. She'd been just about to throw a "Hey, hot stuff," out there.

A half hour later the girls were still lying out when a young Hispanic man with a handsome smile and muscular build approached. "Good afternoon, ladies."

Kendra leaned up and pushed her sunglasses up again. "Hel-loo," she said in a singsong, relaxed sort of way.

"Are you enjoying your stay in Cancun?" he asked them in a smooth local accent.

Jamie re-snapped her bathing suit top and sat up, "Yeah, it's gorgeous."

"As are you three," he responded. The girls knew it was a corny line, but he pulled it off with such confidence they forgave him for it. It was entertaining if nothing else. He reached into a duffle bag he had slung around his shoulder and retrieved three yellow pieces of paper, handing one to each of the girls. "There's a party tonight at *Noche Salvaje* just down the strip. It's the place to be in Cancun and I would like to invite you lovely ladies to come as V.I.P.'s"

Kendra looked the paper over, "V.I.P.'s, huh? How much is the cover?"

"It's twenty dollars cover and we have an option for open bar at forty, all you can drink," said the man. "And we throw the best party in Cancun. All the celebrities party at *Noche Salvaje* when they come here. You don't want to go anywhere else."

Taylor huffed and Jamie immediately handed the paper back to him, "Thanks, but I'm pretty sure we can find some place without cover."

"Ladies," said the man, disappointed. "Oh, ladies, you don't know what you'd be missing. Here," he pulled a pen from his pocket, took Jamie's flier, and wrote something on it, "Give this to the man at the door, and you three will get in free. V.I.P.'s also get their first drink free. You can't come to Cancun and not at least visit *Noche Salvaje*. Once you see what I'm talking about you'll be thanking me. Our club is rated one of the best in the world. There's no other place like it here or anywhere."

Jamie took her flier back, "Well, maybe." She told him. "We'll see."

Taylor read her flier over. Fifty-cent beers, dollar tequila shots, two dollar you call it shots, a million dollar sound system, and the most bumping spring break party in Cancun.

As the man strolled away down the beach to court more potential partygoers, Kendra looked her flier over as well. "I think we should go. It sounds like fun. Do you think they pay that guy to go around looking for pretty girls to invite to make the place look better?"

"Well, yeah," said Jamie, her mischievous smile ever present. "I mean we are looking pretty good, if I do say so myself." She eyed her friends. "Taylor, how the hell are you already tan? We've only been out here like an hour and you're already darker than me."

"I tan fast," she said. She left out she'd been studying by the apartment pool in preparation for wearing her bikini in Cancun. She leaned back and sipped the last of her margarita down with a gurgling noise emanating from the straw, "So let's go, then. Sounds good to me."

They sat out and enjoyed one more round until a gray-haired European couple took two chairs near them. The elderly gentleman wore his Speedo as though he was at home in front of the television, the most natural thing in the world to him. Taylor was horrified to see Jamie's eyes fixated on the man's weenie-wrapper, red-faced and laughter threatening to escape at any second. The old man's equally rotund wife didn't hesitate to strip off her bikini top and proceed to tan stomach up with her sinking breasts resting sadly upon her belly as though they knew they belonged to an old woman and were ambivalent to anyone's opinion about their never-ending struggle with gravity, which they were clearly losing at an alarming rate. The old woman must have been a habitual tanner as her breasts looked like brown, leathery saddlebags someone had burdened her with.

Jamie boob-checked herself. "I'm done," she announced to her friends. As they walked back towards their room she added, "Did you see his . . ."

Taylor cut her off, "Jamie, please. Don't even say it."

"He looked like he was smuggling a tater tot in his Speedo," shot Kendra.

Taylor couldn't help but laugh.

Chapter 6

Taylor, Kendra, and Jamie were dressed to kill. Taylor stood in front of the mirror in the hotel room curling her hair. She wore a white skirt that showed off her freshly tanned legs, black flip-flops, and a black sequined top. Kendra wore tight shorts that accentuated her petite figure. She was busying herself by trying to adjust a padded bra. "I so need some boobs," she said.

"No, you don't," said Jamie, who was currently struggling against her endowments in the mirror. "They can be a real pain in the ass." She was retesting the straps of her tank top to make sure her breasts, which looked like they were clamoring to escape, wouldn't snap free.

"Whatever," said Kendra. "You can give me some of yours any day."

They caught a taxi around seven and headed north along Kukulcan Boulevard to *Noche Salvaje* which sat amongst other hot spots such as the Hard Rock Café, Dady'O's, and Forum by the Sea, a mini-plaza of restaurants and night clubs. There was a huge line outside, but when Taylor walked towards the line Jamie grabbed her by the hand and said, "We're supposed to be V.I.P., remember? V.I.P.'s don't wait in line," and she pulled Taylor to the front of the line with Kendra in tow, pushing people out of the way while flashing her cutest smile as though it were a hall pass that allowed her to cut in front of whomever she pleased. "Sorry, excuse us. Sorry, thanks."

When they got to the doorman, he held up his hand and said, "Line's back there, ladies."

"Yeah," said a terribly sunburned girl with a scowl on her face standing next to them. "We've been waiting half an hour. You need to go to the back," she told them snootily, pointing the way in case they weren't sure where it was.

Jamie pulled out her flier from the back pocket of her jeans. "Here," she said, shoving it into the doorman's hand.

He looked at the handwriting on the flier and then stood aside to let the girls pass.

"Hey!" said the other girl in the line. "How come they get to go in? I've been waiting for freaking ever. Oh, screw this, let's go!" she told her friends, and they stomped off in a huff. "This place isn't all that, anyway."

Jamie gave a wave over her shoulder, "Byeee," as they disappeared into the club.

The dance club was enormous. Shakira was blaring from that million dollar sound system the flier had advertised, "If my hips don't lie then I'm startin' to feel ya, boy . . ." drifted her voice, accompanied by Wyclef Jean and enough bass to mimic an earthquake.

"I love this song!" yelled Kendra.

The center of the dance floor was a sea of half-naked bodies. Lasers and lights lit up the club like a techno alien invasion. Bare-chested guys were groping girls who still wore their bikini tops; compressed air was shot out of various openings cooling tanned bodies slick with sweat everywhere they looked. And large though it was, the club was packed full. Everywhere they looked, people were screaming, dancing, and drinking, drinking, drinking.

"It looks like an orgy in here," said Taylor apprehensively.

"Oh, come on. Let's get this party started!" said Jamie. She grabbed Kendra and Taylor by the hand and headed for the closest bar where a bartender stood atop it like king of the mountain with a funnel and beer. A patron was knelt at the bottom of the bar, connected to the funnel above by a tube than ran down straight into his mouth. He sucked at the tube like a suckling piglet while his buddies shouted, "Chug! Chug! Chug!" The beer disappeared in seconds and his friends cheered.

"Three tequila shots," Jamie shouted over the chaos. Without even looking at her, another bartender whipped three tequila shots towards her. "Three Dollars! Open bar or cash?" He shouted. Jamie handed him a five.

"Hey, weren't you supposed to get the first one free?" asked Taylor.

"Screw it!" She handed Taylor and Kendra both a shot, raised her glass, and said, "Here's to spring break in paradise!"

Taylor looked at Kendra, who merely shrugged her shoulders with a smile. "Spring break!" they echoed, and they whipped the tequila down their throats, licked the salt, and bit the lime.

"Oh," said Kendra with a wince. "That's strong stuff."

"Top shelf," said Jamie. "They know their tequila down here," she laughed.

Two hours later they were all sloshed and having a ball. Kendra had disappeared back to the dance floor for the tenth time with another guy who had nicer abs than the guy before him. Jamie had temporarily lost her mind and was at the end of the bar letting guys put shot glasses in her cleavage and then shooting them with no hands while she laughed. Taylor shook her head disapprovingly, yet couldn't help laughing at the scene. Jamie had four guys eating out of the palm of her hand. They hadn't paid for any drinks since the first round of tequila. The moment any of their glasses got halfway empty, someone was offering to buy them another drink.

Taylor had retreated some feet away from Jamie's new entourage, as she didn't feel like being mistaken for a salt lick in a stag party. So she sat back a bit and enjoyed the spectacle while Kendra was off bumping and grinding.

She saw him coming out of the corner of her eye and thought to herself, *Oh, boy, here's a winner.* Khaki slacks, white, crocodile leather shoes no less, one of the lamest looking shirts she'd ever seen on anyone other than Disco Stew on the Simpsons and perhaps Mr. Furley from the old re-runs of Three's Company, and a thick gold necklace complete with a gold medallion for good measure. *Oh, good Lord,* she thought. She wondered if Steve Martin was about to jump out next to the man and exclaim, *We are two wild and crazy guys!*

"Hello," said the man when he reached the bar, his black hair gelled back and a goatee trimmed neatly on his face, his lips opening into a thin smile revealing a gold molar glinting in the corner of his mouth.

Sexy, she thought. "Yeah, um, hi. I'm waiting for someone," she said automatically.

The man's face became taught, "Oh, really? Because I've been watching you from over there," he pointed, "and I haven't seen you with anyone."

"I'm here with my friends," she said, pointing to Jamie down the bar.

"Well, I'm here with my friends," said the man "So if you wait for your friends here at the bar, may I not also wait for my friends here with you?"

Taylor wanted to be polite but she just really wasn't in the mood for this kind of guy. "Free country, I guess."

"Is it?" said the man with a smile. "I don't know about that." Taylor shrugged. *Weird one.* "Can I buy you a drink?"

"No, thanks, I've got one," Taylor said, holding her drink up.

She turned her back a bit to him and pretended to be very interested in what Jamie was doing, but she could feel the guy standing directly behind her watching her. "What's your name?" he asked.

She turned back to him. "Taylor. Look, I don't mean to be rude or anything, but I'm just here with my friends."

"Well, as I said, I'm just here with my friends as well. I'm Martin," he said, holding out his hand. He'd stressed the *tin* in his name so it sounded like 'teen'.

She shook his hand automatically although her thoughts were saying, *Guy, take a hint.* "Well, nice to meet you, Mar*teen.*" She then turned back around and did her best to ignore Mar*teen* as best she could, hoping he'd buzz away like the annoying fly he was becoming.

But he didn't. Instead she could sense him still standing behind her and it made her uneasy. She took her drink and sucked on the straw, then set it back down. "That's a nice ring," he said, reaching around and trying to point at the cheap silver ring she wore on her right hand. In doing so he spilled her drink and it sloshed against the front of her shirt and down her legs and she jumped backwards. The man quickly apologized, "Oh, damn, I'm so sorry," he said. He reached for a stack of napkins and handed them to her, "It was an accident, really, I'm sorry."

"It's fine," she said, exasperated, taking the napkins and cleaning the icy pina colada from her shorts.

The man called out to the waiter, "Pina colada, por favor."

"No, it's fine," said Taylor, realizing he was ordering her another drink.

"Please, I insist, *señorita*. I've made a fool of myself and the least I can do is replace your drink."

She was tempted to just turn and walk away but he seemed genuinely embarrassed so she did the politically correct thing to do and smiled half-heartedly and said, "Ok, then. You don't need to, though. It's no big deal."

"Ok, then," said the man, taking the drink from the bartender. "Again, I'm so sorry," he said. "I'm going to just go back to my friends. I'm sorry if I bothered you. And I can see you probably need to watch your friend over there," he said with a smile, pointing at Jamie.

Taylor turned and looked to see what Jamie was up to now; nothing terribly unusual. She had a blond boy's face nestled in her cleavage, probably licking salt from somewhere naughty.

"Hey, what the fuck are you doing!!?"

Taylor turned back around to see Kendra behind her yelling at Martin. "What?" she asked Kendra, wondering what on earth had her friend so upset.

"Is this your drink?" Kendra asked Taylor, pointing to the pina colada in Martin's hand.

"Yeah," said Taylor. "Why?"

"Because he was just putting some shit in your drink," Kendra said loudly, staring Martin down with fuming anger. She thrust a finger at him and said, even more loudly, "You were trying to put something in her drink!" Her voice rose loud enough for Jamie to hear, and she immediately separated from the boys and pushed her way to her friends, who she could now see were in a confrontational stance with some tacky looking guy.

"Hey, I think you're mistaken," he said with his hands up slightly in a peace offering.

"Bullshit!" Kendra yelled. "I saw you pull a little plastic bag out of your pocket and dump it in her drink." She snatched Taylor's drink away from him and held it in front of his nose. "What's in here!? What kind of shit are you trying to pull?!"

Jamie leaned over the bar and started yelling loudly at the bartender, "Hey! Hey! This guy just tried to drug my friend! Call the cops or something."

The bartender walked over and Martin scowled at Jamie and quickly turned and started walking away. "Hey!" yelled Jamie. "Hey, where do you think you're going? Hey, someone stop this guy!" she started yelling. "He tried to drug my friend! This guy is spiking drinks!" she yelled, pointing at him. "This guy is trying to put stuff in girls' drinks!" She didn't let up on him.

He kept walking through the crowd with the three girls trailing behind him, Jamie still yelling at the top of her lungs that he was trying to slip a Mickey to girls in the club. He had almost reached the door when Jamie's new entourage, who had noticed something amiss, appeared and one of them reached out and grabbed the man by the shoulder, "I think you better hold on there, pal."

Nobody really saw where they popped up from, but in an instant two other Hispanic men were at Martin's side and one punched the would-be Good Samaritan. One of the victim's friends started for the man who'd hit his friend, but he lifted his shirt to reveal a gun and the young man stopped in his tracks, throwing his hands up and fear draining the color from his cheeks, "Easy, bro."

"Oh, shit, he's got a gun," said Jamie.

She grabbed both Taylor and Kendra and pulled them back the way they came. Taylor had time for only a brief look over her shoulder to see the Hispanic men exiting the bar.

"Let's get the hell out of here," said Jamie. They went back to the bartender and explained what had happened and he disappeared to call security which was currently spread out in the bar. The three girls decided they didn't want to hang around to explain it all again for the cops. Right now, all they wanted was to get back to the hotel. Jamie asked some of her new friends if they'd walk with them outside to hail a taxi. They readily agreed and escorted the three chivalrously to a taxi and the trio headed back to the hotel.

The uncomfortable silence in the car was broken by Kendra. "Well, that was scary as hell."

Chapter 7

Yesenia felt ill. She was disoriented in the darkness, her equilibrium under constant attack with the rolling motion and pulling sensation every time the truck rounded a bend, and she was struck with the onset of motion sickness. Unfortunately, she was not the only one. Someone in the truck had already vomited and the smell was making everyone else nauseated. Someone, presumably the offender, had tried to clean it up and put the shirt they'd used in the corner, but the smell was still wafting around the enclosed space. They'd been in the truck 2½ hours so far. "I have to go to the bathroom," said Silvia.

"Me, too," Yesenia confessed.

"How much longer are we going to be in here?"

"I don't know."

"About three more hours," someone offered, having heard the girls talking.

"I can't go more than another hour without peeing," said Silvia. It was a shared sentiment with others in the truck.

Another two hours slipped by. The morning sun was up and the truck was beginning to heat up. It was only in the low 80s outside, but inside the metal confinement it was in the 90s and rising. People were sweating, the vomit was stewing, at least one person, probably more, had urinated, and no air was being ventilated. The stench that was accruing was unbearable, and no matter what she did, cup her hand over her nose or pull her shirt up over her face, Yesenia couldn't avoid it. She sat with her back against the wall and her legs pulled to her chest, trying not to think about it, though it was impossible not to.

Finally, she gasped. "God, the smell is horrible," she told Silvia.

"I know. I'm trying not to throw up."

"Here," said a woman, who leaned over in the darkness and handed Yesenia a small tube. "Spray some of my perfume under your nose. It doesn't get rid of the smell, but it helps." Yesenia took the perfume and sprayed a little, as did Silvia. The fumes actually made her feel worse for a moment, but as it dissipated she realized it did cover up the smell a little bit.

"Thank you," she told the woman, handing back the perfume.

Occasionally the woman would point the tube upward and let out a spray before finally someone said, "Please, no more perfume. I know it stinks in here, but it's making me sick. Please, no more." And so for the rest of the trip they were stuck with the stench.

"Aren't they going to stop to give us a break?" asked someone. "I'm thirsty and my body aches."

"I can't believe they haven't pulled over for us to use the bathroom," said another.

"Sometimes they stop, sometimes they don't," said another voice. "This is my third trip from the border, but I've never been put in the back of a big truck like this. They'll have to stop for gas, but I don't think they'll open the truck. It's too dangerous for them with all the drugs."

The man was correct. The morning wore on and the situation in the truck worsened. People began to feel dizzy from the smell and the heat. The sweat had no place to go when evaporated, so a haze seemed to drift about inside the truck, its humidity making people sweat worse. The truck did stop once for gas as the man predicted, and some of the immigrants debated about banging on the walls to get them to open up, but having figured they were nearing Houston, decided to tough it out and bear it.

"It's only a little further," said one.

"This hell is almost over," assured another.

Finally, at around 10:00 in the morning, the truck began making frequent turns, having apparently left the highway and now working its way along smaller streets. The mood in the truck lightened as they realized their long trip was nearing an end. The truck paused a moment and they thought they heard the sound of a garage door opening, then the truck moved forward again and they suddenly heard the sound of gravel beneath the tires.

After seven of the worst hours of Yesenia's life, the truck stopped and the engine was shut off. The handle of the doors rocked back and forth and then the doors opened.

The sudden burst of light blinded the occupants for a moment. They'd spent the last seven hours in complete darkness, and as the sunlight spilled over them many had to raise their arms for a moment as their eyes adjusted.

"God," said the man who had opened the door. "What's that smell?" He looked over the passengers as though they were dogs that'd just crapped on the carpet. "Come on, out of there, all of you."

Yesenia climbed out and the blast of fresh air was like slipping into a cold pool after walking across the desert, parched and weary, for untold days. She breathed deeply and her body rejoiced in the stench-free oxygen. She raised her hands over her head to stretch and couldn't suppress a smile. It felt so wonderful to be out of the truck. She felt like kicking off her sandals and skipping about, but of course didn't. The smugglers were still around and they hadn't put away their guns.

As she looked around, she saw they had pulled into the back of a small auto repair shop in a town called Rosenberg, Texas, just south of Houston. There was a privacy fence around the lot where cars sat waiting to be worked on and it afforded the immigrants secrecy as they climbed down from the back of the truck, some practically crawling with their cramped muscles and aching joints.

The smugglers told their passengers to unload the truck first and the fifty bales of marijuana were taken inside the shop and stacked neatly in a little pit normally used by mechanics when doing oil changes. Only then were they allowed to stretch their legs, use the bathroom inside the shop, and get a drink from the water hose, which was then used to clean out the inside of the truck, urine and vomit splashing out onto the ground.

Over the next few hours, cars began pulling up to the front of the shop and ringing a little buzzer. The garage door facing the street would open and the cars would drive through and out the rear garage door into the yard where they happily met the family members they were there to pick up. Husbands and wives, siblings, parents and children, all reunited with hugs and kisses. "*Papi*, you smell," said one little girl as she hugged her father.

"It was a rough trip," he told his wife, who also hugged him tightly but squinched her nose.

Yesenia and Silvia watched with a bit of envy, happy they at least had each other, but somewhat frightened to be in this new country with no family to greet them. They were even more frightened as the rest of the travelers left, leaving the girls alone with the smugglers, one of whom eyed them both hungrily.

The afternoon wore on into the evening and they began to wonder if anyone was coming for them. They were given some chips and soda by the men at the shop but it did little to fill their stomachs. Both could tell the men in the shop were becoming frustrated. Whoever was supposed to pick them up was running late and the one who had been eyeing the girls most of the day was sending shivers up Yesenia's spine.

If he had intentions of taking advantage of the girls, he was thwarted by an older model black GMC Suburban that pulled into the yard. Its windows were tinted almost limo black and the girls couldn't see who was inside, but when its doors opened two Hispanic men got out. They both looked to be in their twenties and they met the other smugglers like old friends. They walked over and looked at the two girls.

"I'm Jose," said one. "That's Hector." He pointed to the other man. "You'll be riding with us from here."

Yesenia and Silvia introduced themselves, but the men didn't seem overly interested. "Got the other stuff?" Jose asked the smuggler with the strange eyes.

"Of course. Ten each, right?"

"Yeah, fifteen loads." Each packed load they'd been carrying was twenty pounds of pot, and with an estimated street value of $300 an ounce, that was a potential $96,000 worth of pot per pack, or just under a 1.3 million dollars total profit if purchased at $10,000 a pack and then sold by the ounce all over the country. Jose and Hector weren't street pushers, but they'd still earn a nice cut just for their part. The cartels weren't likely to cease business any time soon with that kind of profit margin to be had.

The two men were led inside the shop and shown the bales down in the pit. Then they backed their Suburban up to the rear garage doors and put fifteen bales inside. They handed the man with the wild eyes a bag full of money. "A hundred fifty-five. The five is for the girls."

The man flipped through the cash and handed the bag to a man next to him to be counted, "You want a beer?"

"Sure," responded the man.

After drinking a couple of beers and smoking a few cigarettes with the other men, the money was announced counted and correct. So Jose and Hector shook hands with the others and told Yesenia and Silvia to get in the Suburban.

"Where are we going?" asked Silvia.

"Dallas," said Jose.

"Is it a long drive?" asked Yesenia, scooting into the back seat with Silvia.

"A few hours, but you'll be more comfortable than you were in the truck."

"Can we stop to eat?" asked Silvia.

"What, are you two hungry?" asked Hector.

"Starving," said Silvia. "We haven't eaten anything except chips since yesterday."

"You wouldn't believe the trip we had. They didn't even let us use the bathroom. People were peeing in the truck. It was disgusting."

"Hey, rest stops are the easiest way to get caught." The men drove through a McDonalds and handed the girls cheeseburgers with fries and cokes, which the girls devoured with relish. Afterward, with full stomachs, the two leaned in opposite directions on the bench seat, and it was not long until both girls fell fast asleep.

Jose looked back at them and told his friend, "You want to have some fun before we get there?"

"No," said Hector. "She might let you get away with it, but not me."

"How's she going to know?" asked Jose. "We can make sure they stay quiet."

"She'd know. Nothing gets by her."

Chapter 8

The taxi pulled to the curb in front of the hotel and the three friends got out. "That's not exactly how I wanted to start the vacation," Kendra said.

"It's going to be okay," said Jamie. "Let's just put it behind us, but we'll definitely be more careful for the rest of the trip."

"I still can't believe that guy," Taylor said as she got out of the car. Jamie pulled a little cash from her pocket and as she was paying the driver the girls saw headlights barreling down on them from up the street. They looked up to see an older cream colored car skid to a halt in front of the Hutton's driveway, tires screeching. Three men jumped out and Taylor screamed when she realized who it was . . . Martin and his friends.

The men rushed them and one punched Kendra viciously in the face. She dropped unconscious to the ground. The two men with Martin then grabbed Taylor and pulled her kicking and screaming towards the car where Martin stood opening the back door for them.

Jamie had looked up in time to see Kendra drop and the men grab Taylor. She ran around the taxi and flew at the men. "Get your fucking hands off her!" she yelled at the top of her lungs. She lunged at Martin as though ready to rip his eyes out.

Martin reached into his belt waist and pulled out a gun. "No!" Taylor screamed as she was pushed into the car and realized what was about to happen. "Jamie!" she screamed in warning, but it was too late. Martin shot her without a hint of hesitation. Her eyes went wide in surprise, and she fell face forward as she clutched her chest. Then he pointed his gun at the frightened taxi driver. The poor man tried to switch his car into drive and hit the gas, but Martin put two in his head before the car could take off. He then took two steps forward and leaned over Jamie as if to put another bullet in her.

Taylor was being stuffed into the car, her arms and legs held tight, but desperate to do anything to stop Martin she leaned towards the man holding her arms and bit him as hard as she could on his ear. He let out a belligerent scream just as Martin was about to fire, and instead he turned his head, saw what Taylor was doing, and ran over and kicked her in her head. She fell backward in the seat and Martin yelled at the man she'd bitten, "Let's go!" The man ran back around the car and jumped into the driver's seat.

A second later Martin pushed Taylor's legs further inside the car as he slammed the door shut behind him and the car roared off into the night. People began to run out into the street to help Kendra, who was still unconscious, and Jamie, who was face down on the asphalt bleeding to death.

Chapter 9

Yesenia was awakened by flashing lights. Her eyes fluttered open and she saw that the black Suburban was parked on the edge of the highway, its engine idling. The digital clock in the dash read 9:42 P.M. There was an unusual bustle of movement in the front.

"Don't panic," Jose whispered from the passenger seat.

"What do we do?" asked Hector.

"Just act normal. I'll take care of it."

Yesenia looked over her shoulder and saw what had the two men concerned. The flashing lights sat atop a Texas state trooper's car. She watched as the cruiser's door opened and an officer dressed in gray with a matching cowboy hat approached, his right hand resting on his pistol and a flashlight held up in his left. He was a black man with an athletic build and stern gaze.

Unbeknownst to the trooper or the girls, Jose's hand was also resting on the grip of a pistol. He slowly moved it to his lap and slid it beneath his thigh. Yesenia leaned up just in time to see what Jose was hiding away and she gasped. Next to her, Silvia was still sleeping soundly, but Jose had heard her and looked back at her. "Don't say a word," he warned her, his finger to his lips.

Hector rolled down his window as the trooper approached and smiled as though happy to be pulled over. "Was I speeding?" he asked.

"License and insurance, please," said the trooper. The beam of light from his flashlight slid along the interior of the vehicle like a snake looking for a mouse. Jose had his hands visible, one on the center console and the other on the window handle of the door. The trooper angled the light and looked at Yesenia and Silvia a moment before continuing the light towards the back of the vehicle where it fell upon the black tarp. Hector was fumbling with his wallet and handed his license to the trooper.

The light retreated from the car and fell upon the license he now held in his hand. "Where y'all headed?"

"Home," said Jose, speaking over Hector. "We were visiting family in the valley."

"Is that right?" asked the trooper, looking at Hector.

"Yes, sir," he answered. "I'm sorry if I was speeding. We've had a long trip."

The trooper leaned in a little bit, still moving his flashlight about. "You got your insurance card on ya?" he asked.

"I'm looking for it," said Jose as he opened the glove box and rummaged around.

"Whose vehicle is this?" asked the trooper.

"It's mine," said Jose. "We're taking turns driving."

The trooper flashed his light towards the glove box to watch Jose's hands, but saw nothing but a mess of papers. As he leaned in towards the vehicle to keep an eye on what Jose pulled out of the glove box, he suddenly picked up on the aroma of marijuana. The bales had been packed and re-packed as tight as could be, but still that unmistakable smell permeated ever so softy. And the trooper was all too familiar with that telltale scent. From roaches in the ashtray to dime bags people tried to hide in their underwear, he'd smelled it a hundred times before. But he didn't so much as raise an eyebrow to let on that he knew. The tarp in the back indicated this could be more than someone's personal joint he smelled. This could be a runner.

Intending to call for backup he retreated from the window a bit and told them, "Y'all keep looking for that insurance and wait here for a moment while I run the license."

Jose pulled some papers from the glove box, and as the trooper turned around he quietly slipped his hand beneath his thigh. He pulled his pistol and folded the papers around it, hiding it from view. "Sir! I found the insurance, sir!"

The trooper turned back around and flashed his light inside the car. Jose leaned over Hector as if to hand the officer a bundle of papers. As he reached out to take them the trooper glimpsed the bulge of the gun, but it was too late. In the second he realized what the man had in his hand, he went for his own gun, but Jose had already fired, striking the trooper in the neck.

Yesenia screamed as he fell to the ground, his hand grasping the wound as blood spurted out of his carotid artery. Jose jumped out of the Suburban and ran around to where the trooper was lying. Still holding his neck, the officer saw Jose coming for him and tried again to pull his gun, but Jose shot him three times more, twice in the chest and once in the head. His head tilted and his open eyes seemed to be looking at Yesenia. She covered her own to escape his gaze.

"C'mon!" yelled Hector, seeing headlights in the distance in the rearview mirror.

Jose took the license back from the trooper and ran back around and jumped inside, the tires throwing gravel as the black Suburban sped out.

Having heard Yesenia's screams and the gunshots, Silvia was now awake. All around her was chaos. Yesenia was moaning and nearly hyperventilating, the sound of the gun still ringing in her ears. Jose was staring out of the back window with a gun raised, and the Suburban's engine was being pushed to its max. "What happened?" Silvia tried to ask Yesenia, but got no response. Yesenia was crying now and held her hands over her mouth in shock. "What's going on?" she asked Hector.

"Sit back and shut up!" Jose yelled. Silvia turned around and saw the trooper's lights disappearing behind them as they sped away.

"Is that the police?" she asked.

Jose whipped his left arm back and slapped her hard. "I said shut up!"

Silvia flinched in pain and withdrew to the corner of the rear bench seat. Tears welled up in her eyes from the sting and she rubbed her face. She still had no clue what had just transpired, but didn't dare speak another word.

They drove on in silence, speeding through the cover of darkness for miles before anyone spoke again. "They'll be looking for us," said Hector. "Did you have to kill him?"

"Yes, I had to kill him!" yelled Jose. "He smelled it and was going to call for backup."

"How do you know?" asked Hector.

"I just know, okay. The way he put his head in then went right back for his car . . . I just know. Do you want to go to jail?"

"Now they'll all be looking for us," said Hector worriedly.

"Looking for who?" asked Jose. "They don't have any information. He didn't run the license." As they always did, the two men had stolen the license plates on their vehicle from another early model Suburban as a precaution before making the pickup. Soon the police would likely be breaking down the door of a very surprised Suburban owner whose real plates had been replaced with ones from a random car. After all, it was seldom people memorized their own plates or would notice them being changed out.

"We still have to get off the highway."

"There's not much further to go," said Jose. He pulled out a map from the glove box and turned on the dome light. "Just take the county roads ahead. We can take this one and get off the highway and it goes all the way down. Look." He pointed to a line on the map.

"Ok, that will work," said Hector. "But keep a look out. There's going to be cops swarming around here pretty soon."

A few miles later, just as Yesenia looked back and saw a speck of light flashing in the far distance, the Suburban turned down a thin county road. She stared behind her as the black patch of highway began dwindling away. She imagined at any second she'd see a dozen police cars suddenly turn down the road speeding after them. Her eyes stayed glued to the road, her heart trying to decide if she wanted to see the police coming after them or not.

They made a curve around a bend, cutting off her view of the highway, and after a few minutes Yesenia began to breathe normal again as they put more miles behind them. *What have I done?* She asked herself. *How did I let myself end up with people?* It all seemed to keep going from bad to worse and what scared Yesenia the most now was wondering how much worse it could get.

Chapter 10

Ten hours. That's the approximate time it took for all hell to break loose in Cancun. It was like an avalanche that began rolling down the hill that morning. Univision, the Hispanic television channel, broke the story in the United States on their morning news channel, followed by KHOU 11 in Houston. Other students on vacation in the hotel had found out what had happened and via Twitter, Facebook, and a barrage of cell phone calls, the news spread like a wildfire . . . the snowball grew bigger and bigger until finally half the mountain gave way to its weight.

By early afternoon a current affairs news commentator was on the case, tossing accusations around like cheap beads at Mardi Gras and comparing events with similar cases of years past. She had some poor clueless official on her program via satellite ripping him a new one for the incompetence of the local police, barraging him with insults while he stood and gave his approved answers in short, apologetic replies. The tourist strip in Cancun was now littered with Associated Press vehicles while famous newscasters stood outside of the *Noche Salvaje* recounting the last hours leading up to Taylor 's disappearance. By that afternoon, less than 24 hours after the kidnapping, it was worldwide. Parents all over the United States were calling their children in Cancun for spring break ordering their immediate return. The bars and restaurants were at half yesterday's occupancy. People were staying in their hotels and the markets were quiet. Fear and apprehension was on every face to be seen.

Jim and Amy Woodall were sitting at a conference table at the Hutton Cancun. Jim was tall with graying thin brown hair and tanned skin from his weekend golfing getaways. He was 48, but now looked more like 68 under the stress and lack of sleep.

Amy was four years younger, though looked much the same. Her hair was pulled back in a quick ponytail and she wore no makeup. She sat in a chair in a pair of shorts that had been close by when they got the call and a UT orange T-shirt she'd gotten on a recent visit to Taylor's school. She had sandy blond hair, crisp green eyes like her daughter, and a similar complexion to Jim, who she often joined on the weekends.

The hotel's Melbourne Ballroom was now ground zero for the search for Taylor Woodall. It had 9,652 square feet which could be broken up into four separate areas and could hold up to 1,000 people. Barriers and tables were being erected upon its red and tan carpet creating separate designated areas including a media relations section with a podium for when officials needed to make public statements and deal with the press.

The hotel and its staff were still in shock that the horrific event had occurred right outside their doors and the hotel chain's corporate offices in the U.S. had pledged their unequivocal support. Inside, the conference room bustled with activity while outside, a single palm tree stood back-dropped by the azure ocean in a picturesque view.

Across from the Woodalls sat senior officer Juan Ramirez and his partner Hernando Vargas of the Quintana Roo anti-kidnapping unit. Ramirez was 5'8" with a thin mustache and hair that was plastered into place by years of disciplining it with a sturdy comb. His eyes were sharp and he spoke English effortlessly. He was dressed in gray slacks with a white button down shirt and plain navy blue tie. Vargas was slightly older, his dark brown hair accented by gray that began in the part in his hair and slowly worked its way down like spilled paint. He wore a blue suit with a gold and blue tie.

In his hand Ramirez held an artist's rendering that Kendra had provided only hours before. She'd given them enough to create a strikingly accurate picture of the man named Martin. "We have circulated this photo to all the departments in and around Cancun," he was explaining to the Woodalls. On the table sat a picture of Taylor, one she had just taken before the trip for graduation where she wore her cap and gown. "We've also sent both pictures to every police station, gas station, and hotel in and around the district." He tapped the sketch with his index finger, "If this man shows his face anywhere in public, we will know. We will have his picture placed in every newspaper and in every shop window by this time tomorrow." It was already on every television channel in Mexico and the U.S.

"Why haven't they asked for a ransom?" asked Amy Woodall. It was the thought that worried her most. *Why wasn't there a money demand? If someone had kidnapped her, and they didn't take her for ransom, then what did they take her for?* She shook in fear to think of it. At first she was terrified of the idea of a ransom call, but now she was praying for one. Just some news that Taylor was still alive, some hope that she could get her back.

Ramirez had wondered the same thing about the ransom, and the only answer that fit didn't bode well. But it was not something he was prepared to share with the girl's parents. He knew the helpless feeling and the fear they suffered. He had worked many disappearances of young women during his time as an officer in Mexico City and then a detective in Chihuahua State. Usually, they never found the girl, or if they did, it was a body out in the desert. Many of the young women in Ciudad Juarez were forced to travel long ways for the jobs they found, either by bus or often walking across the barren landscape for hours. Hundreds of such women had gone missing, many turning up raped and killed. He'd seen the look in their mother's eyes when they learned what had happened to their missing child. He wondered if he'd be giving the Woodalls similar news in the near future. He hoped not, but the more time that went by without a ransom, the more likely the prospect.

Ramirez had worked in a department called *Unidad de Atención a Víctimas de Delitos Sexuales y Contra de la Familia,* or the Unit for the Care of Victims of Sexual Offences and Offences Against the Family, for three years before being put in charge of a search commission, set up at the behest of Amnesty International and former President Vicente Fox. He was all too familiar with looking into worried family members' eyes and telling them "We're doing everything we can," which is what he said now to Taylor's mother. "I can't say why there has not been a ransom demand."

She wasn't satisfied. "But that's what they do, right? These people, they kidnap Americans or wealthy people and then demand a ransom, right? I've heard about this before. They keep them alive, in a small house out in the country or something, sometimes for months, right? Right!?"

"It is very possible, *señora,*" Vargas told her. "Such things happen occasionally in this part of the world." Off to his right stood an official from the governor's office that shadowed Ramirez and Vargas, then reported back to his superiors. He cringed with Vargas's words.

"Why don't they have better security?" asked Mr. Woodall. "I thought the kidnapping problem you had down here was only in Mexico City or along the border. We would never have let Taylor come here if we knew you had a kidnapping problem here."

"Actually, it is unusual that the victim is a tourist. Normally, what you have said is true," said Ramirez. "This is the first time we've had an American tourist kidnapped in this way from the boulevard."

"We have one of the largest police forces in the world," said the official who now stepped forward. "We take our security very seriously. We will not rest until we have found your daughter and brought any responsible criminals to a swift justice."

This seemed to placate Mrs. Woodall, at least for the moment. She grabbed her husband's hand. "I feel so helpless," she told him. "We're sitting here, just talking and talking, and she's out there, God knows where." She pictured Taylor, lying in the gutter, bleeding and beaten, gasping for air, calling for her parents, and yet here they were, still talking. Or maybe she was in a dark room somewhere, tied to a chair with a blindfold and gag in her mouth. This image didn't seem a much better alternative. To keep from descending into madness, she concentrated on reminding herself what she'd heard about these sorts of things. The kidnappers usually just wanted money and therefore wouldn't be likely to hurt Taylor because if they did there'd be no ransom. Taylor was alive somewhere, uncomfortable and scared, maybe, but alive. She made herself believe that a call would come and they'd get her back. It became her internal mantra, *we'll get her back, we'll get her back.*

But the afternoon wore on with no demand, only hollow assurances of best efforts with no tangible progress. Finally, Jim Woodall couldn't take it anymore. He whispered to his wife "Well, I'm not just going to sit here and do nothing. These people obviously aren't getting anywhere." He picked up his cell phone and stood up to leave the room.

"Where are you going?" she asked.

"To call an old friend," he said, "someone who might actually be able to get something done around here."

Chapter 11

In a posh office in Dallas, a receptionist sat at a large oak desk answering the phone. "Hello, and thank you for calling the Law office of Catherine James, how may I direct your call?"

"Hi, is Catherine in?"

"May I tell her who's calling?"

"Jim Woodall."

"Just a moment, sir."

She transferred the call to a phone sitting atop another larger oak desk where Catherine James sat peering over papers, her black hair pulled neatly back and her blue eyes moving quickly over the pages. She'd just settled a large lawsuit based on an oil pipeline leak and subsequent environmental damage, garnering her client a more than fair deal by having the supplier of the sealant kick in half the damages via their insurance carrier. She was now putting the finishing touches on the release.

Behind her two posters adorned the wall, one of Mukhtar Mai and one of Neda Agha-Soltan, as well as a Rice University bachelor's degree, a Doctor of Jurisprudence degree from the University of Texas, and an enormous and intricately detailed world map. When her secretary told her who was on the phone she picked it up with a pleasant voice. "Jim?"

"Hi, Catherine."

"It's good to hear from you. How are you?" It was a nice surprise to hear from Jim. She hadn't talked to him in almost a year. The annual Christmas card was their usual means of communication these days, though she had sent Jim's daughter a graduation card the year before.

He answered in a tired and strained voice. "Catherine, I have a problem. A big problem." She could hear his voice shaking. "Have you heard the news?"

"What news?" Catherine had been working on her deal for a while now and while the news about what had happened in Cancun had been airing all day on the television, she'd been so focused on the task at hand that she'd paid no attention.

"Taylor's been kidnapped."

Catherine's tone instantly changed. "What!? When!?" She grabbed her pen and a legal pad from her desk drawer as Jim talked. "Wait, wait," she said, trying to get her mind around what he was saying, "Tell me everything from the beginning."

Forty minutes later she burst out her office door. "Get me a flight to Cancun," she told her secretary. "First one you can . . . doesn't matter what time. I'm going home to pack now."

"Now?" her secretary asked, baffled. "But you have an early meeting . . . "

"Cancel it."

Bewildered but ever efficient, her secretary immediately started dialing, "Is everything okay?"

"Not by a long shot," Catherine said. "But I'll have to explain later."

She briskly walked into another office where a young man was busy browsing the internet, doing his best to appear busy while doing so. When she entered, he was halfway through the entertainment section of CNN and looked up, alarmed, to see his boss standing before him. "Teddy, I need you to finish the settlement docs," she told him.

Flabbergasted, the young man looked at her in disbelief. "Me? Um, sure, yeah." He eyed her for a moment wondering if she was about to say *Gotcha!* with a big grin, but she looked anything but joking at the moment. "Yeah, Catherine, you bet. That'd be great! I'll get right on it." As one of three associates, he'd never been asked to finalize anything . . . Catherine always saw the big cases through by herself. She handed him the folder, hoping he was up to the task. He was bright eyed and willing enough, which wasn't entirely comforting. "Jennifer can fill you in on any points you're missing, but I have to go out of town on an emergency. I really need you to be on top of this, Teddy. It's important."

"I got it, no problem," he said, holding the folder as though he'd just been handed his first driver's license.

Before she left she told her secretary, Jennifer, who was on hold with an online travel agent, "Call me on my cell when you get the confirmation." Then she whispered, "And make sure Teddy doesn't screw up."

Chapter 12

Julio and Juan scrambled over the wall of the cemetery, two wiry young boys, one with big ears who moved clumsily and with eyes darting warily on the lookout for police, the other more sharp-eyed and sure moving like an agile tomcat. Juan, the clumsier of the two, lost his grip while climbing down and let out "*Chinga!*" before hitting the ground with a thud.

"Shhh," demanded Julio. "You're going to get us caught." Juan held his hand up apologetically. "Hurry up."

They walked through the monuments, tombs, and headstones, heading to a place they'd been before. It was a large, ornate tomb, with three walls and a roof, but open on one side. It made an excellent shelter where the two homeless boys could sleep.

"I don't know why we have to sleep in the cemetery," complained Juan. "The dead don't like it. It's bad to sleep where they sleep. What if they curse us for it?"

"Don't be so superstitious," said Julio. "As long as we're respectful, they won't bother us." Juan didn't look convinced. "Besides, it's safer here at night than in the street."

"Ghosts walk here at night," said Juan.

"They do not," said Julio. "They sleep. They don't care if we're here." The homeless problem in Mexico had been worsening, and it was Julio who discovered it was easier to find a safe place to sleep in the cemetery rather than try to fight for a bed in a shelter or crouch down in an alley. "Besides, we don't have to worry about being beat up here," he told Juan. It was true. The older homeless boys or adults rarely tried to sleep in the cemetery.

As they walked Juan suddenly stopped. "What was that?"

Julio stopped and listened for a moment, "What?" he asked.

"I heard something."

Julio stood quiet and listened, but he didn't hear anything. "It's nothing, a dog or something."

"Are you sure? What if they have someone watching at night?"

"Nobody's watching. How many times have we slept here? And have we ever seen anyone? No. Nobody stays here at night." Julio went through this with Juan every time they slept at the cemetery. "Just follow me and don't worry so much."

Julio kept walking and Juan cautiously followed, but then he suddenly ducked. "What are you doing?" asked Julio.

"I saw someone!" he said in a whisper.

"You did not. There's nobody here. We're almost there, so come on."

"No, I did, I swear. I think it was a ghost. I told you they walk here at night!"

"There are no ghosts," said Julio. But in truth he was a little frightened. He'd often seen shadows in the night that scared him, and if he walked the streets alone, he probably wouldn't stay here. It was easier for him to put on a brave face for Juan, because Juan's cowardice always made him feel so much braver. And it was never safe on the streets alone. While the cemetery was normally empty, Julio had long learned that around any corner there might always be thugs who were more than ready to beat him up for whatever he might have in his pocket. Even if he had nothing in his pocket, they still might beat him up, possibly worse for having nothing to offer. The streets were a dangerous place, and those who were smaller or not in a gang always had to be on the lookout. Julio trusted no one, save maybe Juan. He knew they were just two little fish in a sea full of sharks.

"Someone was walking down there, I saw them move," said Juan. "If it's not a ghost, then it's someone else, but I saw them."

"You always think you see something. Remember when you thought you saw the *Chupacabra*?" scorned Julio. It turned out to be just the ugliest dog they'd ever seen. Nonetheless, he ducked his head and proceeded quietly. "Come on, I'll show you."

Juan reluctantly followed the other as they sneaked low around the headstones and tombs. As they moved, they suddenly heard voices.

"Aren't you done yet?" said one in a hurried whisper from beyond the end of the row of stones just behind the tomb to their left, far too close for comfort.

"Do you want to get down here and dig?" asked another voice.

"I already had my turn," said the other.

"Why are we burying her here, anyway," asked the digger. "We should have just driven out to the desert or left her for the crocodiles somewhere."

"We hide her here because this is where we were told to put her. They don't want her found and nobody's going to check the cemeteries," said the other. "It was a bad idea to get her in the first place. I don't know why your boss wouldn't listen. Did you see what happened? It's everywhere already. One day and the entire fucking world is looking for her. Looking for me!"

"You can't tell him anything when he's like that," said the other. "Once he makes his mind up, that's it with him. He doesn't think of anything else."

"What's his problem, anyway? Is he fucking crazy?"

"I don't know. He just gets like that. He gets in one of his moods and won't listen to anyone. But don't tell anyone I said so. He'd kill us both just for talking about it."

"There wasn't any reason for this shit. You have no idea how much trouble he's brought us. No idea. He's going to get us all killed, the stupid son of a bitch."

"What are they doing?" asked Juan.

"Shhh," said Julio. "Grave robbers, maybe," said Julio, although he already knew by the conversation they probably weren't. They snuck a little closer and stayed behind a tomb out of sight. In the soft light they saw two men with shovels. One had his shirt draped over a headstone nearby, but had khaki slacks and what appeared to be some kind of dress shoes on. Around his neck a gold chain glinted in the moonlight. The other was equally well dressed. The boys heard a Clunk! And the man digging said, "Finally!" He threw his shovel out of the hole and began brushing the dirt away. Then he opened up the casket.

The other man looked inside. "Huh," he said. "Still fresh."

"He was just buried," said the digger.

"You want some company, *señor*?" asked the other jokingly. "We have a very pretty girl for you." He let out a laugh.

"She was," said the one with the gold medallion dangling from his neck. "And stop laughing. This shit isn't funny." He climbed out of the hole and Julio and Juan watched as the two men walked a couple feet back behind a monument. When next they appeared, they were carrying a body, one holding the ankles the other grabbing the wrists. The boys were close enough that they could see she didn't have any clothes on. Also, she didn't look Mexican. She had blond hair and her skin, while tan, didn't look Hispanic. The men dropped the body by the re-opened grave and the one with the chain got back in the hole. When the body hit the ground, its face turned towards the boys. It was partially obscured by the hair, but the boys could just see the unmistakable mouth, nose, and closed eyes that appeared unnaturally swollen.

Juan made a noise of surprise and shifted his body as if he was going to run, but Julio quickly grabbed him and shook his head, *No.* He held his finger up to his mouth in a silencing gesture.

The man with the gold chain looked up as though he may have heard Juan.

"Hey!" said the other. "Come on, already. Let's get this over with."

"Shut up," the digger responded angrily. "I'm not in the mood for any shit. That's my picture all over the news. It's me they're all looking for, not you."

"Well, you're the one that shot the other girl. Nobody told you to do that. You could have just found someone else instead of taking this one in front of her hotel. That's what got all the news people running stories about it."

He stared at the other man murderously, the steely glint of his eyes matching the metallic shine off his gold chain. "The other one shouldn't have gotten in the way." He paused a second longer to look around again, but hearing nothing then bent down and grabbed the body by the arms and dragged it to the hole. Then each took an end and maneuvered the body until it disappeared into the embrace of the grave's current occupant. A few seconds later the boys could hear a shutting noise as the casket closed again. Then the men in the grave climbed out and both proceeded to start shoveling the dirt back.

Julio and Juan sat quietly while the two men worked, too frightened to move lest they be heard. After a while the job was done. One of the men stretched his back and then sat down on a nearby headstone. The other, however, the one with the golden medallion about his neck, meticulously packed the dirt, poking and prodding as though unsatisfied with its appearance.

"What are you doing?" asked the one sitting.

"It has to look right. What if this man's family comes to visit and notices someone's been digging? They might call the police, and the police may check the grave. We can't have any mistakes. Otherwise, it'll be us that are buried next. You said it yourself. Your boss is a crazy asshole. Hell, we're all dead men either way if we get caught. If your boss doesn't do it, the cops will." There was a slight pause, and then the man sitting stood up and began to help. After a few minutes the one in gold said, "There, that's good enough. I've had enough of this. Let's go." The two men walked off, leaving the boys dazed in the darkness.

"Who do you think they were?" asked Juan.

"I don't know," said Julio.

"Were they grave robbers?"

"No," said Julio. "They were here to bury that body."

Juan seemed to think about this. "Do you think they murdered her?"

"Yes," said Julio.

Juan sat on his butt and leaned against the tomb they'd been hiding behind. "Should we tell the police?"

Julio looked at him. "No. We can't tell anyone," he told Juan sternly.

"But they murdered someone," Juan said.

"Did you see their clothes?" asked Julio. "They're gangsters. If they knew we saw them, they'd kill us, too. We can't tell anyone what we just saw. Understand?" Juan nodded his head, but it didn't seem to Julio that Juan understood how precarious their situation was. "I'm serious," warned Julio. "If we tell the police, then they'll come get the body and those gangsters will know someone saw them. They'll come looking for us and if they find us, they'll kill us and hide our bodies just like that woman." Juan's eyes got big and Julio knew he understood now. "So we were never here and we didn't see anything, right?" Juan nodded. "Say it," Julio told him.

"We were never here and we didn't see anything."

"That's right. Now let's get out of here. They might come back again."

Chapter 13

Shortly after midnight, the black Suburban turned down a dirt road. They had been crisscrossing back roads to avoid any law enforcement, even once cutting through a field when Hector became nervous about headlights ahead. All the while Yesenia and Silvia had sat in silence. Silvia kept looking at Yesenia with questioning eyes, and Yesenia had made the gesture of a gun and pointed back to the horror they'd left behind. Slowly, Silvia began to realize what had happened. She and Yesenia let their eyes do the rest of the talking to one another.

At the end of the dirt road they came to a crude fence with rectangular structures ahead of it. As they approached two large Rottweilers greeted them barking aggressively. Jose got out and called to one of the dogs, "*Hola, Chico.*" The animals seemed to recognize their master and began wagging their tails. The man then opened the fence and the Suburban continued on into a little clearing where four very old mobile homes sat in a makeshift compound. An old woman wearing a muumuu and smoking a cigarette came out of one of the mobile homes followed by a man who looked similar to the two young men who had driven Yesenia and Silvia. The girls were dismayed to see he was armed with a pistol sticking out of his jeans.

The old woman moved like a cow, her chin tucked downward and her stride heavy and slow as her slippers shuffled along, the cigarette held between yellowed fingertips before she flicked it away. Behind her, the younger man walked leisurely with a caballero swagger, sharkskin boots on his feet and an ivory bolero around his neck.

The old woman walked over and kissed Jose on the cheek in greeting. "Everything good?" she asked.

He held his head down slightly. "No, we had problems. It's bad."

"What kind of problems?" asked the old woman as Hector got out of the vehicle as well. The two men looked at one another. "What happened?" she asked them.

"We had to shoot someone, Mama . . . a police officer."

The woman put her hands to her cheeks and gasped. Then, without warning, she rose up on her tiptoes, her slippers remaining flat but her heels suddenly popping out of them, and she smacked Jose hard on his head, "*Idiota!*"

"You killed him?" asked the man with the bolero.

"You shut up," spat the old woman at him, turning back to Jose. "How could you be so stupid?"

"We had to, Mama. He pulled us over and smelled the marijuana," Jose whined as a child might as he rubbed his head.

"And why were you pulled over?" asked the woman. "Were you speeding?"

"No, Mama."

She looked at the two men disapprovingly. "Stupid, stupid, stupid."

"We had the fake plates," said the other man. "And he didn't have time to run the driver's license."

"Did you get the video?" asked the woman.

The men looked confused. "What video?"

She smacked him on the head again, "They have cameras, you idiot. They keep the video in the trunk. You didn't get it?"

"No," he admitted.

She mumbled curses at them before saying, "Well, at least you didn't get caught. You'll have to get rid of this thing, though," she gestured towards the Suburban where Yesenia and Silvia were just getting out.

"It's fine. I can just paint it. I don't want to get rid of it."

She scowled at him. "Fine, paint it, then. But make sure it looks different. It can't look anything like it does now. Put different wheels on it, change everything."

As Yesenia and Silvia got out the two large dogs sniffed around their legs and both girls huddled together. The dogs looked as big as they were.

Jose looked towards them and told the woman, "They saw."

The old woman looked at the girls and walked over, "Oh, they did, eh?" She gestured to the Suburban and told the man who had accompanied her, "unload it." Then she looked to the girls. "I'll have a talk with them." She walked up to Yesenia and poked her in the ribs with her index finger, "And which one are you?" She kept on poking her like a schoolyard bully pushing a smaller child around. Yesenia was so unnerved she couldn't find her voice. "Well? Out with it! What's your name?" asked the woman. One of the dogs had his nose in her crotch and Yesenia remained speechless.

Silvia spoke up instead, "Yesenia. Her name is Yesenia."

The old woman wheeled around and smacked Silvia on the head like she had done Jose, "Was I talking to you?" Silvia cowered and remained silent as the woman turned back to Yesenia. "Now, then, I'm talking to you, girl. What's your name?"

"Yesenia," she finally managed.

"Yesenia Flores, yes?" said the woman.

"Yes, ma'am." The dog was still pressing itself against her and Yesenia stood tense in fear that it would attack.

The woman scolded the dog, "*Oye, Chico.* Hah! Go on, now!" She waved her arms at him and the dog ran off with the other one underneath one of the mobile homes, still wagging his tail as though he'd enjoyed angering the old woman.

Yesenia relaxed a little, but then the old woman grabbed her by the chin. "Well, I know all about you, Yesenia Flores, including your sister in Mexico City." She let go and turned to Silvia, "And you! I know all about you, too." She stared at both the girls menacingly, "So did you see these men shoot anyone?" Silvia looked at Yesenia in confusion, but she caught on as Yesenia shook her head, no. "What's that?" asked the woman. "Speak up!"

"We didn't see anything," said Yesenia.

"I was asleep," said Silvia honestly. "I didn't see anything."

"Ah, well, that's good for you, isn't it? You just remember that." She circled around the girls, sizing them up. "I'm Miss Lydia," she told them. "I run things here. You behave and do like you're told, and we'll get along and things will be good for you. But if you don't," she wagged her finger at them, "things won't be good for you."

She stopped in front of Silvia and stared at her. Silvia felt very uncomfortable and looked to Yesenia for support, but Yesenia kept her head down. Suddenly the old woman grabbed one of Silvia's breasts. She was so shocked she didn't have the nerve to pull away. She stood at attention like a soldier while the old woman felt her up. "How old are you?" asked the woman as she squeezed and pressed on Silvia's body. She moved her hand from Silvia's breast down to her hip and pinched her love handles.

"Um, eighteen," Silvia answered nervously.

"Huh," said the woman. "A little chubby, aren't ya." It wasn't a question. "Well, we'll fix that."

She moved in front of Yesenia and tried to repeat the process, but when she grabbed her breast Yesenia pulled away. The old woman hit her on the head and yanked Yesenia back in place. "Stand still," she told her, and continued her examination. Yesenia complied, her jaw clenched in anger. "Don't be such a prude," said the woman.

She pressed, pinched, and squeezed while Yesenia fumed in humiliation. "You're not so bad," the woman finally said. Then she addressed both girls again, "Now, Arnulfo will show you where you sleep. The other girls will explain the rules to you. You'd better learn them fast, or else you'll learn the hard way. The first rule is you behave and do as you're told. And don't get it in your head you're going to run off somewhere. There's nowhere to go and my dogs let me know if anyone is coming or going that shouldn't be. Now, off with you."

The man with the sharkskin boots told the girls to follow him and led them to one of the mobile homes. It was an odd pink that had become weatherworn to a dreary color, like a red that'd been washed too many times.

"You'll be staying here," said the man as he opened the door.

"Here?" asked Silvia. "You mean this is it?"

"Of course here," said the man. "Where did you think you were going?"

"But this is the middle of nowhere."

"That's how Miss Lydia likes it. The girls will explain things. Just do what you're told and you'll be fine."

Chapter 14

Catherine shifted uncomfortably in her seat. The first flight she could catch ended up being early in the morning and she was already dreading the hours lost. She knew enough about kidnappings to know that the first hours were the most important. Still, it had been the best she could do under the circumstances. It seemed Cancun was suddenly on a lot of people's travel plans, either going to for the media or coming back by the hordes of early departing vacationers.

It wasn't a very long plane ride but she hated the blackout of information. There would be no CNN on this flight, which she'd been glued to the whole night before, and she was still woefully ignorant of what steps had already been taken, having only what she got from the news last night and what Jim told her on the phone the day before. Her clients weren't going to like her suddenly dropping everything, but she didn't care. This wasn't the type of request where you tell a friend you're too busy. *That poor girl,* she thought. *And poor Jim.* She could only imagine what he and Amy were going through right now. She looked down at her watch and groaned to herself. Every minute ticking away was precious lost time. She thought about the one time she'd met Taylor Woodall. It was around the time of her own great tragedy. Her fiancé, David, had been good friends with Jim, which is how she became friends with him. David and Jim were both avid cyclists and rode on the same team each year for the Austin MS-150 charity challenge. But one early morning as David had been on a ride, he'd been struck and killed at a fairly quiet intersection that had a bush that stuck out too far, blocking the truck's view, and a driver who was going too fast, running late for his shift. Several months later she'd been in Houston on a case, and after the trial had called Jim to see if he wanted to get together. Much to her surprise he invited her over for dinner with the family. Taylor had been just fifteen or so, a very pretty girl, she remembered, smart and outgoing.

It wasn't surprising Jim would think to call her. He knew she did a lot of international law involving things mostly a little further south in South America, but occasionally her travels led to Mexico and she knew a few people here and there who were some decent people to know in a crisis. She wasn't sure how much help her casual contacts could be under the circumstances, nor how much help she could be for that matter, but it was something. And right now something was better than nothing.

When the plane touched down she ran into some issues with customs and it took a couple of phone calls to get sorted out. But it wasn't long until she was in a similar taxi to the one that Taylor, Kendra, and Jamie had taken the night before last, and on her way to the hotel where it all happened. She was shocked when she pulled up to the resort. It looked so, well, vacationly . . . not the sort of place anyone would have guessed that something like what had happened could happen. That, in itself, she found unnerving.

Chapter 15

Two days after seeing the men with the body in the graveyard, Juan and Julio were in the market square looking through trashcans for something to eat. "Who do you think she was?" Juan was asking Julio.

"I don't know," he answered. He was elbow deep in an effort to fish out a quarter of a burrito someone had thrown away. He pulled it out, swatted it a few times to get some coffee kernels off of it, ripped it in two, and handed Juan the other piece. "Looks okay," he told him.

Juan took it happily. "She looked white," he said around a mouthful of tortilla.

"She was," said Julio. He thought again about the gangsters and what would happen if they knew the boys had seen them. "I don't think we should talk about it. It's best to pretend it never happened."

Juan finished his piece of burrito in one bite. "I'm still hungry," he told Julio.

"Me, too. Go check that one," he said, pointing to another trashcan.

Juan ran to another bin and began rummaging through it. He held up a piece of bread but then something else caught his eyes. He put the bread back in the trash and called to Julio, "Look!"

"What?" asked Julio perturbed, still looking through the trashcan where he'd found the burrito. "You find anything good?"

"Yes!" cried Juan.

Julio looked up expecting to see Juan holding food, but instead he had a newspaper in his hand.

"What about it?" he asked.

Juan ran over with the paper. "Look at the picture, blond hair."

Julio took the paper and stared at the front page. Neither boy could read, but there were two pictures, one a color photograph of a girl with blond hair wearing a cap and gown, the other a sketch of a man. In the sketch the man wore a chain with a medallion, and next to both pictures, a very big number with the easy-to-recognize symbol for American dollars.

"What does it say?" asked Juan.

"I don't know," said Julio.

"That's them, right? She could be the woman and this guy is wearing a necklace like the guy we saw, right?"

Julio stared at the picture and tried to remember what the body he'd seen looked like. The hair was right, so was the skin tone, but the facial features were hard to match. Still, it was a dead body they'd seen. That might make her look different, he figured. And the sketch did look like the man from the graveyard, especially with the necklace. "Maybe," he told Juan.

"I think it's her," said Juan. "See? That says American, right?" He pointed at the headline, *American Tourist Kidnapped!* He'd seen the word America or American many times, and it was one of the few he could recognize. "And what's that?" He pointed to the reward part, but although they both knew it was a dollar amount, neither recognized the word reward although they figured rightly what it was. "It's a reward, isn't it?"

Julio looked at the girl in the picture and thought deeply. He knew his basic numbers but did not know how much the number in the paper was. It was a lot, though. The more zeros, the more money, he knew. And just like that his curiosity overcame his fear. He wanted to know more.

The boys decided to take the paper to a nearby vendor everyone called Aunty Nita. She worked a little lemonade stand that also sold chicken and beef kabobs. She was old and hobbled about on a cane, spending most of her time sitting in a little plastic chair, either cutting the chicken and beef into little cubes, or cooking it over a little wood-burning stove. Her bad leg kept her from standing all day, pouring lemonade or ringing up sales, and she probably would have been unable to run her little stand if not for the assistance of her niece, Maria, a young woman in her late 20s with a round face and a big smile. Aunty Nita was missing most of her teeth and her tongue seemed to constantly be moving around her gums, as if though she were always checking to make sure her few remaining ones were still there. Her face was wrinkled and her gray hair always pulled back so tight in a bun that it looked like a helmet, and as the boys had learned over time, she was a very grumpy old woman. But she was also a very informed woman, another thing they'd learned about her over time. That tended to be the case with nosey people who were always listening in about others. Plus, her niece was always very good to the boys, so they decided it'd be the best place for them to learn a bit of news.

As they walked up to the counter Maria greeted them with a friendly, "*Hola, niños.*" She looked over her shoulder. Aunty Nita was watching them carefully, stabbing little chicken chunks with a wooden stick. "I can't give you any lemonade," she whispered, "Aunty Nita's watching. But if you wait around, she'll go to the bathroom soon, and I'll give you a cup to share." Aunty Nita had a bladder as bad as her leg. The boys had been coming to the market almost a year, and Maria was one of the few vendors who didn't chase them away and curse them. Instead, she was always kind and sometimes gave them lemonade or the occasional kabob when Aunty Nita hobbled off to relieve herself, something which Aunty Nita suspected and absolutely abhorred. So she was none too happy to see the boys this day.

"Are you giving those little street urchins free lemonade?" she asked from her chair.

"No, Auntie!" said Maria. But Aunty Nita got up from her chair anyway.

"What do you want?" she asked the boys. "Do you have money? If you don't have any money then you have no business here. Go away before you scare away my customers."

"Please," said Julio, "we were just wondering what this says." He pushed the paper on the counter.

Aunty Nita looked at the paper and the boys as if annoyed with them, but she picked it up anyway. Her eyes squinted, and her lips moved a bit as she tried to form the words, her tongue occasionally flicking forward along her gums. Maria leaned over her shoulder, "It's about the American girl that's missing," she said, both to the boys and to Aunty Nita.

Aunty Nita looked at her reproachfully, and then back at the paper again as though swiftly reading it. She handed it back to the boys, "Ah, yes," she said. "So it is. My eyes aren't what they once were, so it takes me a moment to focus is all." She'd already heard about the story, anyway, so she didn't really need to read the whole thing to know what it said. "You shouldn't be so nosey," she told the boys. "But if you must know, a tourist got shot and another one disappeared and everybody's looking for her. They're offering a reward."

"How much?" asked Juan, excited.

The woman eyed them suspiciously. She leaned towards the boys, "Enough. Why? What business is it of yours? Have you seen this woman?" Her wrinkly hand pointed to the picture and her tongue swirled around behind her lips.

Juan's face lit up in a smile and he looked as though he was about to tell them everything, from start to finish, but Julio stopped him by stomping on his foot. Juan, not quite grasping why Julio stomped his foot, quickly responded by kicking Julio in his shin. Julio, unfazed, still managed to recover the situation. "No, we just thought she was a famous singer. I told Juan she was, but he said she was an actress. We were just trying to settle it."

Juan suddenly realized his error in letting his face say too much, so he nodded in agreement. It seemed to have worked, at least for the moment. She looked at them as if waiting for one to crack, but could read nothing definitive in their wide-eyed faces. "Well, if you do see anything, you come tell me and I'll help you boys. You're too young to get a reward, anyways. You'd have to get an adult, so if you see or hear anything, you come tell your Aunty Nita and I'll give you both some lemonade and a skewer each, and also help you get the reward money, okay?"

"Okay, Aunty," promised Julio.

"Okay, then," she told them. "Off with you."

As the boys ran off Juan was practically skipping in excitement, "I knew it! That's who we saw. We know where she is!"

"Be quiet," said Julio.

"I wonder how big the reward is."

"Stop jumping around. She's still watching us."

Juan looked over his shoulder and Aunty Nita was indeed following them with her eyes. As they scampered off and out of sight, she turned to Maria, "I don't want you giving them free lemonade. They're like dogs; they'll keep coming back if you feed them."

"Yes, Aunty," Maria sighed.

Later that afternoon Aunty Nita began to have a gnawing feeling. *Those boys know something,* she thought. She couldn't get Juan's expression out of her mind. He'd been excited when she told him what the paper said. And the way they'd walked away, with him practically skipping and the other looking over his shoulder . . . they knew something. She told Maria she was going to run an errand and went to the *caseta*. There on the wall was the hotline number for Taylor Woodall. She dialed the number and reached the anti-kidnapping unit. "I'm calling because I think these two street urchins might know something." She was transferred to one of the Detectives and told him about the incident. "If they do know something and it leads to the girl, then I would be the one to get the reward, yes? After all, I'm the one calling. Those two are just trying to hide something, but I'm trying to help."

"Yes, yes," assured the officer, "don't worry. Now, are they still there at the market?"

"No, they ran off, but they'll be back. They always come back."

"Here, let me give you my direct number. If you see them again, you call me directly."

Chapter 16

"We should tell the police and get the reward," Juan was telling Julio.

It was something Julio had been pondering since the day before when Aunty Nita told them what the paper said about the American. "Maybe," he said. "It's still dangerous. And Aunty Nita's right. They won't give us the reward."

"Why not?"

"Because, we're not old enough. We would have to have an adult. If we had parents, then they would get the money until we were old enough, but no parents means no money."

Juan was frustrated by this reasoning. "That doesn't make sense. They have money for anyone who knows where the American is. We know. What difference does it make how old we are?"

"It's just how they do things. They won't give two street kids that much money. They'll find a way to trick us and keep it for themselves."

"So what do we do? We could get Aunty Nita to help us. She said she could help."

Julio shook his head, "She'd definitely keep it for herself." He picked up a piece of paper wrapper on the sidewalk and began twisting it in his fingers, thinking deeply. "Maria would probably help, but then Aunty Nita would find out. Let's just wait. We have to be smart. We'll wait until we can think of a way to do it."

"But what if someone else finds her first?"

"Who's going to find her?" asked Julio. "You saw how well they hid her. Nobody knows where she is except us and those gangsters."

Juan reluctantly agreed and then changed the subject when his stomach growled. "Can we at least go back and find some food, then?"

Julio wasn't sure if he wanted to forage under the eyes of Aunty Nita, but decided there was little harm in it. They'd already told her they didn't know anything, and if she tried to talk to them again they'd just leave. "Yeah, I'm hungry, too."

They walked down the streets, the sun cooking the brick of the buildings and beating down on the boys. No sooner had they entered the market and began looking through the garbage than Aunty Nita saw them and told Maria to watch the stand while she walked to the *caseta* and made a phone call.

The boys had found little food today and were just about to leave to go look behind some of the restaurants that would be throwing their lunch trash away when a police car pulled up. A man dressed in a suit got out and was greeted by Aunty Nita. She pointed to the boys and

Julio was suddenly filled with fear. Juan watched with curiosity as the man began walking towards them. Julio began walking away quickly and Juan turned to him, "Where are you going?"

"We should run, Juan," he told him.

"Why?"

"She must have told the police we were asking questions," said Julio. He paused and beckoned for Juan, "Come on."

Juan turned and the man was now briskly headed for them. *"Hola, niños!"* he called to them, "I just want to talk for a moment."

"Come on, Juan," Julio said sternly.

Juan looked at the man and thought about the reward. This was their chance. This was his chance, maybe. For once, he thought Julio was wrong. The police wouldn't care they weren't adults. All they wanted was to find the American. He was convinced they'd give them the reward. If Julio wasn't willing to talk to them, then he would, and he'd bring back the reward and Julio would be embarrassed about being wrong. But Juan would share. Julio was his best friend and he'd bring back the reward for both. For once, Julio would have to admit that it was he, Juan, who had known best. "No," he told Julio. "I want the reward."

The man in the suit was nearly on them, "Come on, Juan!" Julio scolded again.

But Juan stood his ground, "No!"

The man in the suit had reached Juan now and was telling him, "Hello, Hello." He looked at Julio who had backed away some fifteen feet. He smiled friendly and held out his hand, "Where are you going? Come back, come back," said the man, waving him to return. "I only want to talk to the two of you." Julio stood firm, looking from Juan to the man, an awkward standoff of tension. "It's so hot out here," said the man kindly, "Don't make an old man walk anymore, please. Come, I'll buy you both a lemonade and we'll just talk for a bit."

Juan smiled at Julio and also waved for him to come back and join them. "It'll be okay," he told Julio, "you'll see."

But something told Julio to run. He didn't trust the police. He knew Aunty Nita was after the reward and he didn't trust her, either. *Why hadn't Juan listened?* The police would lock them up and make them tell them what they saw, but there wouldn't be any money. They'd drop them back in the streets and the gangsters would come looking for him. Julio was furious with his friend. He wanted to grab Juan and make a run for it together, but it was too late.

"Come on, *niño*," said the man, now a bit more gruffly. He started to walk towards him, and Julio turned on his heels and ran.

"Julio!" yelled Juan. "Where are you going?! Julio!"

He looked back over his shoulder only once to see if the man was chasing him. He wasn't. Instead, he'd gone back and put a friendly arm around Juan, who seemed to be apologizing for Julio, who turned back around and disappeared.

The man and Juan sat in the square and talked over a nice glass of lemonade. Then he told Juan something that made him smile wide. A few minutes later Juan and the policeman drove away together.

Chapter 17

"So you're the new girls, huh?" asked the woman. Silvia and Yesenia had each been given a room already furnished with a bed and dresser. Yesenia's had an ugly orange carpet with a matching bedspread and when she opened the closet to set her bag out of the way, roaches shot out and disappeared behind the wood paneling that lined the walls. She recoiled and smacked the lining, hearing a slight squish sound followed by a large dead roach falling out from under the crack.

Silvia's room was almost identical except done in green. Both rooms seemed like a throwback to the 70s. She had put her bag away and gone into Yesenia's room to try and figure out what was going on, but as soon as she sat down with Yesenia on the orange bed another young woman walked into their room. She wore shorts and a tee shirt with no bra. She would have looked relaxed except she had makeup caked on her face. She stood leaning against the doorjamb, filing her nails and waiting for the girls to answer. "So, you got names?"

Yesenia was still embarrassed about being fondled outside, horrified at the events that had occurred on their ordeal coming here, and downright afraid for her life at this point. She wasn't in the mood to talk, so Silvia answered for them. "I'm Silvia, this is Yesenia."

The woman eyed them. "Where you from?"

"I'm from Mexico City," said Silvia.

"And you?" She looked over at Yesenia who sat stoically without answer. "What's your problem? You don't talk?"

"She's from Mexico city, too." said Silvia. "We had a bad trip. I don't think she feels like talking."

"Oh?" asked the woman. "What was so bad about it?"

Silvia knew better than to tell the woman about the police officer. "It was just bad is all," she said.

"Oh, Jose and Hector had a go at you, huh? I can't say I'm surprised."

"What do you mean?" asked Silvia.

"You know what I mean. What happened? They rape you or something?"

"No!" said Silvia. "Of course not!"

"Oh," said the woman, genuinely surprised. "Well, they're going to have a go at you sooner or later. Those two are a couple of horny little bastards. They're always getting free ones."

"Free ones?" asked Silvia.

The woman laughed. "Oh, shit. Don't tell me you don't know."

"Know what?"

"Do you have any idea where you are?"

"No," Silvia admitted.

The woman found this very funny and laughed even more. "They haven't told you, yet? Wow, that's just fucked up. Neither of you know what this place is?" She chuckled to herself, "Wow."

"Told us what!?" Silvia asked defensively. "What is this place?" She didn't like the way their apparent new roomie was enjoying their confusion.

"*Chinga, chica*, you're in a brothel." Silvia looked confused but Yesenia looked up, suddenly awakened from her shocked state.

"A brothel?" asked Silvia.

"Yeah, you know. A whorehouse," the girl said. "A place where men pay to have sex with women."

"What are we doing here?"

That made the woman laugh even more, "Holy shit, girl, are you serious? You're the new girls, aren't you?"

As the words seeped through, Yesenia's heart sank like a lead weight. She'd been conned. They weren't going to help her find a job here. They were going to try and make her a prostitute. She'd given herself over to murderers and drug running coyotes, and now they had her and there was nothing she could do about it. She broke down in tears.

Chapter 18

It had been a full day and night since Juan left the market with the police officer, and Julio was worried. He'd walked the streets they normally walked together looking for him, but had seen nothing. He had wanted to go back and ask about him, but he was scared Aunty Nita would call the police on him.

Finally, he told himself he had to go back to the square and find out where Juan was. If the police were holding Juan, then he had to consider whether or not he was prepared to risk joining him. He was scared of the gangsters, but he was also scared of life on the street alone. Juan was impetuous, clumsy, and not the brightest person in the world, but Julio missed his friend terribly nonetheless.

He made his way through the streets to the market, but stayed hidden across from Aunty Nita's stand, waiting for her to leave. After sitting crouched in between two other little stands for half the morning, he finally saw the old woman get up from her little chair, tell Maria something, and hobble away. He watched her as she strolled out of the market square, and then he quickly darted out and ran to the stand.

"*Hola*, Julio," said Maria. "I was wondering where you got off to. What was all that about yesterday?"

"Have you seen Juan?" he asked.

"No," said Maria. "Haven't you? He's not with you?"

"I haven't seen him since yesterday morning," he told her. "Not since Aunty Nita called the police and they took him away," he added with a hint of pout.

Maria looked at him sympathetically. "Is that what it was? I was wondering where she had gone when we saw you two back again. I guess I should have known."

"Yes, and now Juan is missing."

She looked at him skeptically, "Missing? You mean he still hasn't come back?"

"No," Julio told her.

She picked up her wooden spoon and stirred the lemonade. "Do you think he's sitting somewhere waiting for you?"

"No, I've looked. He's not anywhere we usually go."

She clicked the spoon against the lip of the large jug that held the lemonade and said, "I'm not sure where he is. I guess maybe they've kept him for questioning, or they may have taken him to an orphanage. That's probably what they've done. I don't think they're allowed to just let a little homeless boy go back on the street." She didn't seem much concerned.

"An orphanage is worse," he told her. "Can you find out where he is?"

Maria seemed to ponder it. "Maybe. Aunty Nita has gone to get medicine from the pharmacy, but she'll be back any minute. If she sees you she might call the police again. She thinks you boys know something and she's hoping for the reward."

"We don't," he said automatically.

Maria smiled at him. "I don't really care, Julio. If you do, then you should tell the police so the American girl's family can find her, but if you don't, you don't. It's really none of my business, but Aunty Nita thinks everything's her business and that could be trouble for you if you do know something. I'll tell you what. I'll go this afternoon to the police station and see if he's still there or if they've dropped him off at the boys' shelter. If you come back tomorrow I'll tell you what they tell me."

Julio thanked her and ran off before Aunty Nita returned. Neither he nor Maria noticed a man who looked like a tourist taking photos of them. As Julio left the square, the man began to follow him and pulled a cell phone from his pants pocket, his fingers already dialing.

That afternoon, true to her word, Maria took a taxi the seven miles to the police station. She was greeted by a police officer who sat in a little booth that looked like an old-fashioned theatre ticket box.

"May I help you?"

Maria briefly explained the situation before she was cut off. "One moment, please." The officer picked up a phone and dialed an extension. A moment later a young female officer came out to greet her and she explained the reason for her visit.

Meanwhile, Catherine James was asking, "Have you circulated the vehicle information outside the district?"

"Of course," said Ramirez. He was holding up fairly well given the amount of pressure he was under. For the past two days he had given two press conferences on their progress, been hounded by the press both at the office and at his home for the few hours of sleep he tried to gather, and sifted through tips, all the while the governor's official shadowing him and coaching him on what was and wasn't okay to say to the press. "Keep it optimistic. Downplay the possibility of her being killed and for God's sake assure them that Cancun is safe." Things had continued to slide for the popular vacation destination. The markets of local wares and crafts had full shelves and empty cash registers. Hotels were having spring breakers exit like herds of cattle as parents were calling their children and demanding their return to the States. The airlines were swarmed with angry calls as people couldn't get their departure date moved forward. The busiest tourist time of the year was becoming an economic black hole as money flew away by the planeload. Ramirez had retreated to the police station for some peace and quiet to review the information they had accumulated thus far, which wasn't much considering how much manpower they had on the matter. He'd expected to have more by now . . . a body, the car, someone calling in who recognized the man immediately, something. But thus far, they had nothing new but some worthless video and hundreds of leads that all seemed to go a thousand different directions, none of them concrete. His quiet moment of peace had been interrupted by Ms. James' visit.

"Interpol has stepped in to assist and has circulated the information to border patrol. Not to mention the media attention. If either the girl or this man appear in public, I have little doubt someone will see them and we'll be notified," Ramirez assured.

As if he hadn't already had enough headaches, Ramirez had recently met Ms. Catherine James, fresh from a visit from the Woodalls and full of focus and dissatisfaction at the progress thus far. Apparently, she was a private investigator the family had hired, or so they had explained. She was polite and professional, but she was already clearly putting her thumb down on important people, which was making things that much more uncomfortable for Ramirez. Plus, there was something about her. It struck him that the she seemed a little too seasoned. She swiftly set into a mode of operation as though she'd done this many times before, and Ramirez wondered just what kind of private investigator she was. She'd already demanded full access to all their information, and much to Ramirez's dissatisfaction, his superiors had agreed.

It wasn't that he didn't think the family deserved the access, but in his opinion having their own person step in like this could cause a diversion to the investigation. The Governor's shadow man, Fuentes, had told Ramirez, "The last thing we want is the girl's family going on the news and telling everyone that the local officials aren't cooperating. The girl's probably dead, anyway, so give their people whatever they want so if we do end up with a body we can say we did all we could." So, acting on his superior's orders, he was now giving Catherine a rundown of where they were on the investigation, Catherine still launching a barrage of questions.

"Someone had to have seen that car around the club before the night of the kidnapping. Have you checked with all the stores along that part of Kukulcan?"

"Yes, we have. And we've pulled as much video as we could find. We have images of the car, but that's all that can be seen. Its windows were dark and it was at night, but Detective Vargas is running down matches."

"I'd appreciate a copy of any video you have," she told him. "Have you sent it to the FBI to see if they can clean up the resolution?"

"We have our own technology division, ma'am. We are not as backward as you may think."

"I'm not making a judgment one way or the other, Detective, but Interpol can send along a copy to Quantico and they have a system there that we need to run it by. How soon can I get . . . "

She was interrupted by a knock that came at the door as the female officer walked in, "I'm sorry to interrupt, sir," said the woman. "But a woman is here asking about a missing boy."

"Well, take a report," he told her with a sigh. This was one more thing Ramirez was having a hard time reckoning. All other investigations were now on hold indefinitely pending a resolution to the Taylor Woodall kidnapping. And while he understood its importance, he couldn't help but feel a pang about telling his officer to take a report about a missing child instead of doing it himself. "I'm in a meeting," he told her, "but get the info."

"I know," she said. "I've already talked to her a bit. She says she's pretty sure Vargas had talked to the kid about the missing girl. She wants to know if we're holding him. I just thought maybe you might know what she was talking about."

"No, I haven't heard anything about it," said Ramirez, surprised.

"Okay, I'll take a message then for Detective Vargas," she said. "He probably knows."

She was about to leave the room but Catherine stopped her, "No, please." She turned to Ramirez, "Why don't you go ahead and talk to her? I need a refill on my coffee, anyway."

Ramirez shrugged, "Okay, if you don't mind. It probably won't take but a few minutes." He told the officer, "Go ahead and send her back and I'll handle it." She left the room and returned a few moments later with Maria in tow.

Maria entered apprehensively, immediately trailed by Catherine who had also returned with a fresh cup of coffee. She nodded to the departing officer and smiled at Maria as she passed next to her and took a seat. Ramirez rose to greet Maria, "*Hola, señorita.* I'm Detective Ramirez, Detective Vargas' partner. Is there something I can help you with?"

They shook hands and Maria couldn't help but to look at the other woman in the office. "This is Catherine James," said the officer. "She works for the missing American girl's family."

Catherine rose, shook her hand, and greeted her in perfect Spanish, "Hello, please just ignore me. I'm just going over some papers." The woman returned her greeting and Catherine sat back down and began reading over a notepad she had with her.

"Now, then, what can I do for you?" asked Ramirez.

"Oh, I was wondering about Juan, *señor*, the little boy Detective Vargas talked to yesterday. I was just wondering if the police are holding him for some reason. His friend came and told me he wasn't back yet and he's very concerned. Can you tell me if he's still here or if he's been taken to an orphanage?"

"I'm not sure, *señora*," Ramirez told her, reaching for his own notepad. "When did Detective Vargas talk to him?"

"Oh, just yesterday," said Maria.

"Are you sure it was a Detective Vargas?" asked Ramirez. "What did he look like?"

"Yes, my aunt called him. I saw his name on a piece of notepaper where she wrote his number. I was going to call but thought I'd stop by instead." She described the man she'd seen talking to Juan in the market. Ramirez listened intently and then recalled Vargas did leave the day before to check out a lead. When he returned, all he said was that it was another dead end.

"Are you sure the boy left with Detective Vargas?"

"Oh, yes, quite sure. I watched them leave together."

Ramirez began rapping his pen against his desk. This was quite odd. Vargas hadn't mentioned the boy. "Maybe he dropped the boy off somewhere at the boy's request," he told Maria.

"Maybe, but I think he would have come by. Do you know if he was taken to a shelter nearby or an orphanage, maybe?"

"Not that I know of," said Ramirez. "Maybe he just hasn't come by the market again yet."

Catherine sat quietly thumbing through her notepad as though the conversation did not concern her, but Maria had the odd sense she was listening quite intently. "Maybe, *señor*. But if so, I am still concerned. You see, Juan and the other little boy, Julio, they go everywhere together. It's not like him to go off on his own." Slowly she began to feel a worry creep upon her, even a dread. The more she sat there telling them why she was there, the more she realized Julio was right. Juan wouldn't go anywhere without him. She was beginning to wonder if Juan didn't get himself into trouble somewhere. "Can you ask Detective Vargas where he dropped him off? He's a sweet boy, but he is prone to get into trouble, probably even more so without his friend. I would like to make sure he's alright."

Ramirez gave her his card with his direct phone number as well as his assurances that he would check with Vargas and that if Maria called back that afternoon, he'd have something for her. As she turned to leave Catherine rose and asked, "May I walk you out?"

The question caught Maria off guard as much as Ramirez, but she saw no reason to protest. Ramirez could only watch in curiosity as Catherine exited with the woman.

"So you are with the police up north?" Maria asked as they walked.

Catherine smiled, "No, not the police. I know Taylor Woodall's parents and they've asked me to help look for her, is all."

"Oh. I'm very sorry for them. I hope they find her."

"As do I," said Catherine. "So this boy, Juan, has he taken off like this before?"

Maria was surprised at Catherine's interest. "Well, he and his friend are homeless so they go around everywhere, but it's not like Juan to go off without Julio. So, no, he hasn't done this before, I don't think. I only really know him from the market, but he's a sweet boy, they both are, though they do get into trouble from time to time. I hope he hasn't done anything foolish. I think Julio keeps them out of trouble for the most part. Juan can be a bit impetuous."

"Do you think something may have happened to him?"

"I don't know," she told her. "I thought he was here, that the police were holding him or took him to the shelter, but if he's not here, then I can't imagine where he's gone. I wasn't very concerned until now."

"Now you're worried?" Catherine asked.

Maria nodded. "Yes, now I'm worried. Something feels wrong."

As they reached the door Catherine pulled out her own business card and wrote a number on the back. "Well, I'm sure it will be okay. I know the police sometimes don't pay much attention to a missing homeless person, though, so if you need a little help getting information, please give me a call. Juan will probably show up soon, though. Little boys are adventurous. And, of course, if you hear anything about Taylor Woodall, I'd be very interested, even something small." She handed her the card which had the number to a pre-paid cell phone she'd already purchased at the airport, one with a local number so she might be available at all times.

Maria took the card and thanked her.

When Vargas came back from lunch Ramirez asked him about the boy. "Oh, that," he responded matter-of-factly, "just boys playing. They had seen a blond woman and thought she looked like the one in the picture. I gave him a ride to show me where they saw her, but it was nothing. Just some tourist they'd seen, probably. Either that or they were making it up to try and get some of the reward money, them and everyone else." They'd already encountered a number of people with off the wall stories trying for the reward. It was all part of the circus.

"Did you drop him off somewhere?" asked Ramirez.

"I offered to give him a ride back to the square, but he said he was fine, so I left him there on the tourist strip, by a dress shop I believe. I think he was upset I wasn't impressed with his story. He was convinced he was going to get a reward. Why, is anything wrong?"

"A woman came by and said he's missing."

"Missing? Missing from where? He's a street kid. They never stay in one place."

"Still," said Ramirez. "She's worried."

"Well, should I go back and look for him?" Vargas asked.

Ramirez sat thinking, his pen rapping again. "No, I suppose he'll turn up."

"I'm sure he will, too," said Vargas. "I'll take a ride back down where I left him anyway and see if he's not still hanging out down there. It might not hurt to talk to some of the vendors again, anyway."

Chapter 19

Julio had bedded down in an alley near the restaurant district. He'd found a half-eaten, lemon-pepper chicken breast in one of the dumpsters, finished it off, and was now in a makeshift tent he'd built by leaning cardboard against the dumpster where it butted against the wall. The smell was unpleasant, but it was good shelter for the night and gave easy access for when the restaurant threw out its breakfast leftovers in the morning. Sleep was not coming easy, though. Julio wondered what Juan had told the police and worried for him as he shifted his weight vying for comfort.

At the end of the alley an old cream-colored Pontiac pulled to a stop. The man who had taken pictures of Julio and Maria earlier was standing on the street and walked to the car. A few words were exchanged and the man pointed down the alley. The driver gave him a handful of money and the man smiled happily and then walked away, back down the street in the direction the car had come.

As Julio tossed and turned he heard an unfamiliar sound in the alley. A car's engine could be heard echoing off the cracked brick walls. He poked his head out from his makeshift tent and saw it slowly creeping down the alley, its headlights ominously off. Immediately, he was filled with fear. He ducked back inside hoping he hadn't been seen and sat quietly listening and waiting.

The car pulled up next to his shelter and the engine died. He heard footsteps approach, their clip-clop noise nearly drowned out by the beating of his heart, which was now pounding in his chest. The cardboard was jerked away, and the first thing Julio saw was a gold medallion flashing before his eyes. He bolted as fast as he could, two hands just barely missing him.

"Grab him, you idiot!" the man shouted to his cohort.

Julio ran with all his might, the sounds of two sets of feet just behind him. "Help!" he screamed, "Help!"

"Damn!" yelled the other. "He's like a cockroach!" Julio was running full speed and despite his shorter legs, was gaining the distance to the end of the alley faster than the men.

"Just shoot him!"

Hearing this, Julio immediately jerked to his side and ducked his head, a bullet just missing him and careening off the wall, its echo resounding sharply. He was near the end of the alley, but just as he was about to round the corner another gunshot echoed and he felt his leg explode in agony, as though he'd just been lashed with a whip of fire. He let out a scream but did not stop, instead stumbling forward, forcing himself to stay on his feet; refusing to allow gravity to take him down.

He rounded the corner and continued running, desperately trying to keep his balance through the searing pain. *I'm going to die,* he thought. He'd never outrun the men chasing him. *It's the gangsters, they found me. Juan told the police and they've found out, and now they're going to kill me.* His leg hurt horribly and was shaking unsteadily with every step. If it wasn't for the adrenaline coursing through his body, he would have already collapsed. He was just about to give in to the pain when he saw a fleeting hope ahead. There on the street was a storm drain in the curb. He ran to it with all the speed he could muster and practically dove inside. It was no easy fit, but he scrambled in, scraping his arm and cheek, but disappearing inside just as the men fired again.

There was a small culvert inside the drain just big enough to fit him and he crawled in just as a face appeared in the opening above him. A hand with a gun attached, probed inside as the man squinted his eyes trying to see where Julio had gone.

"Shoot the little bastard!" The man wearing the golden medallion ordered to the other.

"I can't! He's crawled in a fucking pipe and I can't get my arm low enough for a shot."

"Here, there's a manhole. We'll go in after him."

Julio sat inside the culvert, roaches all around him, crawling up his shorts and falling on his head. A small mouse squeaked next to him in protest of the invasion. He paid them no mind and concentrated his ears on the sounds above him. He could hear the men fumbling with the manhole.

"We need something to pry it open with," said one.

"Find some rebar or something," said the other.

Julio shook and cried in fear. Any moment they might pry the manhole open and drop down in front of him, pointing their guns and blowing his head off.

Then he heard a siren. He wasn't sure if it was the police or some other emergency vehicle, but he prayed someone had heard the gunshots and that the siren he heard was the police on their way.

"Hurry!" said one of them. "Try this!"

Julio heard the sound of something being pressed into the slit of the manhole in an effort to pry it open. He shut his eyes and prayed. He prayed for the police to get here in time or for the men not to be able to open the manhole. He heard the sound of it moving and held his breath. It was too late. A sliver of light beamed down as the manhole began to open. Then . . . Crack! Clank! Just when he expected to see one of the men drop in front of him, something snapped and the manhole, which had just barely begun to open, echoed like a bell as is slipped back in place.

"Damn it!" One of the men said. Above on the street he held the cracked remains of a discarded broomstick handle he'd been trying to use to pry the manhole open. The siren became louder and Julio kept up his prayer.

"Come on!" said the man Julio had seen before. "We'll find him later."

A face appeared again at the drainage opening and a voice called out to him. "Hey! Can you hear me little cockroach? Does your leg hurt? I hope so. I hope you bleed to death down there. It'd be better for you if you do, because the next time I find you I'm going slit your throat and chop you into little pieces. Then I'm going to feed you to the crocodiles in the swamp like I did your little friend."

"Come on!" said the other again.

"I'll see you soon, little cockroach." The shadow disappeared from the storm drain and Julio could hear their footsteps echoing away as they ran back to their car.

He sat crying inside the culvert. He'd never been so scared in his life. He felt his leg with his hand. The bullet had grazed his thigh. It was bleeding and painful, his skin peeled back like a banana revealing his muscle, but it wasn't as bad as he first thought. He'd still be able to walk, but he'd have to put a dressing on it soon to stop the bleeding. As he sat in the culvert, the man's words echoed in his ears. *I'm going to feed you to the crocodiles like I did your little friend. Juan*, he thought. *Poor Juan*. That's why he hadn't seen him in the last few days. They must have been waiting for him outside the police station. They snatched him up and killed him. It was just as he'd warned Juan. He wondered if Juan was still alive when they cut him. He wondered if his friend died screaming in pain as he wept.

Chapter 20

Yesenia didn't remember falling asleep but she had the vague recollection of strange noises in the night. When she awoke she had to look around her orange surroundings to fully recall where she was. She'd hoped it'd all been a dream, some kind of nightmare and she was still asleep on the bus to Reynosa and none of this had really happened since then, but the orange walls were an unwelcoming herald back to reality.

The young woman who had first greeted Yesenia and Silvia was named Evelyn. She was 28 and originally from El Salvador. She had spent all her money four years ago to reach Mexico City, and from there fell into the same trap as they did.

Yesenia saw her in the hallway of the ugly mobile home as she came out of the bathroom. "How long have you been here?" she asked Evelyn.

"Oh, hey," she said. "You must have been tired. You slept for nearly 12 hours."

"I guess," said Yesenia.

"So how long have I been here?" She seemed to think on it for a bit. "Four years, I guess. You never get out of debt, you see. We have to give them everything we make and they pay Miss Lydia directly. Every now and then they'll give you some for clothes or whatever, but not often. Your best bet is if a man gives you a tip, then hide it away. They don't really say much about tips unless it's a big one, but don't get caught hiding a big tip or you'll get sent to the hot box."

"What's the hot box?" asked Silvia, who walked into Yesenia's room after hearing the voices.

"It's this old metal trailer they have outside. If you get in trouble they lock you inside. Imelda's out there now. She spends a lot of time in the hot box, actually. She smarted off to Miss Lydia last night. Trust me; you don't want to go there, especially this time of year. Just a few hours in the summer and you'll be sick as a dog. Plus, it stinks in there. The dogs piss in it."

Their conversation with Evelyn illuminated just how precarious their situation was. The makeshift compound they were at served as both a brothel and a trafficking hub for drug smuggling. Miss Lydia was the madam and the three men were her enforcers when they weren't running the drugs.

"The one with the fancy boots, that's Arnulfo. He's gay or something so you don't have to worry about him trying to get in your pants, but don't tell Jose or Hector. Arnulfo comes over, but he just likes to hang out and talk. The other two don't know, I don't think. He's the only one that's halfway decent. If you give him your tip money he'll get you things in town as long as you keep them hidden so Miss Lydia doesn't find out. I think she knows he does it sometimes, but so far she hasn't said anything. The other two, though, Jose and Hector, you have to watch them. And if Jose is drinking, stay away from him no matter what you do. He's not right in the head to begin with, but I can't even tell you some of the things he's done when he's drunk." She shivered at a memory the girls were sure they didn't want to know.

"I'm not a prostitute," said Yesenia flatly. "They told me they were going to help me get a job as a maid or nanny."

"Yeah, that's what they always say," said Evelyn. "You think I was a prostitute before coming here? I used to work in a hair salon back in El Salvador. I should have stayed put, too."

"How many others are here?" asked Sylvia.

"Well, Miss Lydia lives in that one there," she pointed out the window to a tan mobile home, the only one that didn't seem like it was thirty years old. "Jose, Hector, and Arnulfo stay over there," she pointed to another run down white mobile home. "That just leaves our house and the one next to it. We three stay here, and in the yellow one you have Imelda, Maria, Isabel, and Catalina. Would you like to meet them? Come on, you can't sit here crying all day." Before either girl could protest Evelyn grabbed them both by the hand, yanked them off the orange bed, and ushered them out across the dirt to the yellow mobile home. She knocked twice on the door but didn't wait for anyone to answer, pushing it open to reveal a mobile home much like their own, except slightly larger. Immediately upon entering Yesenia saw two women sitting on an old floral couch watching television, both of whom looked up as she entered.

Evelyn introduced the first girl on the couch, "This is Catalina." She smiled and held up a hand. She was a waif of a young woman with a cleft chin and a friendly smile. "And this is Isabel." The other girl was curvy with short hair bobbed at her shoulders. She looked up and waved, but no smile crossed her lips and she barely paid notice to them. "Isabel doesn't like to talk when her novellas are on," explained Evelyn. "Where's Maria?" Evelyn asked Catalina.

"She's with Arnulfo."

"Shhh," scolded Isabel.

"Come on, we'd better go," Evelyn whispered to Yesenia and Silvia. As they stepped outside they saw a vehicle pull up in the distance by the entrance, and then heard its horn sound. "Uh, oh," said Evelyn, "it must be someone's lunch hour. I hope you two are ready."

"Ready for what?" asked Yesenia.

"We have a customer, and customers always want to try the new girls."

Chapter 21

Yesenia stood with the other girls in a line outside their pepto-pink mobile home. An older white man had arrived in a white Ford F150 and he was now looking the girls over. He wore a smile on his face and smoked a menthol as he passed close by each girl. "Hello, Catalina, how are you?" he asked as he came near to her.

She smiled and said, "I'm okay."

Then he saw Silvia and Yesenia. "We have two new girls," said Miss Lydia, who walked behind the man as though his shadow.

He walked up to Yesenia and smiled. *Please don't pick me, please don't pick me,* went her thoughts. As he smiled she could see the yellow of his teeth and he inadvertently blew smoke in her face. "What's your name?" he asked.

She said nothing and kept her head down, staring at the ground and praying he'd leave her alone. But Miss Lydia walked up and grabbed her by the chin again. "The nice man is talking you," she said in a false sweet tone. "She's a shy one," Miss Lydia told the man, "but her name is Yesenia."

"Well you're just as pretty as you can be," said the man. "I think I'd like to get to know her a little better," he told Miss Lydia. He eyed her like a dog at a table waiting for the scrap to fall. "How'd that be?" he asked Yesenia. She said nothing.

Miss Lydia released Yesenia's chin and spoke for her, "She'd like that very much. I'm delighted you like her, but she's a fresh girl. She's never known a man, so it's something I have to consider. Only one man will be her first, so I can't just let it be anyone."

The man's smile faded and he had a look of surprise. "Never known a . . . ? Oh, horseshit. How much we talking here? I didn't come out expecting to spend my entire paycheck." He looked at his watch. "And I ain't got a lot of time."

"No, it's true. Come inside, come inside. We'll work something out." She led the man towards her mobile home that had a little office in the front. The man looked back at Yesenia as though trying to decide if he was being bamboozled. "She'll be waiting for you," assured Miss Lydia. "Don't you worry." She may have looked like the sweetest little grandmother , but Miss Lydia was more akin to the silver-tongued used car salesperson of the year. She grinned and patted the man's elbow as she led him inside. Then she called out, "Arnulfo, take the girls back inside, won't you, dear?"

Arnulfo herded the girls back in, and stood outside the pink mobile home. Inside, Yesenia was frantic. She couldn't understand the conversation the man had just had since she didn't know English, but the body language had spoken volumes. "What am I going to do?" she asked Silvia. "She's going to sell me to him. I can't have sex with that man. I won't!" Silvia sat silent as she had no answer.

"Have you ever been with a man?" asked Evelyn.

"No, of course not," said Yesenia. "I'm Catholic."

"Well, there's no use trying to fight it," said Evelyn. "The first time is always the hardest, but believe it or not, it does get easier."

Yesenia began to cry angrily. "You don't understand. I can't do this! It'd be better that I should be killed than do something like this."

Evelyn tried to comfort her. "Don't think like that. Look, all you have to do is lay there and let him do his business. It'll be over before you know it."

Yesenia looked out the window. Arnulfo was sitting on the steps of the mobile home chewing on another toothpick. "Don't even think about it," said Evelyn. "You won't get far, and there'll be hell to pay. If you try to run, Miss Lydia will have her son beat you, and then they'll put you in the hot box."

"I have to do something," said Yesenia.

"Don't run," said Silvia. "I don't want them to hurt you. You know what kind of people they are. You saw."

"It doesn't matter," said Yesenia through tears. "I can't become a whore. My Papa looks down from heaven. How could I let him see such a thing?"

She ran to her room and pulled her still unpacked bag from the closet. "You don't know the trouble you'll get in," warned Evelyn. "And there's no place to go. There's nothing but pastures and woods around here for miles."

But Yesenia was in a frenzy. "I don't care!" she practically yelled. Outside, the door to Miss Lydia's mobile home opened and she stepped forth with the man. Yesenia's window was open, and through the screen she heard the affable tones of their conversation. *They've made a deal and now he's coming for me.*

She hurried to the back of the mobile home with Silvia and Evelyn watching on. She tried to push the back door open. "It's nailed shut," said Evelyn, "to keep men from sneaking in or us from sneaking out."

Yesenia hurried into the bedroom that they'd given Silvia. Her window faced out of the rear of the mobile home and Yesenia pressed her fingers against the edge of the screen and pushed upward until it popped out.

"Don't do it, Yesenia," Silvia pleaded.

"Seriously, girl, you don't know how much trouble you'll get into," added Evelyn, following her into the room. She moved forward as if to physically stop Yesenia, but it was too late. She was out the window in a flash. "Oh, shit," Evelyn said. "This is not good," she told Silvia.

Yesenia dropped to the ground and hurried towards a barbed wire fence that separated the little clearing of homes from the woods. She was halfway there when she heard the barking. She looked back and the two Rottweilers were barreling down on her. Then she heard Arnulfo's voice as he strolled around from the front to see what the dogs were going on about. Yesenia managed to make it to the fence and just maneuver in between the wire before the dogs were able to tackle her, but not before Arnulfo saw her. "What are you doing?" he called after her. "Get back here!"

The dogs could easily have slid under the fence to continue after her, but thankfully when Yesenia looked back they merely stood by the fence barking at her and wagging their tails as if it were all a game to them. She tried to push through the brambles as Arnulfo called to Miss Lydia. "The new girl is trying to run away."

"*Dios Mio*," cursed Miss Lydia. "Go get her!" She turned with her salesperson smile to the man. "She only arrived today. I'm afraid we haven't had time to train her properly."

"Well, I don't think I want that girl after all. She don't seem like she's exactly a willing participant, if you know what I mean."

"Of course she is," she told the man. "She's just being a spoiled brat. You know how these girls can be. They get used to getting their way all the time and throw fits when they don't. Come with me and we'll work something else out," and she gingerly escorted the man back to the trailer. He was shaking his head and lighting up another cigarette, but Miss Lydia wasn't about to let his money drive out the gate without getting as much of it as she could.

Arnulfo casually jogged to the fence and flung his toothpick away in exasperation as he carefully climbed through.

Yesenia was still wearing her sandals, and the sticks and thorns kept whipping across her ankles until they were red and raw. She let out a little squeal as she walked face first into a large spider that had been sitting in the center of its web. It rappelled from her chin on its web, scrambling to get away as she swatted at it. Behind her she could hear Arnulfo tromping along in his fancy boots. "Come back before you get into more trouble," he warned her. But she kept the thought of what they intended for her in her mind and pressed forward, determined not to shame herself by submitting to such degradation.

Having grown up always traveling on foot, Yesenia was in excellent running condition. She was not, however, used to trying to run through the woods and was not dressed for it. For nearly half an hour she eluded Arnulfo through the brush. When the brambles let up and she had a slight open area to run, she put distance between herself and his boots, but as soon as the thickets sprung up he closed in again.

Finally, she had hit upon a patch too thick for her to make it through. Berry vines gripped her like barbed shackles as she tried to press through them. She had paid no attention when the poison oak leaves wiped her skin with malicious intent or when the fire ants bit her toes and feet, but the thorny vines were too much. She tried to step over them by lifting her knees high, but the further she went the more tangled up she got. She could feel her skin being slit like a thousand tiny paper cuts with each step. Tears welled up in her eyes as she tried to keep going. Behind her, she heard Arnulfo, "Oh, come on now. Look what you're doing to yourself." He stood at the edge of the thicket watching her like she was a dinosaur sinking into the tar. Finally, the pain was too much and she stopped trying to move her feet.

"Now see what you've done?" he asked her. He leaned down and picked a berry and popped it into his mouth. "Now what do you have to say for yourself?"

She looked back at him with tears falling down her cheek. "I'm no prostitute!" she told him. "I won't do it!"

He seemed almost to have a moment of sympathy for her. "Sometimes life takes us to places we don't like," he told her. "Like into thorns, right?" he said, stepping into the thicket and nearly completely protected by his jeans and boots. Yesenia made herself move her feet despite the pain in an effort to get away, but with a short spurt he had caught up and grabbed her about the waist. She screamed and kicked, but he held her tight. "Enough of that," he told her. "You're in enough trouble as it is. Don't make things worse for yourself. You're lucky it was me she sent after you. Hector or Jose would probably let you keep hurting yourself in here."

"Let me go," she pleaded. "Please, let me go. I can't do what they want me to do. Please let me go. Just tell Miss Lydia you couldn't find me."

"I can't," he said. "Miss Lydia has a contract on you. She's paid a lot of money for you and if I let you go, I would be the one who would be in big trouble." He pulled out the knife from his side and Yesenia's body tensed. "Oh, come, now," said Arnulfo. "I'm only going to cut some of these away." He bent down and cut some of the blackberry vines that gripped her legs like a bear trap. Then he put the knife away, heaved her up over his shoulder, and started walking back out of the thicket. She tried a couple of times to kick herself free, but too much of her energy was already spent.

Arnulfo tried to carry her back, but after a while she began to feel too heavy and he set her down on her feet. "I'm putting you down so you can walk, but don't try to run on me again or I'm going to be very upset with you." As soon as her feet touched the ground she tried to jerk away, but Arnulfo had a handful of her hair and yanked her back hard. "What did I just tell you?" he asked. "Now behave yourself."

They made the slow walk back, Arnulfo directing their progress with his constant hold upon her. Yesenia cried most of the way, pleading with him to let her go, but he simply ignored her and did not answer. Arnulfo didn't seem pleased with his task but he knew if he didn't bring Yesenia back now, not only would he be in a world of trouble, but Yesenia would likely face a much worse punishment if Jose and Hector were sent out to find her and teach her a lesson.

It wasn't long before they came to the fence again and the two dogs came running out from under one of the mobile homes to greet them with their wild barking. As they passed through the fence Miss Lydia came out of her house and walked towards them. She was not smiling anymore. Yesenia could see the white truck was gone and thanked God that she might perhaps be spared for the moment from being stripped of her purity.

"You little bitch," said Miss Lydia. She walked right up to Yesenia, who was still being held by the hair by Arnulfo, and slapped her hard across the face twice. "What took you so long!?" she screamed at Arnulfo.

"She ran a long way," he explained. "Got herself into some thorns and tore her legs up pretty good."

"Oh, the poor thing," Miss Lydia said sarcastically. "Not here two days and already making trouble. Bring her over here!" she said to Arnulfo as she began walking to the open court area between the mobile homes.

"Do what she says and don't talk back," Arnulfo whispered into her ear. "And if she starts hitting you don't do anything. She'll just get Jose to beat you if you do and you're already in enough trouble."

Faces were already at the windows as Yesenia was led towards the makeshift courtyard. As Miss Lydia had wanted, they were all watching to see what would happen to her. Jose and Hector stepped outside with beers in their hand. Jose knew he might be called upon, so he walked over close to where Yesenia stood. "You made a deal with Mr. Ortiz, did you not?" began Miss Lydia.

"Yes," said Yesenia. "But not for this!"

Miss Lydia hit her on the head in the way Yesenia had previously seen her strike Jose and Silvia. "Not for this, eh? Not for what?"

"I'm not a prostitute," said Yesenia, summoning all of her indignation, determination, and steadfast resolve.

Miss Lydia hit her across the face with her palm, a hybrid of a punch and slap. It was enough to cause Yesenia's lip to burst and she was stunned that the old woman was able to generate such force. "I'll tell you what you are!" declared Miss Lydia. "You're a stupid little girl who owes a lot of money. You made a deal and now you're here, but you have to work off your debt. And work it off you will!" she turned to Arnulfo, eyes flashing, "Bring that other new girl out here!" she told Arnulfo. He went inside the pink mobile home and came out with Silvia, who now looked a lot like Yesenia, disheveled and stumbling along with her head down. "Since you decided to run away, I had to give Silvia to your customer." Yesenia looked over at her friend in horror. Silvia looked up at her for a moment and then dropped her head again as if in shame. "And I had to lower the price by half to make up for the trouble. You have to pay back that money, so I'm adding a hundred and fifty dollars to your bill," she told Yesenia. "Plus, another five hundred for running away!" The old woman stepped close to Yesenia. "What do you think about that?" Yesenia said nothing. "Come on," goaded Miss Lydia. "I bet it makes you mad, huh? Want to say something to me? Maybe you'd like to hit old Miss Lydia?" She pushed Yesenia hard in the chest, but Yesenia said nothing and stood still. "Maybe you'd like to try and hit me back, no?" She cupped her hand and repeatedly hit Yesenia on the side of the head with it, but Yesenia heeded Arnulfo's words and did nothing. "Oh, not so stupid after all, are we?" said Miss Lydia.

Down at the fence a horn sounded. "Ah, we have another customer." She smiled wickedly at Yesenia. "Get her cleaned up," she told Arnulfo, "she has some entertaining to do." Turning to greet the new arrival, she sneered at Yesenia, speaking through a clenched jaw. "And if you mess this one up I'll really make you sorry."

Chapter 22

Julio had spent more than half of the next day still hiding in his hole, convinced they were waiting for him to come out. He'd tied his shirt around his leg and the blood seemed to crust over the wound and stop the bleeding, which he was thankful for. Finally, hunger and exhaustion took hold and he crept out around midday. He stole another shirt off a clothesline, filched some food from a trash bin behind a restaurant, and then hid himself away in an empty old building.

As he lay there that night, jumping at even the slightest of sounds, his leg began to feel numb and heavy. By midnight he was feverish, and by morning so sick he could barely summon the strength to stand up. He knew he needed help or he was probably going to die.

The next morning Maria pulled a small wagon carrying the wares of their little store along the street, and Aunty Nita followed along behind with her usual wobble. They opened up their little *tienda* and Aunty Nita settled into her chair and started a little fire in their hibachi and began cutting up the chicken to make kabobs. Maria stood near the front of the store pouring water into a huge jug. She had her sugar and lemons already prepared for mixing and was about to pour the sugar into the water when something caught her eye. Across the square she saw a little flag of some sort being waved around in the shadow between two stands. As she looked a little more closely she could see it was a shirt. A young boy had removed his shirt and was apparently trying to get her attention. Then she realized it was Julio, probably anxious for what news she had. She put her hand up a bit to let him know she'd seen him, and continued mixing the lemonade.

"I have to run to the bathroom," she told Aunty Nita. She headed towards the market's public restroom and gestured with her hand that Julio should go around the other way out of sight and meet her on the other side.

When she turned the corner beyond Aunty Nita's view, she stopped short. Julio had crawled to the back of the store as she had directed, but he looked a mess. Around his leg he had a dirty rag that was encrusted with an enormous patch of dried blood.

"Julio! What's happened to you?" she gasped as she crouched next to the boy. He was covered in dirt and sweat, his eyelids heavy and his complexion awry. She put her hand to his forehead, "My God! You're burning up! And your leg!"

"The men," he told her. "We saw two men in the cemetery. They killed the American girl." He began to cry uncontrollably. "They killed Juan. They told me. They killed him and fed him to the crocodiles out in the swamps." His tears ran down his cheek leaving little streaks of clean skin through the dirt and grime he perpetually wore from his life on the street.

"What happened to your leg, Julio?" she cried, barely hearing what he'd just told her. "Come, let me see." She bent down and began to unwrap the shirt covering his injury. The things he'd told her had not yet sunk in. "How did this happen?"

"One of the men shot me," he told her. "I ran as fast as I could, but one of the bullets cut my leg."

"They were shooting at you!?" she asked in horror.

He nodded his head. "They almost killed me, too. I had to hide in a street ditch. They killed Juan, Maria. They killed him."

"Oh, my God!" she said, both to what he told her and to the sight of his leg which was now revealed beneath the rag. Already, pus had begun to form and it smelled of almonds roasting on a fire. "I have to get you to the hospital."

"No!" he cried. "They'll call the police, and then the gangsters will find me again. Please, no hospital."

"We have to do something," she told him. "You could bleed to death, or get an infection. I think it may already be infected, Julio. We have to do something. I'm going to get Aunty Nita." She stood up to go and get help, but Julio clung to her, his fingers balling the fabric of her shirt in a fierce grip. "No," he said angrily, his tears still falling. "She'll call them. She's the one who called them in the first place. Please. Please. Please."

It'd taken all his courage to come back to the market but Maria was the only person he knew would show him kindness and that he could trust. It'd been a gamble, as he knew if Aunty Nita saw him he'd have to run away even with his leg the way it was. He pleaded with Maria so miserably she did not have the heart to call Aunty Nita or to leave him, but she didn't know what to do. She knew she had to get help. She also thought about what he just told her about Juan. He had a right to be afraid. The police had talked to Juan, and if Julio was right, Juan was now dead. She remembered the card she had on her, the one from the American woman, who suddenly seemed the best person to call. She was an outsider, someone with no ulterior motives other than finding the missing American. Stranger or not, she seemed to be the most trustworthy person in all of Cancun at the moment.

"Wait here," she told Julio. "I'm going to be right back."

"Where are you going?" he asked frightened. "You won't call the police, will you?"

"No, I know someone else to call, not the police."

He still held to her fiercely, "No Aunty Nita and no police! Promise?"

"I promise."

He unraveled his fingers from her clothes and she ran to the *caseta* while Julio crawled back into the shadows between the two little vending stands.

Catherine was already out in her rental car driving the strip, matching up the little dots on her map with the hotels along the way, when her phone rang. "Catherine James."

"Miss Catherine?"

"Yes?"

"This is Maria Ortega, from the police station?"

"Yes, *señora* Ortega, how are you?" Catherine noticed the woman was breathing particularly fast.

"Miss Catherine, I need your help."

She assumed she meant getting the police to cooperate in searching for the missing boy. "Okay, sure. How can I help?"

"I need you to come to Market 28. Do you know where it is?"

"Yes, I know of it. I'm doing some mapping right now, but I can meet you there this afternoon around ... "

"No, it has to be now. It's an emergency."

Catherine was surprised by the urgency and desperation in the woman's voice. "May I ask what the emergency is?"

Maria seemed to hesitate. "If I tell you, you can't tell the police, not even Detective Ramirez. I don't know what's going on or who to trust right now, but I think something horrible has happened to that little boy I told you about." She offered the statement as a contingency, waiting to see if the terms were accepted.

"Okay, Maria, I won't call the police. Can you tell me what this is all about?"

"It's about the missing boy's friend, Julio. And it's about the American girl, too, I think. The boy, Julio, he says the American girl was killed and the two boys saw who did it, and now the men are after them. Julio is here in the square and he's been shot, and he says the other boy who I told you about, Juan, he says the boy was murdered." Her voice began to shake as Julio's words took on meaning for her. "He said they killed Juan, Miss Catherine! I'm scared. Julio wouldn't let me call the police and I don't know what to do. His leg is bleeding and I'm scared the men who did this may come to the square looking for him. I think he's telling the truth. If you saw him the way I just saw him . . . I don't think he's making this up. I don't know what to do! Please, can you help?"

Catherine was stunned by the blur of information. As the words soaked in she tried to organize them into their places. Although she was a bit confused about it all, she felt a stabbing sensation in her gut, as one of the things she'd just heard had been clear enough. If her information was right, Maria had just said Taylor Woodall was dead.

There was nothing she could do now, but get to the market as quickly as possible. "I'll be right there."

"Thank you. I'm sorry. I didn't know who else to call. I'm in the back of the market. There's a public restroom in-between the back of the stores and the street. Please hurry. He's hurt real bad and I don't know how to treat something like that."

Catherine made an abrupt u-turn and hit the gas. When she arrived at the market it was eerily empty of tourists with only a few stragglers milling about shopping for souvenirs. She walked towards the back and found the restrooms Maria had mentioned, but didn't see any sign of her.

"Miss Catherine!" She heard a whisper from the shadows and turned to see Maria crawl out from in-between two little stands. She had tears on her cheeks and a little bit of blood on her dress. "He's in here," she told her, gesturing towards the shadows from whence she just arose.

Catherine poked her head in and saw the little boy.

Julio scrambled away from Catherine when he saw her. "Who's she!?" he asked Maria in fear.

"It's okay, Julio. She's an American. She works for the American girl's family. She's okay. She won't call the police, I promise."

"My name is Catherine," she told the boy. "I only want to help."

Julio had crawled further back into the V shaped shadow where Catherine couldn't fit.

"Come out, Julio, please," said Maria. "We have to treat your leg. Miss Catherine is a friend. Please, come out of there."

"The policeman said he was a friend, too," said Julio. "Juan went with him, and now he's dead!"

"I'm not with the police," said Catherine. "And I don't work for them. You've heard about the missing girl, right?"

"Yes."

Catherine reached into her pocket and pulled out a picture of the Taylor Woodall. "She's my very good friend's daughter," she told the boy, pushing the picture into the shadows where a small hand picked it up. "I'm only here to find her, and am not with any police or other group here. I live in Dallas, Texas, very far away from here. I came to Mexico only to look for Taylor."

Julio was still huddled in the back, but he pushed the picture back out and told Catherine, "She's dead. They killed her like they killed Juan . . . like they tried to kill me."

Catherine let out a sigh and put the picture away. *I hope that's not true.* Part of her wanted to believe the boy was lying, but as Maria had said, the sight of him hiding there in the shadows with his leg wounded made him very convincing. She looked at him and thought about how scared he must be, not knowing who to trust and having no place to go. "I would like to help you if you'll let me," she told him. "I know you aren't sure who you can trust right now, but I promise I won't call the police or do anything without asking you first." Julio scooted forwarded a bit enough for Catherine to see his tear-streaked face. She put her hand towards his forehead, "May I?" she asked.

He nodded and she felt his temperature, dangerously hot. Then she looked at the boy's leg. She could distinctly smell the infection setting in. "Your leg is in bad shape. You've got an infection and it's making you sick. We need to clean your leg and get you some medicine for your fever right away. Some antibiotics, too," she added.

"It's not too bad," said Julio, as though letting Catherine know he could still run away if he wanted. Nobody was buying it.

"Julio, please. Let us help you," said Maria.

He was still apprehensive.

"How about this?" asked Maria. "There's the pharmacy right over there," she pointed to where the pharmacy was, "I'll go and get some bandages and medicine and we'll look at your leg. We won't even go anywhere, but we have to look at it," she told him.

But her words frightened Julio. "Don't leave!" he said. Catherine's story seemed true to the boy, but he still didn't want to be left alone with the stranger. Everyone was a shark to Julio at that moment, and he was but a small fish trying to evade being eaten at every turn.

"I'll go," said Catherine. "You wait here with Maria and I'll go and get some things."

"Okay," said Julio.

Catherine walked to the pharmacy where she bought bandages, iodine, aspirin, antibiotics, and a cream that would keep the bandages from adhering to the wound. She also purchased one of the flashlights that were lined along a shelf.

When she returned, Julio crawled forward enough that Catherine could lean in and treat his leg. The few people who walked by stared at Catherine and Maria curiously, but otherwise they attracted no attention.

Catherine had taken a few first aid courses and tended a few wounded cyclists in her days with David and when she began removing the dirty rag she knew it was going to hurt. Julio had simply wrapped the shirt around his leg and tied it, and now the dried blood held it against the wound like duct tape. It would sting terribly when removed from the tender flesh.

"Can you go get a bottle of water?" she asked Maria, handing her a couple of dollars. "The biggest one you can find." Julio tensed as Maria disappeared. "She'll be right back," Catherine told him. "And we're not going anywhere." A moment later Maria returned with a gallon jug of water. "Perfect," she told her.

She poured the water over the rag hoping it would soften some of the caked blood, but it had little effect. She gave Julio a long drink from the jug and began trying to pull around the edges of the wound where his old shirt was plastered in place. Julio winced in pain.

"I'm afraid this is going to hurt a little," said Catherine. "I have to take off this last bit here, and it's stuck to the skin."

Julio said nothing, only stared at his leg and nodded in acknowledgement of the warning. Catherine worked methodically around the edges and in this way finally managed to remove the rag. Once done, she could see that it was indeed a bullet wound, at least what she imagined one would look like. It hadn't hit straight on, which was very lucky for Julio. But it had cleaved away a good bit of tissue from the boy's skinny leg. It wouldn't have been so bad had the wound been properly dressed, but now a large mound, like a giant boil, had formed under the skin, which Catherine knew was the infection setting in. She poured some of the iodine over it and told Julio, "This bump here is fluid under your skin. I'm going to have to open it so it can drain out. It'll hurt a little, but it will also make your leg feel better afterward. Right now it probably feels stiff and hurts when you move it?" Julio nodded affirmatively.

"I need something sharp," she told Maria.

"I'll be right back," said Maria, scurrying off to a find something.

"You're a pretty brave little man," she told Julio. "Do you know the men that did this to you?"

He nodded, "Gangsters. We came across them in the graveyard burying the girl."

"The graveyard?" Catherine asked. "Near here?" Julio nodded. *That doesn't make much sense.* But as her mind began to reason, she suddenly realized it made a whole lot of sense. What better place to hide a body than someone else's grave?

Maria returned with a small sewing repair kit and opened it, pulling a small needle from its plastic holder. "Will this work?"

"Yes, that's perfect," said Catherine. "This will help," she told Julio. "I'm just going to poke it right here," Catherine prepared him, placing her finger above the bump in his wound. "Ready?" Julio held his breath and Catherine counted, "One, two . . ." but didn't wait for three. Instead, she quickly lanced the swollen target, releasing the contents, which ran out over the wound. Julio had flinched, but it was over so quick he hardly realized it was done, and as Catherine had said, the sensation was one of pressure being released. His leg, while stinging quite a bit, immediately felt better. The yellowish fluid oozing from his leg was disgusting but Catherine assured him it would be much cleaner once the wound had drained. "We have to keep this clean," she told him, "or this infection will get much worse." She knew from her travels how many people died from something as easily preventable as a staph infection in even small lacerations.

She used a bandage with iodine to blot the little hole she'd made, pressing around the edges occasionally, and the wound was well cleaned when she finished. She swathed the area and wrapped Julio's leg in clean bandage. Then she had him take a couple of aspirin tablets right there on the spot along with the other medicine. "There," she told him with a smile and pat on his back. "We'll have you back up and running in no time."

Julio had never really been mothered in such a way and found it very disarming. Despite his streetwise sense, he couldn't help but feel much safer and comforted by this woman.

Maria had watched Catherine work and thanked her profusely. "I don't know what we would have done," she told her.

"Now," said Catherine. "You have a decision to make, Julio. If you're right, there are some bad people somewhere out there looking for you. I can take you somewhere where you'd be safe, but it's up to you if you trust me enough. I don't want to leave you here, but I won't make you do anything you aren't comfortable with."

Julio checked his bandage and tested his leg by moving it a bit. It was painful, but more mobile than just a few minutes ago. His wide eyes fell upon Maria. "I don't know what to do," he told her, seeming, for the first time, like the lost little boy that he was. He was still terribly sick and didn't have the strength to try and go on by himself. He knew he needed help, he just wasn't sure if Catherine was to be trusted. Still, he didn't have a lot of options at the moment.

Maria leaned in and caressed his cheek. "She's a friend, Julio. I can tell. She won't tell anyone where you are. I think you should go with her. I can't keep you safe like she can." Aunty Nita would never allow Julio to come and stay with them if there were truly murderers chasing after him. And given the recent turn of events it didn't seem likely Julio would trust Aunty Nita anyway. "You know I care about you, but I just wouldn't know what to do if something happened. You're safer with Miss Catherine."

Julio looked up at Catherine skeptically. It was either accept her offer or take his chances on the streets. If the men found him again, he couldn't run like before, and even if he could, they weren't likely to give him the chance a second time.

"Okay," said Julio, as he finally crawled out of his little hideaway. It took a little help for him to stand up, but once up he insisted he was okay to walk on his own.

"Okay," said Catherine. "But I'm right here if you need a hand."

When Maria returned to the lemonade stand, Aunty Nita looked at her and demanded, "Where the hell have you been? I've been sitting here alone for over an hour!"

"I'm sorry," said Maria. "I'm not feeling well," she explained as she set about making more lemonade, Juan's demise and Julio's fate heavy on her heart. Aunty Nita scowled, but said nothing more.

Catherine led Julio around the market to where she had parked her car. Julio still wouldn't let himself be carried, which suited Catherine as she wasn't sure she could carry him so far, so he limped along beside her and she patiently slowed her pace. As they were crossing the street another car, the same cream colored Pontiac from the alley, suddenly spun out of its parking spot and barreled down on them. Catherine had just heard the tires and looked up in time to see the car, its engine screaming full throttle as it rushed towards them. Instinct took over. She yanked Julio up into her arms and bolted. She made for her car a few feet in front of them, and as she looked over her shoulder she saw the oncoming car's back window slide down and the barrel of a gun protrude outward. *Oh, God, no.*

She reached the other side of the street and in a surprising display of strength and dexterity, jumped across the hood, sliding off its edge and landing on the other side with a painful thud, Julio still in her arms. She'd made it within milliseconds. Bullets riddled the car like a rainstorm on a tin roof, a blitz of pings and pangs. Tires squealed as the driver slammed on his brakes. "Stay down!" Catherine yelled at Julio. *I'm ready for this,* she told herself. *You can do this, Catherine.* She was overwhelmed by the protective instinct that immediately filled her blood, sending anger, fear, and urgency pumping through her veins in pure adrenaline. *You know what you have to do to protect yourself and this boy.* And she was ready. She'd been to some dangerous places in her travels and had filled out the necessary forms long ago. Kidnapping was rampant in some parts of the world and an attractive, professional woman like her was a prime target. She'd made sure she was prepared if ever she had to defend herself, and today was the day. It was the same reason she'd been held up in customs. Her hand slipped to the back of her smart pants suit and she produced a Glock 25, a .380 ACP pistol, one of the few firearm calibers which civilians could legally carry in Mexico with a proper permit. It was also the same gun she'd carried with her for the last five years whenever she went to a particularly dangerous part of the world. She'd never had to use it anywhere other than the gun range until now, but she had made sure she was familiar with the weapon. She pushed Julio flat on the ground, his hands over his ears and his eyes shut tight in terror.

More shots rang out from the car, which had now stopped in the middle of the street. The shooter opened his door and walked towards them, trying to find an angle to get a good shot as the little flurries of automatic fire repeatedly burst in their direction. Catherine peered through the gap underneath the car they were sheltering behind and saw a pair of tennis shoes. *Shoot, Catherine,* her inner voice was commanding. *Shoot him now before he gets close enough to kill you both.* She took aim and fired a shot, which struck the man where the ankle joined the foot, and immediately the man fell to his knees. *Go now!* Catherine jumped up. The man saw her coming and his expression was one of bewildered fright. The wolf expects the sheep to run for its life so that he might tear it down from behind, not turn and bare teeth of its own. He raised his weapon again. She fired, hitting the shooter square in the chest with the first two shots and a third struck him in the face near the bridge of his nose. The rest of him slumped over and Catherine leaped over him with no hesitation, increasing her speed as she began running towards the assailants' car, attempting to shoot through the rear window at an angle sufficient to hit the driver. She was in full attack mode now, not thinking so much as just acting on instinct. She'd no idea where this intense sense of rage sprang forth within her, but it had filled her over, and was now pouring outward with each step she took, each shot she fired. The tires squealed again and the car lurched forward. Catherine was right behind it, running full speed now. She concentrated on keeping her aim steady as she ran and put three more bullets square into the back of the driver's seat, but the driver didn't lose control. *I'm not hitting him,* she realized. A few seconds later the car had pulled too far ahead for Catherine to follow, weaving through traffic before disappearing from sight.

Catherine was shaking from head to toe. She holstered her gun and returned to Julio who was still on the ground, trembling and immobilized by the pain in his leg and the fear that strangled his heart. "Are you hurt?" she asked him, concernedly.

Julio looked up, clearly terrified, "Are they gone?"

Catherine bent down to check him over and spoke in a comforting voice, "Yes, they're gone. It's safe now." She was still shaking herself as she smoothed out his hair in an attempt to calm him as much as herself. *Jesus Christ,* she thought.

She helped Julio back to his feet, taking care not to exacerbate the boy's injured leg. Julio looked behind Catherine at the body still lying in the street. "You killed him?"

Catherine looked back; surprised a dead man's body was actually there. "Yes," she told him. "Yes, I think I did."

Julio stared. Lying in the street was a man with a gold necklace, a round and shiny medallion glinting in the sunlight, and instantly he thought it was the man from the graveyard, but as he looked he realized something disturbing. Despite the bullet in the face, Julio suddenly realized it wasn't the same man. "That's not him," he told Catherine. "That's not the man I saw in the cemetery."

Chapter 23

Catherine had walked Julio down the street and flagged a taxi, leaving her bullet-riddled rental car at the market. She knew it wouldn't take long before the police ran the tag and traced it back to her. She had to get Julio somewhere safe before she tried explaining what had happened. She wasn't sure exactly what she was going to tell them.

They took the taxi back towards the Hutton, but she began thinking that even though the hotel was in the very heart of activity in Cancun at the moment, it still might not be safe. *They were waiting for that boy,* she thought. *They might be expecting me to take him to the Hutton.* It seemed safe with all the security, but given that an attempt had been made on them both in broad daylight at one of the most popular markets in Cancun; she decided it was still risky. Instead, she had the taxi drop them off several blocks away, then she and Julio walked another two blocks to the Chapa Del Rey hotel. Catherine constantly scanned their surroundings to make sure nobody was watching where they went.

"Why didn't we just take the taxi here?" asked Julio, swinging his hurt leg in front of him like a wooden plank.

"I'm sorry," said Catherine, truly feeling bad for all the walking they were doing. "I didn't want anyone to know which hotel we went to, even the driver. Do you want me to carry you?"

Julio shook his head. His ribs still hurt from being jerked up by Catherine earlier and he was determined to get wherever they were going on his own steam.

Catherine had Julio wait by the elevators while she rented a room in cash under a false name, the desk clerk overlooking identification when Catherine told her to keep the change, assuming she was just another reporter.

"It's probably best if you stay here a while," she told Julio. "Are you hungry?" Julio nodded. He hadn't eaten since the day before.

Catherine ordered chicken fingers and a Coke from room service for Julio and then told him he would have to stay in the room alone for a while. Julio began to protest but Catherine told him, "I've got to go explain to the police what happened at the market."

"Are you going to tell them about me?" asked Julio.

"No. From what you've said, I don't think I'd trust anyone with your whereabouts right now. Nobody knows you're here, and for now it's best to keep it that way." Julio's expression seemed to relax a little. "I'll be back in about an hour," Catherine told him. *At least I hope so.* She wasn't entirely sure of whether or not she'd be arrested on the spot. "But if I'm late, just wait for me, okay?"

He nodded. As she turned to leave Julio said, "Miss Catherine?"

"Yes?"

"Thank you." His eyes were sad and deep, those of someone much older. "They were going to kill me. They're still looking for me, aren't they?"

Catherine flashed a smile, a mask to her true concern. Someone was certainly still looking for the boy and now probably her as well. Things had taken a much-unforeseen turn. She felt overwhelmed. "You'll be fine," she told him in the most reassuring voice she could muster. "Just don't open the door, not for anyone. If it's me, I'll knock like this." She gave a knock on the dry wall, Bump, bumpa, bump, bump . . . bump, bump. "Okay?"

"Okay."

Ten minutes later Catherine had returned to the market where the police were almost finished clearing the mess.

She had called Ramirez and told him what had happened, except she left off everything that had to do with Julio and said she was in the market on an anonymous tip. He wasn't buying the anonymous part of it, but seeing that she wasn't going to offer any more than that, he let it be.

"You left the scene of a crime," Vargas said when she arrived.

"I ran and hid for my life, you mean. I wasn't about to stay here in the open until the police arrived."

Ramirez lifted the sheet to look at the body.

"Do you know who he is?" asked Catherine.

"No, I don't think so." He lowered the sheet. "It's difficult to say, though. You did shoot him in the face."

"May I ask why you are armed?" asked Vargas, who was now smoking a cigar and leaning against their car. "We were told you were a private investigator. I don't believe that entitles you to walk the streets of Mexico armed."

"I have a permit," Catherine said flatly.

"I'd like to see this permit, and your gun, please," said Vargas. Catherine produced both. Her gun, the Glock 25, was the most appropriate weapon for Mexico. Any military-caliber weapon was banned, which included the 9 mm so popular in American law enforcement. Additionally, she had to have a permit issued by a consulate, which she had diligently renewed each year. Vargas looked at the permit skeptically, "I don't see how it's legal for a non-citizen to carry such a weapon on our streets."

"Maybe you should brush up on the law, then, seeing as how you're a police officer and all. Article ten of the Constitution of The United States of Mexico," she explained. "Foreigners can't have *unlicensed* guns or guns prohibited by law. You're welcome to look it up if you're not familiar with it, sir. You'll find my license in order and my weapon perfectly allowable under the law."

Vargas was fuming. "I shall do that."

"You sound like a lawyer," Ramirez told her.

"Well, I am one, at least back in the states, although I doubt that matters."

Ramirez wasn't surprised. He knew there was more to this woman than just being a private detective. She had connections in Mexico, of that he was sure. It wasn't easy for a foreigner to acquire a gun license. "I suppose it's a good thing you were carrying a weapon," he told her, taking the permit and gun from Vargas, checking them both, then handing them back to Catherine while Vargas stared at him in disbelief.

"What are you doing?" he asked. "That's evidence."

"Evidence of what?" Ramirez asked. "She's committed no crime here. This is clearly self-defense. We all know that. The only reason she's still alive is because she was armed. Would you take her only means of protection from her after someone just tried to kill her?"

Vargas looked to Fuentes for support, but he stood silent and motionless, unwilling to put himself out on a limb. He didn't know if Catherine James had done anything illegal or not and wasn't about to have his name brought up if she was falsely arrested. And he knew what Ramirez knew . . . if Catherine James had a license it was because someone in the government had allowed it. Fuentes hadn't gotten where he was by pissing people off who might have connections above his pay grade. Having no support, Vargas relinquished. "Fine, if you think it's acceptable this woman just gunned down a Mexican citizen, who am I to argue?"

"Well, you assume he's a Mexican citizen, right? Since you have no idea who he is," Catherine pointed out. "He could easily be a foreigner, too, couldn't he?"

Vargas was quickly developing a hearty dislike for this woman. "Yes, of course. I would just assume, Ms. James."

"Well, I'd rather we not assume things, detective. That may be part of the reason the investigation into what happened to Taylor Woodall hasn't produced any meaningful results."

Vargas only guffawed dismissively, "Whatever you say, Ms. James. You're obviously the expert here."

"Maybe," added Ramirez. Vargas had meant it sarcastically, but he saw no sign on Ramirez's face that's how his partner interpreted it.

Ramirez examined the body. He was not so much interested in the man's appearance as what he had been carrying. He bent down and picked up a large plastic bag that contained the dead man's gun, a tech nine automatic. "This is a serious piece of hardware. You're lucky to be alive."

"It's a shame you missed the driver," added Vargas. "I suppose we should be grateful you didn't kill an innocent bystander, shooting all over a busy market in the middle of the day."

"It wasn't so much that I missed," said Catherine. "The bullets ricocheted. I suspect the vehicle's interior was modified with metal plating or something similar."

"They went through a lot of trouble to try and kill you, Ms. James," said Ramirez.

It wasn't me they were after. But as she thought about it, she realized he was right. Whoever had planned that attack had taken time to prepare the getaway car for potential gunfire. Their preparedness was discomforting. "I suppose someone is getting worried I might find something."

"That's a bit of a stretch, isn't it?" asked Vargas. "It was probably an attempted carjacking."

Catherine turned and looked at Vargas incredulously. "I hope you're not serious. They put an awful lot of bullets in the car I was standing next to for someone who planned on taking it. And wouldn't they first wait to make sure it was my car?"

"Mmmhmm," agreed Ramirez. "No, I don't think this was any carjacking, either. They were after you, Ms. James. For whatever reason, someone wants you dead." He looked at her as though surmising something was hidden beneath her countenance. "If you have anything you'd care to share, Ms. James, I would appreciate it if you did so now. Because if you do know something you're not telling us, that'd be obstruction. And I think it's pretty evident if you do know something that someone wants to make sure you don't share it, which is all the more reason to get it out now."

"If I learn anything worth sharing you'll be the first to know, Detective," she said coolly.

"What exactly were you doing here at the market?" asked Vargas.

"As I said, following up on an anonymous tip."

"And did you learn anything?"

"I did," said Catherine.

"And what is that?" asked Vargas.

"I learned that I'm close, otherwise why bother to try and kill me?"

Vargas' eyes squared on Catherine as he smoked his cigar.

After answering their questions and awaiting the results of a phone call which verified the authenticity of her permit, Catherine was allowed to leave. Vargas wanted to arrest her on the spot but Ramirez knew that besides the fact no charges would be filed it could potentially turn into a public relations' nightmare, something he didn't mind sharing with Fuentes. "Do you want to explain to the governor's office why every news channel around the world is broadcasting that someone tried to gun down the private investigator hired by this girl's family in the middle of one of the most popular markets?" Fuentes agreed and ordered them both to keep quiet. They'd lose their jobs in half a heartbeat if either of them leaked that what had occurred in the market was related to the girl's disappearance. Already the press was descending. Fuentes could see the headlines now, *Gun Battle in Heart of Cancun, 1 Dead.*" His superiors were going to be furious.

Catherine was sent on her way, but not before Ramirez offered some advice, "This anonymous tip, Ms. James. You didn't say how they contacted you? Look," he added, sensing a scowl hidden in her blue eyes somewhere behind the icy façade, "you would do well to watch your back. People like this aren't likely to quit. You're in a lot of danger, Ms. James. You should consider leaving Cancun. You seem a most capable woman, but I wonder if you understand the type of people that would try something like this here in the tourist district in the middle of the day."

"Thanks for your concern," she told him, "but I can take care of myself." She wondered if that was really true or not.

Ramirez could see she didn't trust him. "Then be careful, Ms. James. And feel free to call me any time. I'm on your side, you know."

"Are you?" she asked.

Ramirez took it as an offense. "Yes, Ms. James. I am. Do you doubt it?"

"I do," she said. "Have you inquired after the missing boy lately, Detective?"

"Missing boy? You mean the one the woman who came to the station told us about? Yes, I have."

"Really?" she asked, incredulously. "And has he been found?"

"Well, he hasn't turned back up recently, if that's what you mean."

"No, Detective. I'm asking you if he has been found. He was reported missing after allegedly giving information in this case and I am asking you if you have found out where that boy is now."

Ramirez ran a fingertip over his mustache. "No," he confessed. "I was told he was dropped off after giving an empty lead."

Catherine peered intently at him. "And who told you that? Vargas? Perhaps you should do a little more checking, Detective. I'd hate to think you've missed something."

Ramirez was left pondering Catherine's advice as she walked back to hail a taxi. She'd need to rent another car right away and had a funny feeling she'd need a different rental company.

When Ramirez returned to his own car Vargas was sitting in the passenger seat still smoking his cigar. "What was all that about?"

"Huh? Oh, she just wanted to give me an earful. She's understandably upset."

"Well, seems to me like she's pissed off the wrong people," said Vargas.

Ramirez turned and sized up his partner. "You think so?" he asked. "I wonder how she's managed that in such a short time."

Vargas shrugged. "Probably been asking the wrong people the wrong questions," he offered.

More likely the right people the right questions, Ramirez thought. And he suddenly had a very uncomfortable chill sitting next to his partner.

An hour later Catherine returned to the hotel with a fresh set of rental car keys in her pants pocket. She hadn't bothered calling the other car company to fill them in on what happened to the first rental. She figured they'd find out sooner or later. She'd also used her company card for the new rental, hoping it would leave a less obvious trail for anyone so inclined to look. She knocked on the door in the prearranged rhythm and was relieved to find Julio safe and sound. She sat down on the bed and said, "Okay, Julio, I need to talk to you."

"Okay."

"Can you tell me what you and Juan saw that has these men chasing you?"

The day's events had erased any doubts the boy had about Ms. Catherine James. Julio was ready to tell her anything she wanted to know. "We saw two men in the cemetery. They had a woman, the American, I think, and they buried her in someone's grave."

"Can you show me where?" Julio nodded. "Okay, let's go."

"Now?" he asked.

"Right now."

As they drove to the cemetery Julio gazed out the window apparently lost in thought.

"Are you okay?" she asked.

Julio shrugged.

"I'm sorry about your friend. How close were you?"

"We were family," said Julio. "Some people made fun of him because he had big ears and he sometimes wasn't too smart, but he was my best friend. He was a good friend." Catherine nodded sympathetically. "He just trusted too easily." He rubbed his hurt leg. "He trusted the police even though I told him what would happen. I told him exactly what would happen. I told him the gangsters would be looking for us and would find us if we talked to the police, but he didn't believe me, I guess."

That was something weighing on Catherine's mind as well. Someone was playing both sides and had tipped off where Julio might be found. She just hoped Ramirez wasn't corrupted as well. But she certainly wasn't going to risk Julio's life in finding out. "What about your friend?" he asked her. "What was she like?"

"Who?" asked Catherine.

"The girl, the American everyone is looking for."

"Oh. She was very beautiful," Catherine told him, "and very kind and intelligent, from what little I know about her. You would have liked her, I think." She smiled at Julio, "And she would have liked you." She wished she knew Taylor Woodall better, now. *How am I going to tell Jim and Amy what's happened to their baby?*

They turned down a side street and pulled up to the cemetery.

"What were you doing here that night?" asked Catherine.

"Juan and I sleep here sometimes. He didn't like it, though. He was afraid of ghosts."

"You aren't?" She just wanted to keep the conversation going so Julio wouldn't feel so frightened about being back at the graveyard. She was on edge herself, her hand making sure it knew where her gun rested. It wasn't at all outside of the realm of possibility that someone was now watching this place.

"I didn't think any ghosts would care. Nobody else pays us much attention. Why would the dead?"

Sharp kid, she thought, *tough life.* Julio led her to the grave. "They put her in here," he said. The name on the grave was Eduardo Villanueva, born in 1938 and died two weeks ago. "They put her in with the dead man."

Catherine eyed the grave. The dirt looked settled at first, but then she saw that it had actually been compacted more recently than two weeks. She stared at it, wondering if Taylor Woodall was really right there in front of her, hidden beneath the dirt. She had no reason to doubt Julio at this point, but the idea of the girl being so near was surreal nonetheless. She looked around, her hand never far from her gun; thankful Ramirez had given it back. That was something in his favor regarding her opinion about him. "Okay," she told Julio. "Let's go back to the hotel. I'll come back with the police."

Catherine felt she had little choice but to contact the authorities. She wasn't ready to tell Jim and Amy what was happening, though. *Not until we know for sure.* Within the hour four men were digging. Ramirez, Vargas, and Fuentes stood by and watched with Catherine. A pair from the morgue stood near, prepared with a body bag and gurney they'd rolled out to the scene. Ramirez was directing the progress. After 10 tense minutes, the casket was once again revealed. The diggers stepped out of the hole and Ramirez jumped in. He finished wiping the dirt away and placed his fingers under the lip of the lid. As the casket opened a patch of blond hair and white skin appeared. Catherine winced as her heart sank. She knew immediately that they had located Taylor Woodall. She was glad they'd found her at last, but now her death was solidified. She'd have to go back to the Hutton and tell Jim and Amy the news; something she knew would break their hearts.

An assistant took pictures at Ramirez's request, and then he turned the body over and brushed the hair from her face. As Taylor's face, swollen and misshapen, was revealed, most of the group began to cross themselves and mutter hasty prayers sotto voce.

"What are the pictures for?" asked Fuentes.

"We need them for the investigation," said Ramirez.

"Then you take them," ordered Fuentes.

The assistant shrugged and handed Ramirez the camera.

"And I want it made clear to you and your people that no one is to speak of this to anyone else. Anyone who talks to the media will be fired and subject to prosecution," Fuentes continued.

Ramirez hated having to take orders from this government weasel, but he was under fire enough as it was and didn't want to complicate things worse than they already were. "Yes, sir."

Fuentes looked at Catherine as if though he was about to ask her to leave, but Catherine merely looked at him and said, "I won't talk to the media but I'm staying." Fuentes did not argue.

Taylor was laid out on top of the corpse of an old man. Her body was bloated with gases but otherwise not far along in decomposition.

Catherine leaned over the grave and looked down at Taylor. "What's the cause of death?"

Ramirez looked closer while taking further photographs. He saw bruising on her neck, wrists, and ankles. "I'm not positive but there appear to be ligature marks around the neck. I think she was choked." Catherine grimaced and looked away.

As the body was removed from the grave, Ramirez noticed something else, a glob of dried blood in Taylor's hair on the back of her head. He stopped the morticians from moving the stretcher and examined it. Catherine stayed back, but asked, "What is it?"

"Not sure," said Ramirez. "Could be a bullet wound." He snapped a photo.

"She was strangled and then shot?"

"Maybe," said Ramirez, eyeing the bruises again and trying to put the pieces together. "Looks that way."

Catherine walked forward and examined the wounds around her neck. "Someone definitely choked her." The eyes were closed but Catherine imagined once opened during the autopsy they'd show to be full of broken blood vessels. She sighed and grabbed a pen from Ramirez's shirt pocket, pointing towards the blood-matted area of the hairline, "May I?" Ramirez nodded. Catherine proceeded to part the hair revealing the bullet entry wound. "It's small," she commented. She'd never examined a corpse before, but she held herself fast knowing that it was a necessary evil. She was the eyes and ears for this girl now and couldn't trust anyone else to either miss or intentionally hide evidence. She decided that she had to get as much information as possible to ensure it wasn't swept under the rug later.

".22 caliber, maybe," Ramirez suggested.

"So maybe they strangled her, but then shot her in the back of the head afterward to make sure she was dead." Ramirez nodded in agreement.

"Well, let's not jump to conclusions," said Fuentes next to them.

"I'm not jumping to anything," said Catherine. "It is what it is." She backed away and began slowly walking back towards her car, fighting to keep from crying in front of the others. Ramirez watched her go with a pang in his gut. He suddenly felt very useless, a feeling he'd come to know a time or two and didn't like feeling at all.

Fuentes walked forward and told him quietly, "Remember, nobody talks to the press yet. Not until we've had time to make a formal public statement." His eyes trailed to Catherine as she got back in her car and drove away. "That includes her."

"I'm not sure how I can stop her if she decides to talk," said Ramirez.

"If she wants to stay involved, it's on our terms," said Fuentes. "You're the head of this investigation. That makes you accountable." He walked off, looking to Ramirez far less in control of things than he'd like people to believe. He wondered how Fuentes planned on spinning this outcome. There was no way the world wasn't going to hear what had happened to Taylor Woodall. He looked up to the sky; as blue and beautiful as it was, he knew a storm was coming.

Ramirez returned to the Hutton to inform the parents, if Catherine James hadn't already, and was surprised to see her still standing in the lobby. Reporters and cameramen still stood about and talked. They'd been low-key enough in the cemetery that nobody was any the wiser for the moment. It was amazing to Catherine as she stood there watching them all that in just a few short minutes they'd be clamoring like an angry nest of fire ants someone stepped on. "I'm sorry about the girl," said Ramirez as he stopped next to her.

"So am I," said Catherine. She tried to suppress her emotions but it was difficult, "I wasn't expecting it to be so hard. That poor girl."

"It's never easy," added Ramirez. "We try so hard to find the victims, but then when you do it's always terrible. And now comes the hardest part of it all. I have had this conversation several times in my career and it's always horrible. I will tell her parents if you wish. There's no reason for you to have to be the one."

She turned and looked at him. "No, it'd be better if I told them."

Ramirez nodded. Catherine was a friend to the family. He understood. "I'll wait downstairs in the conference room. Just come find me after you've spoken to them. I'm ready to answer any questions they may have at this point." He went to put his hand on her shoulder, but held it. "You have my condolences. As does her family."

Catherine said she'd come find him later and went upstairs. The Woodalls were staying in a suite that was being provided gratis by the hotel. With the sudden recent drop in tourism, they were the only hotel in town to still be sold out. Catherine knocked on the door and Jim answered. She walked inside and glanced at Amy, who was sitting on the bed, her arms folded.

"I have some news," she began. Amy looked up at her with hope in her strained eyes. "It isn't good."

She needn't say more. Jim sat down next to his wife and before Catherine said another word, they knew. "No," said Amy softly, stepping off the cliff straight into the abyss.

"I'm sorry," said Catherine. "We found her."

Chapter 24

Later that night Catherine sat in her room deep in thought while Julio slept soundly, probably the first time he'd slept well in ages. She'd found Taylor Woodall, but the outcome had been what everyone feared most. Now she had to make a decision. Did she return to Dallas and leave to Ramirez and the local authorities finding Taylor's killers? If not, what was the alternative? Could she really stalk the streets asking about the girl's murder? If she did find anything she was likely to end up a victim herself. Still, she couldn't leave like this. There had to be something more she could do. She looked at Julio, wrapped up beneath his covers and snoring softly. *And what about him?* The proper thing would be to let Ramirez handle it from here, but her mind kept going back to what Julio had said in the market. *Juan had trusted the police and it got him killed.*

Again, she felt overwhelmed by the weight of the circumstances. This was much more than she had ever expected. More than even she could have imagined. Killer thugs with machine guns had tried to murder her and the boy in broad daylight. An innocent street kid had been murdered, his body still missing and unlikely ever to be found. And then there was Taylor's murder itself, the brutality of the kidnapping and its motives still unclear. *I'm out of my league,* she admitted to herself.

She began wracking her brain, trying to figure out what to do. She knew a few people in Mexico, but they were executives and lawyers, mostly. They might be able to make a few phone calls on her behalf and pull strings here and there, but they wouldn't be much help in finding Taylor's killers. She took out one of the small bottles of whisky from the mini-bar and poured it into a glass. When she finished that one, she poured another. *There is someone I could call,* she thought. *Would he even help? It'd been years now.* She swirled the Jack Daniels around. *Yes, of course he would. That was a stupid question. It's Matt, after all. He'd help even if he didn't owe me one. And this is the sort of thing he knows better than anyone.* She thought about what it would mean to call him after all this time. There was a reason it'd been so long. Was she sure this was a good idea? *I need him,* she finally decided. Their past would just have to be a separate issue, one that couldn't interfere with what needed to be done.

She wondered where he was these days, probably Iraq or Afghanistan. *God, what if he's married? How awkward would that conversation be?* She doubted her chances of even reaching him, let alone that he'd be able to get away from whatever he was doing wherever he was in the world. But still, she had to try.

She put the glass down and called Jennifer, her legal assistant and long-time confidant, at home. "Catherine? Is that you?" said a voice, obviously pulled from sleep.

"Yeah, it's me. I'm sorry to call so late."

"No, it's fine. I've been worried about you. We heard the news earlier. I was waiting for your call but figured you were busy."

"Yeah, not the way we hoped it would turn out."

"Is there anything I can do?"

"Yes, actually. Do you have your laptop nearby? I need a phone number. Things here are even messier than the news is letting on." She quickly filled her in on everything that'd happened so far.

"Oh, my God, Catherine. Are you serious?" Her friend was now wide awake. "Did they catch the driver!?"

"No, they've got nothing on him so far. Everything's gone crazy down here and I'm in over my head."

"What are you going to do?" her friend asked.

"I'm going to see it through."

There was a long pause on the phone. "Catherine, you need to come back. At least for a few days, let things calm down and then look at this fresh."

"I can't right now," she told her. "I couldn't live with myself if I just walked away now."

Her friend sighed heavily, "Catherine, you're going to get yourself killed. Please, just think about this a second. You know how much I respect you. You're as tough as they come but you're not in law enforcement. And you're not a vigilante. You've done what you can for these folks. You found their daughter, for Christ's sake. Let the authorities take it from here."

Catherine had somewhat expected this. "I am coming back for the funeral, which I expect will be soon. But then I have to come back down here and do what I can. I know what I'm doing."

"I know you do. I'm just worried about you is all. Well, we'll talk more when you're here. Now, whose number do you need?"

"Titansteel," she said. It was a strange name for a company, but after the fall of Black Water, those companies still left in the private security sector opted for less sinister names these days. She doubted he was still with their outfit, but it was the only place to start looking if she hoped to find him.

Chapter 25

The very evening she tried to run way Miss Lydia had put a lot of effort into getting Yesenia in bed with another man. The horn that had sounded belonged to a Honda Civic driven by a young Hispanic man who couldn't afford the three hundred dollars Miss Lydia was demanding for the pure Yesenia. After that came an old man with bushy sideburns and gray hair popping out of his shirt like a yeti. Miss Lydia coaxed him into choosing Yesenia and this time lowered the price to two hundred fifty. She wanted that girl whipped into shape and was willing to bargain to do it. But when they were alone in the room together Yesenia couldn't stop crying. She pleaded with him, and though he couldn't understand her, he got the gist of the problem and couldn't go through with it. He felt so sad for Yesenia that he lost his ambitions to have any girl that night, demanded his money back, and wanted to know just what kind of place Miss Lydia was running. "That girl acts like she's being forced to work. Just what's going on out here, anyway? Is that girl here of her own free will?"

"Oh, of course, of course, she's just been having a rough time, lately. I'll make sure to have a word with her."

"Well, I'm tempted to call the police on out here."

Miss Lydia's eyes narrowed. "I assure you that isn't necessary, sir. And besides, you wouldn't want that sort of trouble, now would you? What would your family say if they knew you were here?" She looked at the ring on his finger. "I'm sure your wife wouldn't approve. And the police would wonder what you were doing here yourself, now wouldn't they?"

The man stammered, "Well, uh, well, something just don't seem right is all."

Her friendly smile reappeared, "Don't worry. That girl is just trying to start trouble for everyone, especially you. I caught her stealing from someone earlier today and now she's making more mischief. Her crocodile tears are just a good act, I can promise you."

"Well, all right. Okay, then," said the man, who now couldn't wait to get out of there. The idea of having to explain to family and friends why he was at a brothel was enough to scare him good and plenty. "I guess you're right. Hell, I don't even know what she was talking about. It's best if I just mind my business and be on my way."

She patted his arm in that solicitous way she often did with customers, "Oh, it's fine, dear, fine. How could you know? She's such a trickster, that one. Don't you give it another thought. I'm just sorry she tried to play on your good intentions. I'm embarrassed, really. Most of my girls are such nice girls."

After she smoothed over the man's concerns and showed him the gate, Miss Lydia dropped her grandmother's facade and unleashed her true fury at Yesenia's insolence. She'd had enough of this new girl. She told Hector to let Imelda out of the hot box and lock Yesenia inside for now while she thought on what to do. "I should put a few scars on that nice little face of hers," she told her son.

"I could fix her," offered Jose. The moment he'd seen Yesenia he had started thinking of things he'd like to do to her.

"Maybe," said Miss Lydia. "But I should be able to get top dollar for a pretty girl like that unused."

"Except she won't cooperate," he reminded her. "She's like a horse. Someone needs to break her before others can ride her."

She nodded agreeably. "Broken nice and good," she told him. Then her wicked smile played across her face. "I think I know a way to get her in line and make a few more dollars while I'm at it. I think I know just the customer for our little trouble maker." She smiled at Jose. "That crazy, *pinche* mechanic hasn't been out for a visit in a while. Maybe he'd be a good one to break the girl. I'm sure he'd be happy to help."

Jose smiled, too. He was disappointed he wouldn't get to be the one to break Yesenia, but the thought of what would soon befall her filled him with a sadistic satisfaction. "I'm sure he would."

"I don't know why I didn't think of it before," she laughed, and went inside her home to make a phone call. The mechanic was usually a problem client of hers. He'd given her a number to reach him when she got a new girl, but given his propensity for violence she had never called him. But now, that same trait might come in handy. And she could make a few dollars out of it as well.

Yesenia had sat alone in the hot box for many hours. As night had fallen, it wasn't the oven that she imaged it would be during the day, and though it was uncomfortable and just as smelly as Evelyn had said, in an odd sense she felt secure for the first time since she'd arrived. She sat in the darkness with her legs pulled up to her chest as she had done when riding in the truck from McAllen.

She was just nodding off to sleep when the door opened. She looked up to see Miss Lydia standing next to Jose and a man she'd never seen before. He stood with no shirt on, his arms and chest covered in tattoos, and fidgeted from side to side in an unnatural way. He ran his hands through his short, sandy blond hair and looked her over in a way that Yesenia liked not at all before he said to Miss Lydia excitedly, "Yeah, yeah, I want some. I'll take me some of that and fix her up right. How much?"

Fear rose up in Yesenia's chest. Miss Lydia saw it on her face and smiled. "Let's go talk," she told the man, still grinning wickedly at Yesenia. Jose slammed the door closed. *Not again*, she thought. She rose up and pressed herself against the metal door, but it had no leeway. She'd already tested it before, but now she made a frantic effort to open it. She had to get away. She knew what Miss Lydia and the new man were going to talk about. The way he had looked at her made her skin crawl; something told her she wouldn't be talking her way out of it this time. He was like Miss Lydia, she thought. They both enjoyed other people's misery.

She beat against the metal door and yelled for help, but no answer came. Then, after 15 minutes or so, the door opened again. The man smiled at her and behind him, so did Miss Lydia. "Now, you know the rules," she told the man, handing him a condom. "She has a room in the pink house."

He took it with a smile and unbuckled his belt while turning to Yesenia, "No, we're gonna do it right here, ain't we, girl? Yeah, we're going to have us some fun."

"Don't mess up her pretty little face," Miss Lydia warned him.

"Awww, we ain't gonna do that, are we, girl? We're just gonna play a little tiny bit." He bobbed left to right with the most horrid smile Yesenia had ever seen.

"You'd better make sure," she told the man. "She needs breaking in, but if you ruin my girl my boys will make you pay."

"Yeah, yeah," he told her. "Go on, now. I paid. I get to play now." He took a few steps towards Yesenia and she backed into to the darkness of the metal container.

"You two play nice now," Miss Lydia told them, with one last look to Yesenia as if to say, *let's see how you like this*. Then she turned and waved Jose back to the house as they left the man to do his worst.

"What if she manages to run away again?" asked Jose, concerned since they'd left Yesenia's cage door open.

"She's not going anywhere," Miss Lydia responded.

"*Por favor*," Yesenia begged the man. "*No. Por favor, no.*" But he just smiled.

Yesenia fought with everything she had, from punching and kicking to biting and scratching, but the man had his way anyway.

"Whoo!" he whooped when it was over. "Now that's what I'm talking about! Yeah, I can't wait to play with you again, girl!"

All the rage and fight that had been in her went down deep into a hidden place inside of her. Not gone, only pushed down deep. Yesenia angrily wiped away the tears, forcing her face to become rigid. She wasn't going to give Miss Lydia the satisfaction of succeeding in beating her into submission. She took it all and put it in the well deep in her belly, promising herself that she'd bring it back out when the time was right.

As the man left, Jose and Miss Lydia came back to the hot box. "Are you going to behave now?" Miss Lydia asked. "Or do I need to get you some more like him. I can get as many as you like." Yesenia wiped away a last tear, her expression as stone. "So we understand each other?"

"Yes," Yesenia told her. "We understand each other."

But Miss Lydia frowned. She looked into Yesenia's eyes and where she had expected to see a broken and submissive gaze, she thought she saw a hint of something else, something she liked not at all. Behind the curtains of the expressionless eyes, she saw iron, burning red-hot with a kindled rage. "You better," she warned Yesenia with a wag of her finger, "or I can find worse things for you."

Chapter 26

In a remote area of Colombian rainforest, three men crept quickly through the thick undergrowth. Their faces were painted to match their surroundings and each wore a gillie suit, an outer layer of fabric like a poncho, but filled with lacings in which local vegetation is tied so that the wearer looks like a bush when standing still.

The point man suddenly froze, ducked down, and held up his arm, the other two instantly stopped and ducked as well. They listened quietly, but no sound out of the ordinary could be heard. Still, the point man looked about cautiously. He gestured to the other two that they were going to flank right, but just as they rose to move again, his chest was instantly covered by an explosion of orange goo. The others swung their guns around, but it was too late. Instantly, they, too, were covered in goo.

"You're all dead," said a voice in Spanish. And as if from nowhere, a man suddenly appeared not fifteen feet in front of them. He pulled off his gillie suit to reveal his face, covered in grease paint.

"I looked for your tracks," said one of the orange-painted soldiers. "There were none."

"That's because I look where I step," said the man as he approached. "And I'm wearing these." He held up a leg and the men saw he was wearing very thin leather boots, something like moccasins, which had been dyed black and had no tread. They were full of little holes on the top where air could ventilate. "That's our next lesson," said the man. "You have to get rid of those clunky boots. I could have shot you blindfolded with the racket you were making in those things. Not to mention how easy it was to track you. Look behind you!"

The men looked, but didn't see much. "Here," explained the man. He stepped behind them and pointed to the ground where a slight indentation was. "See this? A decent tracker can not only follow you with this, but he'll know right away you're wearing combat boots because of the heel depth. You've not only been discovered, but you've also been made. The cartel would follow you back to your blind and put a grenade right up your ass. Not to mention those boots will give you jungle rot that'll eat the skin right off your feet if you're humping it for more than a day or two, which you will be. And Torres!" He got up and walked to the point man, "What the hell is this?" He pointed to a group of fronds tied into the gillie suit.

"It's fern," said the man.

"Look around you," he scolded. He pointed to a fern growing nearby, "What's different about that fern and what you've got sticking out your ass, here?" The man looked but said nothing. The other continued by letting his paintball gun fall by the strap to his side and cupping his hands together. "Ferns grow like hair, up and out in a curved shape. You've got a vertical line here that looks completely unnatural. I'd spot that instantly. And if I would, someone else would, too."

"I thought it would look right when I hit the dirt," said the man.

"You look like a peacock trying to get laid. The second you get a shot off, the rest of the enemy is going to spot this ridiculous looking row of fern vegetation and blow your head off." He tore it off the gillie suit. "Unacceptable," he told Torres. "Okay, that's enough for now," he said to all three. "Let's head back to camp. You guys can get a few hours sleep, but at 22:00 hours we're doing some more night training, so make sure you have your night vision goggles. And Torres, I want you to redo this gillie suit before we head out again. I don't want to see any vertical lines on this thing. You're not trying to disappear into a cornfield."

"Yes, sir," said Torres.

They trekked a quick mile back to camp, a well-furnished set of temporary buildings just inside the forest. More than a hundred soldiers were being trained here, all in small groups, learning everything from bomb making techniques to sniper killing, to search-and-destroy missions. It was a school for covert operations and Matt was the hired substitute teacher.

Once inside his tent, Matt noticed his satellite phone was blinking, indicating a missed call. He hit the button and recognized the number. He pulled a Gatorade out of a cooler, peeled off his moccasin boots, then picked up the phone and dialed. An operator answered the phone.

"Titansteel."

"Hey, it's Matt. You guys call?"

"Yes. You had a call from one Catherine James. She said it was urgent and left a number for you to reach her."

Catherine James. He hadn't heard that name in a while. *Wonder what's got her calling me after all this time.* It'd been years since last they talked, and he hadn't been exactly pleasant. He never thought he'd hear from her again. In fact, he thought she made it pretty clear he wouldn't. That didn't matter, though. He'd promised to always be there if she needed anything, and he'd meant it. Besides, if she was calling him instead of the other way around, she must really be in a fix. He took the number, hung up, and then dialed. He recognized the international prefix. *Wonder why she's in Mexico?*

"Catherine?"

She was working on a third Jack Daniels. It wasn't the smartest thing to do, she knew . . . getting drunk in the hotel room knowing armed assailants may very well find out where she was and that she could end up in another gunfight while inebriated. It didn't seem likely, though. They were probably laying low now that it was all over the news. Still, the Glock was on the table next to her, freshly loaded. "Hi, Matt. How are you?"

"Oh, not too bad. The World Peace boys have me out and about teaching some kids their ABC's, but what the hell? Two weeks' vacation and the pay is okay, so I can't complain." The World Peace Organization was a little running joke between him and Catherine. It was their pet name for the miscellaneous companies he'd worked for over the years. Matt was a modern day mercenary. They both knew it. It was one of the reasons she'd left him so many years ago, though it was one incident in particular that had finalized the split.

"And where's here?" she asked.

"South of you," he told her. "Let's just say that."

Catherine knew enough to put a reasonable picture together. He wasn't in the Middle East. He was in South America, probably being paid to train local anti-cartel soldiers in their fight against drugs. Ironic, in a way, considering it was probably the same sort of people she was dealing with in Cancun. *Reagan's war rages on,* she thought, nostalgically.

"I'm surprised you're not someplace with a little more sand," she told him.

"No, not me. I did a round or two over there but that I.E.D shit was enough to send me packing. I saw a hummer go up in front of my face and that was enough for me." Catherine heard there was more to tell in his voice, but that was probably a story for another day. Maybe another life, she didn't know. He used to tell her all his stories, but that didn't work out so well. "What are you up to?" he asked her. "How's babysitting the oilers?"

"Entertaining as ever," she said. "So you're still willing to work down south, huh? I'm surprised after what happened."

He felt a knot in his stomach. *Didn't take her long to bring that up.* "Aw, you know how it goes. I try not to live in the past," he said defensively. *I shouldn't have been drinking for this call,* Catherine told herself. Matt continued, "I cover my ass these days. I make sure I have a plan B. I'm still grateful for what you did, though, Catherine. I think you know that."

"I'm sorry," she told him. "My mind is all twisted up. I shouldn't have brought it up."

"It's fine," he told her. "You know I'm sorry about it. We can't go back, though, right?" He kicked his boots under his bed. "Why are you calling me, Catherine?" It wasn't an ugly question, just honest.

"Matt, I've got some trouble."

"Uh, oh," said Matt. "Wolf snatch another sheep off the ranch?" Several years ago, when one of the Americans working in Belize was kidnapped, Catherine had been called in to consult on the ransom negotiations and liability risks. The company that hired her also hired another company to assist . . . one with a more sinister name at the time. That's how she met Matt. They'd been fortunate on that one. The oil company had insurance which paid the ransom, and the worker had been released. A small transmitter was in with the money, and Matt had led a team that tracked down the kidnappers. They killed two in a brief firefight before the rest surrendered. Whether it was the dramatic circumstances of their meeting or a lingering, adolescent attraction towards bad boys, Catherine and Matt soon began an intense romance. Something happened later down the road that effectively ended their relationship, yet bound them together forever at the same time in a different sort of way.

"Have you heard anything about the missing girl in Cancun?" Catherine asked him.

"Yeah, I heard something about it. Don't tell me you're caught up in that mess."

"She was the daughter of a close friend of mine," said Catherine.

Matt put his Gatorade down. "Hell. I'm sorry to hear that, Catherine."

"I'm here in Cancun," she told him, "but things are getting out of hand. Someone tried to kill me today. I was wondering if there was any way . . . "

"Someone tried to kill you?" he asked, his tone low and ominous.

"Yes. With a machine gun no less." Matt remained silent a moment. "Are you impressed?" she asked, trying to inject humor where none was to be found.

"I'll finish here tomorrow morning," he said. "Do you want to meet me tomorrow evening?"

Catherine breathed a sigh of relief and chastised herself for ever having a doubt. "Yeah, that would be wonderful, Matt. I'm heading to Houston soon with Taylor Woodall's family, but I'm looking after a boy here and can't leave him alone."

"He's not yours is he?" he asked, half joking. It was entirely possible after five years.

"No. To be honest he was the real target today. He's a witness and someone is doing their best to kill the poor kid."

Matt listened as she tried to explain what had happened. "You weren't kidding," he told her. "You are in a mess."

"Yeah," she agreed, "believe, me, I know. "

They made their arrangements to meet. Catherine was definitely relieved, but also a little frightened at what it would mean to see Matt again. "Thank you, Matt."

"I meant what I said," he told her. "I'm always here."

"I know." The intervening pause was sorely uncomfortable for her. "I'll call."

The next morning Matt made a phone call of his own. He used his work connections and hired a sub-contractor he knew about who had a twin-engine private aircraft available.

"Did you have a good stay?" asked the pilot.

"I did."

"Oh, heading for a little vacation?" asked the pilot, reviewing the flight plan.

"Something like that." Next to him Matt placed two bags, one a backpack with two weeks' of clothes, consisting primarily of camouflage. He'd have to buy some civilian clothes when he got there. The other was an army duffle bag filled with weapons that would have set off the alarms in customs like a Fourth of July extravaganza. Luckily, he wasn't going to have to go through customs. The sub-contractor who leased out the plane had a bonus package. It wasn't cheap to upgrade, but Matt had it put on the company's tab. They'd be pissed as hell when they got the bill, but he figured he'd earned them more than enough to cover it with all the hours he'd been putting in.

The plane was headed for a private landing strip with a government clearance. He'd have to be careful, though. There weren't any permits for the things he was carrying and once he drove off that strip he was on his own. He had an M-14 assault rifle, two 9mm's, one Glock .380, the same model Catherine carried except his had a silencer, his thin boots, and a small black knife with no hilt, only a slender unibody that edged out on one end into a razor-sharp blade. It was the same knife he kept by his bed at nights . . . just in case.

Someone tried to kill her, he thought to himself. And he took the knife from his bag and rubbed its edge. *Does that bother you, Matt?* A voice somewhere inside asked. *Even after all these years?* The answer was a resounding yes. *Old feelings die hard,* said another part of his conscience. *And so will whoever tried to hurt Catherine if I get my hands on them.*

Chapter 27

It had been two days since Yesenia's encounter in the hot box. Like a nightmare, it played over and over again in her mind. The smell of the dog piss in the air, the crazy man screaming jubilantly as she did everything she could to fend him off, and of course the pain and humiliation of it all. Jose had all but dragged her, naked, across the ground back to the Pepto-pink mobile home.

"That's what happens when you don't do what you're told," he told Yesenia and the other girls as they helped her inside.

Imelda was furious enough to rip Jose's eyes out. She had gone to Arnulfo, banging on his door. "How can you just let this happen?" she demanded.

"She brought it on herself," Arnulfo told her. "Now go back to your room before Miss Lydia hears you. You don't want to get her any more upset than she already is."

Half the next day, Yesenia slept in a fitful slumber filled with nightmares. It had been the most disgusting, horrific trauma of Yesenia's life. *I'm disgusting,* she thought. The things he'd done to her, the way he used her body as though she were nothing but his plaything.

"Are you okay?" asked Catalina. She had walked over to visit as Yesenia lay listless in her bed, her right eye swollen badly from the mechanic's handling. "I know what he's like. I've had to be with him a few times, and he's always the same, never nice, always too rough. I don't know why Miss Lydia lets him keep coming back. He's on drugs, you know. That's why he jumps around and yells all the time and why he's so skinny. He's skinny but strong. We're all scared of him."

Yesenia rolled over. She didn't feel like responding. "He choked me one time," said Catalina, continuing on. "So hard I passed out. I thought he was trying to kill me. Really. Miss Lydia threatened not to let him come back after that, but he gave her a couple of hundred dollars and she let it go. I don't know what kind of mechanic he is but he makes money, I guess." Yesenia looked out the window, lost in her sadness. "She gave me fifty of it like that was supposed to make it all right. But it didn't. It's not right she lets some of them treat us like that." Yesenia lay limp and un-answering. "He told me to choke him one time," she told Yesenia, who now rolled over and looked at her. Catalina's face lit up. She wanted to desperately to cheer her up. "It's true. He kept saying 'Come on, girl! See what you can do.' So I did. I was scared at first. Scared he'd turn around and beat me up, but he didn't. So I tried to choke him as hard as I could. His eyes started going all crazy and I quit 'cause I thought he might die or something." She rolled her eyes towards the back of her head and thrust her chin up, breathing heavily as though someone gasping, "He looked like this."

Catalina looked like a cartoon character and it was enough to make Yesenia let slip a smile.

Then Catalina stopped her impression and laughed. "I don't know what would have happened if I didn't stop. I think he might have let me keep going 'til he passed out. There are all sorts of weird ones," she told Yesenia. "One man pays Miss Lydia fifty dollars just for one of us to spank him."

"Tell her about Jose," Evelyn said from the doorway as she entered.

Catalina stifled her laugh and shook her head no.

"Go on," said Evelyn.

"If he finds out . . . "

"Oh, he's not going to find out," she assured. "Tell her." She smiled wide and her eyes laughed.

Catalina looked as though she was frightened to speak of it, but she couldn't help giggling at the thought. "Okay, but you have to swear never to talk about it. If he hears us laughing at him, we'll all be in big, big trouble."

"I want to hear," said Silvia, who now also entered the room after hearing their voices from the kitchen. But Yesenia wasn't sure she wanted to know. She had already learned what big trouble could mean.

"Well," began Catalina. "Jose cries sometimes when he does it."

"What!?" cried Silvia, laughing in enjoyment at the idea of big, bad, boogie man Jose crying.

"It's true," confirmed Evelyn. "Cries just like a baby while he tells you how much he hates you." She jumped on Catalina, pushing her back against Yesenia on the bed and then laid upon her, squinting her eyes together, imitating Jose pumping away while bawling his eyes out, "Boo, hoo, hooo. I hate you. Booo hoo hoo. I hate you, whaaaaaaaa."

"Oh, quit, Evy, quit," Catalina cried through laughs. All the girls were laughing, now.

"He tells you he hates you? Why does he cry?" asked Silvia.

"Cause he's a freak!" laughed Evelyn, getting up and leaving Catalina looking disheveled. "That's why you have to stay away from him. He can be a real mean drunk anyway, but when he starts doing that he just cries and yells at you. Boo, hoo, hoo, boooooo, hoooo, hoooo," she mocked, her voice rising higher and her physical imitation more dramatic.

They all laughed and even Yesenia couldn't help smiling. She rather liked the idea of Jose bawling his eyes out.

"Don't ever say anything to him about it, though," warned Evelyn, her laugh quickly fading. "Imelda got in an argument with him once and called him a crybaby. He nearly broke her jaw because he hit her so hard. So for God's sake, never let him hear you talking about it."

Silvia stopped laughing. "I wonder what's wrong with him."

"It's probably because of Miss Lydia," Evelyn said. "She's always pushing Jose around. Can you imagine what she must have treated him like when he was little? She's so mean. I don't know what happened to his dad, but as far as I know, it was always just Miss Lydia and Jose. She's really messed her little boy up."

"I hope he doesn't do that with me," said Silvia.

"If he does, just lie there. Whatever you do, don't look him in the eye and don't laugh," said Catalina.

"Oh, I'd never do that."

"Yeah, well, we all say there are things we'd never do, and then we end up doing them. That's just what kind of happens after you've been here a while," said Evelyn.

Chapter 28

The knock at the door came around four in the afternoon. Catherine and Julio had spent the day talking and getting to know each other more, watching a few movies and ordering food. He was still running a fever, but it was coming down. Except for a brief call to Jim Woodall, Catherine had talked to no one and they'd gone nowhere. She had wanted to be as far off the grid as possible for the moment.

She checked the peephole to make sure it was Matt and her heart raced a bit faster as she saw his squared and stubbly jaw and dark brown eyes under the mop of his dark brown hair. She opened the door with an awkward smile. "Hey," she said.

Matt stood in the doorway looking at her. She was still striking with her black hair and blue eyes, though for the first time since he'd known her, her porcelain features seemed to be wearing. Perhaps it was age catching up, perhaps just the stress. She was still a knockout, though, and he surmised she probably always would be. "Hey," he said back.

Relief swept over Catherine. She instantly felt like she'd just been thrown a life preserver while floundering in the sea. She stepped up to his broad shoulders and put her arms around his neck. "Thanks for coming," she said. "I can't tell you how much I appreciate it. I didn't know if you would."

"Of course," he said surprised, dropping his bag and putting his arms around her. "You know you can count on me."

She felt her shoulders and ribs warm up as though the blood in her suddenly flowed freer, like she'd been freezing in a cold room and someone just lit a fire. "Well," she said, "Thanks just the same." She stepped back and aside to let him in. And as he walked through he saw the little boy she'd told him about sitting on the bed watching them curiously. "This is Julio," she told him. "He's just about the bravest kid you'll ever meet," she said in Spanish with a smile.

"So I hear," Matt told the boy. "I also hear you've been having a hard time lately," he told the boy, hoping it sounded sympathetic. He wasn't used to kids.

Julio nodded, "Yeah, I guess it could be worse. If I hadn't met Ms. Catherine, I'd probably already be dead."

The kid's a straight talker, thought Matt. He appreciated that in anyone. He handed Catherine the bag full of clothes and asked, "Mind helping me put this in the closet?" She knew there must be a reason for the request as Matt could have put it in the closet himself quicker than asking her, but she took the bag anyway and they both leaned in the closet to put the bags down. As they did Matt unzipped the other bag a little so Catherine could see what was inside. They didn't say anything but she nodded that she understood. Then Matt sat down in the chair Catherine had been sitting in just before he arrived and said, "So, what's first?"

Chapter 29

The next day and a half consisted of an elevation of media activity from a county fair Hoedown to a full-blown three-ring circus. Taylor's parents were prisoners in their hotel room. If they so much as ruffled the drapes by the window, a hundred cameras outside zoomed in, prepared to catch even just a glimpse. The sheer enormity of the story was mind-boggling, and everyone wanted some kind of scoop over the others. Reputable reporters had resorted to paparazzi antics in an effort to get the story. Everyone who went in and out of the hotel was surrounded and questioned about whether or not they were involved in the case, and if so, what information they knew. One *Telemundo* reporter went so far as to dress as a hotel employee and sneaked up to the Woodall's room. Security pulled him away as he pounded on the door, "A word! Just a word! What do you want the people to know about what's happened to your daughter?"

"Damn vultures," said Amy Woodall, crossing her arms as she'd taken to doing so often recently. She peered out of the window through a slit no bigger than a dime, then turned and spoke to Fuentes, who had come to visit. "I don't want my daughter to be cut up," she told him. "If an autopsy has to be done, it can be done back in Texas."

Fuentes spoke in his ever-political calm voice, "I understand your concerns, ma'am. While our laws require us to perform an autopsy, I assure you we will take every measure to leave your daughter as she is. I will see to it personally that she is treated with the utmost respect."

"How long until we can take her home?" asked Jim.

"Tomorrow, sir," said Fuentes. "We have arranged a private plane for you. And again, if there is anything we can do to help, please do not hesitate to ask. I'm at your service."

The following day the Woodalls were on their flight back to Texas. Catherine accompanied them, wondering what would be waiting for her when she returned to Cancun.

She and Matt had only talked briefly before she had to get ready to leave. Julio hadn't taken the news that she had to leave for a couple days very well, but she assured him he was in good hands.

She used the time during the trip to try and gain some perspective on everything and organize her thoughts. She believed Ramirez was a good cop, but she had seen the way the officials were sweeping as much of the dirt under the rug as possible. She'd have to remove some carpet when she got back, and was feeling better about calling Matt. He'd have an idea of where to begin rather than sitting around waiting for the Mexican authorities.

Ramirez was at his desk in Cancun in the middle of an angry outburst. He had picked up the phone and called the coroner's office. In his hand he held the official cause of death report. When the coroner answered he didn't waste any time. "What the hell is this?!"

"What do you mean?" asked the coroner, nervously.

"I mean, what is this report supposed to be?"

"That's how the girl was killed, sir. I don't know what else to tell you."

Ramirez wasn't buying it. According to the toxicology report Taylor Woodall had multiple drugs in her system. Even if it was true, they'd conveniently included that information and excluded most everything else. "You can tell me why the hell the rest of the information has been left out. What about the ligature marks? We all know what happened to that girl and you didn't mention any of it in this report. I want to know why!"

There was a long pause. "She died from a gunshot wound. I merely reported the cause of death, sir, as I was told."

"*Told?*" asked Ramirez. "What do you mean *told?*"

Another pause. "I'm sorry if you are dissatisfied with the report, sir. I'm afraid it's out of my hands." And then Ramirez heard a click as the coroner hung up.

Fuentes, he thought to himself. *That son of a bitch.* He ended the call on line one but started another on line two, this time calling Fuentes.

"Hello?"

"Mr. Fuentes, this is Detective Ramirez."

"Hello, Detective, how may I help you?"

"I want to know what you're doing."

"How so?"

"You're covering things up in this Woodall murder. You're intentionally hiding the facts from scrutiny."

"I'm not," said Fuentes defensively. "And I would encourage you to take a moment before making such grave accusations."

"I just got the autopsy report on the girl. All it says is she was highly intoxicated, on drugs, and died by a gunshot wound. It says nothing about her other wounds or the sexual assault, which seemed pretty apparent to me. And I've already told you who the shooter in the market was."

"I see no reason to believe the two are connected," said Fuentes.

"With all due respect, sir, I can't see how you could just dismiss . . .
"

"I will not entertain conspiracy theories in this matter for the media to expound upon. This situation is delicate enough. We're talking about the very lifeblood of our economy, Detective. You do your job, let the coroner do his, and I'll do mine," warned Fuentes.

"And how am I supposed to do my job when information is intentionally being withheld?"

"Stick to your own affairs, Detective. Your job is to bring this mess to an end without causing any more damage than what has already been done." And Fuentes hung up.

Ramirez slammed his phone down as well. *Dammit!* The wheels were turning and he was quickly putting the pieces together. *They're going to cover it up and blame it on the girl.* He could see it now. Soon there'd be a press conference or some other kind of media announcement. They'd detail the drugs and alcohol in Taylor Woodall's system and call the whole thing some seedy drug deal gone wrong. *No, no, it wasn't a kidnapping after all. The girl was obviously an addict and her kidnapping and murder were an isolated, drug related event.* It was going to be a smear campaign, and Taylor Woodall was the target. Cool and calm Ramirez decided he'd about had enough. It was time the puppet cut a few strings.

Chapter 30

Over the next few days men came and went. Yesenia had every intention of running away, but each time either the other girls would talk her out of it or the fear that Miss Lydia would hand her over to someone worse than the meth-head mechanic was enough to scare her from trying. *I need somewhere to go,* she thought to herself. *And some way to get there.*

He'd come back again, the mechanic, though it hadn't been as bad as the first time. He seemed bored with her now. She'd learned from the other girls that it was the fight he wanted, so she refused to give it to him. She just lay with her eyes closed or her face turned off to the side, doing her best to show no emotion, which frustrated him immensely until finally he finished and told her, "Lost your fight, huh? You're just like a limp little fish, now. You ain't no fun." He told Miss Lydia to call him when she had someone more interesting and sped out of the little compound with a roar of his truck.

Jose had come for her the next night, and it was a night, like the first time with the mechanic, that made her sick to think about. He hadn't cried like she'd been told he sometimes did, but he was rough and let fly a laundry list of insults for no apparent reason.

Their little compound, she learned, was located about forty miles northwest of Dallas. Miss Lydia had been running it for nearly two decades, always with illegal immigrants for prostitutes. Her deal with Ortiz back in Mexico City made it easy for her to get a supply of pretty young girls over whom she could exercise complete control. She'd work them until they weren't earning enough to appease Miss Lydia, then most were told their debt was paid and they could leave, although it usually took years before a girl was actually allowed to go. There had been two over the years who weren't so lucky. Miss Lydia thought they were a particular risk if set free, so the others were told the girls had paid their debt and were now free to pursue their own interests, but in truth those two girls just disappeared. The first was found floating in a river five years ago, never identified. The second one Jose crudely cremated and buried in the woods not far from the compound. Neither Hector, Arnulfo, nor any of the other girls, past or present, ever knew about the two who Miss Lydia had ordered gone for good. It was something she'd forced Jose to handle quietly.

The prices were anywhere from forty to a hundred and fifty dollars, of which the girls got only twenty-five percent towards their debt, not that it mattered. Some girls had their debts paid off long before they were allowed to leave, but they were too afraid to contact the authorities. Miss Lydia made them believe they'd be deported back to Mexico where friends of hers would deal with them. "My good friend

Ortiz saves all your information," she reminded them. "And all I have to do is pick up a phone and I can get to you or your families any time I want." The threat worked. The girls were prisoners without bars.

Yesenia knew she could not live this way much longer. With each man she imagined her Papa looking down upon her, his heart breaking and hers echoing. She knew she had to find a way to escape this life. That's when she got the idea for using Armando.

He was a young Hispanic man who had arrived one night in his old Chevy pickup truck, and he absolutely worshipped Yesenia from the first time he laid eyes on her. "I've never done anything like this," he told Miss Lydia while the girls all lined up in the courtyard area.

"Oh, there's nothing to be concerned about," she told him. "My girls are all clean and very pretty, as you can see." Immediately he locked on to Yesenia. "Do you like her?" asked Miss Lydia. He nodded. "Well, I think she's going to like you, too. Come now, let's see if we can work something out." She had led him to her place of business and that was the first night he slept with Yesenia.

He came back the very next night. "You're so beautiful," he told her in Spanish as he lay on top of her, kissing her neck, her ears, and her breasts. His touch was gentle, almost comforting. "You shouldn't be a prostitute. You could be a model or an actress or something," he told her.

It was just the break she needed. Until now, none of the other men she was presented to, save one who seemed too friendly with Miss Lydia for Yesenia to trust, spoke Spanish. Miss Lydia had seen to it to keep Yesenia away from the Hispanic clients. Her sob story might fall on sympathetic ears. But Miss Lydia had let her guard down. Yesenia had been obedient of late and Miss Lydia had begun to think the girl was finally broken in, instead of just biding her time. And Armando was a good mark for a potential opportunity. He didn't know Miss Lydia, and best of all, she didn't know him. He wasn't a regular that she might have information on. If Yesenia stole away with him, she thought it very unlikely Miss Lydia would have the slightest idea of where to look for her. On that second night she began to formulate a plot.

When Armando returned again for the third time a week later, she tested the water. After he reached his climax and lay on top of her panting in deep breaths, kissing her as he had done before, she asked him, "Do you have a girlfriend?"

He kissed her lips as if half dreaming. "Hmmm?"

"A girlfriend. Do you have a girlfriend somewhere?" she asked.

"No," he told her. "No girlfriend."

"How come? You seem like a nice guy. Not like the others."

He ran his fingers through her hair. "I don't know. I guess I'm not that great with most girls. I don't make a lot of money or drive a fancy car. Hell, I really can't afford to keep coming here, but I can't help myself. You're just so amazing."

"What do you do?"

"I work at a big car dealership, washing cars and stuff. It's not very interesting, but it pays the bills . . . well, sort of. I'm going to school, too, though," he added quickly. "At night, I take some college classes. I'm working on a business degree so I can get a real job. You know, one with benefits and all that so I can really take care of us."

"Us?" she asked.

"Yeah, my brother and me. I look after him."

"Is the school hard?" Yesenia had daydreamed about attending college in the U.S. one day. That now seemed an impossible fantasy.

"No, just time-consuming and expensive. They give grants and financial aid, but it still costs so much money you wouldn't believe it."

"You don't live with your family?"

"No, just me and my little brother. Our parents weren't very responsible, if you know what I mean."

"How so?"

It wasn't something he was accustomed to talking about, but he felt at ease with Yesenia. "Our dad took off when we were young and my mom's kind of a screw up. She doesn't live far from us, but my brother and I just couldn't live with her anymore. She's into too much shit. My brother works with me so we saved up and got our own place. Just a little house we rent, about like this," he gestured around the mobile home. "It isn't much, but it works for now."

"What about you?" he asked. "Where's your folks?"

Yesenia leaned against him. At one time the girl she was would have felt bad playing on his sympathies like she was about to do, but that girl had been replaced by a tougher Yesenia, one who was willing to do what she needed to do to survive and escape her hellhole. Men were using her. It was her turn. "They're back in Mexico. They've no idea what's become of me. None of this was supposed to happen."

"What do you mean?" he asked.

She looked deep into his eyes and tried to find the words that would make him help her. "This place. These people. They tricked me," she told him in a whisper, "all the girls here."

"They tricked you? How?"

And there she saw it. In the glint of his eye and the way he caressed her as though he cared for her, she saw her chance. "If I tell you, you mustn't speak a word to anyone else. If they find out, they might hurt us both. They're bad people."

He shifted his body weight and pulled her close. "Who are bad people?"

"Miss Lydia and the men here. You don't know how bad they are." She held his arm and pressed her head against his cheek. "It all started back in Mexico City . . . " she began. She told Armando about meeting Ortiz and about the man that came to the apartment with her bus ticket in his hand, about crossing the river with the marijuana, the truck ride, and what happened when she got to the compound. She left out a lot of things, in particular what had happened to the state Trooper, and she was able to quickly summarize events.

"Oh, my God," he said. "Well, you have to get away," he told her.

"I want to run away," she whispered, "but I've no place to go."

"You can stay with me."

She rolled over on his chest, "Really? Would you actually do that for me?"

"Yes," he told her. "I'm serious. You can't stay here, not after what you just told me. You can stay with me and we'll call your family back in Mexico."

And that was how it happened. She knew he had no idea just how serious a danger he was agreeing to face, and she didn't want the young man to get hurt because of her, but she had to get away and he was her best chance. She knew there'd be consequences, but her desperation was far more potent than her reason at this point. She was ready to accept any risk on her own, but she would have to warn her family immediately upon her escape. She refused to stay a slave in the compound and accept this new horrific life, and exactly what they were all going to do afterward she didn't yet know, but anywhere had to be better than here.

The very next morning, Yesenia felt as though God smiled upon her when she looked out the window and saw rain. She walked as a shadow to the fence, holding her breath the entire way in fear the dogs would raise the alarm, but luckily they had retreated to the hot box for shelter and the rain masked the sound of her steps. She could have simply run down the beaten trail to the fence, but she was too frightened of being seen or heard, so she had snuck through the barbed wire fence in the back and now circled around through the brush.

When she reached the road, Armando was parked in his old pickup truck waiting for her. *Thank God he's here.* She smiled with exuberance. She felt luck was with her and that her escape was meant to be. She ran to the truck and knocked on the passenger window. Inside, Armando jumped. He unlocked the door and opened it. "You scared the hell out of me," he told her.

"Has anyone seen you?" she asked.

"Not that I know. Get in, get in. Let's get out of here."

Yesenia crawled inside and the truck pulled way and headed down the lonely county road. She looked back, worrying that the Suburban might suddenly dart out from the little compound, but no lights came. It was 5:20 in the morning. As most of the brothel's traffic was at night, she knew everyone would have gone to sleep just a couple of hours ago.

As she looked back, she thought about Silvia. She didn't want to leave her, but she couldn't risk Silvia revealing her plans in fear. Miss Lydia's threats and violence had subdued Silvia from the start. Yesenia knew Silvia was far too afraid to risk their captors' wrath after all they'd seen. She'd accepted that she was now the property of Miss Lydia, something Yesenia would and could never accept. *I'll send help back to them*, she thought. *But first I have to warn Ceci in case Miss Lydia calls Ortiz.* She had to make sure her sister's family was safe.

Chapter 31

Funeral services for Taylor Woodall were held the following weekend in Taylor's hometown of Katy, Texas. Police formed a perimeter around Anders Funeral Home keeping the reporters and curious onlookers back. Flowers, stuffed animals, and cards were piled high at the driveway entrance. Hundreds, if not thousands, of people were there. The Governor also attended the funeral after asking if it would be alright with the family, as did most of Taylor's old classmates from high school and new friends from the University of Texas. Also in attendance was Jamie. The bullet had broken her collar bone, ripping through muscle and tendon, but she'd survived . . . thanks to a quick medical response by the hotel staff and of course Taylor's brave last actions. She was looking at a long road ahead of physical therapy, and probably severe arthritis for the rest of her life, but she was able to attend the services of her friend who'd saved her life.

"I've never seen so many," said one of the funeral home directors as he looked out at the sea of mourners that were lined up outside their gates.

"It's big news," said the other. "Did you hear what Shelly said? About the body, I mean?" Shelly was the embalmer.

"No, what?"

"She said that girl got assaulted, had marks around her ankles, wrists, and neck. All that b.s. about a gunshot, Shelly said that came after . . . says the girl was tied down and assaulted, then they shot her."

"Jesus," said the other.

"Makes you wonder about the rest of the young folks going down there every year for spring break, doesn't it?"

The other shook his head, "Whole damn place is going to hell in a hand basket. Used to just be the border was a fun place to go shopping or out for some drinking, now look at it. People getting their heads cut off for no reason, kidnappings, murders all over the place."

"Scary."

The other nodded in agreement.

After the services Catherine met the Woodalls at their home, along with other close friends and family. She was already packed and ready to return to Cancun, though she hadn't yet told Jim and Amy. There were a lot of things she hadn't told them yet, and she wasn't looking forward to having to be the one to break even more bad news to them. *As if losing Taylor weren't enough to bear,* she thought.

The hours ticked away and the visitors thinned out, until finally it was just Taylor's maternal grandparents and Catherine. She was sitting in Jim's study with an old bottle of Chivas Regal, which had sat for years in his cabinet until now, a large glass full of ice, and two smaller glasses, watching CNN on a small flat-screen television in the corner when Jim finally came in and closed the door. She was listening to the reporter nervously. She had hoped it wouldn't be on the news so fast as she had wanted to warn them first and prepare them, but there was no good way to try to explain what he was sure to soon hear, so she just prepared herself for the worst.

"Officials released a preliminary report this morning on the murder investigation of Taylor Woodall that has many stunned," said the reporter. "One anonymous official said a large amount of cocaine and other drugs were found in the girl's system, alluding that her death may have been drug related."

Jim's face turned white as he stared at the television. "Bullshit," he said. "Did they just say what I think they said?" He turned and glared at Catherine, "Did you hear that?"

Catherine clicked the remote and turned the TV off. "That anonymous official was probably Fuentes. If not, then it was probably an intentional leak to the press. His office has been trying to spin this from the moment we found her."

Jim looked shell-shocked before he saw something he recognized in Catherine's demeanor. "You knew," he said accusingly. "You've already heard this and didn't tell me, haven't you?"

"Yes," she told him softly, "I heard. I wanted to tell you privately so you could decide how to approach the subject with Amy. I wasn't trying to hide it from you. We just haven't had time to talk. They just started reporting this earlier today."

"Oh, God, when Amy hears this crap . . . I'm not sure how much more she can take. I ought to sue those bastards for slander. How could they say that?"

"They're looking for any excuse to rationalize that it wasn't the random act of violence it was," she told him. "They want everyone to think Taylor was culpable in some way, but we all know it's crap. The truth will come out. You'll see." Catherine had already heard that Taylor's toxicology report had revealed that she had amphetamines in her system. How it got there, though, was the real question, assuming the report was even accurate. She decided not to get into it at the moment and instead changed the subject. "How is Amy?" She hadn't really talked to Amy since she broke the news to them of Taylor's death a week ago.

Jim was still lost in his own contemplation of what he'd just heard, but he managed to bring his thoughts back to answer, "She's holding up. The doctor has her on Ambien, so at least she can sleep. She's upstairs resting now."

"And you? Are you sleeping?" Catherine filled the glasses and handed one to Jim.

He took it and slumped in his chair behind his desk. "Not really. But I'm fine without it. I don't want to sleep. Every time I close my eyes, I see her." He gulped down his drink and got up to refill it. "I see her like that day in the morgue on the computer screen. I hardly recognized my own daughter," his voice broke and he took a drink from his glass to keep his composure. She was glad he hadn't seen her the way she had. He'd been the one to make the positive identification formally, but at least they'd managed to clean her up a bit before he saw her. "I can't get the image out of my head." Catherine, meanwhile, drank from her glass a little slower, but she wasn't being bashful, either. Both intended on getting drunk. Both needed it. His tears having ebbed, Jim asked, "Have you heard anything?"

"Not much you don't already know," said Catherine. "Except of course this," she said, pointing to the now blank television.

Jim stared blankly off into the distance, "That Fuentes . . . what a little snake. Kissing our ass and then pulling this shit behind our back. Well, they're not going to get away with it. I'm not going to let them turn her into something she wasn't, just so they can tell the world it wasn't their fault and pretend like it didn't happen."

"No, we won't let them," she agreed. "This isn't over, Jim. We've still got a lot more searching to do."

Jim nodded. "What about that boy you found? How's he doing?"

"He's getting better. Luckily, the bullet missed all the tendons and arteries. He really needed to go to the hospital but I couldn't convince him. I can't say as though I blame him. He'll have a nice little scar, but I expect he'll be good as new otherwise."

"You didn't leave him alone down there, did you?"

"No, of course not. He's with a friend."

"Have you found out yet who was after you in the market?"

"Well, I still think they were after the boy more than me, but of course the police down there aren't much help. That guy Vargas wrote it off as a carjacking, which is beyond stupid. I really don't think he could be that big of an idiot. He's shady."

"You don't think we can trust him?"

"Oh, I know we can't," she said. "I'm just wondering how untrustworthy the guy is. Let's just say I won't be walking down any alleys with my back to him."

"Well, you don't think he's in with any of the drug people, do you? I mean, just that he's looking out for Cancun's interest more than us, right?"

"No," she told him, "I mean he's shady in the worst possible way. I don't know it for sure, but I'm getting a distinctly bad vibe from the guy. And then there's this thing with him being the last person the missing kid was with. That's just setting alarm bells off in my head. I don't think we need to have anything to do with that guy and we should probably ask that he not be involved in any further investigation. I don't have any proof he's done anything wrong but there's just too many bells ringing in my ears telling me the guy's bad. You wouldn't believe the level of corruption down there, Jim. The former Chief of Police for Cancun, Francisco Velasco Delgado, was arrested for ties to the cartel and listed as a suspect in the torture and murder of the newly appointed chief of the drug task force."

"You're kidding," said Jim.

"No, I'm sorry to say that I'm not. And he was the Chief of Police. You can just imagine how many more of those cops are working for the cartel. Law enforcement is a for-profit business down there. And it gets even worse. One mayor they had, who had taken leave of absence to run for governor of Quintana Roo, by the way, was arrested for aiding and protecting the cartel. And that's just a few samples of the things that go on down there. You have got college kids tanning themselves on the beach while cartels behead people in the streets. Makes you wonder if the whole damn country isn't run by the cartels these days. There's kind of been an unspoken rule about tourists, though. They bring in the money so traditionally they have been off limits, but obviously that's starting to not be the case. More and more you're seeing kidnappings and ransom on the border. Hell, a top U.S. anti-kidnapping expert who worked to free victims was in Mexico a while back for a speech. He went out to eat with some colleagues, stepped outside for a phone call, and disappeared into thin air . . . kidnapped."

"What happened to him?"

"Felix Batista," she recalled. "That was his name. Nobody knows. There was never a demand. He just disappeared."

"That's what would have happened here, if not for you. At least we know," he added, his voice choking a bit. He cleared his throat forcefully and then asked angrily, "Jesus, how in the hell can they all be corrupt? I mean who the hell can we trust?" The information Jim was hearing was infuriating. He'd always heard about the problems in Juarez or Mexico City, but he never paid attention to Cancun. It was always advertised as a beautiful getaway. Only now, after it was too late, was he hearing what really went on there. "Can we even trust that Detective Ramirez guy, or any of these people for that matter? They keep telling us how they're going to find out what happened and do all they can, but then I turn on the TV and hear this bullshit. Lies, lies, damn lies. That's all we're getting. We wouldn't have ever found her if you hadn't stepped in."

She tried to think about things from Jim's perspective and understood his skepticism completely. She shared his sentiment for the most part, but the jury was still out on Ramirez. "Ramirez seems okay so far. He cares, I think. There are a lot of good people who love their county and who risk their lives on a daily basis trying to get rid of the corruption and crime of the cartels, but it's a hell of a tough fight. I'm hoping Ramirez is on the right side of that fight, but even if he is, he has people pulling his strings. Hence, the kind of stuff we just heard."

"Well," said Jim. "I've got a fix for that. I've got the news camping out on my front lawn. I'm going to go out there and tell them what's what. There's no way in hell this was drug related. Taylor would never be into that kind of thing. And I'm going to tell everyone just what I think of this smear campaign they got running against the victim in this case, my little girl. Let's see how many people I get to cancel their summer plans in Mexico then." And he was so moved by his anger that he put his glass down and made to get up and go right outside then and there.

"No," said Catherine. "Look," she told him. "There are still a lot of questions that need answering before you do that."

"Like what?" he asked, seating himself back down angrily. Catherine paused to gather her thoughts and he grew frustrated, "What else could you possibly not be telling me?"

"There are some things the law enforcement down there hasn't released to the public, certain ugly facts about Taylor's remains. Things they don't want to get out. And I think it might hurt our chances of finding these people if the details did get out."

"Such as?" asked Jim. He'd been told where Taylor was found, and that she had been shot. He also knew her face looked abnormally swollen and bruised when he made the identification, but he didn't know if it was just part of the decomposition that had caused the abnormal appearance or if there was another explanation. After being told she'd been shot he didn't think to ask what else might have happened. Part of him suspected, but didn't really want to know for sure.

Catherine breathed heavily. "I'm not sure how much to tell you, Jim. Knowing all the details won't bring her back."

Jim looked over his shoulder, drank a heavy gulp from the glass, refilled it, and said, "Just tell me. I deserve better than to be left in the dark like this with everyone else knowing things that I have to find out from the news."

"Her clothes were gone," started Catherine. Jim gave no reaction, and that worried Catherine even more.

"And?" asked Jim. Catherine stared at him, trying to decide what to do. Jim looked up from his glass at her. "Goddamn it, Catherine. That was my child. I deserve to know how she left this world."

Catherine killed her drink. She was visibly upset. *He already knows part of it,* she thought. *Why does he want to hear it?* "I'm your friend, Jim. And as such I'm not sure you do need to know. At least not right now. Let me put some more pieces together first."

He leaned in towards her, "Catherine, I can never repay you for what you did by finding her, but I need you to listen to me, now. I am her father. My life, our life, was about raising our child and seeing her on to have her own family, raise her own children, and live a full and complete life. That's gone, now. All we have left is finding the truth. We can't do that if you hide things out of a misguided sense of protection. We're parents who lost our child. There's nothing left to protect us from . . . the worst has already happened. Now we have to pick up the pieces and make them fit. Otherwise, there's no moving on from this. And we can't do that without knowing everything." He reached out and put his hand on her arm, "Everything."

She didn't want to say it, but she knew she had to. She didn't want Jim to know how bad it was, but if she didn't tell him, nobody else was going to, and it was things he might need to know when dealing with the authorities in finding Taylor 's killers or talking to the press. He was right. He needed all the pieces or there'd never be any way of putting them together again. "Taylor was asphyxiated and she had ligature mark on her wrists. The gunshot came after." She heard herself say the words as if in a dream. "And there were drugs in her system like they're saying, though I don't think anyone believes she consumed them of her own free will. More like she was drugged to make her more easily subdued, which is precisely what they were trying to do in the club to begin with, for that matter."

Jim stared at Catherine blankly for what seemed an eternity. He could barely wrap his mind about it. He'd believed she'd been killed early in her ordeal, quickly. He thought it had likely been a kidnapping gone awry after the incident in front of the hotel . . . maybe Taylor had fought and they had shot her right off before asking for a ransom, or maybe they caught her trying to escape early on, but, no. If they drugged her into a stupor, tied her hands . . . . he suddenly understood all too well the horror that had happened to her. He jumped up and threw his glass against the door, shattering it. He punched a computer monitor on the desk, cracking it and sent it sliding off the desk onto the floor.

Catherine thought for a moment of stopping him but she knew at this point it could be cathartic for Jim to release his pent-up frustrations. This was a rage that needed to come out.

He let loose an angry and desperate howl and swiped everything off the desk into a nearby bookshelf, his face flushed, the veins in his neck pulsing.

"Jim," Catherine said. "Amy." She was asleep upstairs and while Catherine wanted to see Jim express his anger, she knew he didn't really want to wake his wife.

It took a moment, but he was able to sit back down again and composed himself as best he could, his hands shaking furiously. Catherine sat quietly, occasionally stirring the ice in her glass around. Finally, he was calm enough to speak again through choked back tears. "They're going to get away with it." He looked at her, helpless, his eyes watery and red pained. "Whoever did this . . . they won't find them. They're out there somewhere, watching all this on the news, laughing to themselves. They're going to get away with it and there's not a damn thing I can do, is there?"

"They won't get away with it, Jim."

"What can we do?" he asked her, the tears in his eyes falling before he quickly and angrily wiped them away. "You've got the boy who saw these people, but what good is that with no suspects? They're probably long gone to some backwater village nobody's ever heard of." Jim looked at her. "I have to ask you a favor, but you can say no if you want."

"I won't," said Catherine.

"Whoever did this to her," started Jim. "I have to find them." Catherine merely nodded. "I know you have a business to run, Catherine. But if you could spare some more time . . ." he knew he was asking more than what was right. But he did so, not for himself, but for Taylor. "We wouldn't have found her without you, Catherine. And I don't think those people down there are going to find these people. You're the only person I know who has connections there and can actually get something done. Amy and I have quite a bit saved. We plan on paying that reward, but we've still got nearly two hundred thousand in our combined retirement accounts, not to mention the savings we were keeping for Taylor's tuition and rent."

"Stop it," said Catherine, angry. She'd been slapped by what he'd said and stood up to let him know it. "Why do you think I'm here, Jim? You can't hire me like this is a job. This isn't about money. This is about what's right and wrong. I'm not here because I feel obligated or because I'm expecting to be paid. Don't insult me, Jim. This could never be just another job for me. The people who did this have to be found, or they're going to do it again, Jim. They killed Taylor, they killed a homeless child, and they tried to kill me and that child's friend." She knelt down in front of him and grabbed his hand, squeezing it hard. "This is about right and wrong," she told him again. "I'm staying because I want these people found and punished, because that's what's right and just. Don't you dare think you need to offer me money to stay."

"I'm sorry," he said. "I know you have your own life, though. You have a successful business to run . . . "

"It can run itself at this point," Catherine said. "Believe me. I've got a secretary that can run that office blindfolded without me. She's not a lawyer but she knows more than most attorneys out there, and my associates know what they need to do while I'm out."

"They almost killed you," Jim said, looking at his friend in awe. "I've got no right to ask this, Catherine, and I know it. But I can't live with doing nothing."

"Neither could I," she said. "And that's the point. We're in this together, all of us."

Jim leaned back in his chair. "I don't know how I'm ever going to repay you, Catherine. Honest to God, I don't."

She returned to her seat, her heart still racing. She knew he didn't mean to offend her but the idea that he could even think she was here for the wrong reasons had stung. "Don't thank me just yet." She watched him with her striking eyes. "I have a condition, and you're not going to like it."

Jim looked at her curiously, "What's that?"

"You and Amy can't go back with me."

"Like hell," started Jim, but Catherine cut him off.

"Hear me out. Besides the fact that she's heartbroken and in shambles and you're needed here to take care of her, you won't be any good to me if you do come. Your face has been plastered all over the news. We couldn't take two steps down there without everybody recognizing you. Nobody who might know anything would talk to us. Not to mention we'd be shadowed everywhere by the media." She shook her head, "No, it just can't happen, Jim. It'd never work, especially with Julio, the boy, with me. Your presence would put him in danger. We don't have a right to do that to him. I've got to be a ghost down there, never seen until I'm ready. It's bad enough I've been seen as much as I have. It's got to be this way, Jim. Nobody is going to talk to someone who is going to bring unwanted attention."

Jim wanted to protest, but Catherine's words were powerful. He knew she was right. "What will you do?"

"Start shaking the trees and see what falls. I'm going to do everything I can to find whoever did this. I'll make some calls, put pressure on the authorities, and make them stay on it. We'll find out what really was behind her abduction, who it was and why Taylor was their target. And we'll clear her name. We'll expose this for what it is, not what the powers that be down there are trying to make it look like."

"I want these people caught, but don't want to see you go down there alone. They've already tried to hurt you once, Catherine. I can't ask you to go there without us."

"I won't be alone, remember? I have a friend down there now with Julio."

"Who?"

"His name's Matt. We've known each other for years as well. Longer than I've known you, in fact. It's kind of a long story. If things get dangerous, though, I'll be safe with him. Trust me, he's the kind of guy that's used to being in bad spots."

"What's he do?"

"Well," started Catherine, "That's kind of a long story, Jim. And it'd probably be a little difficult to explain."

"I'd really like to know you're in good hands, Catherine. I would never have asked you to stay and help without me and the authorities down there with you."

"Okay," she told him. "Well, Matt's basically a soldier for hire."

Jim was taken aback. "A what?"

"He's a veteran marine who now works on and off for security companies. You know, escorting diplomats, providing security detail for wealthy foreigners, etc."

"You mean he's a mercenary?" Jim asked. "Are you serious?"

She knew how it sounded. "Yes, I guess you could call him that, although they prefer 'private security team' I think."

"How in the world do you know someone like that?"

She almost laughed. If Jim only knew of some of the shady characters Catherine had met over the years. She could only imagine what he'd think about what she was about to tell him. "He was the man I was with before I met David."

Jim look dumbfounded. "You mean you used to date this guy?" He was wondering why he'd never heard this side of Catherine's life. It wasn't as though they were extremely close friends. Hell, they rarely talked more than once or twice a year until this happened, but still, it was an unexpected bit of information.

"Do you really want to know?" she asked him, almost daring him with the first smile of the evening, still working on her Chivas.

"Yes, if you don't mind telling me. David never told me anything like this."

"That's because David never knew," she said with a nostalgic laugh. *Wouldn't he have been surprised.* "I surprised myself, to tell you the truth. I wouldn't have thought I'd go for that bad boy type, but I did. I guess we girls tend to have a soft spot for them, what can I say? Several years back some extremists had kidnapped an American in South America. I was handling the risk management aspect for the company and they hired Matt's company. A ransom was paid but Matt was still tasked with tracking down the kidnappers, which he did, I might add. We ended up dating for a while after that."

"Really? So what happened?"

Sitting in the quiet den with so much sadness and life's contemplations in the air, she decided to tell Jim what she'd never told anyone before. "What always happens with the bad boys, I guess. He did something bad. Well," she laughed, "in his case that was kind of an understatement. We had our ups and downs, you know. He was a good guy at the core, really, but there was a reason he did the kind of work he did. He'd been in the original Gulf War when he was still just a kid. Got so wrapped up in the military way of life he didn't let it go even when he was back in the real world. That's what led him to the kind of work he was doing when we met. I'd have been okay with that, you know? Except, it got the best of him. It's true what they say about some of the people who go off to war. Some just can't cope afterward. Matt was one of them."

"How so?"

"Well," she sipped from her glass, now severely feeling the whiskey's effects. "He went crazy, is probably the easiest and most accurate way to say it. Some rebel nuts attacked and killed some workers on a pipeline, taking two of them for ransom, typical political propaganda bullshit extremists. It was the third such attack. Normally they just shot from the cover of the forest and ran off, but this time they took hostages, so of course the company hired Matt's company in an attempt to track the guerrillas down and recover the workers." Catherine sipped on her drink some more, "It was all hush-hush, of course. The country's government announced they were attempting to track the guys down, but the company understandably didn't want to leave it up to them. Imagine, right?" she said with a smile, "They didn't trust the government there, either. They figured they were more concerned about the economic ramifications than finding the hostages."

"Yeah, sounds familiar."

"Yeah," she said. "Anyway, he picked up their trail and followed them through the forest for nearly a week before finding the bodies of the Americans, decapitated."

"They were killed?"

"Yes," said Catherine. "See, the oil company had paid the ransom. That was the first thing they had done, but the extremists killed the hostages anyway for a political statement. I remember they issued a statement via local radio saying they'd released the hostages. Everyone breathed a sigh of relief and the missing workers' families were celebrating, only to find out the radio station hadn't heard the man correctly. He had said he released the hostages, but without their heads."

Jim merely shook his head, feeling lightheaded from the Chivas and still feeling the burning embers of his own grief inside his belly, swirling with the drink.

"Well, it gets worse." Her body language became more emphatic. "Matt took it personally. He told me later he found a picture on one of the bodies in the rear pocket, typical family photo. Something just kind of snapped in Matt. "

"What happened?"

"He goes AWOL. Well, the civilian equivalent to AWOL, I guess. He continues tracking them down despite being told to come back. Then he finds the guys, sees them all camped out. So he sits and waits for night to fall. They took turns standing watch, one up while the rest slept. I think there were seven of them if I remember correctly, a small ambush team.

Anyway, Matt sneaked in and choked the lookout guy out cold. Then he walked through that camp and shot all six of the other men in the head with a silencer. None of them woke up. He could have called in and told the authorities where they were. He could have just followed them until the military arrived to arrest them. But he didn't. He killed them in their sleep, one after the other, all but one."

Jim stared in shocked disbelief, but said nothing.

"He lost it," she said, much quieter, almost a whisper to herself as she shook her head remembering, ". . . totally lost it."

"What about the last one?" came a voice from the door.

Jim and Catherine had been so caught up in their conversation they hadn't heard Amy's footsteps. She was standing at the door and had apparently been listening for a little while.

"Amy," said Jim. "I thought you were resting."

"I heard some loud noises," she said. "I thought I better check on you." She looked like a husk of a body, her eyes circled in weariness.

Jim looked around at the mess he'd made. "I could break everything in this house right now, but I don't think it'd make me feel any different."

She looked at him numbly. She felt it, too, only it manifested differently with her, Catherine knew. Where Jim was volatile and on the edge of his rage every moment, Amy was detached and distant. Numb. Numb was worse. Catherine knew numb once. It ate people up from the inside out.

"Your friend," Amy asked with a distant expression. "Did he kill that last one, too?"

Catherine looked at Jim who could only shrug. Amy had as much right as he did to be in this conversation, and if she wanted to hear old war stories, then who were they to tell her no?

She figured she'd told them this much, she might as well finish the story. She would never have started telling it to begin with if not for the drink, but now that she was telling them, it felt good to get it off her chest. It was helping her put things in perspective in an odd way. It made the prospect of seeing him again soon less intimidating. "No. He left him alive so he could spread the word. Matt wanted to scare any other extremists so bad they'd never think of kidnapping anyone else again. He also knew they were very superstitious people, so decided to use that.

Matt tied the guy to a tree. Then he used a machete and decapitated the ones he'd killed, just as they had done the hostages, and placed their heads in front of the man to see when he regained consciousness." Jim looked a little set off by the thought, but Amy stood impassive. "I don't know how long it took the guy to free himself from the tree, but it was probably morning when he finally did. That's a long time to sit and stare at Matt's parting message."

"How do you know all this?" Jim asked her.

"He told me," she said, "after I was given a report on what the government had found in the jungle. They wanted to know just what kind of madman we had let loose in their country. It was a real nice mess. Matt was in serious trouble looking at spending a few decades in a South American prison. What he did down there is the kind of thing psychopaths do."

"Damn," said Jim. "Guy sounds nuts. He actually did that and didn't go to prison?"

"Yes, he did. And no, they didn't arrest him, although they certainly wanted to. And as to his being nuts, well, I thought so, too," said Catherine. "That's why I ended it. I'd asked him what happened out there . . . I wish I hadn't because he told me the whole story beginning to end. It was more than I was ready to deal with. I did what I could to help, but I couldn't stay with him after that. The country's government wanted to file charges on Matt for murder and the company he was with was going to hand him over. They weren't going to lose future contracts because Matt lost it. But I threatened to expose the whole thing if they did. It cost me my contract, but I didn't care.

The government had known who those extremists were and did nothing before the attacks to stop them. They forced that company to hire someone like Matt by their inaction. And the company knew the kind of people they were hiring. These were war-worn vets that were sent out, sometimes alone like Matt, to handle the kind of job that would terrify most normal human beings. He'd definitely gone too far, but would never have been there if the government had done their job and protected those workers in the first place, or if his company had given him more support instead of sending him out there alone in the jungle with no link to sanity. It was a perfect recipe for disaster."

"What happened to the rest of the extremists?" Amy asked.

"I don't know," said Catherine. "But as far as I know they never attacked the pipeline or its workers again. Matt had accomplished that much."

Amy just stood at the door, staring ambivalently. "I don't think what he did was so crazy," she said. "If he stopped them, then he did the right thing." She stood a moment longer in ponder, an eerie silence about the room, then turned and walked away.

"She doesn't look well," Catherine said, watching Amy shuffle quietly back upstairs.

"I know. I'm worried about her, but her folks are here helping me keep an eye on her." They finished their drinks during a quiet moment of thought. "So this guy, Matt. You really want him with you down there? Contrary to what Amy might think, I think someone like that is a loose cannon. What if he loses it again with you in tow? He sounds dangerous."

She had asked herself that same question and thought long and hard before calling Matt. She knew it would be difficult for anyone who didn't know Matt like she did to reconcile what he'd done with the other side of Matt, the caring and loyal side she'd fallen for so many years ago. It was something she'd never quite been able to do herself. But despite that, she was going with her gut on this one. "He is dangerous, but not towards me. I trust him."

"And he's the one watching the boy for you?" Jim asked, worriedly.

"He'll be fine," assured Catherine. "Matt's a bit of a kid himself, sometimes."

Jim found that hard to believe. "If you say so." He wondered what their old friend David would have thought about Catherine's ex-flame.

Chapter 32

"Where is she!?" cried Miss Lydia.

The girls were all lined up in the yard as usual, except this time there was no customer waiting. There was Miss Lydia, flanked by Jose and Hector. Arnulfo stood off to the side shaking his head. *She's really done it now,* he thought.

"I'm not going to keep asking!" warned Miss Lydia. "I want to know where that little bitch went!"

"She obviously ran away," said Imelda, always the feisty one.

Miss Lydia scurried up to her like an angry crab and knocked her on her head, something that Imelda was entirely used to by now. "I can see she's run away! I want to know where!" None of the girls spoke. "You!" she cried, charging over to Silvia, "What did she tell you?"

"Nothing, ma'am," said Silvia.

Miss Lydia knocked her on the head as well. "Don't you lie to me! You tell me what she said."

"I swear, she didn't tell me anything!"

"Liar!" she screamed. "You're all a bunch of liars! Every last one of you!" She turned to Jose and told him, "Put them in the hot box!"

"All of them?" asked Arnulfo.

She wheeled around on him. "Yes, all of them! They're all in this together. Ungrateful little whores, the lot!"

"She didn't tell us anything," said Evelyn. "I swear Miss Lydia, not a single word."

"Even if she didn't, someone here still knows where she went. Who?"

Nobody said anything. Silvia had an idea of where Yesenia might have gone, as did Evelyn. They'd seen the way Armando had been looking at her and heard their whispers in the dark. They also knew what would likely happen to Armando and Yesenia if Miss Lydia found them. "I don't know," said Evelyn.

Miss Lydia glared at her. "Hot box! All of them!" And Jose and Hector herded the girls towards the hot box.

"This is such shit!" said Imelda. "I don't even live in the same house as her! How would I know where she went?"

"Well, maybe you'll figure it out after you spend a while thinking about it," said Miss Lydia. "Maybe you can talk to your little friends here because someone is lying. Someone knows."

After the girls were locked in the hot box Miss Lydia had a meeting with the men. "I can't believe you let this happen," she scolded them. "What do I pay you for if you can't keep an eye on these girls?"

"What are we going to do, Mama?" asked Jose. "She knows what happened to that trooper."

"And whose fault is that, too? Eh? It's your fault. You two idiots got pulled over. And you were the one who shot him and you're the ones who just slept away while that girl waltzed right out of here, free to tell the world what she saw. She knows who we are, where we are, everything! I've told you time and time again to take shifts. Someone has to be awake at all time around here. You know that. Who was supposed to be awake?"

"I was awake," said Hector. "But it was raining this morning, so I was inside."

She hit him on the head. "*Pendejo!*"

"How was I to know?" He asked. "The dogs are supposed to bark, but I didn't hear a thing. She must have been so quiet not even they heard her."

"Tsssh!" the old woman spat. "A lot of good you all are, deaf dogs and blind men. It's a wonder every girl we've had hasn't run off. Who would notice? Not you idiots."

"Should I search the woods again?" asked Arnulfo. "She might be hiding out there somewhere."

"Yes, go look again," she told him.

After he left, she told Jose and Hector, "If that girl goes to the police, we're all finished, not just you two. We've had a good thing going here and made good money doing it, but she could ruin it all."

"What do you want us to do, Mama?" asked Jose.

"I want you to find that girl. That boy she was with last night, he was taken with her. He couldn't stay away, could he? I knew it was a mistake letting him pick her again. He was too smitten by her, too vulnerable to that girl's charms. He's helped her, I know it."

"What can we do if he did? We don't know where he lives or how to find him."

"We know some," she told him. Miss Lydia had sharp eyes and noticed even small details about people, including the community college parking sticker on the boy's truck when he pulled in.

"But how can we find them?"

"Leave that to me," she told them. "I might know how to find the boy."

"Then what?" asked Hector.

"If we find him, I want you to follow him and see if she's with him."

"And if she is?" asked Jose.

She seemed to think some more. "Get rid of her," she finally decided. "She's too much of a risk to keep around here. She'll just keep trying to run away and we can't risk her ruining everything."

"And the guy?"

"If she's with him, then get rid of him, too." She waved her hand as she tried to think through the possible consequences. "I don't like all this killing business. It might raise far too much attention, but we can't risk everything. If they're together, then she might have told him too much already." She looked at Jose and then patted his head like he was one of the dogs. "You have to listen to Mama this time and do as she tells you. If you find her with him, make it look like he walked in on a burglar. Don't leave any sign that she was ever there. I want you to take her out to a field somewhere and do what must be done. Burn her so there's nothing left to recognize." She gave him a knowing look, "You know what to do. She won't have any fingerprints or dental records, so we don't have to worry about such things. Just make sure about that young man she's with. There can't be any link between him and us. Everyone has to believe he walked in on a robbery." She took a deep breath. "Let's clean up this mess and be done with it."

"Okay, Mama," said Jose like a good little son.

But Hector looked peaked. Miss Lydia glared at him, "You don't have a problem with that, do you?" she asked him.

Hector looked up. Jose and Miss Lydia were both eyeing him. "No," he said. "It's them or us." Miss Lydia smiled.

Chapter 33

Matt stood upon the balcony looking out at the ocean. It was another clear day and he enjoyed the view. Three stories directly below him were a couple tanning themselves by the pool. He watched the man get up and dive into the deep end of the pool below him. *It'd be nice to go for a dip on a day like this,* he thought, *if I wasn't babysitting.*

Julio sat on the bed unwrapping his leg just as Catherine had shown him. He'd been told to replace the bandage three times a day. Matt came back in the room and sat next to him, watching the cartoons the boy had turned on in amusement. He was getting a kick out of listening to Hank Hill talk in Spanish. *"Ay, Bobby! Que hace?"*

When Julio had all the dressing removed Matt leaned over and took a peek at the wound. It was healing nicely. "That's going to be a good one," he told Julio, who looked at him as though still unsure of the man. He'd been a little leery of Matt ever since Catherine had introduced him the day before. After Catherine had told him more about Taylor's murder, Juan's murder, and the attempt on both Julio and Catherine's life, all Matt had said was, "You should have called me sooner."

"Here, check this one out," Matt rolled up his pant leg revealing a quarter-sized scar on his calf muscle. "AK-47," he told Julio, "went right through." He showed him the other side of his leg, which had a twin scar. "Got that in a coca field in Colombia a while back. It's actually pretty nice down there except for all the gangs and drugs."

"Same here," said Julio. That made Matt laugh. "We didn't used to have gangsters, but I guess we do now."

Matt nodded, "That's how it goes. It's like fire. It starts off small some place, but if you don't put it out fast, next thing you know it's everywhere." That seemed to make Julio a bit sadder and Matt wished he hadn't said it. "Want to know how I got shot?" he asked. Julio only shrugged. "There was this little old lady pulling weeds at dawn, just the most innocent looking old granny you ever saw. I was hiking out of the area and accidentally ran into her. I didn't think twice about her, which was my mistake. I just told her to be quiet and went on my way, but the next thing I knew she picked up an AK she had stashed nearby and took some shots at me. I took off running but she got me right here."

Julio looked at the scar. "Did it hurt?"

"Did yours?" asked Matt. Julio nodded his head. "Well, there ya go. Feels like a hot poker held against your skin, even hours later, doesn't it?"

"Yeah, it really hurt. Mine got infected, Miss Catherine says. She popped it and a bunch of pus came out of it."

"Sounds gross."

Julio nodded again with a smile. He saw another scar on Matt's leg, a long burn mark. "What happened there?" he asked.

"Oh, that," said Matt, a little embarrassed. "Well, speaking of burning sensations," he was almost laughing. "I was camping on a beach in Saipan and had a little too much to drink. I accidentally tripped and fell in the campfire." He touched the rubbery scar with his finger. "Smelled like chicken." Julio wasn't sure whether or not it was okay to laugh, but when Matt smiled he did, too. "People taste like chicken, ya know?" Matt told him. "If you cook'em right. I've had to eat one or two in my day. Not really that bad once you get used to it." Julio's smile disappeared in an instant and Matt let out a laugh, "Na, I'm just messin' with ya, kid," and he ruffled Julio's head.

Julio smiled the biggest smile yet. Mr. Matt, as he'd been told to call Matt, was funny, but in a morbid sort of way that still made Julio a little uncomfortable. "You've been to a lot of places, huh?"

"Yeah," Matt said, "quite a few."

"How come you go so many places?"

"Well, that's my job. I travel around a lot."

"What do you do?" Julio asked.

Matt thought about it a few seconds. "I teach people how to keep themselves safe."

"Oh," said Julio. "So that's why she called you. I guess that's good, then. She's done a pretty good job so far, though. I mean, I'm not dead or anything yet."

"Yeah," said Matt, "That's always a good start."

"When is Miss Catherine going to come back?"

"Oh, probably tomorrow." Matt got up and retrieved a beer from the little fridge. He'd removed all the hotel's sodas and little liquor bottles and replaced them with beer, sandwiches, and some of his own sodas from the store. "You want one?" he asked Julio.

The boy looked at him skeptically, but curiously, "Okay." Matt tossed him a beer. "Is it any good?" Julio asked.

"Try and see."

Julio cracked open the beer and took a sip, his face squinting in uncertainty. "Did it go bad?" he asked.

"Why?" asked Matt, chuckling.

"This tastes like something in a dumpster after it's gone bad," he told him.

Matt just laughed some more. "Well, maybe you should give it some time. Beer's like girls. You might not like them now, but in a few years you'll constantly be trying to get your hands on one or the other, both if you can." He walked back to the fridge and retrieved a Dr. Pepper which he tossed to Julio.

Chapter 34

A knock came at the door and Ceci opened it. It was the little girl from the *caseta*. "There's a call for you, *señora*," she told her.

"For me? Did they say who it is?"

"She said to tell you it was your sister." The little girl disappeared down the hall and ran back down the stairs.

Yesenia? "Humberto," she called to her brother-in-law. "I have a phone call. Can you watch the kids?"

"Fine," he said. "But be quick. Alisa and I want to go out for a bite."

"I will." She walked down the stairs and to the *caseta* where a woman gestured to the receiver sitting on the counter. "Hello?"

"Ceci?"

"Yesenia!? Oh, it's so good to hear you. I've been worried about you. How are you!?"

"Ceci, listen to me very carefully. You have to leave your apartment."

"What? Yesenia, where are you? What are you talking about?"

"I'm in Texas, but listen to me, Ceci. You have to leave quickly. It was all a big trick."

"Texas? Where are you living? Are you working?"

"Ceci, listen to me!" cried Yesenia. "You have to leave."

"Leave? What are you talking about?"

On the other end of the line Yesenia was sitting on the bed trying to make her sister understand. "The flier," she told her, "That man, Ortiz, all of it. You were right. It was all a big trick! They sent me to a whorehouse."

"A whorehouse!? Oh my God, Yesenia, are you okay?"

"Yes, I'm okay. I ran away, but you have to listen to me, Ceci, this is very important. *Señor* Ortiz made me give him your name and address. I didn't know what it was for, I swear. He said it was in case something happened to me and I was so stupid I thought it made sense. I don't know what he's going to do when he finds out I ran away. He might send people to your apartment or something."

"To our place? What for? Why would he want to know where I live?"

"I don't know," said Yesenia. "I'm just scared for you is all. They said I owed them the money for bringing me here and had to work it off."

"Did they make you do anything?" asked Ceci.

Yesenia was quiet for a moment. "Yes," she told her sister. "They beat me and locked me in a trailer where a man raped me."

Ceci held her hand to her mouth in shock. "He raped you!?" she cried. The woman behind the counter of the *caseta* spun around with eyes wide but Ceci paid no attention. "Yesenia, where are you? You should call the police right now."

"I can't call the police. You don't know what these people are like. They're dangerous people, Ceci. Please, I think you need to leave your apartment. Go soon, all of you, and don't tell anyone where you go."

Ceci was horrified at what she was hearing. "Yesenia, what have you gotten yourself into? What have you gotten us all into? Are these people going to come after me and Roberto for the money you were going to pay?"

Yesenia already felt guilt and shame for all that had happened, and to hear the fear in Ceci's voice made it that much worse. "Yes, Ceci. I think they will. They're bad people. Please, just leave that apartment. As fast as you can."

"What about you? Yesenia, what will you do? If you can't call the police, then where will you go?"

"Don't worry about me. I'm safe. I met someone who is letting me stay with him."

"Who? A man?"

"It's okay. He's a nice guy, your age. I'm much safer here than where I was, I promise. But Ceci, there's something else I have to tell you." Armando had helped Yesenia reach her sister, but then he excused himself to the living room so she might have some privacy. Yesenia worried he might be listening in, though, so she cupped her hand over the phone and whispered. "I saw the men who brought me here kill someone . . . a policeman."

"What!?" said Ceci. "Oh, Yesenia!"

"We got pulled over and they shot him in the street."

"Oh my God," exclaimed Ceci. "Yesenia, you have to call the police."

"I know, but it's just not safe right now. The police might arrest me for being there. I don't know what they'll do."

"Well, you have to tell someone."

"I will. I'll figure it out, but you need to leave, Ceci. Promise me."

Ceci thought of her children and what her husband would think of all this. She knew Yesenia was right, though. Nothing might happen if she stayed, but if something did, she couldn't risk someone hurting her family. "I will. I'm going to go home right now and tell everyone. We'll go. I don't know where, but we'll go."

"I'm sorry," said Yesenia. "I never meant for any of this to happen."

"It's okay," said Ceci. "Roberto's going to have fits, but I'll worry about him. You just take care of yourself. You come back home if you can, Yesenia. I should never have let you go out on your own like this. I knew it was too dangerous. I'll tell Lysette where we go so you can find us." Lysette was one of Ceci's best friends. "You come back home, Yesenia. Come back safe. And if you think you're in danger, you call the police. Don't you wait until it's too late."

"I will," she said. "And I'm so sorry."

"It's going to be okay," Ceci told her, though she wasn't truly sure of that herself. "Just be careful."

"I will," she said again. "Take care, too. I'd better go now."

"Okay," she said. "I love you, Yesenia. Be careful. Come home."

"I'll try. And I love you, too."

As Ceci hung up the phone the woman behind the counter saw her wiping tears from her cheek. "Is everything okay?"

"No," said Ceci. "My sister," she started, but could say no more as more tears rolled down her cheek.

"Is there anything I can do for you?" asked the woman. "Should I call the police?" She hadn't heard everything but she had heard enough to know there was trouble, bad trouble.

"No. Thank you, but I think they're already involved," she lied. Ceci started out the *caseta* but then a thought crossed her mind. "There is one thing you could do that would help a lot, if you don't mind."

"Of course," said the woman.

"Bad men may come here looking for us, some coyotes. If anyone comes asking about us, will you tell them we moved to Cuernavaca? And please, don't mention to anyone I had a phone call."

The woman was disturbed by such a request, but she'd known Ceci and her family for years. "Yes," she promised. "If anyone comes looking for you I'll tell them you all moved to Cuernavaca. And if they ask, you didn't have any recent phone calls here."

"Thank you," said Ceci.

"Are you really leaving?" asked the woman.

"Yes," she said, "we have to." *But definitely not to Cuernavaca.*

The woman came around from the counter and gave her a hug. "You take care, Ceci. I'm sorry for whatever is going on."

"So am I," she said. "Thank you again," she told the woman.

That evening she told her husband Roberto about the phone call, along with his brother Humberto and his wife. It was a heated debate filled with curses and disagreements, but in the end they agreed they had to leave and find somewhere new to live. "We all know how these coyotes can be," said Roberto to his brother. "I don't like it anymore than you do, but we can't have thugs breaking down our door demanding thousands of dollars from us. We don't have it and we have the kids to think about."

"But why do WE have to leave?" asked Alisa. "This is her sister's problem," she said, pointing to Ceci.

"If we stay here it might become our problem when men with guns show up. Did you hear what I said about the American policeman? Think about it. Men who do that, what won't they do? Do you want to stay and find out?"

And that settled Alisa. She stomped into the bedroom furiously and began taking their clothes off hangers and folding them up, ready for packing.

"I'm sorry," Ceci told Humberto and Roberto.

Her husband hugged her, "It's not your fault. And it's not Yesenia's fault, either. At least she was able to call and warn us. It may be nobody comes around, but you're right. There's no reason to take the risk."

Yesenia had hung up the phone hoping her sister could forgive her, not only for bringing trouble on them but for what she told her sister she'd become since last they talked. She sat for a moment, the phone in her lap, then took a deep breath and looked around at her new surroundings.

Armando lived in a dark green frame house with navy blue trim in a Dallas suburb called Greatwood. It was modest as measured by middle-income America standards, but Yesenia thought it a little slice of heaven. She had clean sheets for one, no more disgusting stains. And roaches didn't crawl over her as soon as the light was out. She didn't find their droppings all over her clothes and undergarments. And best of all, the refrigerator was full of real food. Except for the burger and coke that first day, she hadn't had a decent meal since arriving in the U.S. Miss Lydia kept the girls on a strict diet to keep them thin for the Johns. She'd had her fill of raw vegetables and fat free cereal in skim milk. And Armando had gone and purchased a treat. She was too scared to go out with him yet, but after leaving for the store, he soon returned with several bags of groceries, including a few pounds of snow crab and sticks of butter with ice cold beer which he proceeded to make for dinner. And as she sat down to the feast before her, Yesenia gorged herself.

"Hungry?" He asked her jokingly.

"This is so good," she told him.

"You act like you've never had crab before."

"I haven't," she said with a smile. "It's really good."

Yesenia had told herself that once they got away from the brothel she would strike out on her own, but she quickly realized the benefit of staying where she was, at least for a while. Armando was turning out to be a saint compared to what she had expected. She had thought she was going to have to be some sort of servant for him, at least until she figured out her next step. But he wasn't like that at all. *And where am I going to go?* She asked herself. The little house offered her a refuge from her problems, a place to sit and think about what to do next.

There was one hiccup to the arrangement. Armando's younger brother sat next to them on the couch while they all went to work on the crab. He held a meaty leg of crab in one hand and his beer in the other, staring at them both skeptically, "So, you're Armando's girlfriend?"

"Ummm, I guess so," she told him. "You could say that."

He looked at his brother and then back at her. "How come I've never met you before? I've never even heard of you before." He looked back at his brother. "Exactly when did you get a girlfriend?"

"What, I can't have my own life?"

"Where'd you meet?" he asked Yesenia, who suddenly felt like a witness being cross-examined.

"I told you, she's friends with one of the guys from school. He introduced us," interjected Armando.

"When?"

"A while ago," his brother said flatly.

"How come I didn't hear anything about it until now."

"Well, maybe if you weren't holed up in your room playing World of Warcraft all the time you might have known sooner. Hell, maybe you'd have a girlfriend yourself."

That settled him. "So what, you're moving in?"

"Hey, shut up and eat," Armando told him. "You're being rude. It's a long story, okay. I'll tell you later. She just needs a place right now, okay? It's no big deal."

Ricky, who was about Yesenia's age, merely shrugged. "Whatever you say, I guess. I mean, don't get me wrong, you seem cool and everything, I'm just surprised is all." They finished their meal and afterward Armando brought out something else Yesenia had never tried . . . a bottle of Vodka. "Oh, snap," said Ricky. "It's about to get wild up in here." Armando played the bartender role and before long all three were drunk, yet another new experience for Yesenia. She was prepared to get even more plastered as she began to realize its pleasant numbing effect to the swirling storm of thoughts and emotions going through her mind, but Armando cautioned her that another one would likely send her praying to the porcelain god. The three of them talked and joked for nearly two hours . . . two blessed hours where Yesenia forgot about the rest. She soon passed out on the couch in a heavy stupor, free for one night from having to deal with all the horrible new memories in her head as she snored loudly, much to the humor of the two brothers.

"She snores louder than you do," Ricky said.

"Yeah," smiled Armando, "but she's cool, right?"

"Yeah," Ricky said. "And I hate to admit it, but she is hot, bro. She's gorgeous. I still don't understand why she's dating you."

"Fuck you," his brother laughed, tossing a crab shell at him.

The next day Yesenia awoke to discover she'd been tucked in with a clean sheet and pillow. After a good shower she settled back on the couch, a little confused as to what to do next. She ended up spending most of the day watching television, none of which she understood except for the one Spanish station she'd found. So when Armando returned that night, she asked if he'd help her pick up some more English. They sat together on the couch and he began translating everything they watched.

That night Armando ran her a hot bath filled with white, fluffy bubbles and complete with a candle in the corner. When Ricky had to step in to use the facilities, he smirked, "Dude, really?"

"Shut up. She'll like it."

He led her to her oasis by the hand and she reacted with an "Awww." She was wearing shorts and stepped inside and waded around, played with the bubbles a bit while Armando sat on the toilet with its lids down and watched her for a moment. "This is sweet," she said. He smiled.

She looked at him wondering what to think of this guy. On one hand, he was another horny guy, not unlike some she'd known back home. On the other, he was kind, intelligent, and very openhearted. He'd taken her away from the brothel and into his home, despite her being a prostitute. Something she could not have seen herself doing if the roles were reversed. Until she became one, she'd had no empathy for prostitutes. After a moment he said, "Well, enjoy. I gotta take off. I got class," he said, leaving her to undress in privacy and relax in her spa treatment. "I'll make sure Ricky doesn't try to walk in on you," he added before closing the door behind him. He'd caught his younger brother staring at Yesenia more than once. He wouldn't put it past his bro to 'accidentally' walk into the bathroom.

What am I to do? she wondered.

After her bath she toweled off and put on some new clothes Armando had gotten for her earlier. She laughed when she saw herself in the full-length mirror. It was nice having something new to wear. She'd had to recycle the same four pair of underwear for the last three weeks and was glad to be rid of them.

She watched TV with Ricky for a bit, who she noticed was stealing the occasional glance at her legs, before excusing herself to go to sleep early.

Just as she was dozing off she felt Armando slip in beside her, his arm gentle around her waist and his nose nuzzling her hair, inhaling softly. "Hi," she said.

"Hi. That shampoo makes it smell even nicer," he told her. "Not that it wasn't nice before. " He seemed embarrassed by his own compliment. "I'm not trying to imply you smelled bad or anything."

She giggled. "I did smell bad. It's okay, I know. I really needed a good bath." She felt clean for the first time in a month. "I never felt clean even after a shower back at that place. You could never feel clean there."

Armando turned on a small television in the room. "Try not to think about it," he said. "The past is past and tomorrow is another day."

She smiled, "Yeah, it is." She looked up at the small television screen and saw a picture of a man in uniform. He was black, young, with a square jaw and a focused expression. "Who's that?" she asked.

He looked over. "Oh, it's just the news," he told her. "That's some trooper that got shot a while back. I can't believe they're still running this story." To Yesenia's horror, the picture changed to a grainy video of a dark colored SUV parked along the highway. "Watch this part," said Armando. "This is messed up." The trooper was walking back towards his car, but turned around and went back to the window. Then a flash of light like a camera or miniature arc of lightning erupted inside the vehicle, and the screen went black before the trooper fell. Then the video appeared again as a shadowy figure ran around the front of the SUV. The trooper had fallen just off camera, only his boots visible. Yesenia began to tremble as she realized what she was watching. She knew that if it hadn't been for the dark tint on the back of the windows of that SUV, she might well catch a glimpse of herself. "Crazy, huh?" said Armando sadly. Yesenia began to shake.

"Are you okay?" Armando asked. "You're shaking."

"I'm . . . I'm just scared is all." She suddenly realized she had tears coming down her cheeks. "I don't know what those people from the brothel will do if they find me."

He wiped her tears away, "Hey," he said. "Don't cry. It's going to be all right. Nobody's going to find you here."

"I know," she said, although she had her doubts.

She looked back at the news report as it ended . . . "Authorities are still searching for leads," remarked the reporter before a commercial took over. She didn't dare tell Armando the truth. She had no idea what might happen to her if she did. Would she be sent to prison? Even if not, they'd at least send her back to Mexico. And then she'd have people after her. People like the coyote with the strange eyes. People like Miss Lydia's son, Jose.

"You're okay," he told her. "Nobody's going to hurt you here," he promised, "and you can stay as long you like. I'll take care of you."

Chapter 35

Catherine was back in Cancun and had met Matt at the hotel. It was less awkward than their first meeting. This time they exchanged a brief hug again as she set her luggage down and pinched Julio's cheek. "Have you two boys been behaving yourselves?" she asked.

"Yes," Julio assured.

"We've been sharing some war stories," Matt added.

Catherine wasn't amused. "I certainly hope not."

"Just a few."

Catherine felt Julio's head and had a good look at him. "You're doing a lot better," she told him.

"I feel a lot better. How much longer are we going to stay here?" he asked. He'd enjoyed the hotel room at first, a good place to sleep, safe, not to mention it had room service, something he took to rather quickly. But now that his leg was feeling better he was growing restless.

"Well, that's a good question," Catherine told him. "Let's talk about that." They ordered up some food and were just about to sit down to discuss what came next when Catherine's prepaid cell phone rang. It was Ramirez.

"Ms. James, I'm sorry to bother you but I have some information for you."

"Oh?"

"Is there any way that you can meet me? Not in my office, but out somewhere where we can talk a little more freely without having to worry if others are listening in on us."

Catherine was intrigued, "Where did you have in mind?"

"There's a little *taqueria* on Del Mar and CiFuentes. I could meet you there."

"When?"

"Can you meet me now? I think we should talk sooner rather than later."

"Sure," she told him. He gave Catherine directions. "I guess I have to take a rain check, boys," she told Matt and Julio. "I've got a hot date."

"I'll go with you," Matt said.

"No, better not. Can you wait here? It's the Detective on the case and he wants to talk. I'm not sure he'll be quite as open if you're there scaring the hell out of him. Plus, I don't think he wants to see any new faces. It sounds like he's got something on his mind."

They were speaking English so Matt didn't have to worry about Julio. "Catherine, I've been watching out for the kid here the last couple of days, which I don't mind, but that's not why I came here. I'm not here to babysit. I'm here to make sure you're safe."

"I know," she told him. "Just this time. I need him to feel comfortable enough to share whatever he's got. Then we'll figure out a safe place for Julio so you and I can start having a look around." Matt wasn't satisfied. "Please," she told him. "I don't want to leave Julio here alone, either. He may not act like it, but he's a scared kid and who can blame him."

"Okay," he said. "But hurry back. And be careful," he added as she stepped out the door.

At 3:00 she met Ramirez and the two sat down over a late lunch. "You've got good timing, Detective," she told him.

"How's that?"

"Never mind. So why are we meeting here?" asked Catherine. "Not that I mind. I'm just a little curious is all. Who, exactly, are we avoiding?"

Ramirez thumbed his mustache as he did when thinking. "I'm in a precarious situation, Ms. James. I have information but am not being allowed to act on it. My superiors are concerned with how this information could affect the city's image. Anymore negative publicity and we could see the tourism income drop off completely, and that would devastate the local economy. Nothing scares my superiors more."

"I see," said Catherine, entirely not surprised. "And you?"

Ramirez looked at her, "I'm here, yes? I think catching the criminals instead of pretending they don't exist is the best thing for the city. But I'm not sure that's going to be possible. Not right now, at least. Not while my hands are tied."

She eyed him suspiciously. "Do you know who they are?"

"We know one," said Ramirez. "Alberto Thomas, the shooter in the market. He's a member of a gang in Mexico City called the Barrio Boys."

Yes! She thought. *Finally, a lead.* "The Barrio Boys? And you're familiar with them?"

He nodded. "There was a popular band in the early 90s by the same name. I assure you this isn't them, *señora*. These guys are about as bad as it gets."

"This Alberto Thomas, I take it he has a record?"

Ramirez pushed a file towards Catherine, "Oh, yes, though nothing recent. His last arrest was in 2003 on suspicion of murder, but it was dropped for lack of evidence. There was a witness but apparently that witness ended up dead in a dumpster not long after giving the police his account of what happened to his friend."

Catherine picked up the file and thumbed through it. "What do you know about these people?"

Ramirez looked around as if concerned someone might be eavesdropping. "Ms. James, before we go any further I need to ask you something. Do you really want to get involved in this?"

"Of course," said Catherine. "I'm already involved. I want as much information as you can give me."

He ran his fingers over his mustache again. "They're more than a gang, they're organized crime. They started out some years back like any other gang, pick pocketing tourists, robbing stores, carjacking, things like that, but they've stepped things up considerably in recent years. They've gotten more organized and more ruthless. They're killers, Ms. James. There's really no better way to describe them. They don't care who you are, who you know, man, woman, young, old, they just don't care. From what I've learned, that reputation has acquired them a position as muscle for a larger organization now."

"Cartel?" she asked.

He nodded again. "It's always about the drugs these days, isn't it?" he asked rhetorically, sadly. "They run illegal smuggling of just about everything, including people. They have one of the largest immigration operations in Mexico. Then there are the drugs from South America, counterfeit goods from Panama, kidnappings, and murders, pretty much anything that turns a high profit. These are very dangerous people, Ms. James. They have a lot of members, money, guns, connections, and they have no fear of the law."

"What kind of connections?"

"I would say some of the street police, at least. Probably some of the higher-ranking officials. It's hard to say, really. What I can tell you is this: every time we arrest one of these bastards, the charges are always dropped. Either there's not enough evidence, no witnesses, or they have a rock solid alibi. They're more connected than your average gang."

"So you can't really touch these guys is what you're saying."

The words offended Ramirez, true though they may be. "Look, I've done some checking on you. I visited your office website and made some inquiries." His tone bordered on an accusation. "You're not really a private investigator, are you, Ms. James? You're some sort of legal consultant."

"I never tried to hide my occupation," said Catherine, wondering where this was going.

"Just what kind of consulting do you do?"

"Risk management, mostly," she told him.

He scoffed, "Risk management? You don't seem very good at your job, then."

"And what makes you say that?"

He leaned over the table. "Do you have any idea what you're getting involved in? This isn't just some thug street gang that attacked you in the market. These people are cartel. You may not know what that means, but I assure there is a difference. Gangs are disorganized, violent but skittish in the face of government authority. Cartels aren't. They kill cops in broad daylight, judges on the steps of the courthouse. They blow people up in their cars, poison others in a crowded restaurant when they're out for a nice dinner with their family. You're a businesswoman, Ms. James. I must say you handle yourself very well, but you're still a businesswoman."

"I know, Detective," she said. He huffed indignantly. "I do know," she said again. "I'm out of my league," she admitted. "I recognize that."

"Then what are you doing here?" he asked. "Why are you back down here? You can't go around looking for these people. Believe me, I've seen what they do to people who go looking for them. It's beyond your imagining what they're capable of doing."

She closed the file and leaned over the table. "Tell me, Detective. What would you have me do? Let them get away with it? I appreciate you sharing this information with me, but I'm not sure what your motivations are. If it is your intent to convince me that these are dangerous people and I should go home, then I need to let you know up front that's not going to happen. I'm not leaving here until I find the people who murdered Taylor Woodall. And as for me acknowledging my lack of experience in these particular matters, that's not to say that I am without resources, Detective. The first rule in business is to find the right resources, and I'm exceptionally good at that."

They locked eyes for a moment. Then Ramirez leaned a bit forward as well. "My motivations, Ms. James, are to let you know what kind of people you are looking for. You may not want to find them."

"They're the ones who started this," reminded Catherine.

"And they would gladly finish it if you give them the opportunity."

"So would I!" she said, now rising half out of her seat. *Who the hell does this guy think he is!?* "I'm not leaving until they're caught! Period! And if your people aren't going to do their job then you can bet your ass I will!" She slammed her hand down on the table hard. "They don't get to get away with this one, Detective. Do you understand me? Not this time! I don't care who they are. And I'm not going to sit here and listen to you try to intimidate me. If these people think I'm just such an easy target then let them come give it a try. Oh, wait, that's right. They already have, haven't they? That's what's wrong with you all down here. You let these groups get too big, too powerful, and now they're running amok while you all hide in your little cubby holes pretending not to notice. It's a disgrace."

Ramirez leaned back again and softened his tone. "Yes," he told her, "you're right, I'm afraid. And it is a disgrace." He motioned for her to sit back down. "I know how you are feeling right now, Ms. James."

"Like hell you do," she spat, still furious at him. "I'm getting real tired of hearing what the authorities can't do around here, Detective. I refuse to believe that your entire government can't do a damn thing about these people."

"Believe me, I do understand. Some of us are trying, Ms. James. And I know all too well the price of our failures." He reached into the pocket of his sport jacket and pulled out a photograph, worn and creased. He handed it to Catherine. "Her name was Anna Cruz." Catherine took the photo. It was a young girl with a bright smile and thick brown hair. "She lived in Chetumel with her mother, Juanita. A few months ago, Juanita asked Anna to go to the store for her, but on her way there three gang members snatched her off the street in front of a dozen witnesses. They gang raped her and then sodomized her with a metal pipe one of them had been using to beat her with." His voice trailed off.

"She died?" asked Catherine.

"Twelve days," said Ramirez. "Twelve days she survived in the hospital, and Juanita wouldn't leave her side. I've seen many cases, Ms. James, too many cases in Juarez and now even here in Cancun, but Juanita was a fighter. When her daughter died, she went to the police for help. When she didn't get it, she called me. I sat with her, as I am sitting with you, now." He stared at his coffee, a look of shame crossing his face. "I told her much of what I just told you, but she didn't listen. I tried to help but the police had nothing on the men. We all knew it was them, everyone knew, but nobody would make a formal statement or testify. Whenever I tried to talk to people, they ran from me, as though I were the criminal. They ran in fear of their lives, because they knew if they talked to me the cartel would kill them. And so when she asked me if we were going to catch the men that had killed her daughter, I made the worst mistake of all."

"What'd you do?" Catherine asked.

He took back the photograph. "I told her the truth. Not long after, she bought a gun and went after the men that had killed her daughter."

Catherine began to suspect where the story was going. "And did she find them?"

"No." He locked eyes with her. "They found her." Ramirez picked up his napkin and began twisting it in his fingers. "They heard she was looking for them and found out where she lived, and then attacked her in her own apartment. They beat her to death with, what else? A metal pipe." Through the window, Ramirez watched a moped as it sped down the street. "I imagine they thought it was pretty funny. Neighbors certainly heard the attack, but for 20 minutes they beat Juanita to death in that apartment while her neighbors hid behind closed doors, pretending not to hear. Nobody would help her," he said, "and nobody would talk afterwards." He looked at her with a look she recognized. Detective Ramirez had known numb as well. "Juanita was my sister, Ms. James. It was my niece they murdered, my own flesh and blood. And I did nothing. My own sister had to take it upon herself to bring justice to those men. But it should have been me. I should have done what needed to be done in the first place and my sister would still be alive today."

Catherine didn't know what to say. "I'm sorry," she offered after a long pause.

Ramirez sighed, long and sadly. "Not as sorry as I am, Ms. James."

"I can only imagine what that must feel like for you to know the men who did it are still out there, that they may never be brought to justice. I guess you do understand how I feel."

"Oh, yes," he said. "Even more than you know." Ramirez eyed her, trying to decide just how close he wanted their relationship to be. Given what they were up against, he decided to go for broke. "Those men didn't exactly get away with what they did to my sister and my niece." He balled the napkin he'd been playing with up and flicked it to the side. "The men that killed Juanita and Anna got drunk at a bar one night not too long ago, and when they got back in their car someone was waiting for them on the street. Someone shot those men while they sat in their car. All three were killed."

"Who did it?"

"Well, that's a mystery, isn't it?" said Ramirez. "The police don't know. The cartel doesn't seem to know. I suppose nobody does."

Catherine began to understand. "Do you know, Detective?"

Ramirez took the picture of Anna and returned it to his pocket. "What I do know, Ms. James, is that someone decided if those men couldn't be brought to justice, then justice should be brought to them. Some crimes can't go unpunished."

"I agree," said Catherine after a pause.

Ramirez shrugged. "Who's to say if it was right?" Then he shook his head as though considering it. "Who's to say if it wasn't revenge, not justice." He looked at Catherine wondering what she thought of this. "Whoever killed those men broke the law. They murdered three people."

"Three people who were murdering rapists," she added. "Three people who probably would have killed young women and mothers and sisters if they hadn't been stopped. Whoever did it probably saved lives. They did the right thing," she told him, suddenly hearing Amy Woodall's words echoing in her mind.

"Perhaps," he said. "Perhaps not." He looked at his watch. "I should go now. If you do decide to stay in Cancun, I hope you take care and are safe. I would advise that you take special care to avoid men wearing the gold chains with medallions that Mr. Thomas here was wearing," he tapped the file that held the photo of the gunman Catherine had killed. "It bears a striking resemblance to the one the man in the sketch was wearing, doesn't it? I read a report that suggested the Barrio Boys have a way of identifying their hierarchy. The report suggested tattoos or clothing, but I did some checking back on old mug shots and crime scenes and noticed something very interesting, Ms. James. It seems the gang has a penchant for jewelry. The low members of the gang often wear silver necklaces. I saw a few pictures of boys wearing thin necklaces, but as they get older and more ruthless, the chains they wear seem to get thicker. And a medallion? My guess would be they get that when they commit their first murder. It's just a guess, of course. But if I'm right, then it might explain who gets to wear the gold medallions."

"The lieutenants?" she asked.

Ramirez nodded. "It's just a guess, as I said. They're mainly centered in Mexico City and up along the border, but it appears they've made their way here to Cancun, which is very troubling. As an officer of the law, and as someone who doesn't want to see you hurt, I advise you to return home, Ms. James. But if you do stay, I recommend you keep your gun ready and your back to a wall at all times. These guys don't play fair."

"I'll remember that," said Catherine, "and thank you, Detective. I'm glad we talked."

"Goodbye, Ms. James," said Ramirez as he rose from his seat. "I enjoyed our talk as well. I hope we get to do it again someday."

Chapter 36

Catherine returned to the hotel that evening and told Matt what she'd learned.

"This is really something," said Matt. "I just left one cartel. I didn't figure to be getting wrapped up with another."

"I know," responded Catherine. "I didn't see this coming, either. I'm still trying to figure out how Taylor crossed paths with these people. You think they just singled her out in the bar for some reason? Maybe this whole thing happened because that guy was mad Taylor turned him down."

"People get killed for far less logical reasons," he told her.

"Starting to look that way." said Catherine. "I can't believe they would do this to her all because she wasn't interested in the guy."

"They're used to getting what they want and doing what they want without consequence. It's quite possible this guy decided to kill her when she wouldn't return his advances. We'll get him," said Matt. "Where do you want to start?"

"Ramirez said this is the first he's known of them here in Cancun. They're mostly concentrated around the capital, but I think the first thing to do is to find the one that got away, the driver from the market. We can start by trying to find that car."

"What about Julio?" asked Matt.

Julio understood that whatever the two were talking about had something to do with him. "My leg's much better," he offered. And he flopped it around like a bad hokey pokey just to prove it. "Are we going somewhere?"

"Yes," Catherine told him, "but we're going to have to find you another nice place to hang out for a while."

Catherine was surprised to find Matt had a possible solution of what to do with Julio. "I think I know of a place. I can call an old amigo of mine who retired down in Playa del Carmen. We can probably take him over there."

"You think it'd be safe?"

"Safer than most anywhere else." Matt made a phone call and 30 minutes later was happy to report his old marine pal was willing to help out. "He got put on government disability two years ago after an IED in Afghanistan. He took a little R and R down in Playa del Carmen and ended up marrying some cute little *mamacita* down here and never left. He'll take good care of Julio for a bit."

A knock came at the door. Catherine looked at Matt, "You order room service?"

"No," he said.

They both looked at Julio and Matt asked him in Spanish if he had. "No."

"Are you sure?" Catherine asked.

"It wasn't me," Julio swore.

Matt immediately grabbed his gun and Catherine did the same.

"Yes?" asked Catherine loudly. There came no response. Both he and Catherine stood with their guns raised. She motioned to Julio to get on the other side of the bed and lay down.

Another knock came.

"Who is it!?" Catherine asked, louder this time. No response. She began silently walking towards the door as though to look out of the peephole, but was stopped by Matt's arm. He was shaking his head and moved Catherine behind him. Then he picked up a tourist magazine from the little table and waved it in front of the peephole. As the shadow moved across the little circle of glass, a bullet ripped through the glass eye, tearing through the magazine and disappearing into the sheetrock beyond.

Matt instantly answered by placing his own gun to the hole and firing. They heard bumping noises outside and someone cursed. "Kill the bitch!" someone yelled in Spanish.

The door reverberated with the sound of someone kicking it. Then a barrage of gunfire splintered the lock and wood frame of the door. Catherine and Matt were at the ready, though. As the door flew inward, the invaders were met with lead bullets. The first person through the door fell dead with two in the head.

Behind him two others were scrambling. A fourth lay sprawled out in the hallway having received the bullet through the peephole.

One of the two remaining men yelled in fright and began shooting wildly while making a hasty retreat. The other one, apparently not realizing his companion was fleeing, tried to rush the door solo.

Catherine and Matt had to get out of the line of fire, so moved directly behind the door as the man tried to rush in again over his fallen comrade. Catherine waited until he was halfway through, and then kicked it as hard as she could, keeping pressure applied. The shooter was slammed in-between the door and its frame. During the moment he was stuck there Matt darted out from behind the little desk. He pushed the shooter's hand up just as he fired, and then Matt placed his own gun near the man's armpit and gave him a round of his own. The bullet ripped between two ribs, exploded a lung, and tore through the heart. The shooter managed a gasp then coughed up blood as he fell over dead, still caught in the door.

Catherine lowered her leg and the man slid to their feet. Matt bolted out of the door yelling, "Stay here!" It happened so fast Catherine didn't have time to respond.

She turned and dropped to her knees to check on Julio, who had taken refuge beneath the bed. "Are you okay?"

He looked up and nodded quickly, too frightened to say anything.

Matt was running down the hall and pushed the door open into the stairway. Below him, he could hear the footfalls of the last shooter running for his life. Matt leaned out over the railing, aiming his gun carefully, but could get no shot.

The fleeing man was already a floor down and Matt knew he'd never run fast enough to catch him before the man reached the bottom floor and disappeared into the street. He momentarily thought to give up the chase when another idea struck him. *It's a good day for a dip, remember?* He thought to himself. *Ah, hell. This is not a good idea,* thought another part of him. He bolted back down the hallway and through the door of the room. Catherine stared in shock as Matt flew past her with a very determined grimace on his face. "Be right back," he told her as he passed. He opened the sliding glass door to the balcony in one quick motion, tucked his gun in his pants, slung himself over the railing, and then, like the *clavadistas*, or cliff divers, of Acapulco, he jumped outward from the balcony with all his strength. "Matt!" Catherine cried in surprise, running to the balcony edge and watching Matt fall.

Down at the pool a woman was trying to convince her husband she'd just heard gunshots. "Honestly, honey, I think I heard gunshots," she was saying worriedly.

"Probably just a car, dear," her husband responded absent-mindedly, his eyes glued to the pages of a novel he was reading.

"Matt!" Catherine shouted in horror as she watched him crash into the pool below in a cannonball position that became more of an awkward back flop when he landed. *Jesus, he is crazy.* It was not the graceful leap he had hoped for, but he luckily didn't break his neck. "Matt!" She called again. Matt popped up in the water with a grimace of pain. "Are you okay?" She yelled from above. *Idiot.*

He'd hit the water harder than he thought and struggled for breath. His buttocks and tailbone had hit bottom and he wondered for a moment if he'd broken bones. *Stupid shallow pool,* he cursed. But when he kicked his legs they obeyed, albeit not without some protest. He pulled himself up and gave Catherine a wave like a stuntman who'd just missed his mark but wanted the crowd to know he wasn't dead. *Man, that hurt,* he groaned to himself, holding the small of his back as though it might snap in two if he didn't. *I told you it was a bad idea,* a tiny voice whispered in his ear, but he paid it no mind.

"Are you okay?" asked the woman who had told her husband she'd heard shots, who had gotten up and was now approaching Matt like an angry hen. "That was a fool stunt . . . ." she began. But when Matt pulled his gun out of his waistband she turned back the other way in a hurry, "Oh, my!" she cried, her husband finally raising his head from the book to spot Matt coming towards them with a gun in his hand. He dropped his book and then scurried away with his wife. "I told you!" she was screaming at her husband. "I told you someone was shooting!"

"Just run!" her husband responded.

Matt took off around to the front of the hotel in an ugly, limping run, ignoring the pain throbbing through his chest and down his lower back. He passed a few shocked tourists heading to the pool, sending them screaming out of his path, and he reached the front door of the hotel just as the fourth shooter came flying out.

The man was so concerned with speed and who might be behind him that he gave no notice to what was in front of him and Matt delivered a head-splitting strike to the man's skull with a dull thwack, dropping the man to the floor like a wet burlap bag of sand, out cold. Witnesses disappeared into the closest doorway they could find. It was the Hutton all over again, many thought, screams being heard as people disappeared behind halls and doors. He tucked his gun away and was at a loss what to do. The police would be there any second. How the hell was he going to get Catherine and Julio out of the hotel and manage to haul this guy with them before the cops got there? He didn't want to hand over the only lead they had to the police, but he was about to resign himself that he had no other choice. Then he noticed it. Idling outside of the front door of the hotel was a car with nobody inside, very unusual indeed. Further inspection revealed it was an old red Pontiac with a fresh set of paint and a new back window. It had some new seats in it as well but they had left a pitted and scarred metal plate behind the driver's seat. "Is that yours?" he asked the unconscious man. "Yeah, that's yours," he smiled, grabbing the man's arms and dragging him towards the car. "You don't mind if I borrow it, do you?" He put the man in the car but not before borrowing his cell phone. Then he drove off, still soaking wet, while he called Catherine's pre-paid cell phone. Memorizing her number was one of the first things he had done when he arrived in Cancun. She didn't answer the first time, but when he hung up and dialed again he heard a brisk, "Yes!?"

"Catherine, it's me."

"Matt!? What the hell? Where are you? We have to get out of here!"

"I'm already gone," he told her. "Sorry, but I didn't have much of a choice. I got the last guy. He was nice enough to loan me his car. I think you know it, an old Pontiac? Anyway, sorry to take off on you like that but our unconscious little friend made quite a scene downstairs. You and Julio need to get out of there right now. How fast can you grab our stuff and get out?'

"Fast," she told him, hanging up and grabbing a bag. "Come on, kiddo!" She yelled to Julio. "We gotta get out of here."

Julio ran, hobbled, and skipped after Catherine just as fast as his little leg would let him.

Chapter 37

Yesenia was beginning to get used to her new surroundings. While Ceci and her family were settling into a house they had rented on the other side of Mexico City, Yesenia was also settling into the little frame house in Dallas. She unpacked her bag and cleaned the house for Armando and Ricky from top to bottom.

"You didn't have to do that," he told her with a smile when he came home.

"It's the least I can do," she said.

"Hey," said Ricky, looking around and then flopping himself on the couch. "This is pretty nice. The place cleans up pretty good."

"You would, too, you know, if you didn't always wear those baggy pants and sweaters," Yesenia offered.

"Hey, don't start cramping my style, woman," Ricky teased with a grin. "Unless you got a hot friend you want to hook me up with or something."

That made Yesenia smirk. Her new gal pals from the compound could certainly show Ricky a thing or two.

Yesenia had been too afraid to go out of the house for the first couple of days, but finally Armando convinced her to come with them to the Super Wal-Mart so she could pick out some more clothes. It was the most amazing thing she'd ever seen.

"I can't believe how much stuff they have," she told him, marveling at the endless aisles of wares. "And all the clothes!" she walked through the clothing department like it was Tiffany's. "It's like an entire market back home all in one building. Two markets, even, with air conditioning."

"It's really not that special," he tried telling her. "There are Wal-marts all over the place, and they all look like this."

She seemed in disbelief. "Papa was right. Americans are rich."

Armando laughed. "Trust me, we aren't. Some, maybe, but not us," he added, pointing to Ricky.

That night, for the first time, she lay with a man because she wanted to. Part of her did it because she felt it was expected, but another part of her because she genuinely had developed an emotional attachment to Armando. It was different being with him that night. She had a choice for one.

She knew his initial infatuation with her had been purely physical, but she felt they were genuinely starting to have something together. He was different than any other guy she knew. He worked hard, took care of his brother, watched out for their mother the best he could, and all the while was still warm, caring, and even funny. She still wasn't sure exactly how long she was going to stay with Armando, but she knew she was beginning to like him more than she ever planned on liking him.

She was feeling safe for the first time in a long time and it felt unbelievably good. She felt as though she might actually be able to put that hellhole behind her. *No*, she told herself. *You can't forget about Silvia and the others. They're still there. I have to do something.* But what, she still could not say.

Chapter 38

Catherine met up with Matt just outside of the city behind an old gas station and they transferred the unconscious man to the rental car. The vehicle was a Ford Taurus with a trunk release latch, which Matt promptly pried off with the car's lug wrench.

"God, nobody's ever going to rent me a car again," said Catherine, watching as he threw the pieces on the ground.

"Well, we can't have him jumping out of the trunk like a stripper out of a cake at a bachelor party, can we?" She helped him load the guy in and they slammed the trunk shut.

"You think it'll hold?" she asked.

"Oh, yeah," he said. "He's not going anywhere."

"They must have been tailing Ramirez," said Catherine as they were back in the car cruising down the road. She'd been pondering how they found them at the hotel. "At least, I hope that's it."

"Either that or he sold you out," said Matt.

She thought about Juanita and Anna. Could it all have been a lie? A ruse to gain her trust, find out how much she knew, only to have her tailed back to Julio? She didn't want to believe it. "If he was lying about that story he told me, then the man missed his calling because he'd make a genius actor. But if he's not in on it, then they're following him. That doesn't bode well, either, if he is actually on our side." She thought about the implications of either being true. "This sucks."

Matt only nodded, "Yep."

She looked at him. "Thank God there's at least one guy I can trust around here."

"Two," said Matt with a smile. Catherine looked confused a moment until Matt gestured at Julio in the back seat, who smiled brightly when she turned back to have a look at him.

"You're right," she smiled. "Two." As they rode along, she thought of more things in her favor. "I'm glad I used a different name for the room. I don't think all the permits in the world would help me explain that one."

Julio sat back in his seat watching the gnarled trees along the road as they went.

"Well, that solves one problem," said Matt.

"What's that?"

"We don't have to go looking for them anymore now that they've come looking for us. I'm sure we'll get a lot out of Pedro back there."

Julio only caught the one word and could only wonder who Pedro was, but he decided if the adults were talking in English they probably had a good reason. He was happy to leave the planning up to them at this point. It was twice now Miss Catherine had saved him, and if she wanted a little privacy to talk to Mr. Matt, he certainly wasn't going to complain.

Playa del Carmen was only an hour's drive from Cancun, and when they arrived Matt's friend greeted them warmly. *"Hola, Amigos!"* he yelled from the porch of a small hacienda. He had bushy red hair thinning on the top and didn't stand to greet them. He had been pale once upon a time and was covered in freckles, but had apparently spent most of his recent days out in the sun and was now dark orange, similar to an Oompa Loompa right out of the chocolate factory. As they walked up Catherine noticed further that he had a couple of terrible black spots on his shoulders and when she couldn't help but let her eyes fall on them, the man answered her curiosity. "Basal cell carcinoma," he said with a shrug.

"Cancer?" asked Matt, grasping the man's extended hand and shaking it while giving each other a half hug.

"Oh, it's harmless," said the man. "Just ugly as sin. Wife hates it, though. She's always on my ass to go get it taken care of, but you know how I feel about those damn doctors! Can't afford it, anyway. Disability only goes so far."

"You know the VA hospital back home could probably help," offered Matt, "and it'd be free."

"Yeah, I know. But this is home, now. I'll be fine."

Catherine hadn't noticed the man's missing left leg until she was already on the porch being introduced. "Catherine, this is Patrick Reynolds, one of my old marine buddies from back in the day."

She shook hands with the burly man. "It's nice to meet you," she told him, making sure not to stare at his missing limb.

"Pat, this is Catherine James."

"The Catherine James?" Patrick asked. "Oh, I've heard about you, I have," he told her with a big grin.

"Yeah, Pat. *The* Catherine," Matt said sarcastically, but a little flushed.

"Matt tried to talk me into giving you a ring some years back. Said you might be a good somebody to help me find a job. I told him he was fucking crazy if he thought I was going to babysit a bunch of rich oil pussies. No offense. So I went back over for another tour." He pat his leg, "Guess I should have babysat instead, huh?" he said with a laugh.

"No offense taken," said Catherine with a half-hearted laugh. "We do get some whiney ones now and then."

"And this is Julio," said Matt. "Julio," he addressed the boy in Spanish, "This is my good friend Mr. Patrick. He and his wife are going to look after you for a couple of days while Miss Catherine and I try to fix things so the bad men will leave you alone."

"Hello," Julio told the man.

"Hello, yourself," Patrick answered in Spanish. "I got a boy about your age. He's in the house playing. You want to go play with him?"

"Okay."

"How do you have a boy his age?" asked Matt.

"Step kids, *amigo*. But I treat 'em like my own. Pretty good kids unless they feel like being little shits for fun," he smiled. "Their father left 'em when they was just babies, so now I'm their dad. Pretty fucking amazing, huh?" *It's going to be an interesting childhood,* Catherine thought. But at least he seemed to be really attached. "Just go on in and tell him his daddy said you're gonna be staying with us for a while," he told Julio.

He ran into the house with a pronounced limp, his leg still bandaged.

"What happened to his leg?" asked Patrick.

"He got shot," said Matt. "It's a long story," he added quickly, cutting off Pat before he could ask. "Needless to say he's had a hard time."

"Well, hell! A boy after my own heart already, I see," he grinned. "At least he got to keep his. We'll try and take it easy on him, then," said Pat. "Well, bring your asses on in here and have a beer with me!" He started to get himself up on his one leg. "I got a prosthetic in the house but I hate that damn thing. Rubs the shit outta me."

Matt stopped him from getting all the way up, "Actually, Pat. We really can't." Pat looked dejected. "We ran into a little trouble earlier." He whispered, "We've got a gang banger in the trunk of the car."

"Oh," said Pat, his eyebrows rising. "For a minute there I thought it was me," he let out a laugh. "Well, we'll make it a quick visit, then. I see you all got a lot going on. Aracely!" he screamed towards the house. "Bring us out some beers, woman! And bring my leg out while you're at it."

A moment later a woman in her early 30s came out of the house carrying three bottles of Carta Blanca beer in one hand and a metal pole with a shoe on one end and a blue receptacle on the other where Pat's thigh would rest when he wore it. Pat handed both Catherine and Matt a beer. "This is my wife," he said proudly. "Wife, meet some friends of mine."

Aracely smiled politely, "Nice to meet you." She turned to her husband and said, "Here, love, I'll help you with your leg." And she knelt down and slipped Patrick's leg on for him, rolling up the overly large sock on the top that came up to his hip.

"Ah, thank you, dear," he told her. "I'll be in, in a bit."

"It was nice to meet you," said Catherine as Aracely disappeared back into the house with a polite wave.

"Good woman, that one," he told Matt. "She'd have to be to put up with my ass, right? Sweet as an angel, cooks like a chef, and screws like a . . . oh, sorry," he remembered, looking to Catherine. "Well, she's a good woman. I'll just leave it at that. Now why don't you tell me a bit about what's going on?"

Catherine decided that if Matt trusted Pat, then that was good enough for her, so she didn't protest when Matt basically summarized everything that had happened up to that point. "Yeah, I heard about that girl," he said. "Damn shame, that. And you think these fucking gang bangers . . . what do they call themselves, Barrio Boys?" Catherine nodded. "So these Barrio Boys are the little sons of bitches who did it, the kid saw, and now they're trying to off all of yah?"

"That about sums it up," said Matt.

Pat laughed. "Well, hell! They just don't know who they're fucking with, do they?"

"No," said Matt. "But they'll be finding out soon enough."

"We're just trying to find the ones who did it," said Catherine, not overly pleased with the way Matt had said that. "We need closure for the family and to clear Taylor's name of the false accusations they are claiming contributed to her murder. We're not on a vendetta."

"Right," Matt said, reservedly.

Pat looked at Matt, then Catherine, then back at Matt. "Uh, huh. Well, don't go letting one of them gang bangers get a lucky shot on yah. You haven't gotten rusty, have you?" he asked Matt.

"Oh, he's not rusty," said Catherine.

Pat laughed again. "And what about you, Ms. James? Are you up for this kind of stuff after sittin' on your ass all day in your fancy office?"

Catherine wasn't offended. She had known men like Patrick Reynolds before and knew he meant well, even if he did curse like it was going out of style. She smiled and told him, "I'll do what I can."

"Well don't go getting my friend here killed," he said, still laughing. "Then I'd have to start killing me some gang bangers and it'd really turn into a cluster fuck. I can still move the ole stump around if I have to."

"Don't you worry about me," said Matt. "This is just the kind of vacation I've been needing!"

"You would say that! By God, you're still a crazy son of a bitch, aren't yah, Matt?"

"He jumped off a three-story balcony into a pool earlier today," added Catherine.

"Was that before or after you killed the other three gangbangers?" Pat asked. Just hearing it out loud made Catherine cringe.

"After," said Matt. "Nearly broke my ass doing it, but the guy had a head start on me."

Catherine found the direction of conversation troubling and Pat seemed to get a bit more serious for the first time in their conversation. "You two be careful. This is some serious shit you're caught up in. If I didn't think the missus would have my ass, I'd probably go with you. You sound like you could use the help. I got the family now, though. And this leg thing does slow me up a bit."

"We know," said Matt. "Watching Julio is a huge help. He's a good kid."

Pat's severity waned and he chuckled again, "Barrio Boys . . . what kind of stupid name is that, anyway? Sounds like a boy band or something." Catherine smirked in spite of herself, as she remembered Ramirez saying there had been such a band. "Hell's Angels, now that's a name with some meat to it."

They finished their beers and made their goodbyes. Catherine made sure to explain about the necklaces the Barrio Boys wore and about how dangerous they were. "We made sure we weren't followed," said Catherine. "And I can't thank you enough for looking after Julio. We certainly don't want to cause you or your family any problems."

"Oh, hell. Quit kissing my ass, woman. I don't mind one bit. And if any of those gangbangers do show up around here, don't you worry. I got something for their ass. I may be getting fat and lazy in my old age, but I'll still drop a sonofabitch before he knows what hit him, one-legged and all. You just remember about what I said about being careful." And despite his antics and the beer belly jiggling over his Bermuda shorts, something about him told Catherine he was probably telling the truth.

As Catherine and Matt pulled out and onto the street he asked her, "Ready to have a chat with our friend, Pedro?" The man in the trunk was conscious now and they could hear his movements as he tried to untie himself.

"Yes," said Catherine. "It's time we got some answers about what the hell started all this to begin with and who killed that poor girl and Julio's little friend."

Chapter 39

"Look," said the man. "I just did what they told me to, alright? I didn't hurt anybody."

"Well, you tried to kill us," said Catherine.

The man shook his head. "No, no, I didn't try to kill anybody. I was just there, okay. I'm the driver, that's it."

"Oh, yes, you did," said Catherine. "Tell us who killed the girl."

"I already told you I don't know what you're talking about."

"Taylor Woodall, who killed her?" She asked coolly, for about the twentieth time now.

"I don't know what you're talking about, okay. I don't know anything about that *pinche gringa*." His eyes drifted downward to the metal ring Matt had placed around his finger. Matt had finally convinced Catherine it was time to try a new approach.

Matt pulled the wire tighter and the man screamed in pain. The wire cut through his skin and Matt kept applying pressure and then pulled downward and layers of skin filleted outward like a peeled banana, the man screaming. "I told you it was going to hurt," he told the man, "and I really wouldn't talk about the girl like that in front of my friend here."

When Matt stopped pulling, the man looked down and could just see the white of his bone beneath the few remaining layers of skin on his finger. He began to sway. Catherine tried her best not to let her face reflect how horrific she thought what they were doing was. *We don't have a choice*, she thought. *There's no way this guy will talk without resorting to this.*

Matt smacked the man on the face gently to keep him conscious. "Hey, hey," he told him. "You paying attention? You ready yet to start telling us what we want to know?"

"I told you! I don't know nothing about that girl!" the man screamed. "I swear!"

"What do you think?" he asked Catherine, turning and looking at her. She only glanced back at him, trying to hide her discomfort with torturing the man. "Nope, I don't believe him, either," said Matt, pulling a bit more causing the man to cry out again. Catherine turned away briefly. She didn't like resorting to these tactics, but the man had been uncooperative up to this point and they needed to know what he knew.

They had found an empty metal building down a lonely road from the highway and decided to use it to question the man. So far, they'd garnered nothing. They'd started off with just questions, then a more forceful cajoling, but all he had offered was insults and curses. So now they were at the point of last resort.

Matt worked the man's hand like a fish boner preparing fillets, pulling the skin away from the pink flesh slowly but surely. Blood splattered on the floor, at first a trickle, but then it began dripping profusely like a broken faucet. "That looks painful," Matt noted, staring at the man's exposed muscle and bone past the third knuckle of the man's index and middle fingers. "And we've really only started. Sure you don't want to start sharing?"

The man's head bobbed around as though his neck muscles were no longer working. A thick silver chain with an etched silver coin hung about his neck. It looked like a silver dollar someone had machined and re-tooled with a new design, two small exes in its center. She had a suspicion what that meant.

"Look at me," said Matt, who seemed a little too at ease for Catherine's liking. *This is why I called him,* she reminded herself, *to do what I can't.* "Start answering truthfully." The man stared at Matt with venom in his eyes, hate pouring out like the blood from his hand.

"Tell us who put the hit on the boy, then," Catherine said. "Tell us something before we have to start cutting things off!" She demanded, her voice rising in frustration.

The man had drool coming from his mouth from trying to hold in his cries of pain and now spit upon the floor, still eyeing Matt. "I don't know who."

"You're still lying," said Matt, pulling some more until the finger was now a quarter smaller in diameter from the skin that'd been pulled away while the man screamed and cursed some more. "You keep lying like this and there won't be anything left."

"Who?" asked Catherine again.

When Matt let go this time, the man was crying. "I don't know, I don't know," he whined. Matt put the circle of wire around a third finger and began to tighten it. "Wait!" he said. "I don't know, ok! I don't!"

"Who!?" Catherine demanded. She grabbed him by the back of his head, a large clump of hair between her white knuckles, "No more of this shit! Tell us now or I'm going to have him cut your fingers off one by one. Tell us!"

He shook his head in tears and Matt tightened the wire. Again, the man screamed.

Catherine was now truly wondering if the man was a dead end. Surely he would have said something by now. Catherine had had enough. She was going to stop Matt, but then . . .

"Ortiz!" Yelled the man. "Fernando Ortiz!"

Finally. "Who is Fernando Ortiz?" asked Catherine. "And where do we find him?"

The man sat quietly crying, his breaths rapid and labored.

Matt went back to the wire, pulling it just a hair more, cutting more of the top layer of skin away, "Where!?"

He winced in pain, "Mexico City! Fuck! Mexico City, okay?"

"Where in Mexico City?" asked Catherine.

"I don't know. Come on," he moaned. "I told you what you wanted to know, already. I don't know any more."

"Not yet you haven't," Matt said.

"Tell us how to find him," Catherine said.

The man's head began to bob around again as he moaned to himself. "I bet you'd really like this to end, wouldn't you?" asked Matt. "You're almost there. Just tell us what we need to know and we'll leave you alone." The man said nothing, only moaned some more. "Or," said Matt, pulling the wire down and stripping the skin from the man's finger bringing a renewed screamed of pain. "You still have seven more fingers to go and I've got all night."

The man's entire body clenched in agony. He looked down at his right hand and saw that now three of his fingers were without skin, three alien looking appendages with blood and tissue shooting needles of excruciating pain through his body. The bloody stumps that were his index and middle finger looked like bits of bloody salmon after a bear had had its fill. He nearly retched at the sight of them. "Oh, fuck, man. Stop! Please stop!" *They killed Taylor, Juan, and tried to kill us,* Catherine reminded herself. *Let Matt handle this.* Matt began to wrap wire around the next finger. *Just tell us,* she thought. *For God's sake, let's end this.* "No," said the man. "Please stop, man. I'm fucking begging you, please. I can't. They'll kill me."

"What do you think I'm going to do if you don't tell us?" asked Matt. "And I've got all day to kill you. You really want to see just how painful I can make it?"

"They'll kill my brother and mother," he said. "Please. I can't tell you anything more. You don't understand what these people are like. My whole family, man, they'll kill my whole family."

"Oh, we're getting a good idea of what they're like," said Catherine.

"Just kill me," said the man quietly. "Just kill me and get it over with."

Catherine hated the fact this man was able to elicit empathy from her, but she couldn't help it. "You're one of 'these people' just in case you forgot. How many brothers and mothers have you killed?"

"They won't kill anyone if they're dead," said Matt. "Now either you talk, or I keep pulling layers away until your right arm is nothing but bones. Do you want to see? I'm a bit curious how long your fingers will stay attached at this rate. Maybe we'll try some of your toes afterward, see which ones last longer. I think the toes will stay on longer. What do you think?"

Catherine walked over and leaned down in front of the man much the same way she had with Jim in his study, "Do something right while you still have the chance," she told him. "If you want to save your family, tell us where we can find Ortiz so we can put a stop to all this once and for all."

The man looked up and gave her a horrible smile, "You thinking killing him is going to stop anything?" He shook his head.

Catherine only stared at him until his eyes once again met hers. "Tell us. That girl didn't deserve to die like she did. Someone has to atone for all this. You have to atone for it. Now tell us what we need to know."

Still, he said nothing. But as Matt began to put the wire on the fourth finger, the man gave in. "Okay. Enough. They're just going to kill you anyway, same as me. I don't know how to find Ortiz, okay, but Miguel does."

"Who's Miguel?" asked Catherine.

"Miguel Valencia. He runs the gang, right? He's Ortiz's guy. He'll know where to find him. Everything goes through Miguel. Ortiz doesn't talk to anyone else in the gang."

Another name to find, thought Catherine. She was having trouble believing all these people were involved in Taylor's murder. *Why?*

"And where do we find Miguel?" asked Matt, skeptical the man may throwing false names out there in order to end his ordeal.

"Luna Azul," said the man.

"Blue moon?" asked Catherine. "What's that, a restaurant?"

"It's a strip club," said the man. "Miguel owns it. He's always there. Miguel loves the ladies."

"Where?"

"Mexico City, man. He's in Mexico City."

"He lives there?" He nodded. "Where?"

"I don't know where he lives, just go to the club. You'll find him there."

"Does he have a car?" she asked.

"Mercedes. Black. He parks it behind the club when he's there."

"You wouldn't still be lying to us, would you?" asked Matt, pressing again on the tender areas of stripped skin.

"No, man!" he cried. "I'm telling you the truth! It's all I know, man. Come on, please, let me go. That's all I know, I swear."

Matt looked at Catherine and they seemed to reach an agreement in their eyes. They'd gotten what they needed from the man. Matt removed the slim wire from the man's finger and they walked together towards the back.

When they were out of earshot, Catherine asked Matt, "What do you think?"

"He might be full of shit, but I don't think we're going to get much more out of him."

"I agree," said Catherine. "And it sounds like a good lead, at least."

Matt looked back towards the man sitting in the chair. He was moaning, "Let me go, man. I want to go home. I just want to fucking go home."

Catherine looked back at him, too. "We can't let him go," said Matt. "He knows Julio's in Playa. He may have even heard us talking to Pat." He looked into her eyes. She was already shaking her head. "Catherine," he whispered. "This is the cartel we're dealing with. The first thing he'll do if we let him go is run back to his gang. Then they'll know everything he just told us and everything he's heard and seen since we took him."

"I didn't come here for this," she told him. "I don't know if this is right. Who are we to decide this man has to die?" Back home, this guy would have been sent to prison for the next 20 years, but Catherine had to remind herself she wasn't back home. She thought about what Ramirez had said about charges never sticking to these guys. If they handed him over to the police in Mexico, he'd probably never even see the inside of the police station. He'd be back with his buddies before breakfast.

"No," he told her. "This is war. I don't know how Taylor ended up a victim of it, but make no mistake, Catherine. This is war. And these guys," he said, pointing back at the gang member, "are the enemy. I know how you feel about these things, but sympathy will get you killed. I'm not saying we do this because the guy deserves it or because it's justice. We simply don't have a choice. If he goes free and tells the rest of them what's happened, it could get Julio killed, Pat killed, his family . . ."

"Enough," she told him, shrugging his arms off her. "I get it." She looked back at the man, still moaning in pain. *Who's to say if it was justice or revenge?* She thought of the implications of their actions, and then she knew he wasn't going home. As much as she hated to admit it, Matt was right. The man was a cartel henchman. There was nothing they could do to stop him from warning Miguel or coming back to Playa with a dozen armed thugs to find Patrick's house if they cut him loose. Even if they locked him up somewhere, the risk of his escape meant too much. And no matter what he promised, as soon as the risk of losing his life was gone, he'd be right back to the Barrio Boys. *Take a life to save lives,* she told herself, hoping she wasn't deluding herself into becoming a coldblooded killer.

"Go on," said Matt. "I'll be right behind you."

"Wait," she said. If they were going to do it she wanted to know one more thing, first.

She walked back to the man. "Just let me go," he pleaded with her. "You'll never see me again, I swear. I just want to go home."

She knelt down in front of the man again and lifted his medallion up to better see the little exes engraved. "Two?" she asked him. "Who were they?"

The man looked down at his medallion disheartened. "Nobody. Just a rival gang, you know."

"Yeah," said Catherine, now having her suspicions verified. "I'm sure that's what they were," she told him, rubbing her fingers along the etchings, "not two innocent people you and your buddies murdered, surely." Then she turned and walked away, ignoring the man as he begged after her.

As Catherine walked out towards the car, a single gunshot reverberated against the thin metal walls. The moment had reaffirmed a few things for Catherine. She had called Matt because he possessed the things she couldn't accept about him years ago. She needed him now for all the reasons she'd left him then. And in some ways, being involved and up close to the fray, she understood him better now. Maybe he wasn't a bloodthirsty killer. He'd just been around them so long he'd learned that to survive them sometimes meant playing by their rules. *God, maybe Amy was right. Maybe what he did back then was the right thing to do.* But then she wondered, *But how far can you go before you're no better than the enemy?* It was a slippery slope and she felt herself losing her footing.

Chapter 40

Jose sat in the Suburban and lit another Marlboro as he kept watch over the parking lot of Richland Community College. He turned his *tejano* music up and leaned back. He'd been at this for days. There were no less than nine Dallas Community College locations, but Mama had told him to stick with the three on her list. "It's one of these," she'd told him. "If he goes to classes, it'll be on the north side." He'd been starting to think Mama was wrong on this one lately, and had settled for spending his recent hours dozing off. But right when he was about to assume his most relaxed of positions, he spotted what he'd been waiting for. Armando's pickup truck came pulling into the parking lot. *There you are*, Jose thought. *Leave it to Mama.* He got out his notepad and wrote down Armando's license plate as Mama had told him. Then he lit another cigarette and waited.

A few hours later Armando pulled out of the parking lot and the Suburban, to which Jose had applied a horrible tan paint job using spray paint, shadowed him from several car lengths back. Armando stopped off at a gas station and after pumping gas went inside to pay. Jose kept his distance and followed Armando back to the little house. He wrote down the address and then pulled away. He didn't want to stay on the street long enough to be conspicuous. He drove to another nearby gas station and pulled in. Then he picked up his cell phone to call his mother.

"Any news?" she asked.

"Yes, Mama, I found him. It was just like you said. I found him at one of the schools. I followed him to his house and wrote down the address like you told me to."

"Good. Is she there with him?"

"I don't know. I didn't see her, but she might be in the house."

"Where are you right now?"

"I'm parked at a gas station down the road from where he lives."

"Good. You did a good job, *hijo*," she told him. "Now, I want you to go back and park down the street, close enough so you can see if he leaves, but not so close that he'll see you. And go to the opposite end of the street from the way he will most likely go to leave so he doesn't pass by you. Do you understand?"

"Yes, Mama."

"If you don't see anything by the time it gets dark, then park a little closer and try to look in the windows. But don't get caught!"

"Okay, Mama."

He hung up the phone and returned to the subdivision where he sat and waited. He smoked his cigarettes and ate a meal of chicken and rice Miss Lydia had packed for him, but for the next two hours nothing happened. Then, someone emerged from the front door of the house. It was Armando and some other young man, and directly behind them came Yesenia.

Jose dropped his Tupperware container in the passenger seat and picked up the cell phone again. When his mother answered he told her what he was seeing. "She's with him. They're getting into his truck."

"I knew it," said Miss Lydia, immensely pleased with herself. "I knew the little bitch had help. Tell me where they go, but don't be seen."

Yesenia sat next to Armando fiddling with his radio. "There are so many stations," she said. "Oh, I like this song." Lady Gaga belted out a tune and Yesenia sang along.

Armando looked at her funny. "What?" she asked. "Do I sound bad?"

"No, but you're singing in English," he reminded her.

"I guess, but I don't know what all the words mean." Catalina had a Lady Gaga CD one of her customers had given her and it was one of the only English songs Yesenia knew.

As they drove along Armando would point things out and tell her the English word for it. When they pulled into a parking lot she asked, "How do you say '*restaurante*'?"

"Restaurant," he told her.

"That's it?"

"That's it."

They ate dinner at the *El Patio* Restaurant, laughing until late. Armando felt swept away by Yesenia. Despite knowing where she'd been, he couldn't help but feel he was falling in love with her, if he wasn't in love already. "Hey," he whispered to his brother. "Why don't you stay over at Mom's tonight?"

"What for?" Ricky asked.

"I want to have a night with her, you know. Just the two of us. I'll give you twenty bucks, bro. "

Ricky smiled, "Man, you got it bad for her, huh? Okay, fine." They both visited their mother about once a week but rarely spent the night anymore. Ricky didn't mind, though. It might be good to check on his mom, see if she was on a binge or not.

Yesenia was curious about their exchange. "What are you two up to?"

"Nothing," Armando told her. "Ricky was just wanting to know if we could drop him off at our mom's on the way home, weren't you Ricky?"

"Yeah, I'm going to go hang out with her tonight and see how she's doing."

Out in the parking lot Jose was once again calling Miss Lydia. "They're just eating at a restaurant," he told her.

"Good. If they're going out to eat, then they aren't worried about us looking for them. You can catch them off-guard. Come back and get Hector. You two have business to take care of tonight."

Chapter 41

Catherine and Matt flew to Mexico City the next day, following the lead they had garnered from the Barrio Boy. They used Catherine's company card again to charter an old Cessna with a pilot who flew as hazardously as most of the taxi drivers in order to bring Matt's toys. The pilot hardly spoke two words to them throughout the trip, and Catherine surmised it probably wasn't the first time he'd flown strange foreigners with large bags who didn't want to go through airport security. Catherine thought for sure they weren't going to make it during the landing as the plane dipped up and down, side to side, rocking back and forth as they made their approach. "Is fine," the pilot told her as she pointed and tried to make sure he knew he was about to send the plane into a cart wheeling ball of fire on the tarmac. Even Matt had to force himself not to lose his breakfast, but somehow, magically, the plane plopped down evenly on both rear tires, the nose following smoothly afterward as the plane came to a swift halt, sending both passengers lurching forward in their seats. Luckily, both were wearing their seat belts. "See?" remarked the pilot. "Is fine."

They didn't bother checking into a hotel. Instead, they rented yet another vehicle and went in search of the Luna Azul strip club. When they found it, they drove slowly down the back alleyway and saw a black Mercedes parked under an awning.

"Looks like he was telling the truth," said Matt.

"I know I shouldn't, but I'm still wondering if what we did back there was right," said Catherine. "That's strange, isn't it? Considering what these people have done . . . what they do. And still I question myself."

"That's not strange," said Matt. "That's what makes you so different from them. Don't dwell on it. He would have killed all of us and wouldn't have lost a wink of sleep over it. All that pleading and promises . . . you think the two exes on his coin got a break?" She'd explained to him earlier the significance of the etchings, as she'd been able to confirm from the man in his last seconds.

"No, I'm sure they didn't."

Outside of the Luna Azul, a young teenager wearing the trademark silver chain, a very thin one at that, was watching over the car. They stayed well back in the alley so as to not arouse his suspicions.

"Look at him, he's just a kid," said Catherine. "These 'Barrio Boys' are probably a bunch of inner city kids who couldn't find work. They see someone like this Miguel guy with his nice car and a pocket full of cash, and get sucked right in."

"Doesn't matter," said Matt. "You have to remember, Catherine. It doesn't matter why someone ends up staring you down through a gun sight. Once you're there, it's you or them."

Catherine looked at him. "Is that really how you see it? You don't think it matters who that person is or why they picked up that gun in the first place, even if it's just some punk kid like that one there?" She wasn't trying to be accusing, but this was a point they'd long disagreed over, and she'd never second-guessed herself over it until recently.

"If I stopped to think about those kinds of things I wouldn't be sitting here today, Catherine. I'd have been picked off a long time ago. When you have a gun and they have a gun, it's whoever shoots first. Hell, you know the only time I've been shot was by that old woman in the field, and that was the only time I was dumb enough to let down my guard. I joke about it now but she was trying to kill me. It didn't matter that she might have been someone's grandmother. I should have looked closer to make sure she wasn't armed and maybe I would have seen that AK hiding in the grass like a snake. It was a mistake that nearly killed me."

"Yes, I know," said Catherine. She looked back to the kid watching the car. "I just don't know what I'd do if I saw a kid like that on the other end of my gun."

Matt looked at her. "If you're ever in a situation like that, don't stop to ask yourself who they are or where they're from because it doesn't matter by that point. There's no second place ribbon in that race, unless you count a toe-tag."

She knew Matt was probably right, but she couldn't help but think there was always hope for kids like the one they were looking at. It couldn't be too late for them. People always had time to change their ways, pick a different path, change who they are.

There was Matt's side to consider, though. These weren't people to feel sorry for, especially since they were responsible for what had happened to Taylor. Still, the thought troubled her that if she saw someone so young on the other end of her gun, she'd hesitate. She didn't think it'd be possible not to. She might not be able to pull the trigger at all. Her conscience wouldn't let her. "I'm glad you came, Matt," she told him. "I couldn't do this without you."

A moment of silence passed between them as they watched the boy, each with their own ideas of what he represented. "You want to go in?" he asked.

"No. Let's wait for him to leave. There's no telling how many Barrio Boys he's got in there, and even though I understand everything you said, I'm in no hurry to have to shoot at them. I'm after the men who took Taylor Woodall, not every stupid kid wearing a necklace. Let's try to catch Miguel alone."

"Sure," said Matt. "That's probably the better way to handle this. There's no reason to go after anyone who wasn't directly involved." She turned her head and watched him for a long moment. "What?" he asked, a bit unnerved.

"I misjudged you before," she told him. "You know, what happened with the guerrillas and the pipeline workers. I misjudged you. I still think it was pretty horrific what happened, but I think I understand why it happened, now. And I shouldn't have been so quick to judge. I'm sorry for that."

Matt was speechless. Catherine had no idea what her words meant to him. "You were right about a lot of things," he told her. "But it's a complicated world sometimes. I shouldn't have done what I did. But when I saw that picture in that guy's wallet, him standing there with his wife and kids, and then me looking down and seeing his headless body . . . it was hard. I got angry."

"I know," she said. *I know.*

They waited in the car until the hours of the night were nearly gone. At four, a tackily dressed young man came out of the club. The kid who was watching the car was nearly asleep by now, and Catherine watched as the man kicked him in the shin to wake him up, and then scolded him.

"Looks like our guy," said Matt.

Catherine couldn't see him well enough from their vantage point to know if he was the man in the sketch, but as she watched him get into the car and it pull away like a sleek shark stalking prey upon the streets, she felt confident they had found their man. *God, let it be him,* she thought as they started the car and followed.

They had to remain quite a ways behind the Mercedes to remain unnoticed due to the light traffic of the late hour. The Mercedes eventually pulled into a large high-rise condominium complex, nicer even than the one Catherine lived in back in Dallas.

"Who says crime doesn't pay?" remarked Catherine.

"Oh, it does," said Matt. "Until it catches up with you."

"I guess it's about to catch up to him," Catherine mumbled, wondering what they were going to do with Miguel. *It just depends on what he says,* she told herself. *Nothing is decided.* Although in her heart she doubted that was true.

They parked across the street and entered the condominium building. Inside, the beautiful lobby with travertine floors, deep wood furniture and a warmly glowing crystal chandelier was empty save for a security guard who greeted them politely behind a small podium.

"Hello," he greeted them in English. "Are you here to see someone?" he asked, pulling a pen and placing it on the next vacant line of the guest registry.

"Miguel Valencia," said Matt.

The man's smile faded somewhat. "And may I have your name?"

Matt firmly but calmly took the pen from his hand. "No, I'm afraid you may not."

The security guard looked from Matt to Catherine and realized they weren't expected. Matt pulled his gun and the guard quickly held his hands up. "I'm not armed," he said. "You're Americans, yes? I know why you're here," he continued, an eerie silence capturing the moment before he offered, "I thought it was him. I would have told someone, but I couldn't. I have a family."

"What do you mean?" asked Catherine, her heart racing, hoping he meant just what she thought he meant.

The guard now looked scared. He wasn't sure if he'd jumped to the wrong conclusion. "We're here about a girl," Matt told him, "a girl who was murdered in Cancun." And the security guard's face told them they were all on the same page.

Yes! thought Catherine, *it's him.* "What unit number is he in?"

The man gestured to a tablet on the podium. Catherine picked it up and began going down the alphabetical list. "Top floor," he told Matt, eyeing the gun in his hand fearfully. "We have four penthouses on that floor, sir. Mr. Valencia is in number three, the second to the right from the elevator."

Matt smiled at Catherine. The security guard acted as though he wouldn't mind a ringside seat. Whether it was the gun pointed at him or just that he was happy to see Miguel about to face the music, the security guard was being quite accommodating. *Or maybe he'd already pressed a hidden button and warned Mr. Valencia.* Either was a real possibility, Matt decided, but he thought the former more likely than the latter.

"I'm sorry," said Catherine. "But we're going to need to put you out of the way for a while."

"I understand," said the man. "There's a janitor's closet down the hall. I would be happy to remain there until your business with Mr. Valencia is concluded."

He showed Catherine and Matt to the closet and unlocked it with his key, which he then handed to Catherine.

"We have to tie you up, I'm afraid," she told him.

"I understand." There were garbage twines in the closet and the guard practically put them on himself.

"Is that too tight?" Catherine asked him after he was tied up.

"No, ma'am. I'm fine." They turned to lock him in. "Oh!" said the guard. They looked back at him. "I believe he lives alone and I didn't see any guests this evening, if that's of any help. But I would expect he's, um, prepared for visitors such as yourself, if you know what I mean."

Again, Catherine and Matt exchanged an odd look. They didn't know who the guard thought they were, but as it was to their advantage, they didn't ask. As they took the elevator up to the top floor, Catherine was almost chuckling over the man. "Well that was easier than I thought it'd be."

"Let's hope that security guard isn't trying to herd us into an ambush." He checked his gun and made sure it was chambered. Catherine didn't think the guard was pulling a fast one, but she followed Matt's lead just the same.

When they reached the top floor, they quietly approached the door. Matt stayed low and put his ear to it. There was no sound. He pulled Catherine off to the side a bit. "Do you want me to kick it in, or try to pick the lock? I'm a little rusty but might be able to. I brought a pick just in case."

"Let's try to get in quietly if we can," said Catherine. Matt reached into his back pocket and retrieved a small black pouch. From it, he pulled two small pieces of metal, one straight, and one with a tiny L-shape on the end.

"How many times have you done this?" asked Catherine.

Matt smiled. "It's been a while."

They returned to the door and Matt put the hook shaped piece of metal on the top of the dead bolt lock and then began searching for the tumblers with the other. As he pressed his ear to the door, he heard the first clicks of the tumblers. Catherine stood behind him with her gun at the ready. Then Matt heard the click. He held up his finger as if to say, *that's one.* Then he repeated the process on the lock of the doorknob. It took a little while, but after a minute or so he turned the knob and the door opened silently. Luckily, the building's maintenance staff kept the hinges of the penthouse doors well oiled, and as they entered, the door gave away nothing.

The front entryway was dark but they could see light spilling out from the master bedroom. They stalked towards it, Matt's eyes scanning the shadows as best he could so as to not miss Miguel if he was crouched down somewhere ready to shoot from an unseen vantage. As they entered his bedroom they could hear water running. Again, luck was on their side. Miguel was in the shower and he hadn't bothered closing the bathroom door.

A Browning Buckmark .22 pistol with a Dragonfly silencer sat on the nightstand. *Interesting choice,* thought Matt, pointing it out to Catherine. She didn't know what kind of gun it was, but she did notice it was a .22 caliber.

As they passed by the closet, near where he'd discarded the clothes he'd worn that evening into a dirty hamper, they saw a Mac-10 with a Bowers CAC-9 silencer. *Guy's got an arsenal,* Matt thought. He pointed to the gun and then held his finger to his lips as if to say, *these are quieter.* Then he grabbed the machine gun while Catherine walked to the nightstand and put her pistol away, trading it for the silenced Browning. She quietly checked its clip and chamber, which was loaded as she'd expected. Her face went red as she held the gun. *Was this the same .22 that had been used to kill Taylor?* She knew by picking it up she'd likely tainted it as evidence, but that didn't much matter after what Ramirez had told her. The police weren't going to be coming for this guy. Even if they did link him directly to the crime they'd never risk the cartel's reprisal. If Miguel was going to pay for what he did, they'd have to be the one serving up his bill.

They walked into the bathroom. It was wall-to-wall marble with a large Jacuzzi bathtub in the center of the wall at the rear. To the left was the large shower with multiple showerheads spraying warm water. A mist of steam floated around the shower like a fog and they could just make out the silhouette behind the frosted glass.

Matt grabbed the shower door and opened it up to a shocked Miguel. "Shower's over," he told him. Miguel's hands froze in his hair, shampoo bubbling down his face as he squinted trying to make out who it was that had just got the drop on him. As the suds streamed away from his eyes he stared at them in shocked disbelief. He had no idea who they were, but he knew they were white and they were both pointing his own guns at him. He couldn't understand how he didn't hear them coming in. The door was always locked.

"Out," said Matt.

Miguel recovered his composure and stared at them with a cocky glare as he lowered his arms and rinsed himself off as though Matt and Catherine were expected to let him finish at his leisure. "You know who I am?" he asked in English.

Catherine had been eyeing him closely. She had to be sure. But when he spoke, she knew. She knew and it set off a powder keg of rage. "You son of a bitch!" she cursed, charging towards him. She snatched Miguel by his hair and slammed him against the back of the shower, driving her knee as hard as she could into his bared groin. Miguel dropped to the floor of the shower in pain.

"Does that answer your question?" asked Matt. He'd never seen Catherine explode in such a violent outburst. Catherine was grinding her teeth as she stood over the doubled over Miguel, the shower still pouring water on them. Then she stepped back and put the Browning level with Miguel's downcast head. For a moment, Matt thought she might actually pull the trigger. "Catherine . . . " he began, "Catherine, easy now. We still have questions."

She lowered the gun, but kept clenching her jaws against one another angrily. "So we finally found you, Miguel," she told him, "or would you prefer it if we called you Martin?"

"Come on," said Matt. He handed Catherine his gun and snatched one of Miguel's arms, twisting it around his back, and placing a gnarled forearm around Miguel's neck as he marched him out of the shower. "Be glad she didn't shoot 'em off," Matt told Miguel as the man moaned in pain from his aching balls.

"The day's not over," said Catherine, disgusted.

Chapter 42

When they returned from eating that evening, after they had dropped Ricky off, Yesenia and Armando were talking about her immigration status. "Maybe we could get you a student visa or something," he told her. "We'll find something." He turned the key in the lock and they walked inside. "I think the first thing would be to find a job. That's kind of tough without papers, I think, but we can do some checking around."

As they walked into the living room Yesenia froze. Armando was still talking and nearly walked into her before he realized she'd stopped cold. He looked up and saw two men standing near the entryway to the kitchen. Both had guns drawn.

"Hello, Yesenia," Jose said with an evil grin.

Armando reacted without a thought. "Run!" he yelled to her, and he snatched a little glass bowl where he kept his change off the end table he was standing by and threw it as hard as he could. It happened so fast that Jose was taken off guard and the bowl, full of quarters, dimes, and innumerable pennies, smashed off his head like a chunk of iron with a candied glass shell, exploding on impact. At the same moment, full of fear and with her heart nearly bursting through her chest, Yesenia bolted. She heard two gunshots behind her and saw Armando drop to the ground just as she looked back. "No!" she yelled as she spun around. She was about to run back to him but Hector raised his gun and fired a shot which whizzed through her hair, skinned her ear and missed killing her by an inch. She turned and fled again, out of the door and into the street.

The two men ran after her but Yesenia was wearing new tennis shoes this time. All those years of walking everywhere and running up and down the river bank in Santa Rosanna gave her long and lean leg muscles which now propelled her like a gazelle taking flight. By the time Jose burst out of the front door Yesenia was already across the adjacent lawn and had disappeared between the two houses. He and Hector followed but their boots slowed them down. Each time they rounded one corner to catch up to her, she was disappearing around another, putting more and more ground between them.

They thought they had her at one point when a six foot privacy fence blocked her path, but Yesenia jumped up and over it like she was running a playground course and it was her favorite obstacle, and by the time they reached it, Jose was so winded from his smoking habit he didn't have the strength to scale it. "I'll go get the truck," he told Hector. "Go get her."

Hector grunted and pulled himself over the fence and saw Yesenia darting out of the gate. Behind her a Labrador was barking ferociously.

It turned away from Yesenia when Hector entered the yard and jumped on him instead, biting his arm and trying for his neck.

"Fucking dog," Hector cursed, yanking his gun back out and then shooting the dog dead. An old man in boxer shorts and a T-shirt came running out of the back door as Hector got to his feet. "Lady, what's wrong?" The old man asked, addressing the dog. He saw Hector and then he yelled "What are you doing here!? I'm calling the police!" Then the man saw his dog sprawled on the lawn, its tongue laid out between its teeth, its chest not rising, and then the man saw the gun in Hector's hand. "Lady!" he screamed. "You son of a bitch!" the man yelled at Hector. "You shot my Lady!" The man ran back into the house cursing and wailing furiously, nearly blubbering, and Hector made for the gate.

By the time he passed through it, there was no sign of Yesenia. Hector looked both ways hoping to catch a glimpse of her running between the houses, but she was gone.

He stood in the alleyway listening intently for any sound of her, but heard nothing. "Shit," he muttered to himself. He began walking down the alley with his eyes darting in all directions when the man in the boxer shorts suddenly reappeared behind him. Hector turned and was greeted by a shotgun blast aimed right at his gut. The irate old man had retrieved his twelve gauge from next to his bed. "You killed my Lady!" cried the man again in tears. "You God damn son of a bitch! I hope you rot in hell, you bastard!" The old man kicked away Hector's gun and stood over him still yelling as Hector lay on his back, seeing nothing but the old man's red face, tears streaming down it, spit flying from the man's mouth, silhouetted against the sky above. "Die, you bastard!" the old man yelled. And with a second blast from the shotgun, Hector obliged.

"That's for my Lady!" the man screamed. A widower for four years, Hector had just unknowingly killed the old man's only companion in life, his beloved dog, Lady, who he'd let out for a bathroom break and to run around the yard a while. It could have been any yard in the neighborhood Yesenia had led him into, but unfortunately for Hector, they'd fallen in Lady's.

Jose pulled perpendicular to the alley on a nearby street, but when he looked down the alley and saw the old man holding the shotgun, still crying and yelling hysterically, Hector sprawled out on the ground with a pool of blood around him, he cursed, "What the hell?" He put his truck back in drive and drove away. Police sirens could be heard in the distance. *What happened?* he thought to himself. *What am I going to tell Mama?* He wasn't exactly sure how Yesenia had managed to escape them or how Hector had ended up dead, but he knew explaining it wasn't going to be easy.

In a nearby yard beneath an upside down kiddie pool, Yesenia lay in a fetal position with her hands pressed tightly over her mouth to stifle her sobs.

Chapter 43

He had a new haircut and had lost the cheesy goatee, but Kendra had been spot on with the police sketch in all other regards. "So you're the son of a bitch who killed her," she said. "I can't tell you how happy it makes me to finally meet you," she told him ominously.

"Killed who?" Miguel laughed. "I didn't kill anyone."

She eyed the gold medallion around his neck. "Liar, liar," she told him. "I know what that is. You're a killer, alright. And you killed Taylor Woodall. Now you're going to tell me why. Why did you kidnap that girl off the street? Why'd you kill her for no reason?"

"I don't know anyone named Taylor," he said.

"The American girl in Cancun," said Catherine. "We'll be happy to jog your memory if you like."

"Hey, you got the wrong guy. I haven't been to Cancun since I was a kid. I'm telling you, you guys are making a big mistake. I don't know any girl named Taylor and I haven't been in Cancun in over 10 years."

"Save it," Matt said. "Let's get him out of here." He sat Miguel down in the living room, "Watch him a sec, will you? And if he screams for help just kill him." Catherine kept her gun on Miguel and Matt had the impression she just may actually do it if the man yelled. He went to the closet and retrieved a pair of pants and a button down short sleeve. "Put 'em on," he told Miguel.

They both kept their guns pointed at him while Miguel put the slacks on. "What do you guys want?" he asked them. "Money? Drugs? You're obviously not with any law enforcement. You working for someone?"

"Taylor Woodall," Catherine said. "We're working for her."

"Shirt," said Matt, throwing it at him.

While he put it on, Matt took some of Miguel's silk ties from the closet. Then he went to the dresser and took Miguel's cell phone. By the television he saw a DVD, *Scarface*. He almost laughed to himself. *Of course.*

After Miguel had his shirt on Matt bound his hands behind his back with one of the ties. As he did, he noticed Catherine staring at the .22 in her hands. "Here, let me have that one," said Matt, trading guns with Catherine.

They led Miguel out and into the elevator. He was still talking. "Do you have any idea what will happen to you if you do this?" he asked. "Not only will you be killed, but your friends, your family, everyone you know will be hunted down one by one and executed. There won't be bodies. There'll be pieces. Everywhere."

"I said save it," said Matt. "You're the one who doesn't have a clue who you're talking to."

"No, *you* don't!" he yelled, like a five year old trying to win an argument with the same line over and over again. "I run this city! You're in my country, *pendejo*! You think you can just come in here and take me out!? My boys will kill everyone, EVERYONE you so much as know! It'll be war, mother-f . . . " but he didn't get to finish. Matt punched him in the mouth with the butt of the gun, knocking a front tooth loose and bloodying Miguel's lip. "Fucker!" he yelled at Matt, as though finishing his last sentiment. "You're a fucking dead man!"

Matt grabbed him by the throat, stifling him. "Keep talking, big man, and you won't even make it to the car." He wanted to gag him with another tie, but couldn't risk a passerby in the street noticing the gagged man being led away. It was only by fortune of the hour they were able to take him from the building without anybody witnessing.

Miguel stopped making his threats, but he glared at his captors with murder in his eyes. Catherine stared back at him with equal vehemence. She so desperately wanted to hit him but knew if she did she not might be able to stop herself.

They left the building figuring the security guard would be fine until morning when someone would hear him, and when they reached the car, Catherine kept a gun to Miguel's back while Matt gagged him and bound his legs. They had rented yet another car with a trunk release button inside the trunk, but this time Catherine insisted they not destroy the car unless absolutely necessary. So instead they threw Miguel in the back seat. Catherine drove while Matt kept his attentions on their new friend. He wasn't about to turn his back to Miguel, not even for a second. "Comfy?" he asked. Miguel scowled.

They drove to an industrial part of the city where ancient rail cars sat unused. Their rusted husks wasted away near abandoned tracks without another soul in sight. They parked next to them and pulled Miguel inside of one. Then they leaned him against the back wall and un-gagged him.

"Now," said Matt. "Before we start talking to one another I want to make a few things very clear for you, Miguel, or Martin, or whatever your name is. We're going to ask you questions and you'd better answer them truthfully or I'm going to start removing body parts."

Miguel sat with a smug look on his face. "Go on, then. Ask."

"Did you kill that girl?" asked Catherine.

"I already told you I didn't kill anyone." Matt held the silenced Browning in his hand. As he bent down and leaned in towards Miguel, the smug expression evaporated. "What, man?" He asked. "I'm telling you. It wasn't me."

"What about the boy?" asked Matt. "Why did you send your boys after him, then, if you don't know anything about the girl?"

"Boy, boy, boy, what boy?" he asked. "You two are fucking crazy. I don't know what the hell you're talking about."

"The little homeless kid some of your Barrio Boys shot," said Matt. "They shot him in the leg while he was running away. Remember him?" Matt knelt down by Miguel and cocked the hammer on the pistol.

"What are you doing?" Miguel asked. "Come on, stop fucking with me."

"That's the thing, Miguel. I'm not fucking with you." Matt looked to Catherine, and Catherine nodded. Miguel was a different animal than the last man they'd questioned. She had no moral conflicts when it came to him. They were going to get answers and if that meant Miguel died a slow and painful death, then that was his choice for what he had done to Taylor, so far as she was concerned. The silenced gun barely made a thump, but then came Miguel's scream of surprise and pain. "Hurts, doesn't it?" Matt asked loudly of the yelps. "I know, I know. That little kid and I were just talking about it the other day. Burns like hell. Now you know how he felt. And this is just a little .22."

"You shot me!" cried Miguel in shock. He tried to grab his leg but couldn't since he was still bound at the hands and feet. All he could do was roll around in his agony. "You fucking asshole! You shot me!"

"Of course I shot you," said Matt. "Just like you shot my little buddy. Did you think I wouldn't? Did you think we were going to try and scare a confession out of you, then give up and say, 'oh, well, we tried, better let him go.' This is just the beginning, Miguel. If you don't give us answers, you're going to be introduced to whole new level of pain in your life. I don't like you, Miguel. And when I don't like someone, I can be a real rat bastard."

"What do you want!?" he yelled at them.

"We've already told you," said Catherine. "We want to know about the girl! Tell me how you raped and killed her, Miguel! Tell me why you chose her and why you did what you did to her! Tell me why this happened, all of it." She kicked Miguel in the knee where he'd just been shot. "Tell me!"

"It wasn't me!" Miguel cried.

"That sure tastes like more bullshit you're feeding us, Miguel." Matt grabbed him by the hair and cocked the gun again. He put it to Miguel's other leg. "Wait!" He cried. "I'm telling you the truth! It wasn't me. It was Arismendez!"

Matt kept the gun to his knee, but didn't fire. "Who?" he asked.

"Victor Arismendez!" he cried. "Him and Ortiz."

"Fernando Ortiz?" asked Catherine.

"Yes," said Miguel, unpleasantly surprised they knew the name already.

Shit, you gotta be kidding me, Catherine thought. If Miguel wasn't the killer . . . . *damn. He's lying. He's got to be lying.* "Okay, so which one killed Taylor Woodall?" Catherine asked.

"And who is Victor Arismendez?" Matt added.

"It was fucking Arismendez," groaned Miguel, his leg tormenting him. "He's a crazy fucking guy back in Cancun, Ortiz's partner. He told Ortiz to get the girl. Ortiz told me. It was all Arismendez, man."

"What kind of partners?" asked Matt.

"They share things . . . trucks, runners, people, safe houses up north, all that shit."

Her heart sank at the prospect Miguel was telling them the truth. "How does it work?" asked Catherine.

Miguel hesitated. "I don't know specifics . . . " he shifted his leg in pain. "Oh, you guys are so dead. You have no idea who you're messing with. Arismendez is crazy."

"There you go hurting our feelings again," said Matt. "You know what your problem is, Miguel? You've been watching too many movies. I bet you sit up in that high rise of yours jerking off to *Scarface,* don't you? Is that what it is, Miguel? You think you're Tony Montoya? Well, do you remember the ending of that movie, Miguel? Do you remember what happened to Tony Montoya?"

"Go fuck yourself," Miguel spat.

"You just aren't getting this, are you Miguel?" Matt asked. He pulled the trigger on the gun, shattering Miguel's other knee as he screamed. Catherine flinched and shot Matt an angry look. They were just now getting some answers. The small hole on the surface belied the damage the bullet did as it tore through the bone and cartilage. As he tried to roll around in pain, his legs flopped about awkwardly like broken hinges at the knee. Matt put the gun to Miguel's hand. "You want to see what happens when I shoot your wrist?" Catherine grabbed Matt's arm and shook her head, but let go when Matt gave her a firm stare that faded slightly into one of recognition. He was going too far. They were after answers, not his screams of pain. *Okay,* his eyes said. "Tell me about the girl," he told Miguel again, more calm. "Start from the beginning."

Miguel writhed in pain reminiscent of the last man that Catherine and Matt had had a talk with. Finally, he spoke again. "I told you, Arismendez was the one that offed her," he said. "He threw some fancy dinner party down there during spring break, invited all the bosses. He's got a big fucking spread out there off the island. We stayed late trying to work some deals with him. He's got connections like crazy. But he didn't want to talk business. He just wanted to party. He started talking about all the white girls that were in town, started talking about how hot they were and how he wanted one. Ortiz offered to get some girls, prostitutes, the expensive ones, but Arismendez wouldn't hear it. He kept saying it had to be a white girl with blond hair and green eyes, someone exotic, like a model, not a prostitute. He got obsessed about it." He trailed off as he saw that his legs were bent in ways they couldn't naturally be bent. "Oh, shit, man," he whined to himself. "I can't believe this shit. I'm freaking bleeding all over the place, man." The pain was unbearable, as though his legs had been ripped away.

"Keep talking," warned Matt.

"We tried to talk him out of it," said Miguel. "*Tio* told him there'd be too much heat, but Arismendez was snortin', man, and the higher he got the more crazy he got about it. He told *Tio* to go get him a white girl with blond hair and green eyes. He told him to do it or he wouldn't make any deals."

"*Tio*? You mean Ortiz?" asked Catherine. Miguel nodded. "He's your uncle?" Catherine asked again to confirm.

"Yeah," Miguel confessed. Then he shook his head with a painful smile, "fucking millions of dollars on the line and all the guy would talk about was getting laid with an American chick. He just went on and on and on. He wouldn't shut up about it."

Catherine and Matt exchanged a look. Some of the pieces were slowly coming together, strange though they were. Miguel was just a glorified errand boy. "Go on," said Matt.

"Finally, *Tio* told him we could go party at some of the clubs and maybe he'd get lucky. Throw around some coke and cash, you know, but Arismendez wouldn't listen. He was high as hell. Plus the guy's a real ugly, fat bastard. There was no way he was picking up any of those chicks. We tried everything, man, but the guy wouldn't listen. He told *Tio* to either go get a girl or to go back to Mexico City. So *Tio* told me to go find a girl so he could get Arismendez to shut the hell up about it and start talking business. *Tio* needed some new supply and better transport up north and Arismendez had it. Fuck, man! I'm dying. You got to get me to a hospital, man."

"No. No hospital for you, *amigo*. Not until you tell us everything. Keep talking."

"If I die, you won't get shit," he told them.

Matt grabbed him by the throat. "If you don't talk, then you're no good to us alive anyway, and I'll just kill you right here."

Miguel managed to talk despite the python-like grip Matt had on his throat. "You're just going to kill me anyway," he gasped, his face turning red.

"That's probably true," said Matt. "But there's an easy way and a hard way." He grabbed Miguel by the knee and dug his thumb into the bullet hole. Miguel's eyes went wide in pain. "You don't even want to know what we did to the guys you sent after us in Cancun. I skinned one of them myself, flayed his flesh right from his bone."

He let go of Miguel's knee and throat, and Miguel immediately vomited on himself. He'd never imagined the human body could hurt so much. "Tell us the rest," Matt prodded.

"What happened to Taylor Woodall?" asked Catherine. "What *exactly* happened."

Miguel was nearing semi-consciousness and Matt untied the gag that had fallen around his neck and used it as a tourniquet on one leg, then he used his own belt for the other. A large pool of blood was already forming and he was worried Miguel might bleed out from the second shot sooner than he thought. *Why is he bleeding so much?* He wondered. "You were drinking tonight, weren't ya?" he told Miguel as he tightened the belt around Miguel's leg. "Tsk, tsk. Your blood's all thinned out, but these will let us keep you around for hours." It was an over-exaggeration, but he needed Miguel to believe his hell could go on indefinitely.

"Go on," said Catherine. "Tell us about Taylor."

Miguel winced in pain as the belt cut off the blood supply to his legs, but he spoke. By now, he would have done anything to avoid being shot again. "Tio told me to go out to the clubs and find a girl that fit the bill."

"Why her?" asked Catherine.

"Arismendez was being picky. He wanted an American girl with blond hair and green eyes, tan and pretty. He wanted the hottest girl we could find. If we didn't find the right girl, we could fuck off, that's what he said. She just had the look, that's all."

"She just had the look?" Catherine asked. "Is that what you're telling me? You raped and murdered that poor girl because she just had the look?"

"I didn't do any of those things! It was him. We didn't know what he was going to do. We didn't know any of this shit was going to happen. We were just there to talk business. It was that stupid Arismendez who wouldn't listen."

"What'd you put in the drink?" asked Catherine.

Miguel started moaning again. "Speak up," said Matt, holding him upright by a handful of hair.

"Ribs."

"Ribs? You mean Rohypnol?" asked Catherine.

"Yeah, Arismendez had some. He's got everything. *Tio* told me to use 'em so we could knock a chick out and make it quiet." Catherine clenched her jaws. Her anger was building rapidly again and she pressed her will against it to keep from raging out of control. "But that other chick saw me. I knew we should have just bailed."

"Why didn't you?" she asked him.

Miguel looked her in the eyes. "I couldn't," he said. "There were millions of dollars on the table. If I came back without a girl, we were fucked."

"So you kidnapped her. You shot her friend and you snatched that poor girl right off the street . . . all because you were told to go find a pretty girl?"

"I had to," said Miguel.

"Bullshit," said Catherine. "You didn't have to do any of it. But you wanted the money. What'd you do to Taylor after you snatched her away from her life?"

Miguel sighed and turned his head away, but Matt was quick to grab his leg again, sending spears of pain shooting through his nerves. "I brought her back!" he said, Matt releasing. "She wouldn't stop fighting in the car so I pushed a few ribs down her throat. Then we took her back to the villa. She was out of it by then and Arismendez was pissed about it. He mixed up a shitload of coke with water and made her drink it. Then he took her to a bedroom and told us all to go have a drink by the pool, stay in the guesthouse if he didn't come down. I don't know what happened." Miguel's head began to sway back and forth.

"What'd he do?" Catherine asked, but Miguel began moaning again, this time in choking breaths.

"I'm dying," he began to cry. "I'm going to fucking die." Tears began to roll down his cheek. "Don't kill me. Please, just drop me at the hospital. I'll tell you whatever."

Matt grabbed his leg again, and Miguel jerked and twisted. Then Matt let go and grabbed Miguel by his chin, "Hey. Hey, look at me. You tell us everything you know until you're done and we'll decide then," he said, releasing his grip.

"I wasn't there, alright? I don't know what happened. She was a tough chick. She bit the shit out of one guy in the car and when Arismendez came back down he had marks and shit all over. She bit him, too, on his ear and his eye was all fucked up. He came outside told *Tio* he'd make a deal, but that some shit had happened upstairs. He wanted the girl gone. He said she was unconscious and we needed to get rid of her. We didn't even know what he did until we went upstairs to get her. She wasn't unconscious, man, she was dead. He'd choked her or something."

Catherine sat against the wall of the rail car to the right of Miguel. She couldn't help but to see images of Taylor's last moments. It'd been a long and drawn out death. "How long were they in the room before he came back down?" she asked.

"I don't know," Miguel said, now sobbing miserably. "He had her up there a couple of hours, maybe, I don't know. I don't want to die, man. Please. I don't want to die."

"You should have thought of that before you let that girl die," said Matt.

Catherine began to cry. *A couple of hours. Oh, God.* She knew what had happened to Taylor, but hearing it now conjured such a horrific image. She could more than see the attack. She could feel it in her soul. Anger returned and replaced her tears as she wiped them away. "Who shot her?"

"*Tio* told me to make sure she was dead," said Miguel.

Catherine looked up again, and Matt caught her glare. "So it *was* you who killed her?" She stared down at the gold medallion hanging around Miguel's neck. It had five x marks etched on its face. "Which one is she?" Catherine asked. She grabbed the medallion in her hand and slapped Miguel hard across the face, "Which one is she!?"

Miguel shook his head. "No, man, she was already dead. You should have seen her, she was dead. He choked her to death, plus all the drugs he made her take. I shot her like I was told, but he had already killed her, I swear."

She might have been alive, Catherine thought. *She might have made it!* She stood up and clenched the gun in her hand, wanting so badly to use it now.

"Why the cemetery?" asked Matt.

"Heat was everywhere. *Tio* left and told me to handle it, so we tossed her in a bathtub in the guesthouse until we could figure out what do to do. We decided to wait until the next night when there wouldn't be so many cops all over the place. The cemetery was close by and *Tio* said we should take her there, dump her in a fresh grave. He told me Arismendez was going to bring us all down with this shit." He laughed in spurting breaths. "He was right, huh?"

"And then you went after the kid," Matt reminded him.

"Yeah, those fucking kids," said Miguel, still chuckling pathetically. "We thought the cemetery was empty."

"Who killed the other kid? The one named Juan?" asked Catherine. Miguel began shaking his head. Catherine kicked him in one of his knees, "Who!?"

He looked down at his medallion and Catherine knew the answer. "I had to."

If he said *I had to* one more time, Catherine thought she might kick his teeth in. "I see. Who gave the kid up?"

"Some cop."

"Vargas?" Catherine asked.

"I don't know. Just some cop *Tio* bought." Miguel was beginning to fade in and out. "Let me have some water, man. Come on, get me some water." His eyes rolled around and he could no longer focus on anything. They rolled upwards and his head lolled to the side. "Just a little water, man, come on."

Matt pointed to his watch and made the international death sign to Catherine, an index finger crossing his throat, to indicate Miguel was likely not going to be with them much longer. The alcohol in his system had thinned the blood so much the tourniquets couldn't keep him from bleeding out. Even if they had decided to let him live, it was too late. There was nothing they could do to stop it now. He wouldn't make it to a hospital even if they were so inclined, which they weren't.

"Where's Ortiz?" asked Catherine.

"Just a little water," Miguel mumbled.

"Come on, Miguel. Where's your *Tio*?" asked Matt.

"*Tio*?" Miguel asked, dazed.

"Yeah, *Tio*. Where does *Tio* live?"

"*Tio*'s rich," he mumbled. "He lives in a fucking mansion."

"Where?" asked Catherine.

"*Tio, Tio, Tio*," he mumbled. "Good ole *Tio*. 'Trust me,' he said. Now look at me. And Arismendez, that fat, fucking asshole."

"Where's *Tio*, Miguel?" Matt asked. "Where's his mansion?"

"Fat fucking asshole," he mumbled again, this time barely audible.

Catherine knelt down by him and held his hand. "Tell me how to find *Tio*, Miguel."

"Fuck you," he said, his eyes rolling around like marbles. "I don't care anymore. Fat fucking asshole," he said melodically, as though it were his new favorite rhyme.

Matt looked at Catherine. They were about to lose him. "Tell me where *Tio* lives and I'll kill the Fat Fucking Asshole for you, Miguel," said Matt.

Miguel stared up at the railcar's metal ceiling, and then he coughed and made a gurgling noise.

"Miguel!" Catherine yelled, kicking his leg again. "Where's *Tio*? How do I find Arismendez!?"

His eyes settled on her for a moment, and he smiled. Matt was still holding him upright, but he felt the slack weight and tried smacking Miguel on the cheek. "Come on, Miguel. Wake up. Miguel? Wake up!" But Miguel didn't move. He just lay there staring upward blankly. Matt looked at Catherine and his eyes told her they weren't getting any more out of Miguel.

"Damn it," said Catherine.

"It doesn't matter," said Matt. He let go of Miguel's head and the body slumped to the side.

"What do you mean 'It doesn't matter'?" she asked angrily. "He didn't tell us where they are."

"You think all those officials back in Cancun don't know where this Arismendez guy is? You heard him, he's right in the heart of the city. Everybody there knows who he is."

That wasn't a comforting thought. "Okay, but what about Ortiz? He's somewhere here in Mexico City."

"We have Miguel's cell phone. I'm sure Uncle Ortiz is in here somewhere." He pulled out the phone and began going through the address book. "Bingo!" he said, turning the phone to show Catherine. "We got *Tio*'s home and *Tio*'s cell. These guys aren't worried about hiding. They don't think they have to. He'll be easy to find."

Catherine looked at him with a smile, but it turned into a worried curve of her lip after a moment. "What's wrong?" He asked. But he had an idea of what it may be from her expression, "Are you up for more of this? We can stop any time. Pass this along to someone else."

"Who?" she asked. Matt said nothing, only looked back at Miguel's blank stare. "Exactly," she said. "It's us or it's nobody." The idea that Arismendez had been sitting in Cancun this whole time was making Catherine's innards boil. And he'd just been left to carry out his business, murdering people left and right, untouched by anyone.

Matt turned back to meet her gaze. "Then it's us."

"Yeah," she said. "I guess so. But how the hell are we going to be able to keep this up?" She was daunted. Miguel was supposed to be the last link in the chain, but now they'd found out he was just a rung in a ladder that still kept going. She wasn't cut out for the running around killing people for more names to run around and kill. It was all starting to seem like a bloody road with no end. How long before a Mack truck bowled them over, just two more carcasses on this highway of death? Even if they did make it through, avoiding all the dangers involved, how long until she no longer recognized herself?

Matt put his hand out and cupped her chin, "We can do this," he told her. "If you want to keep going, I'm with you. But if you've gotten the answers you were looking for and are done, I'm with you there, too. We know who did it and we know why, now. That's something. It's a big something. I don't think anyone could ask more of you than what you've already done. And I don't think the Mexican government will look the other way if they find out Arismendez is the one who killed Taylor. They're not going to give up their tourism."

Catherine held her hand up to his and turned his hand over, kissing it affectionately. How thankful she was he was here. She thought for a moment and then said, "Nobody is asking me to keep going, but I just feel like I have to. I couldn't go back to my life knowing these people were out there despite what they've done. They can't get away with it," she decided.

Matt smiled at her warmly. "Then we won't let them."

Chapter 44

Yesenia had lain under the plastic kiddie pool for hours, scared that the moment she came out from under it Jose or Hector would be waiting for her. She had listened to the sound of vehicles in the alley and had heard people talking, but kept herself as quiet as the leaves of grass upon which she lay. Her terror and tears had exhausted her and for the space of but a few precious hours, she allowed herself to feel safe in her hideaway as though it were a fortress beneath a mountain, and had drifted to sleep somewhere along the way.

When she awoke several hours later it was well past midnight. She poked her head out and saw there was nothing but the night and a few ruthless mosquitoes around her. She crept out from underneath the child's play pool to see the yellow tape and masked outline of a body in the alley, a rusty Rorschach of bloodstain on the concrete. She'd heard the gunshots and the sound of a strange voice yelling something in English, but she did not know exactly what had happened. Did Jose and Hector kill someone else? Did someone kill them? That was too much to hope for. She walked towards the marked outline of body in white spray paint upon the dirt. *Someone did get killed,* she thought. She hoped it wasn't someone trying to help, someone else like Armando. She felt a hole rip in her gut at the very thought of him.

The emptiness around her reminded her that she was now alone. She had no one left to turn to, no place to go, and no one left who cared if she was alive or dead. They had murdered the one person who had tried to help her.

She walked between the shadows of the houses until she could see the little frame house where she'd been staying. The crime unit and police had left the house sealed with the yellow tape. *Armando,* she thought. *It's all my fault. I got him killed.* She couldn't stop the tears that came. She crossed her arms over her chest and pulled tightly into herself as she stared at the house. *It's all my fault.* She wiped her tears away angrily, like she'd done that night in the hot box. She was tired of crying, tired of being a victim. And at that moment she made up her mind. It was time Jose and Hector and Miss Lydia and all of them learned that she wasn't a scared little girl. Not anymore! She was going to see them pay.

She walked down the street of the quiet subdivision and out to the main road. She had considered walking to Armando's mother's house and getting Ricky, but she wouldn't know how to tell him what had just happened and how it was all her fault. She also didn't want to endanger him more than she already had. So she walked down to the same Shell station Jose had parked at the day before. Its door was locked but there was a woman behind the glass working the graveyard shift.

"*Hablas Espanol?*" Yesenia asked the woman.

"Yes, what do you need?" The woman responded in Spanish.

"Can you call the police for me?"

"The police? Is something the matter?" asked the woman.

"Yes. I witnessed a murder. Two murders, actually. A couple of bad men I know killed my friend tonight. They're also the ones who killed that policeman that's been on the news."

The woman behind the glass eyed Yesenia warily as she dialed 9-1-1.

Yesenia sat down on the curb to wait, her arms across her knees holding them close to her chest. She didn't care if she went to jail for being with them that night they killed the policeman. She didn't even care if they sent more people after her for calling the police. It was her turn to step up and do the right thing. Armando had done it for her and now she was going to do it for him . . . for all the girls Miss Lydia had turned into prostitutes, for the poor policeman they'd killed, and for herself. Her resignation to whatever fate would befall her filled her with a sense of calm. She no longer worried about what to do or what would happen. Ceci would be gone by now. So, now all she had to worry about was herself. And to Yesenia, that meant making sure to do the right thing while she was still able. What would happen then, only the stars knew, as she used to say in happier times.

Chapter 45

Catherine and Matt left Miguel in the rail car, still staring into the nothingness, and checked into a hotel. Both were exhausted and hadn't slept in nearly 30 hours. Catherine slept uncomfortably, having dreams of Taylor being assaulted, seeing the faces of the men she'd help kill in the last couple of days. When she woke in the middle of the night, she saw Matt was sleeping like a log. *How strange that someone can be so good, yet so comfortable with killing.* As she looked at him, she wished she could take back some of the past. *I didn't understand. How could anyone unless it happens to them?* She got up, dressed only in her nightshirt and underwear, and walked over to his bed, quietly slipping beneath the sheets.

He woke up, startled, "Catherine? What's wrong?"

She kissed him tenderly. "Nothing," she told him. "I just can't sleep."

He kissed her back, timidly at first, but then more passionately as he felt the warmth of her tongue caress his sweetly. He held her close and they made love, far more intimately than they ever did when they were dating those many years ago.

When they awoke late the next morning, they ordered up a lunch and Catherine called her office.

"Law office, how may I direct your call?" came the familiar friendly voice.

"Jenny, it's me."

"Catherine, thank God! I've been worried sick. Are you okay?"

"I'm fine. How are things there?" Her old business routine seemed a remnant of another life.

"They're going well. That guy from Petroconnex called for you. I told him you were on extended vacation, but he wouldn't talk to anyone else. He's really worked up about this deal, Catherine. Do you want his number?"

"No, not right now. He's just going to have to deal with it. I do need something, though. Can you run a number for me and find out whose it is and what address?" Ortiz may not feel the need to hide but something told Catherine she wouldn't just be able to stick in the phone number on an internet search and the guy's address would pop right up.

"Sure," Jenny said. "What's the number?"

"It's here in Mexico," Catherine said, reading off the number stored in Miguel's cell phone.

"When do you need it by?" she asked.

"As soon as possible," said Catherine. "Also dig me up whatever you can find on the guy, license picture, and bank accounts . . .

whatever. But make sure it's discreet. I don't want any red flags going up."

"Okay, I'll do what I can. You're being careful down there, right, Catherine?"

"Yes," she assured her friend. "I've got some protection with me."

"Good. I'm glad to hear that. I hope you hired some good guys."

Catherine smiled, "The best."

"Is there a number where I can reach you?"

She thought about it but decided it was best if they didn't know where she was at for the moment. She trusted Jenny entirely, but being that this was the cartel, there was no telling if they'd managed to have her office bugged or something along those lines. It was highly unlikely, but no point in an unnecessary risk, she told herself. "Actually, I'm going to be mobile for the next few hours," she said. "Why don't I call you back in about an hour?"

"Sure. Is there anything else?"

"No. Thanks, Jenny. I'll talk to you soon."

They hung up and Catherine began eating her lunch. Matt sat at the little table in their room drinking a beer and eating a po-boy sandwich. "You know getting to this Ortiz guy isn't going to be easy."

"I know," said Catherine.

"If he's head of even half the operation like Miguel said, he may have some seriously armed bodyguards."

"I made a promise to Taylor's parents. I didn't think we'd have all this to deal with, but it's not something I can let go. Besides, after hearing what these people did to that girl, what they did to Juan, also . . . . I couldn't just pack up and go home now, even if I wanted to."

"Are you going to tell them what happened? Her parents, I mean."

It was a question Catherine had already asked herself. "Not right now."

Matt took a long sip. "Then there's Arismendez."

"Yes," said Catherine. "And then there's him."

"He's going to have even more security, I'm thinking. We may need some help with him."

"But who?" she asked.

"I don't know yet. We'll just have to see what we're up against, but we'll figure that out after we deal with Ortiz."

"Okay," she agreed.

Chapter 46

Miss Lydia was in the middle of a furious tantrum. "How could you let this happen!?"

"I'm sorry, Mama," apologized Jose. "It happened so quickly. We would have had the girl if not for that crazy gringo with the shotgun. I don't know who he is but he came out of nowhere and got the drop on Hector."

"And where were you!?"

"I told you! I was getting the truck. The girl took off running and we couldn't catch up to her. She was like a deer the way she was running and jumping over fences. Rafa Marquez himself couldn't have caught her."

Miss Lydia rose up on her tip-toes and hit him on the head. Then she hit him again. And again. And again. Screaming at the top of her lungs, "Moron! *Pendejo!* How could you be so stupid!? Didn't I tell you how to do it! Must I do everything for you!?"

"Please, Mama, stop hitting me," he said with his arms deflecting the blows as best he could. "I'll find the girl, I swear."

"Don't be stupid!" she yelled at him. "Now she's seen you kill two people! What do you think she's going to do? Just dance back here and apologize and forget the whole thing? We had one chance! One chance to get that girl! And you blew it!" Jose said nothing as his mother boxed his ears with her cupped hand. "You've ruined everything!"

Finally she let her anger subside and quit pounding on her son. His thick skull had left her hand throbbing in rhythm to the vein that protruded from her forehead.

"I'm sorry, Mama," Jose said again, cowering in the face of his mother's wrath.

Miss Lydia eased herself back into her couch and suddenly a tender sadness came over her. "How many years have we been here? All this time and no trouble. Never once have the police driven past that gate," she scolded, pointing in the direction of the road. "Never once before now have we even had a girl get away from us like this. And now look." She dropped her bullish head between her shoulders as though she were going to cry. "Ruined. All ruined."

Jose sat on the coffee table across from her, hanging his head in shame. "Don't cry, Mama. I'm sorry."

"Sorry, sorry, sorry," she echoed. "What good is sorry now?"

He looked out the window and cracked his knuckles in anger at the girl that had caused all this. *If only I could get my hands on her,* he thought. "What do we do?" he asked.

She sighed deeply. "The only thing we can do. We leave."

"Leave?" he asked. "There must be some other way . . . "

"No!" she snapped. "You saw to that when you didn't do as I told you. That girl's out there now with enough information to ruin us all. If she opens her big mouth, we'll all die in prison. You have two murders on you, now. And me, well I'm an old woman. How do you expect your mother to survive in such a place?" He had no response. "And now you definitely have to get rid of that stupid Suburban you love so much. Painting it won't do any good this time. Get rid of it. We'll have to get us something else."

"Yes, Mama." Jose did as he was told. He drove the Suburban down an old country road that became a rutted trail, and then out into a nearby clearing while Arnulfo waited for him in his truck. Jose got out and took the two gallons of gasoline he had in the rear of the truck and doused the SUV. Then he stood back, lit a Molotov cocktail he'd brought, and chunked it at the Suburban, which went up like it was made out of papier mache.

Then Arnulfo drove them to a used car dealership called Amigo Auto Sales where they purchased a used truck under a false I.D. Miss Lydia had used for many years.

When they returned to the compound, Miss Lydia began putting things in motion. Catalina was looking out of the window and saw Jose pull the metal trailer around. "I wonder what they're going to do with that?" she asked Imelda.

While Jose and Arnulfo began packing only the essential things, Miss Lydia retreated to her office. She didn't know where she was going to go. She had close to two hundred thousand dollars in cash and wondered if she shouldn't just take it and retire back home to Mexico. Would there be consequences, though? She was a link in a chain of traffic. If the link breaks, so does the chain. There were powerful people who would be affected by recent events, people who might look to her for an explanation for their interrupted cash flow. Before she could even consider going back to Mexico, she needed to know what would be waiting for her. She picked up the phone and began dialing.

Chapter 47

Fernando Ortiz's phone number returned a match for an upscale home in San Angel, a once-quiet village which had been consumed by the behemoth city with cobblestone streets that was now called home by some of Mexico's most rich and famous. San Angel was a hodgepodge of the old and new. It had a lively night life, yet just down the street from some of the most exclusive nightclubs in Mexico City one might find El Carmen Monastery where the bodies of well-preserved nuns slept in the cellars. One side of the street might have an old world *hacienda*, while the other held a brand new mansion full of every conceivable amenity to satisfy even the most demanding of well-to-dos.

Catherine and Matt arrived and parked across the street from their target. Large, black wrought-iron gates stood before them, along with a security guard who sat in a small check-in station, not much larger than an outhouse. The home itself was like the suburb, a mixture of old and new. It was built in the *hacienda* style with stucco and stone, but one could tell it had been built in the last 10 years and the security cameras atop its walls displayed some of its modern technology.

"What do you think?" asked Catherine, discouraged.

"Difficult, but not impossible," said Matt. "There's a guard station there at the front and cameras at all four corners of the wall, probably covering all angles, but I think we can make entry there on the east side," he said, pointing. "My guess is he has a guard or two inside the wall, too, probably around back."

"What about the cameras?"

"Basic closed system. I need a digital video camera and we may be able to get around it." She marveled at how he could look at what she was seeing and think that gaining entry with anything less than a tank was even possible.

"And the security system? I'm sure he's got a good one."

"That's a little trickier. To be honest, we're not going to get around it. We don't have the equipment or the time we'd need to bypass a bunch of motion sensors. A twenty-dollar motion sensor is way harder to beat than security guards and cameras. I could get by the door or window contact, but not the motion sensor."

"Can we cut its power?"

"No, it'll all have a backup battery worth several hours, and the moment we tried it'd go off."

This is crazy, she thought, *we're never going to sneak in that place.* "So what do we do? Wait for him to leave and grab him while he's out somewhere?"

"Not necessarily. Going inside the house gives us a better chance of catching him alone and off guard. Assuming we don't set off any alarms, of course. I'd say our best bet is to get him during the day when he's home so the alarm system will be off. We just have to make sure we're not seen. This neighborhood probably has a significant police patrol. If someone spots us going over the wall, we'll be surrounded before we can get out. There's a big soccer game tomorrow afternoon, Mexico is playing Bolivia. It'll be the best time to try."

Rush the house in broad daylight? Catherine wouldn't even have considered it an option. Still, it made sense. Even if the system was activated, they'd at least have the motion sensors inside the house turned off . . . hopefully.

They went back to their hotel room and began making arrangements. Catherine called Patrick in Playa del Carmen and asked how Julio was doing. "Oh, he's fine," said Pat. "He and my boy are in there playing on the Playstation. He just loves that thing. Took to it like a fish to water. Leg's much better now, too. They get outside and start running around like little monkeys. He's gonna be fine."

"That's great, Pat. You all be safe, now."

"Same to you. No worries here, we're all doing just fine. He's a good kid."

"Yes, he is," she agreed.

Afterward, they went to an electronics store and Matt purchased a JVC digital camcorder with direct connection AV's, and a converter box.

Catherine had found a rental van that met the specs Matt suggested which they'd pick up the next morning and they'd also put in an order at a local sign shop. They returned to the *hacienda* in the afternoon, this time parking a few blocks down the street. "I'm just going to do a quick walk by," said Matt. "When I get a block past it, come pick me up." He got out and began casually walking down the street. If anyone took notice, they would probably have assumed he was just another *gringo* tourist enjoying the cobblestone roads or the shade of the leafy trees.

As he neared the first corner of the fence that surrounded Ortiz's lot, he pulled the small camcorder from his pocket and hit the record button. The security cameras on the lot looked inward to catch anyone who was entering over the fence rather than outward. This way, the entire interior of the lot was under surveillance at all times, but there was no visual on who was standing outside the wall. Matt slung the camera over his shoulder by its small strap, gave a quick glance around, and then, with a small jump and few quick upward motions, pulled his head up level with the ledge where the security camera sat. There he placed his little camcorder, dropped back to the ground, and continued walking.

When Catherine picked him up, she was a bit confused. "You're just going to leave it there? What if someone sees it?"

"It'll be okay," said Matt, nonchalantly. "I stuck it back a bit. It's got 10 hours of video time and an 80 hour battery, more than enough. We'll just need to grab it sometime tomorrow and charge it back up."

Trusting in Matt's experience, Catherine asked no further questions. They returned to the hotel, had a few drinks over a conversation about old times, trying to recall how many times they'd slept together, and then turned in for the night - but not before adding another one to the count.

The next day they picked up the van first. "This one's on me," Matt said, pulling out a credit card that read T.S., Inc. "Company card," he told Catherine. "For business use only," he laughed. He tried the card, but it was declined. "Oh. Well, crap. I guess I shouldn't be too surprised. I bet they're really pissed off at me right now for taking off."

Catherine smiled, "It's the thought that counts. Step aside, cowboy."

They returned to the mansion and repeated the process from the day before. Matt got out and walked down the street, suddenly jumping and pulling himself to the ledge after a quick look around, retrieved the camera, and then continued on his way. They stopped off at the sign place to pick up the magnet and two iron-on patches they'd ordered, having to pay through the nose for the short notice, and then a uniform supply store and purchased two matching uniforms, both a size too large for them, with matching caps. Then they visited a hardware store and purchased a ladder, tool belts, and miscellaneous tools.

"I'm never going to pull this off," she told him, looking at the uniform. "This will look ridiculous on me." Her stomach was full of butterflies . . . or more like hairy gray moths with stubby, prickly legs crawling in her insides, trying to dig a way out, if she'd been asked to describe it. *We're going to stick out like sore thumbs.*

"Don't worry about it," he told her. "If anybody says anything to us, I'll do the talking."

Lastly, they went to another security supply store, something not all too uncommon in Mexico City, and purchased two flak jackets. The man behind the counter eyed them curiously. "You try being a *gringo* in this city," Matt told the man, which made Catherine smirk.

They had lunch at the hotel while the camera recharged. "You really think nobody's going to say anything if we put a ladder against the wall and start messing with the security system?" asked Catherine after Matt explained what they were going to do.

"You'd be amazed by the power of uniforms," he told her. "People just assume you're supposed to be there doing whatever you're doing when you're wearing a uniform. And hardly anybody pays attention to maintenance people in these upscale neighborhoods." Catherine lived in a pretty upscale condo herself back in Dallas and had to admit, she never thought twice about the comings and goings of the various maintenance people in the building. She'd pay more attention in the future, she decided. Assuming they had a future, she also reminded herself.

Matt ironed the patches onto the uniforms. The custom patches read "Alusa", the name of a local security company whose decals they'd copied exactly. He smiled at Catherine while he worked.

"What?" she asked, defensively. "I told you I don't iron. I don't even do my own laundry for Christ's sake. That's why God invented dry cleaners. If someone wants their corporation's contract looked over, I'm your girl. But if they want their clothes done or dinner made, best to look elsewhere."

"No problem," he said. "I like to do some cooking, if you remember." She did. And he was pretty good at it.

The magnetic sign was a matching logo to stick on the van.

When the camera was fully recharged, they donned their flak jackets and pulled the uniforms up over them. Catherine kept shifting the vest and trying to get the uniform to look just right. "I don't think they make these things for women," she said about the vest. Matt just grinned. He wasn't too keen on having Catherine in harm's way, but she was his only support and he couldn't ask for a better backup. He still had his duffle bag with his arsenal, supplemented now by Miguel's additions.

As they made their way through the lobby of their hotel, Catherine was amazed to see that nobody gave them a second look despite the fact she thought they must look entirely conspicuous. "I told you," Matt said, not bothering to whisper. "Uniforms."

They pulled the van right up to Ortiz's lot and got out, carrying the ladder and a couple of toolboxes, along with Matt's electronics and weapons. Catherine was nervously looking about, but Matt was whistling as though he was just enjoying the day on his way to work. They set the ladder against the wall and Matt climbed up. Catherine handed him the camcorder and converter box, and Matt began splicing the wires of their camera into the wiring of the existing system.

He was just hooking up the converter box when a police car pulled up slowly to the curb. Catherine tried to look nonchalant, but she felt sure they'd just been busted. *Oh shit, oh shit, oh shit,* went her thoughts.

"*Que paso?*" asked one of the officers.

Matt looked down with a smile as though he hadn't a care in the world and told them in perfect Spanish, "Stupid camera acting up again. Don't worry, though. We're going to fix it up right this time. Going to put a brand new one in, shouldn't have any more problems."

The officers glanced at each other in the car. *They're never going to buy that,* thought Catherine. But then, with a smile and a wave, they drove away. Catherine's heart was racing ninety miles an hour. *That was too close,* she thought. Matt just kept whistling while he worked. "Easy, Catherine," he told her in a low voice. "You're looking too nervous. That's a dead giveaway."

"They didn't think it strange neither of us are Mexican?" she asked. Matt, she could almost understand, with is tanned skin, dark stubble, and mop of dark hair. But she didn't look a bit like a local.

"It's all about walking the walk and talking the talk."

Having connected the converter box, he screwed the original camera back in place, but this time it wasn't connected to the system. He then turned on their video camera, which was playing a recording of the day before, and flipped the switch on the converter box while quickly fastening his spliced wires together. "There," he said. "Now they're watching yesterday." Luckily the weather hadn't changed in twenty-four hours, which could have caused a delay in their plan. He looked around the lot and all was quiet. "We're good to go," he told Catherine, and then quickly scrambled over the wall. Catherine gave a quick look around and then followed up the ladder. When she reached the top ledge, she pulled the ladder up behind her and handed it down to Matt before dropping down herself.

"Here," said Matt, handing her one of the Glocks, which he'd kept in the fake toolbox he had. "I've got the silencer, so I shoot first if we have to."

"What about the Browning?"

"No, I don't think a .22 is going to cut it. The Glock may be loud but it'll get the job done if you have to use it. But if we get in a scrape let me take the first shots."

"I'm fine with that," said Catherine.

They crept through the lot toward the east side of the house, and thankfully no alarms went off. Matt quickly set up the ladder and scaled it to the second roof, Catherine just behind him. This was where they were most vulnerable. Looking down towards the front, Catherine could see the security guard's little station, which meant if whoever was inside looked out the window towards the roof, they'd be seen. She needn't have worried, though. Inside the little station, the security guard was watching the soccer match. He was joined by Ortiz's other two bodyguards who were supposed to be watching the house, but had snuck away for the game. The three men sat smoking and cheering the Mexican team.

Matt and Catherine made their way to a nearby window, their feet stable over concrete roof tiles, designed to look like old clay tiles but much thicker and heavier. Catherine had worried a tile would come loose and fall crashing to the ground giving them away, but they didn't budge.

Matt worked quickly with his knife, prying and then cutting the window's lock away. He held his breath as he slid it open and he gave Catherine a slight smile when no alarms were heard. They looked towards the guard's station to see if anyone was coming out, possibly being notified by a central monitor, but nobody exited.

"It could be a silent alarm," he warned her. "But I think we're okay."

Once inside, they made their way out of a bedroom most likely used by one of the guards, given its messy condition, and entered a long hall, checking each door as they passed to see if anyone was about. When they were sure nobody was upstairs, they descended down the long stairway. Oil paintings lined their descent, a *hacienda* in an old world village, another artist's rendition of The Man with the Golden Helmet, and another of horses drinking from a river.

As they neared the bottom of the stairwell, they heard a television emitting a play-by-play of the game. Ortiz was watching the game in his study. As they approached they heard him on the phone, "I don't need these problems, Lydia! I have problems of my own. This is one of the reasons why I'm sick of messing with this business with the girls." The voice paused as if listening. "Well, your livelihood has put mine at risk. And I don't appreciate that, Lydia, not one little bit. Your girls are a drop in the bucket. And you had better remember that I have people to answer to as well. What am I to tell them? That I can't send them their product because you lost one of your little prostitutes?" Matt gestured toward a doorway off to the right of the stairwell. It led into the study where the voice was coming from. "I'm well aware of that, Lydia, and yes, you have always been reliable. That's the only reason I agreed to help you with your business in the first place. I found quite a few girls for you over the years, have I not? And all I asked in return is that you get our goods delivered to the right people on time. Is that too much to ask!?" His voice suddenly became angry. "Yes, and that was your stupid son's fault! He panicked! What am I to do with you? You can't control your son, you can't control your girls . . . you're putting me in a very difficult position, Lydia!"

Matt and Catherine entered through the door of the study. There at the desk sat Ortiz, leaning back in his chair watching the game on a 47" hi-def LCD mounted to the wall. He looked up in surprise and said, "What is this? Who are you?" Matt put his finger to his lips and gestured for Ortiz to hang up. Suddenly, it dawned on Ortiz that he was in serious trouble. His eyes seemed to fall in surrender. "You're on your own, Lydia. I have bigger problems at the moment." He hung up the phone.

"That's a bit of an understatement," Matt suggested.

"You are Fernando Ortiz?" asked Catherine.

"I am," he said, slowly turning his chair a bit. "And who, may I ask, are you?" He spoke cordially as if at a business meeting, but slowly his hand began drifting towards the edge of the desk.

"Keep your hand on that desk or I'll blow your fucking head off right now," said Matt. He quickly maneuvered around the desk and pulled Ortiz's chair away from it. On the underside of the desk was a panic button for the alarm system.

"I have no weapons," said Ortiz. "I'm completely unarmed."

"Be glad you are," said Matt, "or you wouldn't be breathing."

"May I ask what this is about?"

"It's about Taylor Woodall," said Catherine.

Ortiz's heart seemed to stop in his chest, his eyes wide. Then he took a long sigh. He looked, for a moment, as if though he was going to try to claim ignorance as Miguel had, but then something changed. "I received a phone call that my nephew was missing. Police found the guard from his place tied up in a closet. Do you know something of this?"

"We do," said Matt.

"Is he dead?" Ortiz asked, flatly.

"He is," said Catherine.

He dropped his head. "I see. And I suppose I'm next?"

"That remains to be seen," said Catherine.

"Who are you, if I may ask? Who are you working for?"

"Taylor Woodall," said Catherine. "You know, it's funny. Your nephew asked that same question."

"I see. So the girl's family hired you?"

"Something like that," said Matt. "But let's just say we have a personal interest in the matter. You're safe to assume you shouldn't have killed that girl."

"I understand your anger," he began.

"You understand nothing," interrupted Catherine. "Don't think for a moment you can apologize for what you've done. Nothing you can say will undo what happened to that girl. Nothing will bring her back or end the grief her parents are going through right now. We're not here to listen to any more excuses."

"You're right, of course," he said. "I truly regret what happened to Miss Woodall. I can assure you I had no idea of what was to befall her."

"We've already heard this story," she told him.

He nodded. "Yes, Miguel. I'm sure he would have told you the truth. You may not believe this, but I am not the man at the top of the food chain. The man who killed that girl enjoys that pleasure and we had no clue he was going to do what he did. We would not have indulged him if we knew."

"You stood by while he raped and murdered Taylor Woodall," said Catherine. "You might as well have done it yourself."

"So Miguel has told you what happened that night? We didn't know, as I've said. We were outside with our drinks and conversation. We figured he'd have his way with her and we'd drop the girl off somewhere. She'd have a sad story, yes, but alive, safe and sound. We couldn't have known."

"Safe and sound? Are you kidding, you sick bastard?"

"Did Miguel tell you why he took the girl? It wasn't at my direction."

"I had to shoot his kneecaps off, but yeah, he talked," said Matt. "And if I recall, he said it was at your direction. Arismendez told you, and you told Miguel."

Ortiz cringed. "Please. He was my dear sister's son. I understand that what's done is done, but please, I do not wish to hear of his suffering. I'm sure you understand," he added, looking at Catherine.

"You don't have my sympathy," Catherine responded.

"Nor do I ask any. I merely ask that you refrain from celebrating his murder while we talk," his said loftily with an air of self-importance.

"Shut the hell up, you pompous ass," said Catherine. "Who are you to talk about murder?" She cut to the chase. "You're going to pay for what you did, but first you're going to tell us what you know about Arismendez."

"Ah, Arismendez," he said with a look of disdain. "Okay, I'll tell you what I know. I'll give you all the information you want about him. But first, I'd like to propose a deal. I have a floor safe hidden in that bookshelf," he said, pointing to the wall unit behind him. "In it, I have my files and half a million dollars in cash, American, of course."

"We don't want your money," said Catherine.

"You're not buying your way out with us," added Matt.

He raised his hand, "Please, hear me out. I understand that you have a personal interest in this matter beyond money. What I am proposing is to trade my life for information."

"What sort of information?" asked Catherine.

"If you allow me to live," said Ortiz, "I'll give you everything you want to know about Arismendez . . . where he lives, the layout of his place, his security, even where he likes to go and what restaurants and bars he likes to frequent, everything you'll need to get close enough to kill him. And you will need my information to get close enough, I assure you. He's a very cautious man and his bodyguards are much more numerous and attentive than the idiots I've apparently hired. Additionally, I'll also give you several other lives."

"Lives? What lives?" asked Matt skeptically.

"I have intimate knowledge of close to two dozen young women working as sex slaves in the United States. I know who they are and I know where they are. Allow me to live, and I'll give you their information." Catherine and Matt exchanged glances. "Think of it," said Ortiz. "These girls are the same age as Taylor Woodall, some as young as sixteen. Right now they are locked away in hidden places all across the U.S., forced to live under terrible circumstances, raped night after night, sold for a few measly dollars to anyone who'll pay. It's too late for any of us to save Miss Woodall, but you can save others."

"Who are they?" asked Catherine, angered by this new turn of events and the prospect Ortiz might actually have a viable bargaining chip.

"They're just girls," he told him. "Girls who, for one reason or another, gave everything up here to try and find a life in America. But once they get there, they were forced into slavery."

"Forced by you!" she said, angrily.

Ortiz was unfazed. "I do not deny I have had a small role in this. I merely connect them with the people who run such places. These are desperate girls who'll do anything to get across the border. I'm a business man. I merely supply when there is a demand, no more, no less."

"And how much do you sell them for?" asked Catherine, indignant.

"A pittance, I assure you. Many of the brothels are located in places we use as transit stations for the drug traffic. That is my true business, ma'am, as I'm sure you've guessed by now. It is by mere coincidence it has brought me in connection with flesh peddlers." He spoke as if though he were equally disgusted by them, a farce that only angered Catherine further. "I was speaking to one such operator when you entered. As we speak, a young woman who ran away from one such place is now running for her life. If I'm killed these people will track down this girl and kill her, I promise you this. She will suffer the same fate as Taylor Woodall did, worse even. The only thing that can save her is the information I can give to you. It's your choice. You can do for her what you couldn't do for the American girl. Save her. You can save all of them. All you have to do is let me live. Hand me over to the authorities. My life spared to save others. Surely you can see the logic in it."

"Authorities . . . a lot of good that will do," she said.

"I can write out a full confession right now. I won't be able to buy my way out if they have a confession, not with the world watching. I'll do my time. But I'd rather live in a prison than die here, now. Spare me and I will help you. That's a small price in the grander picture, isn't it? And besides, it's not me you want, anyway. It's Arismendez. I am clearly the lesser of two evils."

Ortiz rose from his chair. Matt tensed and held the gun on him, but Ortiz didn't advance. "Think of these young women," his eyes locked on Catherine. "Think of how you would feel if you knew Taylor Woodall was still alive somewhere, being forced upon night after night. Isn't it worth letting me live to save those girls? One life for a dozen. I'll give you everything . . . the money, the information in my safe - which includes a list of every individual we have in our pocket, from the police, to judges, mayors, you name it. It's all in there. And I'll tell you how to find the girls. There is no other way without what I can tell you. And I'll help you get Arismendez. I'll give him to you on a silver platter. He's no friend of mine and I certainly don't want to die for his actions. It's he who deserves your retribution. My people would never have done that to that girl. I'd be happy to see him pay for his crime. If I'm lying, you can always kill me later. You're obviously quite capable."

Catherine weighed the man's words. He spoke of trading the girls' lives as though trading in a car. Still, he was smooth. And he was right in that the information he had did have significant value.

"He's probably lying," said Matt.

"I'm not," said Ortiz, still looking directly at Catherine. "I think you know that already." If there was a soft spot to be found, Ortiz had quickly surmised it would be with her. "If you'll give me your word that you'll allow me to live, I'll give you some of the information this very moment."

Catherine considered the deal. "Okay," she said at last. "If your information is accurate, we'll let you live."

"I have your word?"

"You do." Matt looked at her in frustration, but he could tell by her tone she'd already made up her mind.

"Okay," he said. "As that is all I am able to ask for at the moment, I will trust you to keep it. And I will uphold my end," he said pointing to where the floor safe hid. He looked to Matt who motioned him and then he went to the wall unit and opened a door at the bottom. Matt kept his gun on him the entire time.

Ortiz removed a false bottom from the cabinet and there below it was a large floor safe mounted into the very foundation of the house. He turned the dial around, left, right, and then left again, and opened it.

"Move," said Matt, pushing Ortiz against the wall. He leaned over and inspected the contents, making sure there were no hidden weapons. "Looks clear," he told Catherine.

Catherine moved forward and while Matt kept Ortiz covered, she began emptying out the contents of the safe. First came a large leather binder, full of papers. "Those are my records," said Ortiz. "You can find the name and information for each girl in there, but I'm afraid their location is not included. You'll need me for that." Next came stacks of cash, tightly-wrapped American hundred-dollar bills. Catherine began to realize how deep the safe was as her arm kept reaching lower and lower to remove the piles of money. "Four hundred and seventy thousand, I believe," said Ortiz. "Last time I counted, anyway."

The final item to emerge was a small coin bag, but it wasn't heavy enough to be filled with coins. "And this?" asked Catherine. "Cocaine?"

"Diamonds," he answered. "About a quarter million dollars' worth, good for transporting large sums without the need for bulky cash. The highest quality."

Catherine sat on the floor and began thumbing through the brown binder. It was divided into sections. The thickest appeared to be transactions between Ortiz and Arismendez. Numbers scrolled down the pages. "The dates, quantities, and amount of money exchanged," said Ortiz helpfully. Catherine's eyes paused as she saw one of the most recent entries. *H. Vargas. Thank God it doesn't say Ramirez,* she thought. "Ah, yes, Detective Vargas," Ortiz offered, seeing where her finger rested on the page, "Arismendez had me deal with him, as you can see. He called it a cost of doing business." Catherine had been infused with doubt about Ramirez ever since she'd been followed back to the hotel after their meeting, but now she was satisfied. He'd probably been telling the truth about Juanita and Anna. She decided it might be a needed break. She needed someone local to trust and it would have to be Ramirez.

She flipped to another section, which contained one-page summaries of information on the girls. It had their names, ages, family members' names, addresses, and amounts. At anywhere from two to three thousand per girl average, Ortiz was correct that the drugs were his primary income. Catherine felt flush with anger as she read through the names. Marissa, Silvia, Erika, Yesenia, Lucia, the names went one and on, twenty-seven of them now scattered from Texas to Georgia, and all the way up to New Jersey. "You can help each and every one of them," said Ortiz. "We can help them together."

Catherine held the ledger in her hand and thought about her options. What could they do with Ortiz? If they turned him in, he'd only beat the system. She knew any confession he wrote wouldn't be worth the paper it was written on. He'd say he was under duress, for fear of his life, and it'd be tossed in the garbage. That's if it even went that far. More than likely he'd pay someone off and the charges would be dismissed before he spent so much as a night in jail. If he had this much in his floor safe, he surely had more hiding in accounts somewhere in the world. So what if he did actually make it to a trial? He'd find a way to use his resources to beat the charges. Plus, he had a gang on call. If he couldn't bribe or pay off a judge or jury, he could have them threatened or killed. But if Matt killed him now, what would become of these girls? She cursed the predicament. If they let him go now, they'd never get close again. And if they called the police, they'd be the ones arrested. But there were the girls to think about. And there was still the matter of Arismendez. She looked at Matt for help.

"There's no question," he told her, understanding completely what was going through her mind. "You know that."

She nodded.

Ortiz had seen the look between them and watched Matt raise the gun, "Wait!" he cried, the silver tongue suddenly sounding like a rusty hinge on an old fence about to fall off. "We had a deal. I have your word!" he yelled in anger, "And what about Arismendez?"

"We'll figure it out," said Matt. "We're pretty good at that."

"But the girls? What of them? Are you going to just leave them to their suffering? Your word! You gave me *your word*!"

"No," said Catherine. "We'll look for them, I assure you. But, we'll do it without you. The best thing we can do for those girls right now is to make sure you're out of their lives permanently. And make sure you don't make this list any longer than it already is."

"But, your word . . . ." Ortiz said again, his mind spinning for something, anything, else to offer.

"On any other day it would be true," she said. "But not today . . . not with someone like you. Oh, you may find this interesting. That's the same gun your nephew used on Taylor when you told him to make sure she was dead," added Catherine.

Matt couldn't resist. He smiled at Ortiz. *I like this new Catherine*, he thought.

"Wait, please, let's . . . "

"Let's not," said Matt, pulling the trigger. A small hole punched through Ortiz's head right between his eyes and he stumbled backward, falling into the bookshelves.

Catherine and Matt stood for a moment looking at Ortiz's body. She thought again about the slippery slope. "I'm losing it, Matt," she said. "That was too easy." She looked into Matt's eyes. "I wanted to see him die. I don't think that's a good thing."

He put his hand at the back of her neck, "Maybe not, but it's a natural thing given what he is, what he's done. There's only one more to go, Catherine. But it's your call." He thought about killing the men in the jungle so long ago. "I'm already who I am, but you don't have to go down this road."

She sighed. "No, let's finish it. This isn't about me. It's about Taylor, and Juan," she held up the notebook, "these girls somewhere out there, and everyone else who's suffered or would suffer because of people like this. There's one more out there. I can't call it quits until I know he's not out there anymore."

"Okay," said Matt. "I'm with you all the way." They sneaked out the back, eyes darting left and right for any guards, but the game was still playing and Mexico was winning. Both were relieved to not find a SWAT team waiting for them as they made their way back to the fence. The streets were quiet as the *Alusa* security van drove away.

When they returned to the hotel, Catherine called Ramirez and told him what they'd learned so far; leaving out the coercive measures they used to garner such information. Ramirez was understandably shocked. "Arismendez!? Yes, I know of this man, but I would never have imagined his involvement. He's well known in Cancun. He runs several businesses, though I confess I heard rumors that he pays large sums to the cartel. Still, I never thought he was one of them."

"Not just one of them," said Catherine. "He's at the top of the food chain."

"He has bodyguards and security which includes off-duty officers he hires on the side. I know people who work for this man . . . people I consider friends. But that's not terribly unusual for someone of wealth in Mexico. I just assumed he was a successful, but legitimate, businessman. How did you learn all this?"

"I'm afraid I can't share that with you. You wouldn't want to know, anyway. It'd probably place you in a difficult position. Let's just say a measure of justice has been dealt out to those who might otherwise not receive it."

"I see. Well, it's going to require some significant evidence before my superiors will allow me to arrest Arismendez."

"We'll be returning to Cancun shortly and I have something to give you, a ledger of sorts. I think it will be enough to convince your superiors. Ortiz seems to have kept track of everything in it, including all his transactions with Arismendez. There's something you should know," she said. "Miguel told us a police officer in Cancun turned over the missing homeless boy, Juan, to the Barrio Boys. I figured it was Vargas but wasn't sure until I saw his name in the ledger. Ortiz paid him twenty five thousand dollars recently."

There was a pause on the other end of the phone as Ramirez thought about this news. He lowered his head in sadness. He had long suspected improprieties, but this was almost too much to believe. "Are you certain?" he asked. *What have you done, Hernando? And how did I not see?*

"There's an entry the same week I met you in your office. H. Vargas. $25,000. You do the math," said Catherine.

"I just can't believe he would do such a thing," said Ramirez. "He's an ambitious man, but to kill a witness . . . a child, no less. I find it hard to believe."

"Believe it," said Catherine. "And you know he has to be held accountable."

"I know," he said, still shocked. "It shall be handled. I must make certain of his role, but if he is guilty, he shall pay for his crime."

"We're going to need your help, Detective. I know you may have your hands tied, but I think you may be one of the good guys. There are not enough of us right now. We need more good guys. Can you help?" She wouldn't have been surprised if he declined. What she was asking for could likely end up with Ramirez's head on the steps of the police station. It'd happened before. But Ramirez *was* one of the good guys. And he was tired of the bad guys killing off the good guys and getting away with it.

"I will help," he said. "But Arismendez has better security than most governors. We will need assistance and I'm not sure who I can call about this. I'll have to do some thinking. We can talk about it when you get here."

"Be careful," she told him. "We'll see you soon."

Chapter 48

Yesenia sat at the Dallas Police Department's downtown office retelling her story. "And you say you saw, with your own two eyes, this man Jose shoot Trooper Daniel Shoal on the evening of April the third?"

"Yes," she told him again. "I saw him do it." In the corner of the room, a video camera was recording every word and gesture she made. Across from her sat Detective John Zuniga, an 18 year veteran of the force who had been assigned for both his proficiency in Spanish and his way of handling both suspects and victims with respect and sympathy, earning their trust.

"Now Yesenia," said Zuniga. "Tell me again how you ended up at this compound you were telling us about. You said it all started with a flier you had seen in Mexico City?"

"Yes," she told him. "It's all a big trick. They promise you a job, a place to stay, but it's all lies."

"Tell us more, Yesenia. What did they do to you?"

The tears came down her face as she spoke. She relived the entire nightmare from its beginning. She talked about her conversation with Ortiz who she met through the man from the flier. Then she told them of her trip to Texas. She told them about the coyotes and how they were ready to let the little boy die at the river to save their drugs. She told them about being locked in the cargo truck for the long drive to Houston, and then about Jose shooting the trooper on the trip north to Dallas. She even told them about Miss Lydia, the compound, and about being raped by the crazy man known only as The Mechanic.

With each word she spoke she felt a great weight being lifted from her shoulders. She let the words flow like the Nigales River back home. She talked about how Armando had helped her run away, but then Jose and Hector had somehow found them and been waiting inside the house. Lastly, she told them how they gunned him down as he told her to run. "He saved my life," she said. "Twice, really. He saved me twice."

By the time she finished, Zuniga was leaning over the table hanging on her every word. Finally he spoke, "You're a brave young woman, Yesenia. You just wait here. I'm going to talk with my colleagues for a few minutes."

Outside of the little room, Zuniga stood repeating Yesenia's story in English for his captain. "What do you think?" asked his superior when he was done summarizing.

"I think she's telling the truth," said the detective. "Look at her." They could see Yesenia crying on the little monitor. "I think every word she told me was true."

"Get a map and have her show you where that compound is," said the captain. "We'll get started on a warrant."

Yesenia was taken into protective custody and after she pointed out on a map about where she thought the little compound was, the police handed the information over to the Dallas SWAT team.

"They're going to raid the compound tomorrow," explained Zuniga. "We'll take you to a safe place tonight, but tomorrow they might need your help."

"Of course," she told him. "Did anybody call Ricky?" She wondered if he knew about Armando's death and how he and his mother were doing.

"Yes," he told her. "He took it hard, of course, but we've got some good folks with them. We'll take care of them best we can."

Yesenia spent the night in a solitary confinement cell. "It's just until we can figure something else out for you, but in the meantime, if you need anything at all, just knock on the door." Zuniga ordered a pizza and a 2-liter of coke and gave Yesenia what magazines they had lying around. She fell asleep with a *Cosmopolitan* open on her lap, the colorful pictures of glamorous stars smiling up at her as she dozed off, a promise of the America she'd only heard about, and not at all the one she'd found. She slept that way, tomato sauce still on her fingers.

The next morning she was greeted by Zuniga, who had brought her a fresh change of clothes, the tags still on them, along with a new hairbrush, toothbrush, toothpaste, and dental floss. "I hope it fits," he said, handing the bundle over to her, "Courtesy of the Dallas Police Department. I'm afraid you'll have to do without a shower until this evening, but I promise better lodgings for you tonight."

Yesenia changed her clothes and brushed her teeth and was soon standing in a room surrounded by police and detectives, her nerves vibrating as everyone seemed to be following her lead. She stood looking down at an aerial photograph of Miss Lydia's compound with a sergeant from the Swat team. "We took this photo this morning with our helicopter," he told her. "Now, what I need you to do is to point out which mobile homes have the other girls, and which one we're likely to encounter the armed men you told us about."

She pointed on the map, but as she stared at it she looked at the photo and realized something was wrong. "It's missing," she told him.

"What's missing?" asked the officer.

"The trailer - Miss Lydia's hot box. It was here," she pointed on the photo where the trailer once stood, now nothing but a big brown patch in the grass.

"What was in the trailer?" he asked.

"Nothing. It was where she sent us if we misbehaved. She would lock us inside."

"Okay, let's not worry about it for right now. Now, what else can you tell me about this compound? Is this fence here electric?" Yesenia told him all she knew of the compound and those inside of it. She made sure to mention the two Rottweillers. "Do you know how many guns they have or what type of other weapons may be present?"

"I don't know," she told him. "I just know they have guns. I'm not sure how many, though. I'm sorry. You'll make sure none of my friends are hurt, won't you? And the one man, Arnulfo, he really didn't seem like that bad of a man, I guess. He kind of tried to be nice."

"It's okay," he told her, marveling at how a young woman like Yesenia could go through the hell she'd been through yet maintain such a selfless disposition. "We will make every opportunity to keep your friends safe. And, as for Arnulfo, as long as he doesn't try to hurt any of the officers and does what we say, he'll be fine. If he doesn't, well that's another story. We have to keep our officers safe, you understand."

Things seemed to happen quickly after that. Yesenia sat in the police station as the Dallas SWAT team geared up for their charge. They had rented a hotel room for her, but she felt safer in the police station, at least for the moment. The anxiety of what would happen began to make her stomach churn like a lava lamp. She worried for the girls. She thought about Armando, and what Jose and Hector had done to him. She kept seeing images of the dead - Armando and the trooper Jose had shot that first night. She didn't want anyone else to die. She just wanted it all to be over and to never see such violence again. While she sat wondering what was happening, the police were moving in.

The SWAT team had two armored vehicles, which they planned on strategically placing near the compound. Several vehicles, including the armored ones, approached the compound, and at the order of the sergeant, the lead armored vehicle crashed through the gate. Inside, a police officer scanned for activity while the vehicles rushed in. The dogs came running towards them immediately and barked and growled at the vehicles, not entirely sure what to do about so many unfamiliar intruders.

When they reached the mobile homes, one officer rose up on the turret ready to fire upon any hostiles. The other SWAT members began to pile out of their vehicles with guns drawn. *Chico* made the unfortunate mistake of trying to attack the strange men and was put down immediately in a hail of gunfire, scaring the other dog so much it ran away as fast as its legs could carry it. Then the officers kicked in the door to the mobile home where Jose, Arnulfo, and Hector had stayed. They found it empty.

Next they kicked in Miss Lydia's door, and it, too, was empty. "Clear!" they yelled, going from room to room and then on to the next mobile home. In a matter of minutes, they confirmed that the compound had been evacuated. Not a soul remained.

"Damn it," said Zuniga. "They knew we were coming." He scolded himself for not acting sooner, but he had needed time to get the warrant and set up the strike.

When they returned to the police station he questioned Yesenia. "Do you have any idea where they might try to go?"

"No," she said worriedly. "What about the other girls?"

"Gone," he told her. "They've all left."

Yesenia sat wondering what had happened. Would Miss Lydia take Silvia and the others, and just set up shop somewhere else? Or maybe it was worse than that. What if they had killed the other girls because of her? She couldn't help but to think it would be all her fault for running away. *Oh, Silvia. What have I done?*

Chapter 49

Catherine and Matt decided they'd return to Cancun in a bit more style. They used ten thousand dollars of Ortiz's money to rent a Cessna XLS, a state of the art jet worlds apart from the single engine 70s-era Cessna they'd arrived in. "I'm probably going to need some of this cash to pay for the rental cars we've damaged," she told Matt.

"Yeah, and I may need to reimburse my company for the trip up here. I'm sure they're good and well pissed off at me at the moment."

Before they left she called Jim. She left out all the gory details, but told him everything else, including who had kidnapped Taylor, why they'd picked her, and most importantly, that Victor Arismendez was the man who murdered her. She preferred to wait until it was over, but there was the chance she and Matt might come to an unfortunate end, and if that should happen, Jim deserved to know who had taken his daughter's life. She could only wonder how unbelievable this sounded to Jim. She could hardly believe it herself as she heard the story unravel from her lips.

"It was completely random, Jim. There was nothing more to it than she was the prettiest girl in the place." She wondered if it was of any comfort to him. Probably not. "We're about to head back to Cancun now," she told him, staring out the car's window at the sleek jet waiting for them. "I'm not entirely sure what our next step is, but we're going to get the guy. He may think he's untouchable but we'll get him, I promise . . . even if we have to hire our own private army. We've got the means to do it at the moment thanks to Ortiz."

"I can help," Jim said. "I can call up the news and tell them everything you just told me. They'll have to take action if the world knows it was him."

"No, don't do that," she said, concerned. "He'll run. And if he runs we may never get him. He may end up in some village in Peru nobody has ever heard of, or worse yet, Venezuela. We'd never get him. No, just let us figure it out. We'll get down there and assess the situation. I know it's tough, Jim, but I just need a little more time."

"Okay, but I can't just sit here. Wait," he said. "I can contact people here, the governor's office, maybe. Hell, I can probably get him on the phone personally, he was at the funeral. If I explain to him what you just told me, maybe he can help. Our government can put pressure on theirs - quietly, though, no media."

"Maybe," she said. She didn't like the idea of involving any Mexican government officials considering there was no telling if someone would tip off Arismendez, but she knew he was going to be a lot harder to get to than Ortiz. "Try the governor's office, then," she decided. "But be careful who you talk to and what you say. They need to understand just how well connected this guy is down here. If someone tips him off, we'll likely never catch the guy."

"I will," said Jim.

As she hung up the phone, Matt escorted her to the plane, "Your chariot awaits."

Once on board, he tossed her a Coke. "The governor, huh? I'm not so sure about that one. We may end up on the wrong side of that call. We've left a mess of a trail lately, if you recall. They might be sympathetic to the cause, but we're well outside of legal parameters."

"I know," she said, the newly-departed Ortiz still fresh in her mind. The thought made her queasy. She popped the top of the soda can and took a sip. "You've been amazing. More than amazing. But we need help, Matt. We can't keep running around like a couple of vigilantes, not with this guy. There are some good people around, but they're scared. We need to light a fire, something to bring them together and take this guy off the streets."

"That's awfully optimistic." He smirked.

She smiled. "I know what you're thinking. Maybe it is naïve, but I'm a believer, Matt. I think I understand now that sometimes doing the right thing means getting dirty. But at some point people have to get out of the bloody mud pit and stand on their principles. It's not okay for so-called civilized people to turn a blind eye to people like Arismendez. If they do, more like him will keep coming, keep kidnapping people for ransom, keep killing innocent people in a crowd without the least bit of fear. Did you hear the story about the cartel in Sinoloa? They skinned a man's face off, stitched it to a soccer ball, and left it on the steps of city hall."

"No," said Matt. "I can't say I'm surprised, but no, I didn't know that."

"They were making him an example," she said. "And that's the point, Matt. They're winning because they're setting the bigger, scarier example. We need to do something else here. Even if we could get to Arismendez by ourselves, the greater good here is for those who are supposed to be protecting people from someone like Arismendez to actually stand up and do it. Otherwise, who's going to stop them? You and I are just two people. We're lucky we haven't been killed already in all this. There has to be a reckoning for these killers, Matt. There's no stopping them if they think society can be kowtowed against standing up to them."

"So you want to make an example out of Arismendez?" he asked.

"If it's possible, yes. I want the world to see there are good people here that are willing to stand up and say enough is enough."

Matt leaned back, contemplating. "It's not a perfect world, Catherine."

"I know," she said, looking back out the window. "Believe me, I know."

"Well, it may be a little naïve, Catherine, but I still admire you for it. I can't say as though I agree with you, but part of me wishes I did." The jet's engines roared as they raced down the runway and then lifted up into the sky.

Chapter 50

Around 11:00 that morning Zuniga got a call from a small auto dealership in the Dallas area. "We got this sheet you faxed over about the people you're looking for."

"Yes? Have you seen them?"

"Yes, sir. Two of them, at least. We sold them a truck the other day." The fax had been sitting on the dealership's machine and the manager had grabbed it and was ready to throw it in the garbage until the name jumped out at him.

"Are you sure it's them?" Zuniga asked.

"Yes, sir. No doubt. I already checked with the salesman on the description. It was an old woman and her son and they put it in her name. Paid cash."

"Do you have information on the truck?" asked Zuniga excitedly. He snatched up a pen and quickly wrote down the truck's description and VIN number. As soon as they hung up, he gave the information to dispatch and issued an A.P.B. on the new description, a white Chevy C1500 extended cab, possibly pulling a metallic trailer.

Meanwhile, a truck matching that exact description sat parked at a secluded camping area in the Guadalupe Mountains National Park, 2 ½ hours away from the border. Miss Lydia was wracking her brain trying to make a decision. Should she continue on westward within the United States, set up shop in New Mexico, possibly? Or should she cut and run, take her money and head for Juarez? Ortiz hadn't been any help, jumping off the phone saying something about having his own problems to deal with. She cursed him again under her breath.

They had stopped and picked up some food, and the girls were all sitting around a picnic table eating. They were becoming difficult to handle, as she'd put them in the trailer for the long drive which meant they had to make periodic stops to give them a rest from the heat. The girls were not happy and Miss Lydia eyed them suspecting that they might be plotting something.

"Keep an eye on them," she told Arnulfo. "I don't trust them."

"It's too hot in the trailer," he responded.

"That's why we're getting some air. They'll be fine."

Inside the truck Jose was picking his fingernails clean with a pocketknife, listening to a police scanner for signs of trouble. Suddenly, he heard it. Over the police scanner, a state trooper was asking for confirmation of the tag numbers on the truck Jose was driving. He had a possible match at a truck stop, but after the info was relayed to him, he confirmed it was not the correct truck. "That's a negative. It doesn't have temporary tags and no trailer," the officer said.

Shit! He jumped from his seat and ran to Miss Lydia who was sitting at a separate picnic table from the girls, trying to decide the best place to go.

"Mama," he told her. "They know about the truck. I just heard it over the scanner. They've got all its information and they know about the trailer."

Miss Lydia cursed. They had little chance of continuing west now without being seen, even at night. The police would be looking everywhere for them, and even the truckers out on the roads would know what to look for. The minute they passed someone, they'd take one look at the truck with the metal trailer and it'd be over. *It's time to make the hard decisions,* she decided. The only chance was to lose the trailer and make a run for Juarez. But what to do with the girls? She couldn't fit them in the truck, and even if she could, at this point she didn't trust them to keep their mouths shut if something happened. *They'll give us up to the police the first chance they get,* she thought. She pulled Jose aside and began whispering to him.

"What do you suppose they're talking about?" Catalina asked the other girls, spying the furtive meeting being held and taking note of Jose's inability to keep from glancing at the girls as his mother spoke to him in inaudible tones.

"Probably where to go," said Silvia. "Do you think they'll let us go?"

"Not her," said Imelda, referring to Miss Lydia. "I don't know what's going on, but I smell trouble. Yesenia must have called the police. That's why they're running." As she watched the old woman, she began to have suspicions they might be planning something terrible. She took the opportunity to visit with Arnulfo, with whom she'd always had something of a friendship. "Arnulfo, what are they talking about?" she whispered.

"I don't know," he said. "Just go back with the other girls. Don't bring attention to yourself."

"But Arnulfo, look at them. They're up to something."

"I'll find out," he told her, "but please, go back with the other girls. Now is not the time to risk getting Miss Lydia upset. She's already on edge."

Imelda did as she was told, but she picked up that Arnulfo was also worried. He might even be scared, which made her even more concerned. "Something's up," she told the other girls, "but he doesn't know what."

Eventually, Miss Lydia walked over to the girls, speaking in her false grandmotherly voice. "Well, it seems things have not gone as we hoped. You girls have been like a second family to me, but Yesenia has sold us all down the river. I'm sad to say we'll all have to say goodbye soon." She acted as though she was close to tears over the matter, but Imelda wasn't fooled. *What is she up to?* She wondered. "I have decided to go home to Mexico," she told the girls. "We'll all drive down to El Paso and from there, you girls can go where you wish. Your debts are all forgiven. You're free to go where you like. As for me, this old woman is going to go back to the village where I lived as a young girl."

The others looked at each other skeptically. Could it be true? Were they all going to be released in El Paso? *Then what?* Silvia asked herself. She had no desire to continue living as a prostitute, but she had no place to go, either. She had no papers and would surely be deported as soon as someone stopped her. Still, what was the worst that would happen? She might get sent back to Mexico? Her old life was a hell of a lot better than the life she'd found in the north. She just wanted to be free now. She didn't care where.

As she looked around, she saw the other girls were also trying to absorb the news. Catalina's eyes were bright with excitement, as were Maria and Isabel's, but Imelda looked disturbed. "So come on, now," continued Miss Lydia. "Let's go ahead and get going."

"Miss Lydia, it's the middle of the day. It'll be too hot in the trailer," said Arnulfo.

She gave him a sharp look. "It'll only be for a little while. We need to start moving."

Imelda gave him a look that said, *I do not want to ride in that thing in this heat,* but he only shrugged his shoulders.

Jose herded the girls back into the cramped trailer and they all climbed in. Imelda was the last to go in and she made sure to give Jose a look which clearly let him know she'd be perfectly content if he went straight to hell. She also gave one to Arnulfo. "This is such bullshit," she told the other girls as Jose clamped the doors shut and locked them in.

"It's only for a little while longer," said Catalina. "Then we don't have to deal with them anymore," she added with a whisper.

The truck started up and pulled out of the campground, the girls bumping along as it went, but before heading back to the main road, Miss Lydia pointed to a dirt road and the truck turned down it. "Where are you going?" Arnulfo asked.

"Back way," was all she replied.

Only a few minutes later the truck went down a small incline and Miss Lydia told Jose to stop. Arnulfo said nothing but in his mind he was becoming very concerned with these odd actions. The three got out of the truck and Jose went to the back and began unhitching the trailer from the truck. "What are you doing?" Jose used all his strength to pull the little trailer back a few inches and then the trailer tongue dropped to the ground, the girls jostled hard with the thump. "I said what are you doing?"

Miss Lydia stood next to him and put her hands on his shoulders in that false grandmotherly way she conjured so often. "It's the only way," she told him. "The police are watching for the trailer and we can't trust the girls anymore."

As the realization of what Miss Lydia was planning set in, Arnulfo's eyes widened. "No! You can't just leave them! Not in this heat."

"They'll be fine," she told him. "Park patrol will probably be along soon and see them."

"But why lock them in?"

"Because, we need time to make it to the border. If we don't, the girls will flag someone down and call the police. We're not trying to hurt them, we just need some time."

But Arnulfo wasn't buying it. "But there's nobody else out here! Why not at least leave them at the campground, not here! There's nothing here! They'll die in there."

"They'll be fine," Miss Lydia assured him. "Come now, let's be on our way."

"No!" he yelled, so loud that inside the truck the girls heard it, too.

"Arnulfo?" Imelda asked. "What's going on out there?"

"Stop it, Arnulfo," Miss Lydia hissed. "You're going to get them all excited."

"Miss Lydia, please. We're in the desert and so far from the trail. How will anyone find them in the next few hours? They won't. You know they won't. You can't do this. We can't do this."

"Get in the truck," said Jose, walking up behind Miss Lydia.

"I'm not going to leave them here," said Arnulfo. "Not like this. Please, let's just leave the door open. They can walk back to the park entrance or something. It'll take them hours, at least. Why can't we just do that?"

Miss Lydia glared at him. "You're just one of the girls, aren't you?" she said maliciously. Arnulfo looked stunned. "Don't think I don't know," she told him. "I've always known about you. You don't think I know some of the places you've gone to for your little outings?" Jose said nothing, confused at the exchange but ready to do whatever his mother wished in an instant. "You've forgotten your place. Which is it, Arnulfo? Are you going to be one of the girls or are you coming with us?" He said nothing. "Get in the truck," she warned him.

Arnulfo decided. He glared back her. "What's the matter with you? You've always been a bitter old woman, but this is too much. We're not going to leave these girls to die in this heat. Now open the trailer."

"Or what?" asked Jose, pulling his pistol from his belt.

Arnulfo stared at him.

"Hold on," said Miss Lydia. "Let's not get carried away." She kept her eyes on Arnulfo. "It's them or us, Arnulfo. You can come with us to the border, or you can be locked in with them. Think carefully."

He did. He knew Jose was fully capable of shooting him and he also didn't want to be left here with the girls, either. There had to be a way. "Fine," he told them. "We'll leave them. But we have to call the park when we reach El Paso and tell them where they are . . . the moment we get there."

"Of course," said Miss Lydia. But as she turned, Arnulfo saw the twinkle in her eye, as though she were almost winking at Jose. He knew it was a lie. Miss Lydia had no intentions of calling the park rangers. Not only did she know full well that it was unlikely the girls would be found that day, or possibly even the next day, the old woman was counting on it. She was getting rid of evidence. She wanted them to die in that trailer.

As Jose turned to walk towards the truck, Arnulfo reached into his own belt to pull his gun, but Miss Lydia saw him and called out, "Jose!"

Jose whirled around and saw Arnulfo pulling the pistol. He fired one shot and it hit Arnulfo in the chest. He fell to the ground, his ivory bolo covered in blood.

"Why'd you do that?" Miss Lydia yelled at the dying Arnulfo, walking over and standing over him, "*Idiota*! Why!?"

His only answer was his last exhale.

Inside the trailer, the girls had heard the gunshot. It seemed Imelda knew immediately what had happened. "Arnulfo!?" she tried to yell through the metal chamber. "Arnulfo!"

"What happened?" asked Silvia. "Did they shoot him?"

Jose could hear Imelda's cries. "We should just get rid of all of them right now," he told his mother.

"No, someone may have heard that gunshot. Let's just get out of here," said Miss Lydia. And they quickly got back into the truck, desert sand taking flight as they sped away.

"Arnulfo!?" Imelda yelled one more time, but only the silence answered. She began to cry, as did the other girls, both for Arnulfo who'd tried to help them, and because they now knew they'd been left to die in the trailer.

Chapter 51

Catherine and Matt touched down in Cancun about two hours after leaving Mexico City. Ramirez and two other men they'd never seen before met them at the airport.

"Oh, shit," whispered Matt. "Let's hope we don't get arrested."

Catherine looked at the other two men suspiciously as they approached. One was an older, stern looking man in a military uniform. "This is Vice Admiral Luis Alvarado," Ramirez explained, "of our Navy." *The navy?* Catherine thought. "And this is Agent Alberto Rojas of the *Agencia Federal de Investigación*, or AFI, as I believe you're familiar with it," said Ramirez, introducing a short, thin man with not a single hair on his head.

"Pleasure," said Catherine, shaking hands in a professional manner. Matt said nothing, only stood behind her like a personal bodyguard. They eyed him curiously, but accepted his silence without pressing.

"These men are here at the request of our government," said Ramirez. "It seems our president received a call from your governor. Ms. Woodall's family has indicated that you would be arriving with information. They've been asked to review that information, and if confirmed, to assist in the arrest of Victor Arismendez." She knew immediately Ramirez had not shared their previous exchange with the two men.

Catherine turned and looked to Matt, who merely shrugged as if to say, *you let Jim call them. It's your gamble.* She turned back to them, "I'm going to need a moment, please. We'll be right back." The two men with Ramirez stared at one another in confusion as Catherine grabbed Matt by the arm and led him to a nearby table in the airport's lounge. They were further miffed when she said back to them, "Mr. Ramirez, would you mind joining us for a moment?"

Ramirez appeared a bit flushed as he excused himself from his two superiors. The three sat down and Catherine quickly whipped out the book, going through the names in the ledger as quickly as she dared without missing any. "This is a surprise," she told Ramirez, still checking to make sure the two men who had accompanied him were not in the ledger.

"I agree," he told her. "But it was not my doing. I got a phone call from an official in Mexico City. He said to expect Vice Admiral Alvarado and Agent Rojas, and told me they would accompany me to meet your arrival. I wasn't sure how they could know of it. I must admit, I was worried the wrong people may have already been on to you."

"They might be the wrong people," added Matt.

Catherine finished the list, "Well, I don't see their names in here. Not that that doesn't mean they're not in another ledger someplace else, but I don't think we have much choice here, do we?" she asked, turning to Ramirez.

"No, I don't think so," he said. "They know you allegedly have information that Arismendez is the man responsible. There's no hiding it, now, it's already out. But these two men are not your typical officials. They report to the President. I'm pretty sure you can trust them."

"Pretty sure?" asked Matt.

Ramirez held his hands up slightly, "What can I tell you? We are dealing with a very influential man. I believe these men are who they say they are, but I'd be lying if I said I could guarantee it. I'm in as much of a predicament here as you are."

Matt wasn't satisfied, "Even if they are who they claim to be, that doesn't mean they're on our side."

Catherine looked over Ramirez's shoulder at the two grave men who were eyeing them impatiently. "I guess pretty sure will have to do. We can't do this alone and we have to put our trust in someone sooner or later."

Matt said nothing, but Catherine knew what he was thinking. She was thinking it, too.

She returned with Ramirez and Matt to the two men who were standing and talking together, both looking at the book Catherine held clutched in her hands. "I have here a ledger detailing the accounts of one Fernando Ortiz. I'm not going to explain where I got it or by what means, but inside is a list of names of corrupt officers and government officials. We also know that Victor Arismendez ordered the kidnapping of Taylor Woodall and personally carried out her murder. It's my understanding that Mr. Arismendez was injured in the attack on the girl, that she bit his ear and wounded his eye. I believe we will find significant DNA evidence at the home of Mr. Arismendez. I further believe that officer Hernando Vargas of the Quintana Roo anti-kidnapping unit, whose name appears in this ledger, was paid to hand over a witness in the case who was then murdered and that it is likely if he is arrested we can acquire his testimony in this matter." The two men stared at her, utterly dazed. Catherine handed the ledger to the AFI agent and waited for their response, her breath held tight in her chest.

Agent Rojas took the ledger, began looking through it, quickly scanning at first but then slower and slower, his finger running over the lines in the book as the Vice Admiral stood next to him, reading as well. When next he looked up he said, "We are in your debt, Ms.

James. I have been trying to find evidence of *señor* Arismendez's crimes for quite some time." Ramirez looked up at him surprised. "We've long known of his affiliation with the cartel, but never could get enough together to charge him with anything. I'll start with Officer Vargas. I'll get a warrant issued for him first and hopefully he'll provide us enough information to finally pen Arismendez down. Will you come with us, please? We have much to discuss."

As they walked with them Matt whispered to Catherine, "I hope you know what you're doing."

"I'm improvising," she said. "Remember?"

Chapter 52

Miss Lydia and Jose arrived in El Paso less than three hours after leaving the girls to die in the metal trailer. Jose wanted to drive the truck into Mexico, but Miss Lydia knew better. "Don't be stupid," she told him. "They're just waiting for this truck to come through. We were lucky to make it here." She couldn't have spoken truer words. Little did they know they had come within an inch of being caught on their way to the border. The highway patrol had been sitting under an overpass observing the traffic, waiting for the truck should it come by. At just the right moment, though, they'd been pulled away by an accident, and the truck had escaped through their net.

They parked on the edge of a lot near the bridge where tourists often left their vehicles on the American side while enjoying a day of shopping in Mexico. "Get our bags," she told him, "I'm going to the bathroom."

As she walked away and Jose began unloading the few things they'd brought with them, including the bag containing all of Miss Lydia's money, a passing border patrol agent noticed the truck and checked its plate against the report they'd all been given. When he realized it matched, he quickly jumped on the radio. Just as Miss Lydia was coming out of the bathroom, a half-dozen police and border patrol cars swarmed into the parking lot and surrounded Jose. Without more than a passing thought of remorse for her son, Miss Lydia quickly turned and disappeared into the crowd of people crossing into Mexico.

Jose could only watch in shock and fear as several men with badges began screaming at him and coming towards him. He looked for his mother and caught just a glimpse of her as she walked away towards the bridge. He was just about to call for her, but was tackled to the ground. One officer kept his knee on Jose's face while another yanked his arms behind him and began cuffing him. "What'd I do?" he asked in feigned innocence. "What'd I do?"

In all the commotion, no one seemed to notice one more little, old Mexican woman crossing the border. She showed her identification at the checkpoint, but the Mexican guard seemed so interested in what was happening across the border that he barely glanced at her.

Less than an hour after he was arrested, Jose was under interrogation by the Texas Rangers, but he wasn't talking. The authorities knew from Yesenia that the truck had left with the trailer, but had been found without it, so while they interviewed Jose they had aerial units attempting to traverse the highways and troopers checking truck stations and rest areas, but so far were turning up nothing. And time was running out.

"Look at the clock," said one of the rangers. "With each passing minute, one of those girls might die, Jose. And if just one of them dies, that's capital murder."

Jose shifted uncomfortably in the little chair. "I don't know what you're talking about. You've got the wrong guy."

The ranger leaned over the little table. "I have a witness, Jose. And our witness has told us absolutely everything we need to know to put you away for a long, long time."

He began to sweat. "Who?"

"You know who," said the ranger. "She's not afraid of you any more, Jose. And if any of those other girls have come to harm, you're going to pay for it, Jose." The ranger pointed his finger at him. "You, Jose. You're responsible."

Jose shook his head. "No. No, I wasn't the one who left them."

"Left them where?" He stayed silent. "Do you understand what's going to happen here, Jose? Are you aware of the penalty for capital murder? Are you aware we can pursue the death penalty in a capital murder case, Jose? Are you ready for that? Are you really prepared to face those kinds of charges because you're stupid enough to sit here with your mouth shut while these girls are dying?"

"You can't," he said. "I'm not a citizen. You have to send me back to Mexico."

"Oh, we can and we will, Jose. Haven't you ever heard of Angel Maturino Resendiz, the rail car killer? He tried to tell us the same thing. Do you know where he is now, Jose? He's dead. We tried him, we convicted him, and he was sentenced to death. Make no mistake here, Jose. We're going to charge you with capital murder for the death of Trooper Daniel Shoal. And if any of these girls die, we're going to charge you with capital murder for them, too. You're going to stand trial, and if convicted, you will face the death penalty. But it's up to you. If you want to try and make a deal, you'd better speak up now, because pretty soon it's going to be too late. If those girls die, you won't have anything to bargain with, Jose. If they die, what do you think is going to happen to the person responsible? You tell me, Jose. What do you think a jury in Texas will say about someone like that?"

Jose dropped his head. "Okay," he said. "I want a deal, but first I want a lawyer."

They worked quickly to get him one and, of course, the public defender immediately wanted the death penalty off the table for any exchange of information.

"We get the girls back alive and he testifies against any other defendants if and when we find them, as well as whoever else was involved, and we'll agree," said the assistant district attorney. "Your client is a cop killer. This is the best he's going to get and it's contingent on those young women being found alive. If they're not, I will be asking for the death penalty."

With that, the deal was struck. "Now, where did you leave those girls, Jose?" asked the ranger.

"At the park," he told them. "Guadalupe Mountains park, a mile or two off the main road."

"How long ago?"

Jose looked at the clock on the wall. "About five hours."

The ranger passed Jose a blank piece of paper and a pencil. "Draw me a map, Jose. And you'd better make it a good one."

Chapter 53

There was a look of sheer disbelief on Vargas' face when an armed unit of five AFI agents walked into the police station, past stunned faces and cries of surprise, and right into Vargas's office with their weapons drawn. They were led by Agent Rojas. "Hernando Vargas, I have a warrant for your arrest."

"You can't be serious," he told them. "What for?"

"Murder. You accepted twenty five thousand dollars from the criminal Fernando Ortiz in exchange for handing over the minor known as Juan who was murdered to prevent him from telling the authorities information regarding the kidnapping and murder of the American, Taylor Woodall. Deny it if you wish. I assure you we have irrefutable proof and you will only be punished more severely."

They took him into custody and led him out in a walk of shame the likes of which had not been seen before in the station. And when they had him seated at the AFI headquarters, they confronted him with the ledger and the testimony they'd already acquired from Maria and Aunty Nita about the phone call that had led Vargas to Juan. The evidence was overwhelming and Vargas cracked within an hour.

"Did Victor Arismendez tell you to find and turn over the boy?" Rojas asked, making sure to mention Arismendez nonchalantly to imply he already knew who was behind the crime.

"No, Arismendez had some other guy call me," Vargas confessed. "His name's Ortiz. I've worked some outside jobs for Arismendez here and there, and when the news broke about the girl, this Ortiz guy called me up and told me Arismendez gave him my number. He said he wanted me to tell them everything we learned as the investigation went along, quietly. He told me I was to call him directly, never Arismendez. He said if I did, that after the investigation was over I'd have enough money to retire if I wanted. After I talked to the boy and realized what he knew, I called the guy, and he told me to just drop the kid off in the city. There was a car waiting. I handed the kid over and they gave me an envelope. That was it. I didn't do anything other than that."

"What was in the envelope?" He lowered his head in silence. "Vargas, what was in the envelope," Rojas asked again.

"Twenty five thousand dollars. I didn't know they were going to kill the kid." Vargas put his hands over his face in defeat. "I didn't know, I swear."

"Did you ask?" asked Rojas. Vargas didn't answer. Rojas stood up and walked out of the interview room, but halfway through the door he turned and looked back. "Would knowing what they were going to do really have stopped you, Detective? Somehow, I doubt it." He left Vargas alone with his thoughts to think on it.

Catherine, Matt, Vice Admiral Alvarado, and Ramirez had all been outside the room watching the interview on a monitor when Rojas came out. "We got him, right?" Catherine asked. "He said he got paid twenty five thousand, which matches the entry in the ledger. That should be enough evidence to get a warrant for Arismendez."

"Well, he said he talked to Ortiz, not Arismendez," said Rojas. "But I think the information in the ledger along with the fact Detective Vargas said Arismendez gave Ortiz his contact information is enough, yes."

"Don't call him Detective," said Ramirez. "He's not one of us. Not anymore." Rojas nodded.

"So what happens now?" Catherine asked.

"Now is where I come in," said Vice Admiral Alvarado. "If agent Rojas is able to secure a warrant based on this testimony, I will be in charge of the arrest. We will have the full resources of the military at our disposal."

Catherine didn't fully understand why the Mexican Navy was apparently going to be in charge of apprehending Arismendez, but she decided she wasn't going to question how Arismendez was taken down, so long as he was taken down.

Chapter 54

In the heart of Cancun a massive force of military personnel and AFI agents appeared on Lopez Portillo Street. Two hundred Mexican marines amassed, supported by a naval helicopter and two tanks. All police were ordered to stand down and Cancun was put under military control. The helicopter hovered over the city as the military force began its march forward. Cancun now looked less like a vacation resort and more like a city in the heat of battle in Afghanistan or the Gaza strip.

Victor Arismendez quickly caught wind of the incoming assault when first it appeared in the city and ordered his security to call everyone, every gang member, bodyguard, and soldier they had. By the time the military reached his compound, he had no less than forty armed men holed up with him.

What followed next seemed unreal to Catherine. She and Matt remained at AFI headquarters watching the assault on the news. It was all out war. Armored vehicles rammed the walls of the compound, met by a hail of automatic gunfire. Grenades were tossed from both sides. An insane news caster stood on a street corner only a few blocks away narrating the chaos as bombs exploded behind him.

"Jesus," said Catherine, completely amazed by the spectacle.

"I guess you were right," Matt told her. "This guy's got his own personal army."

The siege wore on late into the afternoon, with considerable casualties on both sides. Mexican Special Forces soldiers were seen being carried out on stretchers, images of bodies of the cartel members were on every channel, nothing censored. On and on it went, the multi-million dollar compound being reduced to rubble by the bullets and explosions until finally half of its structure came tumbling down in a cloud of dust and debris. The Special Forces stormed in. Marines rappelled down from the helicopter to the roof while a separate assault team followed a tank though a new gaping hole in one of the walls. More gunfire was heard, then two grenades . . . . then silence.

That evening, Matt, Catherine, Ramirez, and Jim and Amy Woodall all sat a large conference table at the AFI headquarters. Agent Rojas sat across from them with other military officials and, to Catherine's chagrin, the governor's man, Fuentes. "Shortly after 7:00 this evening our forces made entry into Victor Arismendez's compound," he was explaining. "We encountered several armed men and our forces threw two grenades into the room in which they were barricaded. Afterward, a search of that room revealed four bodies. I'm sorry to report that Victor Arismendez was not among them. We are still searching the premises, but our people found a tunnel located in the wine cellar which led to an adjacent property. It appears Arismendez was able to escape through this tunnel, possibly even before the assault began."

A collective sigh of disbelief and disappointment passed among them all. "No," whispered Amy. Matt looked to Catherine, the only one in the room that could look beyond his icy façade to the disappointment beneath - and while his was a face of stone, Catherine's anger and disappointment was written out neatly upon her features.

"We should have known," she said. "Of course he would have an escape route."

"Don't blame yourself," Matt told her, "There was no way to know."

She wasn't comforted. "He's right," Jim offered. "We've come this far. We'll get him."

"We have every resource available looking for him and while he may have had a few hours, he isn't likely to be able to go far," offered the agent. "We have military at the airport, the local marinas, and stationed along the main roads out."

All told, the siege had taken just over four hours and had netted sixteen AR-15 rifles, nine AK-47's, 12 handguns, a few shotguns and other miscellaneous firearms, a cache of grenades, nearly two thousand rounds of ammunition, a quarter million American dollars, and a vast assortment of drugs and drug paraphernalia. But of course, no Arismendez.

They spent some time in the room discussing what would come next. After the military, AFI, and Fuentes left the room, Amy asked the rest who remained, "What's your honest opinion at this point?"

Catherine's heart had sunk when she'd learned Arismendez had escaped. In her gut, she felt they had the one chance and had missed, but she didn't have the heart to say it. Neither did Ramirez. It was Matt who spoke, instead, "They probably won't find him," he told her truthfully. "He knows better than to just get picked up in some public location." Amy began to cry angry, silent tears. Jim reached over to comfort her. "But we won't give up," he continued. "The authorities may not find him, but we'll keep on the hunt. He'll run. He'll go someplace that he feels is safe, and then he'll get careless. It may be a while, but eventually he'll pop his head up, and then we'll find him and end this."

The mood was somber, the group in silent reflection for some time before Ramirez excused himself with his sincerest apologies to all for the turn of events. Then Jim and Amy left for their room for yet another night of restless sleep and unresolved despair. "Drink?" Matt asked.

"Let's have it back in the room. I need to sit for a while and think." She got up to leave, but paused as they were walking out, looking up at him, "When you said he'll show up again, but it may be a while . . . how long do you think . . . really?"

He put his brawny arm around her. "Years, maybe." He felt her sink in on herself. "I'm sorry, Cat. We did our best."

Chapter 55

Zuniga sat with Yesenia after she'd heard the news. Silvia, Maria, Isabel, and Evelyn were all dead. She wept miserably. "You did all you could," Zuniga told her, trying to comfort her as best he could. "I know it's hard, but we were able to save two thanks to you."

"No," she said, "I shouldn't have waited. It's my fault. If I'd gone straight to the police after they chased me in that alley, you would have found them in time. But I hid! I hid and now they're dead because of me."

"You hid because you were scared, and rightfully so. Those men were trying to kill you, Yesenia. Imelda and Catalina owe their lives to you. Many people wouldn't have had the courage to come forward after what you've been through. And Trooper Daniel Shoal's family now has closure because of you. We now have his killer in custody, all thanks to you. I know this is hard, unbelievably hard. But you did a brave thing, Yesenia. You stood up even though you knew you were risking your life. That takes courage, Yesenia." But still she cried inconsolably. "You know they have a visa called a T Visa," Zuniga told her, putting his arm around her in a fatherly sort of way. "It allows a victim like you to remain here if you help law enforcement, which you definitely have. We can get you, Imelda, and Catalina an application. We'll write you out a reference and I'll even testify for you if I can."

"No," she told him. "I'm going home. I just want to go home."

Chapter 56

After leaving the conference room in utter defeat, Catherine and Matt had retired to their room, poured themselves two Jack and Cokes from the little mini-fridge, and were sipping their drinks in quiet contemplation of the day's events when the room phone rang. Catherine looked at it curiously before picking it up. "Hello?"

"Hello, Ms. James. Bad news this evening, I hear."

Catherine looked at Matt with a frustrated yet curious expression. "Who is this?"

"I have a gift for you, Ms. James."

"And what would that be?" she asked, now wary of this mysterious new turn of events.

"Victor Arismendez," he said.

The pause was palpable. "You know where to find him?" she asked.

"I do," he said. "He had tried to leave the city, but it didn't work out for him." Catherine listened with keen interest. "Mr. Arismendez is now sitting in room 403 of the Cancun Palace Hotel, just a few miles from his former residence."

"That's impossible," she said automatically.

"See for yourself," said the man.

"He wouldn't be that stupid. There's no way."

"What's the one place the military aren't going to be out in full force, Ms. James?"

"The resorts," she answered.

"Precisely. He's hiding in plain sight. You're welcome to see for yourself. There's a couple of bodyguards in the lobby on lookout. I'm sure you can spot them easily enough."

"Who is this?" she asked again, more fervently. There was something about the voice . . . something peculiar she couldn't place. He spoke with no accent. He sounded American enough with his deep voice and perfect English, but there was something inexplicable in the way he spoke that just didn't sound right.

"His men are well armed, but I'm told there's only about six of them with him. Good luck, Ms. James. You and your friend are going to need it." The man hung up before Catherine could ask anything more. She looked at Matt with wide eyes, the phone still in her hand.

"What?" he asked, returning her stare. He'd done his best to try to figure out what she might be hearing on the other end of the phone from her responses, but to no avail.

She put the phone back on the receiver as she spoke, "You're not going to believe this . . . hell, I don't believe it."

Chapter 57

Catherine repeated verbatim everything that the mysterious man on the phone had told her. "There's no way, right?" she asked him. "I mean, his face is plastered all over the place." She was genuinely confused and stood with her arms folded trying to put the pieces of her recently exploded mind back in place. "Is it a trap, you think? One last try to take us out for bringing the military down on him?"

Matt was equally lost in thought. "Could be. But then again, could be the truth. Whoever was on the other end of that phone is right, the resorts are the one place they're not looking for the guy. I wouldn't have thought it, but from what we've heard, Arismendez just might be arrogant enough to try it."

"I still can't see it," she said. "And I don't like it," she added, shaking her head. "This just doesn't make any sense. Who the hell was that guy?" Her blue eyes met his brown orbs under the darkened brow, "What do we do?"

He shrugged. "We do like the man suggested. We go see for ourselves."

They put their shoes back on, grabbed Matt's bag of toys, and jumped into the latest rental car.

They pulled up to the Cancun Palace Hotel, the fountain in its circular drive sending jets of water upward in a cordial dance. "If the guy is right then there's some guards in the lobby area."

"It's not going to be very busy in there at this hour and they don't know my face," said Matt. "You wait here and I'll go have a look." She didn't like it, but she knew she'd been seen enough with the Woodalls at this point that someone could recognize her. Matt, on the other hand, was still a ghost. Except, of course, to the man on the phone, apparently.

He returned only a minute or two later, jumping back in the car with a brisk step, "Yeah, there were two guys in there sitting with line of sight to the entry. They were dressed down, no obvious necklaces this time, but they're hired guns."

Catherine noted something she didn't like in the information. "Why are you saying 'were'?"

He cocked his head to the side. "They made me. They went straight for the elevator as soon as they saw me looking at them."

"What!? Oh, crap. I thought the whole point of me staying in the car was so you could check it out without drawing attention to yourself."

"It was."

"So what the hell happened?"

"What can I say? These guys know what they're doing. As soon I walked in, they took one look at me, said something to each other, and it was over."

"Dammit," she spat in frustration. "Now what do we do?"

"We improvise," he said, reaching for the bag of guns.

"We gotta stop improvising; it's making me a wreck."

"Sorry, Cat. Shit happens."

"Okay, so do we have anything remotely resembling a plan? You think he'll bolt or dig in?"

"He'll bolt," said Matt. "He can't risk another assault here. He doesn't have the manpower to withstand it. In about 90 seconds he and his bodyguards are going to be running for the back door to this place."

Catherine looked out on the massive hotel. "There's gotta be twenty 'back doors' to this place, how do we know where he's going?"

"We're not going to let him get that far," he told her, handing her Miguel's Mac-10 sans the silencer. "From what we've heard, he's too out of shape to bolt down the stairs," he told her. "They're all going to hit the lobby by the elevators in a minute."

She stared at the determined glare in his face and realized what his plan was, "Matt . . . there's only the two of us."

"That's how it's been most of the way," he said. "It's either this or we let him go underground and hope we get another shot." Matt was already pulling on his flak jacket and handing her the other. "What do you want to do, Cat? It's now or never. There's no time to call in the cavalry. We literally have one minute to decide if we do this or not."

She stared at the Mac-10 in her hand and then at the flak jacket he was holding out. She snatched it, and began putting it on quickly. Matt was already back out the door. "We need to make a lot of noise. All we have to do is keep them pinned down long enough for the military to get here." He had his Glock in his hand and Catherine's in his belt ready to be pulled when needed, along with two clips. Catherine clasped the last fastener of her jacket and jumped out of the car with him.

As soon as they entered the lobby, Matt started shooting the ground. The desk staff on the midnight shift ran for cover around a corner, immediately dialing for the police just as Matt had hoped. The military was on alert and were sure to arrive much quicker than authorities did at the Hutton incident just two weeks before. Matt and Catherine positioned themselves behind a column with a view of the elevators.

"Get ready," Matt whispered.

No sooner had they put their back to the corner wall than the elevator doors opened up and several men all cramped inside exited. As soon as the doors closed again, Matt and Catherine made their move. Matt took the first two out with a quick and deadly accurate *Pop! Pop!* Catherine depressed her trigger and the Mac-10 sent a sporadic barrage across the lobby, which was now vacant except for Arismendez and his men. Arismendez, who was behind the pack, was dragged back and away by two of his guards. The others now had their guns drawn and began shooting back.

The tiled walls cracked and pieces flew as Matt and Catherine ducked back again. Matt crouched down and peered around the corner for just a split second, but long enough to see two men on the ground, three standing, and Arismendez being led out the back way by two more guards. "He's running," he told her.

Catherine swept around Matt and poked the Mac-10 around the corner ever so slightly, and let loose another, more controlled spray. At the same time Matt popped his head back out again. The three remaining guards were running for cover, still shooting, but wildly now. One caught Catherine's fire in his back and dropped. Matt took another one out just before he reached the corner, but the third disappeared around it.

"They're out of line of sight!" he told her, now pressing forward with her following. They put their backs to the corner the men had just turned. Catherine pointed to an elevator across from them, and in its pristine façade, they could see the reflection of the last man turning yet another corner. Arismendez and the three remaining guards would be out of the hotel in seconds. "Come on," he told her, running for a closer rear door.

They exited at the same time the last guard exited another door, Arismendez and the other two guards could be seen over his shoulder already heading for the side of the building. The guard took aim but Matt was already behind a column, but when Catherine appeared a split-second later, his eyes went wide in terror as he realized he'd left her open to gunfire. He jumped back in front of her just as a bullet struck his back. Matt whipped her around the column with him and Catherine screamed, "Matt!"

He'd hit the ground behind the column but said, "I'm fine. Jacket got it," though breathing hard and clearly in pain. It was lucky the shot had been aimed for Catherine's head, at which height it met Matt in the center of his back between his shoulder blades. He rolled to the left and jumped back up. The guard was now running as fast as he could. Catherine took flight as well, but she was no match for Matt as he was already several steps ahead of her.

The guard turned the corner around the side of the hotel and turned to aim. Matt saw him just as he flew around the same corner in rapid pursuit. He immediately dove to the ground, another bullet barely missing him. The guard took aim again and had Matt squared in his sights, but Catherine suddenly blazed around the corner and drew the guard's gaze. She'd seen Matt dive and knew there was only a hair's breadth to spare. The Mac-10's clip emptied its last three bullets, one hitting the guard in his pelvis. He jerked his arm and Matt seized the chance, finishing him off with one to the chest.

Exhausted as they already were in the chase that had spanned less than 90 seconds so far, Matt and Catherine bolted again. Arismendez had a good head start on them and his guards had managed to push, pull, and drag him quickly enough to the street where they'd stopped a passing taxi by stepping in front of it, guns drawn. One was now jumping in the driver's seat as the other pushed Arismendez's girth into the back, the taxi driver left on the pavement, killed without a moment's hesitation by Arismendez's men. The taxi then scored the road in skid marks as it tore away, Matt sending a few shots into its trunk.

Catherine didn't hesitate. There was no way she was letting Arismendez go this easily. While Matt put a few rounds into the car, she was busy stopping another car, a passing Toyota. The terrified driver slid over and out the passenger door as she came around screaming for him to exit, a menacingly deceptive, empty Mac-10 in her hand. She moved the vehicle up towards Matt, its passenger door still open, and he jumped in. He didn't have to yell "Go!" or give instruction of any kind. They were in perfect sync as they gave chase.

The traffic was light but still present as the two vehicles raced along. As the taxi flew past a patrol car that was racing towards the hotel, it skidded to a halt. Catherine and Matt raced past it just as it was attempting to turn around. "Hope he's radioing someone," she said.

As they raced along the main road heading out of Cancun, she got her answer in the form of a military helicopter, most likely the same one used earlier, as it appeared overhead. Soon they saw more lights appearing behind them.

The taxi hit a side road, then an alley, and back out to another side road and went right, no longer on the main road. "Where's he going?" she asked.

"Airport," said Matt. "They're trying to lose the helicopter."

As they neared the airport Catherine looked up. It appeared the military aircraft either had permission to enter the air space or didn't need it as it did not turn away. Arismendez's ill-fated decision to try and lose the aircraft at the airport was further illustrated when the taxi came to a screeching halt, three military vehicles and a line of soldiers with guns pointed their way blocking the road ahead. Catherine hit the brakes as did the police vehicles behind her. Officers jumped out. The officers in the rear were now pointing their weapons at Catherine and Matt's car, not knowing if they were friend or foe. The military soldiers in front were aiming at Arismendez's car. Nobody exited the taxi and Catherine and Matt remained in their vehicle, engine running. Matt chuckled, taking Catherine off guard. "What the hell could you possibly find funny right now?"

He smirked at her. "Mexican standoff. Literally."

She couldn't laugh. "Jesus, Matt, really?" She concentrated on the vehicle in front of them which was still idling. "He's going to give up," she said, the ramifications of it being quickly calculated in her mind. Even if he hadn't decided yet, Catherine knew he didn't have a choice.

She looked to Matt. He wasn't smiling anymore. "It's your call," he said. Both knew if Arismendez surrendered, he'd have a long trial with a lot of time to plan. Maybe they'd try him, convict him, and he'd spend his life in a Mexican hellhole. But the other possibility was that he'd use his money, his scare tactics, all of his contacts and resources to find a way to squirm out of the imminent charges. They looked at each other, both making sure the other was agreed, both knowing what it meant. This could easily be considered a severe crime, not to mention it could get them killed. Arismendez was preparing to give up. To attack him now would be to interfere with the Mexican government's judicial system. But the possible alternative . . . he'd slipped away once already. The risk was too much for her. Catherine hit the gas.

There had been a sufficient enough gap between the vehicles that when they barreled into the back of the taxi they were nearly up to thirty miles an hour. Glass shattered on the road as the stunned authorities closed in but were dazed by what had just occurred. None of them knew what to think. "Hold your fire!" someone on the military line yelled out.

To Catherine's horror, Matt put one Glock on the dashboard and the other in her hand, and then stepped out of the car before she could stop him, completely unarmed. "Stay here," he said. "But make sure you shoot them before they shoot me."

"What are you doing!?" she cried. He held his arms high and looked as though he were headed for the taxi's rear door, over a dozen guns on his every move.

"Get down!" someone yelled at him, but he kept walking. "Get down on the ground now!" But Matt kept approaching the taxi.

"Jesus, Matt, get on the ground," Catherine whispered. She was halfway tempted to get out and go after him.

"Don't fire!" one of the police officers yelled.

But while the military and police were holding their fire, one of Arismendez's men opened the passenger-side door and made to point his gun at Matt. Catherine saw him move just in time and instantly fired her weapon through the windshield.

As he fell back in the car the taxi lurched forward, its mangled rear dragging the exhaust pipe in a cloud of sparks as the last spooked guard, who was driving, tried to take off with Arismendez in the back seat. As it bore down on the soldiers in front of them, Matt hit the ground. Catherine knew what was about to happen next and she quickly followed suit, throwing her gun out of the window and holding her hands out for the police behind her to see.

A split second later came the rain. Bullets shred the taxi like it was an aluminum can. It was over in seconds. Then the police approached the Toyota and hastily removed Catherine, slamming her head against the top of the car as they cuffed her. They treated Matt with the same affection, but neither cared. They were alive. Catherine looked on while the authorities removed Arismendez and his driver. Arismendez was a bloody mess. Innumerable bullets had reduced the kingpin to a mangled corpse. She then looked to Matt, and wasn't too surprised to find that even with a boot on his back and his head pressed down into the glass-strewn asphalt while they slapped on the cuffs, Matt was smirking.

Chapter 58

The day Catherine landed back in Dallas she had passed an attractive young Mexican woman in the airport who was being walked to the gate by a detective. Catherine had barely glimpsed the badge and gun peeking out from under his jacket as they passed. It was enough to snap her out of a thought she'd been lost in, something that had been occurring fairly frequently since she had shared an awkward goodbye with Matt in Cancun. The last few days had stirred up a whirlwind of thoughts. She and the young woman's eyes met for the briefest of moments, and then they were past each other, each returning to the home from which they had traveled so far. Catherine pulled the headphones from her pocket and plugged them into her phone/mp3, letting the music clear her head a bit.

She and Matt had visited Julio again before heading home. He was thriving at Patrick's home, and in an unexpected result she couldn't have hoped for, Patrick said he and his wife had decided they wanted to take the boy in permanently. "He's already just like family," Pat explained.

"Are you sure?" Catherine had asked in surprise. "What about your wife?"

"Hell, whose idea do you think it was in the first place? She just loves that boy. She took to him like I took to hers. She said she'd be damned if she let him go back to the streets and I can tell you right now that kid ain't going to sit still in no orphanage. If they try putting him in one he might stay for supper but he'll be long gone by bed time. He's not having any part of 'em and I can't say I blame him."

"And you're okay with it?" she asked him, tentatively.

He smiled and shrugged, "He's a good kid. We'll figure it out."

Catherine could hardly believe it but she instantly had an idea of something she could do, not only for Patrick's generosity, but also for Julio. She decided to give them a hell of a going away present . . . the diamonds from Ortiz's safe as well as the money left over. She took some out for the damage to the rental cars and a fair bit she insisted Matt take for a rainy day, but the rest she handed over to Patrick along with the diamonds. "Holy shit on a stick, are these real?" he'd asked, holding up a round diamond twinkling in the sun.

"Oh, yes. The finest of quality, I've been told." Then he looked in the bag she handed him full of money.

"Jesus!" he exclaimed. "I can't take all this from you two!"

But Catherine wasn't taking no for an answer. "It belonged to the man that killed Julio's friend and tried to kill him, so I'd say he's owed. And if you're going to be watching after him, then you'd better hold on to it and use it for your family."

"And go do something about that skin cancer, will you?" Matt added. "It looks like hell."

After much convincing, he accepted. "I'll make sure we put it to good use. I suppose I will have to go get this looked at now," he said, nodding towards his shoulder. He smiled at Matt. "Asshole, now I have to go see a doctor."

Matt smiled back, "Quit being a puss." The two shook hands and Patrick couldn't help but keep peeking inside the bag and shaking his head in amazement.

It was a hard goodbye with Julio. She'd grown quite affectionate toward the little man, and promised to call and check in with him now and then.

The goodbye with Matt had been less conclusive. They'd had to stay a few more days, thanks to an enormous amount of paperwork needed in order to satisfy the authorities. But given that they'd single-handedly handed Arismendez, albeit dead and riddled with bullet holes, back to law enforcement after he'd already escaped their grasp, the Mexican government turned out to be quite appreciative. They'd extended many thanks and contrary to the fear of reprisal that had crossed their minds, Catherine and Matt were told in no uncertain terms they were welcome back to Cancun anytime they liked. Even so, they didn't book any immediate travel plans to return.

As for Yesenia, she didn't think twice about the raven-haired woman with the blue eyes when they passed each other in the airport. She was lost in thoughts of her own. She'd stayed long enough to put her testimony down on tape for the police and visit Imelda and Catalina in the hospital, but she longed for home. The other girls who hadn't made it were to be sent home for a proper burial with their families, assuming Zuniga could determine where each one's home had been. Yesenia knew Imelda would probably be able to help provide their information once she was well enough. Zuniga had been nice enough to see her off to the airport and they walked together in silence towards her final departure.

She was headed back to Mexico City . . . the first time she would ever fly. She'd always imagined flying in a plane would be exciting but given all she'd been through, it now held little appeal. Once back, she had plans to stay with Ceci for a bit. She wasn't sure if she'd stay in the city or go back to Santa Rosanna, but after the hell she'd found in el Norte, a quiet life back in her small town seemed much more satisfying to her now than it had a few months ago.

Chapter 59

A month after things had settled back to normal Catherine sat in her office looking over a new contract. An oil processing plant was being built in India and she was one of hundreds of attorneys and consultants hired to look over their particular parcel of information. She let out a long sigh and pushed the contract away. Then she opened her desk and pulled out a fresh Newsweek magazine which contained an article about the Taylor Woodall murder.

Following the shootout in the street near the airport, a massive investigation had been launched which resulted in the arrest of twenty-seven police officers and officials, all charged with aiding and accepting bribes from the cartel. It was a start.

She looked at the small picture of Detective Ramirez and her fingers ran over the sub-caption *Detective Assassinated in Revenge Killing*. He'd been coming out of his front door not two weeks after she left Cancun when a car pulled up and opened fire. He'd been struck several times. A banner had been left on his doorstep warning others of interfering with the cartel's operations. Arismendez or no Arismendez, the cartel was already back at work. *I'm sorry,* she told him in her thoughts. *You were one of the good guys.*

After Catherine re-read the Newsweek article for at least the tenth time, she put it away in her drawer. Then she picked up her phone and made a call.

"Hello?"

"Matt?" she asked.

"Catherine . . . hi, how are you doing?" Matt had since returned to his little house in the Florida Keys where he spent his leisure time fishing, snorkeling, and occasionally treasure hunting for lost Spanish bullion. He never found much, a silver coin here, a ceramic cup there, but he enjoyed it, and after the war they'd been through in Mexico, he decided it was time to take a nice long break from work. He'd reimbursed Titansteel and after they'd learned what he'd been up to in Cancun, and what he'd accomplished there, he was more in demand than ever.

"I'm good," she said. "I'm doing okay. Thanks to you."

"Any time," he said. "I hear the tourists are already returning to Cancun."

"Yeah," she told him. "Unbelievable, isn't it? The Association of Hotels down there slashes prices and starts advertising the city corruption has been wiped out, and people start showing up in masses."

"Marketing," he said with a melancholy laugh.

"I guess. Hey, Matt?"

"Yeah?"

"I've been thinking about a long overdue vacation. And since Mexico is definitely not in my travel plans any time soon, I was wondering . . . how's the weather down there?"

He looked out his window on a perfectly miserable day, gray and pouring rain. He smiled, "It's perfect."

Catherine smiled on the other end of the phone. "Good. I'll see you soon, then."

Epilogue

A few days later Catherine was busy going over her schedule, making sure everything was in order for her getaway to Florida to see Matt, when her cell phone rang. "Hello, Ms. James."

"Who is this?"

"Did you know, Ms. James, that the translation of the word Cancun in ancient Maya is *nest of snakes*? It's a shame, really. It's a beautiful land. I'm quite fond of it. People forget its history, its culture. It saddens me to see the *narcos* infecting such purity."

At first she couldn't quite understand what was happening, but suddenly it clicked who was on the other end of the phone. She'd heard this voice before, that odd mechanical English with no hint of accent or origin. She wasn't quite sure what to say. She had so many questions, but somehow she knew he wouldn't answer most of the ones she wanted to ask. But there was one she ventured to try. "How'd you know?"

"Which part, Ms. James? How'd I know where Arismendez was? Or how did I know who you were and how to reach you?"

"Both."

She could almost hear the bemused smile on the other end of the line. "Well, we all have our secrets, I suppose. I think it best if I keep mine. I must say, though, I was particularly impressed that you and your companion found a way to prevent Arismendez from surrendering to the authorities. You even managed to get them to finish him off. I still can't decide if that was brilliant or dumb luck born of complete lunacy. Either way, I confess I didn't know as much about you as I thought I did. Why did your companion do it, if I may ask? Why did he get out of that car unarmed? I've tried to imagine what was going through his mind to inspire such an act of faith. He very nearly got you both killed. I hope you realize how close you both came to being shot to pieces out there."

Catherine thought back to that moment. Then she thought about everything else they did and what Matt had done in the jungle so many years ago which had ended their relationship. Right or wrong, she at least felt like she understood things more now. "I suppose he just thought it was the right thing to do at the time."

"And you, Ms. James? Some would say you have blood on your hands."

"Some might. But I did what I thought was right, too. Sometimes there just has to be a reckoning, not just for Taylor Woodall, but also for a little boy named Juan, for all of it."

There was a long pause before the man on the other end of the phone spoke again. "You humble me, Ms. James. You truly do."

Catherine thought now a good moment to try one more burning question, "Who are . . . "

Click.

Fuentes clicked the End Call icon on his laptop and the phone conversation ended. He'd made the call over the web through a program which would take the most skilled of computer forensic analysts to track down its origin. It also allowed him to control the tone and pitch of his voice, slowing it down so it sounded deeper and further eliminating his accent, which he'd already become adept at doing over the years.

He took the piece of paper in his hand, the hand gun permit for one Ms. Catherine James, complete with an old cell phone number that hadn't changed since the last annual renewal, and put it back into a large envelope marked Woodall, T.

The rest of the governor's office was empty save for him. He shut down the laptop and put it into his briefcase, then pulled out an ashtray from his desk drawer, the pack of cigarettes and lighter therein, and lastly the little bottle of scotch he kept for late evenings such as this when he was alone at his desk thinking about the state of affairs of his station. He lit up the cigarette, took a long drink, and looked over the file one last time.

A nest of snakes, he thought to himself. He was in one of the most beautiful places in the world, connected to it by the blood of his forefathers and by his personal choice to call it home. He wasn't going to give up. He loved his country, loved his people, and loved Cancun. And like Ramirez, he was going to fight for it.

But he was not so enamored that he couldn't see the venomous vipers who called his home their home as well. Fuentes knew how risky it was to bring attention to himself. What had happened to Ramirez only solidified that belief. He was right where he wanted to be, behind the scenes and rarely noticed, but with enough authority to effect action when needed. It was a delicate balance.

When Arismendez wasn't found in the compound, he'd given the police dispatchers strict instructions from the governor . . . . well, him, but they need not know that . . . to inform him immediately if anyone called in a sighting matching Arismendez's description. So when two men with no luggage appeared at the Cancun Palace Hotel check-in asking for three rooms as close to one another as possible, the astute check-in clerk knew something was amiss. Her suspicions were confirmed when she saw four other man escorting a rather rotund man to the elevators, so she made a phone call.

Fuentes had thought about calling in the military, but such an action would have resulted in Arismendez's location soon being broadcast on scanners and unknown informants to the cartel may have tipped him off before they could get to him. So Fuentes took a chance. He watched Catherine and her companion when they left the conference room and saw what room they went to. He then made the anonymous call tipping them off. He wasn't sure what would happen, but he figured the woman had already proven herself remarkably resourceful. He'd hoped she'd wait for Arismendez to leave and follow him, maybe taking him out well away from the tourist district quietly so they could avoid any further public incident, but that obviously hadn't happened. Still, it had turned out to be a good bet. Catherine James had indeed surpassed his expectations.

When he caught wind of the chase, he'd ordered the officer in charge to tell his people the Americans were not to be harmed if at all possible, which had been lucky for Matt when he stepped out of that car.

The criminal Arismendez had been brought to a swift end and the media would report it was the Mexican authorities who had accomplished the deed, displaying the state of Quintana Roo's commitment to safety and security in the area.

Taylor Woodall's murder and the media tsunami which had followed had devastated the tourism industry, but he hoped now things might settle back down. Fuentes thought about what Marcus Aurelius had once said, that poverty was the mother of all crime. If that was true, he could think of no better defense against cartel infiltration than a booming economy, and tourism was key.

Fuentes finished his cigarette and his drink. Then he took the folder marked Woodall, T., and placed it in a file cabinet next to an assortment of other folders with ghosts of their own. He'd played his part in slandering the poor girl in the media, and for that he wasn't proud. He tried not to dwell on the decisions he'd made, the constant weighing of pros and cons to each action or inaction.

As he put away the file and prepared to leave for the night, he passed by a functioning scale of justice model on a coffee table in his office, both scales on equal plane symbolizing the fair standing of each one's side. He paused and looked at it a moment before reaching into his pocket and pulling out a 10 peso coin which he then placed on one of the scale's brass platforms, causing the scale to tip to one side.

"Nicely done, Ms. James," he said, and closed the door.

Author's Note: Thank you for reading. If you enjoyed *Border Crossings*, I hope you'll consider leaving a review. Unlike my first novel, *The Ghosts of Varner Creek, Border Crossings* didn't go through the traditional publishing process and was instead Indie published . . . which is a fancy way of saying publishers passed so I published it myself. If you found any errors, I hope they were few and didn't ruin the story for you. I very much hope you enjoyed this book and thank you again for enjoying a read with me.